PRAISE

"[A] gripping novel of suspense from Elliot . . . Elliot skillfully unravels layers of intersecting stories, each one integral to the overall story of the Mills family and their small-town secrets. Readers will want to see more from this author."

—*Publishers Weekly*

"Elliot succeeds in creating both a thrilling mystery and a fascinating character study of the people inhabiting these pages."

—Bookreporter

"With her riveting, narrative-driven, deftly crafted storytelling style as a novelist, Kendra Elliot's *The Last Sister* will prove to be a welcome and enduringly popular addition to community library Mystery/Suspense/Thriller collections."

—*Midwest Book Review*

"Suspense on top of suspense. This one will keep you guessing until the final page and shows Elliot at her very best."

—The Real Book Spy

"Every family has skeletons. Kendra Elliot's tale of the Mills family's dark secrets is first-rate suspense. Dark and gripping, *The Last Sister* crescendos to knock-out, edge-of-your seat tension."

—Robert Dugoni, bestselling author of *My Sister's Grave*

"*The Last Sister* is exciting and suspenseful! Engaging characters and a complex plot kept me on the edge of my seat until the very last page."

—T.R. Ragan, bestselling author of the Jessie Cole series

PRAISE FOR KENDRA ELLIOT

"Kendra Elliot is a great suspense writer. Her characters are always solid. Her plots are always well thought out. Her pace is always just right."

—*Harlequin Junkie*

"Elliot delivers a fast-paced, tense thriller that plays up the small-town atmosphere and survivalist mentality, contrasting it against an increasingly connected world."

—*Publishers Weekly*

"Kendra Elliot goes from strength to strength in her Mercy Kilpatrick stories, and this fourth installment is a gripping, twisty, and complex narrative that will have fans rapt."

—RT Book Reviews

IN THE
PINES

ALSO BY KENDRA ELLIOT

COLUMBIA RIVER NOVELS

The Last Sister
The Silence

MERCY KILPATRICK NOVELS

A Merciful Death
A Merciful Truth
A Merciful Secret
A Merciful Silence
A Merciful Fate
A Merciful Promise

BONE SECRETS NOVELS

Hidden
Chilled
Buried
Alone
Known

BONE SECRETS NOVELLAS

Veiled

CALLAHAN & MCLANE NOVELS
PART OF THE BONE SECRETS WORLD

Vanished
Bridged
Spiraled
Targeted

ROGUE RIVER NOVELLAS

On Her Father's Grave (Rogue River)
Her Grave Secrets (Rogue River)
Dead in Her Tracks (Rogue Winter)
Death and Her Devotion (Rogue Vows)
Truth Be Told (Rogue Justice)

WIDOW'S ISLAND NOVELLAS

Close to the Bone
Bred in the Bone
Below the Bones
The Lost Bones

IN THE
PINES

KENDRA
ELLIOT

Text copyright © 2022 by Oceanfront Press LLC

Published by Montlake, Seattle

www.apub.com

Amazon, the Amazon logo, and Montlake are trademarks of Amazon.com, Inc., or its affiliates.

ISBN-13: 9781542029711 (hardcover)
ISBN-10: 1542029716 (hardcover)

ISBN-13: 9781542006781 (paperback)
ISBN-10: 1542006783 (paperback)

Cover design by Caroline Teagle Johnson

Printed in the United States of America

First edition

For my girls

1

"I'm glad we're busy, Chief, but all these tourists are lousy tippers."

Police chief Truman Daly looked up as Sara frowned and topped off his coffee.

"And it's every single one of them—bunch of tightwads," she continued. "Do you think if they find the treasure, they'll still be rotten tippers?"

"Probably. Can't see that habit changing. Sorry, Sara." Truman made a mental note to leave her a couple of extra dollars.

Three weeks ago a lawyer had posted online a rambling ten-line composition titled "In the Pines" that supposedly led to a $2 million hidden treasure. The lines had been written by recently deceased millionaire Chester Rollins, and the public had voraciously tackled the mystery, speculating about which words were actual references to the treasure and which were red herrings. This week Truman's tiny Central Oregon town had been swarmed as some of the treasure hunters decided one line was an allusion to the city of Eagle's Nest.

Two more strangers came through the diner door. They all had the same look in their eyes. Hunger—but not for food. They were all hungry for money.

Truman watched as Sara led the newcomers to a booth at the far end of the diner. They looked like a married couple who were down on their luck. His hair was shaggy, and his tennis shoes heavily worn.

Faded shorts hung on her thin frame, and her backpack was grimy and frayed. She clutched several papers in one hand, and after they sat, they put their heads together, studying the pages and casting furtive glances at other diners.

The clues.

Truman admitted the treasure-hunt hype had caught his attention. He had reviewed the clues but didn't quite understand how people had decided they pointed to Eagle's Nest. They were full of vague references and twisty language, not clear-cut references. It was like reading a stoned college student's attempt at poetry.

The press was also trickling into town. The treasure hunt had become a national story. That morning he'd seen three different news vans from Portland TV stations.

He finished his breakfast and sipped his coffee, watching out the window. The Fourth of July was the only time he'd seen this many people in town before, and that was still a month away.

The door opened again, and a young teenager came in. He stopped and scanned the occupants, clearly looking for someone. Truman's radar locked on the unfamiliar boy.

Beat-up boots. Shirt too big. Jeans too small.

Something about the boy made Truman think of Ollie, his unofficial son. There was an awareness in the boy's stillness, a caution in his posture. This was a boy who looked out for himself. Possibly out of necessity.

Just like Ollie.

The boy's gaze fell on Truman and dipped to the badge on his chest. Truman expected him to bolt, but instead the boy approached, intense focus on his face. He stopped a few feet away, studying Truman from head to toe.

"Are you the sheriff?" he asked.

"No, I'm the police chief," Truman answered evenly, keeping both hands wrapped around his coffee mug. The boy's caution reminded him of a wild animal's, and Truman didn't want to make any sudden moves.

Relief crossed the young teen's face.

"What can I do for you, son?"

He swallowed and lifted his chin. "My mother is missing. She left to visit my uncle and she hasn't come back."

Truman frowned. "When did she leave?"

"Almost two weeks ago."

Truman's hands flinched, sloshing coffee over the rim of his mug. "That long?"

The boy nodded.

"You haven't heard from her? Did you try to call her?" Truman leaned forward, concern filling him as he wiped up the coffee with a napkin.

"She doesn't have a phone."

He looked sharply at the boy, confirming his first impression: the boy's family was poor. "What about your dad?"

"He passed away recently. And no, I don't know how to reach my uncle." The boy was articulate, his eyes intelligent. Again, Truman was reminded of Ollie.

"You've been living alone for two weeks?"

The teen shrugged, unconcerned. "My sister Charlotte is there. She's eleven."

Truman pushed away his cup and stood. He pulled out his wallet and tossed plenty of cash on the table. "Let's go over to the station, and you can tell me what happened. We'll figure out what happened to your mother."

"And my littlest sister."

His eyes narrowed on the teen. "A sister is also missing?"

"Mom took the baby with her when she left."

"Baby?" Truman's fingers grew cold as he placed his hat on his head.

"Yeah, she's one and a half."

Missing child. I need to notify Mercy and the FBI.

2

FBI special agent Mercy Kilpatrick slowed her Tahoe as she entered the Eagle's Nest city limits. After Truman's phone call, she'd sped from her office in Bend to the tiny town a half hour away. Outside of Bend, Central Oregon was made up of small rural towns connected by long, deserted stretches of narrow highway.

The Cascade mountain range separated Oregon's blue cities from its smaller red towns to the east. Bend was a bit of an exception: a good-size city with prime outdoor recreation areas that attracted tourists from across the US. It offered skiing during the winter and every lake and river sport imaginable during the summer. Its high-desert location and stunning year-round snowy mountain views had exponentially expanded Bend's population over the last thirty years.

The city offered modern art and popular concerts along with feed stores and rodeos.

Mercy passed the abandoned sawmill and the high school, noticing that the traffic was quite heavy for the tiny town—meaning she'd met five vehicles traveling in the opposite direction. She continued past the John Deere dealership and tiny movie theater and then parked next to an ancient Ford truck in front of the Eagle's Nest Police Department.

On the door under the department's name were the words TRUMAN DALY, POLICE CHIEF.

My husband.

It'd been six months since their wedding, and it still felt foreign to her tongue.

Truman's call an hour earlier had both alarmed her and piqued her interest, so she'd driven to Eagle's Nest to meet the thirteen-year-old. Mercy had done a quick DMV search on the boy's mother, Bridget Kerr, but hadn't found a current driver's license. Mercy's partner, Eddie Peterson, was digging deeper while she interviewed the boy.

Mercy stepped out of her SUV and into the warm sun. June was perfect in Central Oregon. Warm, long days and cool nights with nearly constant blue skies. It was difficult to work at the office during the summer. Today she wished she could go for a hike in the woods or a float on the river.

"Hey, Mercy!" Inside, Lucas Ingram, the huge office manager, greeted her with a smile. The twenty-year-old was highly efficient, driven, and one of the most cheerful people she knew. The former high school football player had taken over the desk job when his grandmother retired. He had no desire to be a police officer; he preferred to organize and make the department run smoothly. "Truman's in his office with the boy."

"How's your mother?" Mercy asked as she stopped at his desk and noted the perfect alignment of keyboard, notepads, and pen holder. As usual.

"Good. All good. Cooking up a storm as she always does."

"Say hello for me." Mercy headed down a long hall, passing framed photos of previous police chiefs and officers.

Truman's office door was open six inches, so she did a quick knock and pushed it open. Her gaze went immediately to his, and he grinned. Her stomach did a subtle flip-flop.

His smile still did that to her.

A thin teen holding a Rubik's Cube sat in a chair across from Truman's desk. He stood as Mercy entered and gave a quick nod, his brown gaze holding hers.

Manners.

His solemn, dark eyes seemed familiar, and she wondered if she knew one of his relatives. She'd grown up in Eagle's Nest and often ran into people from her past.

She held out a hand. "I'm Mercy Kilpatrick. I work for the FBI."

He gave her hand a solid shake. "Theodore Kerr, ma'am."

"Do you go by Theo?"

"Theodore, please," he said emphatically.

An old soul stared at her from his eyes; the formal name fit him.

Mercy recognized his type. A rural kid. Raised to be independent. She had been brought up the same, and he reminded her of her brothers and Ollie. If he was scared because his mother and sister had been missing for weeks, he didn't show it. Mercy suspected the decision to ask for help from the police was one he had weighed for days.

Mercy took the chair beside him. He sat, keeping his back impossibly straight in the chair, his fingers spinning and twisting the cube. The boy's hair had been shaved in a buzz cut several months ago and was in need of a trim. She opened her bag and fished around for a notepad, watching the boy out of the corner of her eye.

He silently studied every inch of Truman's office as his hands continued with the puzzle, his gaze lingering on personal photos. A wedding photo of her, Truman, Ollie, and her niece Kaylie held his attention the longest. The candid picture was a favorite. The four of them had their arms around each other as they laughed at a joke Ollie had made. Mercy loved it more than the formal photos.

"Chief Daly called me because your mother and sister are missing," Mercy started. "Missing children are one of the responsibilities of the FBI. We have more resources to help find them."

"Molly isn't really missing," Theodore said. "She's with my mother. But Charlotte is at home."

"That's your other sister?"

"Yes. She's eleven."

The two of them have been alone for weeks?

"Your mother left to visit your uncle, correct?"

"Yes, ma'am."

"Chief Daly said you don't know his name. Or your mother's maiden name."

The teen's shoulders drooped. "That's right. She never talked about him. Whenever I asked about grandparents or relatives, she would tell me she didn't want to discuss it."

"You've never met your grandparents? What about on your father's side?"

"No. I know my mother has a brother, and I only know that because she was going to visit him. She never mentioned him before."

Did she make him up?

"Did your mother appear excited to visit her brother?" Mercy asked. "Or nervous about the trip?"

"Both. She said she hadn't seen him since before she got married."

"Her brother knew she was coming, right?" asked Truman.

Theodore shook his head. "She wasn't sure how to reach him, so she was going to show up at his house."

"So she had an address. You didn't find the address written down somewhere?" asked Truman.

"No, sir. I looked."

"What if he'd moved?" asked Mercy.

"Then she'd ask where he'd moved to," Theodore said logically.

His naivete made her wonder how isolated his family was.

"Theodore." Mercy paused, wondering where to start. "Where is your home?"

He frowned. "Why?"

"Your address gives us a place to start an investigation."

"My mother isn't there." He focused on his cube.

"I know." Mercy tried a different tack. "Theodore, when I was growing up, my parents told very few people where they lived. They liked their privacy, and they had stored a lot of supplies for our family, which they didn't want people to know about. It was to keep our future safe."

The dark gaze met hers; she'd struck a chord.

His family are preppers.

The same as Mercy's. Now his hesitation to give his address made sense. Preppers were highly protective of their hard work. If there was an emergency, they didn't want people stealing their stores. They dedicated most of their life to being prepared for any big emergency. Wars, power grid crashes, pandemics. It was a lifestyle.

"You don't have to tell me right now," Mercy said. "But I do need to see your home. Your mother might have left something that indicates where she went, and I'm really good at finding things like that. If you'd prefer to lead us to your home instead of giving us an address, that is fine with me."

The boy thought for a few moments and then nodded. "I walked, but it'd be much faster with ATVs."

"I can't drive there?" Truman asked.

"No," the boy said quickly. "Not the entire way."

"I'll load up the two department ATVs," said Truman.

"I'll help you," said Mercy. "It's a good day for a ride." She stood, pleased she'd reached an agreement with Theodore and gotten the investigation moving forward.

And I'll get that outdoor activity I crave.

3

"Even *I'm* lost," Mercy muttered as she followed Truman's ATV through the woods. Theodore rode behind Truman, giving directions.

Steering among the trees, Mercy appreciated their sporadic shade in the midday heat. The scent of drying pine needles and warm sagebrush filled the air. Mercy knew the general area they were riding through and noticed Theodore had guided them through several unnecessary turns, essentially making a big circle at one point.

He doesn't want to lead us straight to his home.

She understood. People who chose to live this deep in the woods generally did it to avoid other humans, and Theodore had obviously been trained to protect their privacy. After an hour's ride, they entered a large clearing, and Mercy was surprised at the sight of the well-maintained cabin. It wasn't new, but its roof was in perfect condition, and its windows sparkled in the sun. Beyond the home she glimpsed a large barn and several smaller outbuildings.

There has to be a quicker route. Theodore definitely brought us the long way.

She parked beside Truman and removed her sunglasses, brushing off the Central Oregon dust covering her pants and shirt. She took a drink from her water bottle, rinsing the unavoidable grit out of her mouth.

Kendra Elliot

"He wants us to wait outside a minute," Truman said as Theodore headed to the house.

"Did he say anything on the ride?" she asked.

"Not really. Just gave directions. Did you notice he led us in a circle?"

"Yep."

"I suspect there is a main road closer than he said." Truman studied the house. "This home wasn't built with supplies brought in by ATV."

"Agreed." She set her hand on Truman's arm, making him look at her. "Theodore reminds me of Ollie."

He nodded emphatically. "I saw that immediately."

"I don't think my brothers were that independent when they were younger, even though we were raised off the grid."

"But you kids went to school. I don't think Theodore has spent much time around other people. Ollie definitely didn't."

"He's changed a lot," Mercy said, thinking of Ollie. "I hate to use the word *blossomed* to describe him, but it's accurate." The orphaned teenager had lived alone in the woods for a few years after his grandfather died. Truman had bonded with the teen and given him a home.

"Kaylie has been a big influence," said Truman. "Mostly for the better."

Mercy grinned. Her outgoing niece's goal was to fully integrate Ollie into society. "Those two are closer than siblings. I overheard them have an in-depth conversation about the treasure hunt. Both are convinced they can figure out the clues."

"So does half the town and every recent tourist." A wry smile lifted his lips on one side. "I'll be glad when it's over and Eagle's Nest is back to normal." He looked back at the little house. "Do you think we can persuade Theodore and his sister to leave their home until their mother returns?"

"I hope so," said Mercy. "But if his sister is as stubborn and taciturn as Theodore appears to be, I suspect they'll dig in their heels."

10

"I agree," said Truman. "But it's not like they're town kids who never look up from their video games. These kids have been doing fine on their own. I almost hate to disrupt that."

"Some of today's kids can barely find a grocery store, let alone cook a meal."

"Yep. I think—" Truman stopped.

The door was flung open, and a girl marched out of the house. Theodore was a few steps behind her, annoyance on his face. She was several inches shorter than her brother, but her head was up and her chin was set. Her blonde ponytail bounced with each determined stride.

His sister definitely has an opinion.

Mercy bit back her grin and watched the duo approach. The girl wore faded shorts and a tank top, her arms and legs toasted brown from the sun. She stopped a few feet from Mercy and Truman, put her hands on her hips, and scrutinized them.

"Theodore says you don't know where our mother is."

"Not yet," said Mercy. "We've just started looking."

"It doesn't appear that you're searching for her and Molly. It appears you're simply standing around."

Truman made a quiet, strangled sound, and Mercy hid another grin. "We have people back in town looking for your mother and sister. We came to see if something here will help us discover where her brother lives," she said evenly.

Charlotte exchanged a glance with Theodore that Mercy couldn't interpret.

"Would you mind if we talked inside?" Truman asked.

The children shared another look, but Charlotte nodded and gestured for them to follow her as she turned back to the house. She glanced at Mercy's feet as they walked. "What brand of hiking boots are those?"

Mercy blinked and looked down at her red boots. "Oboz."

"Thought so. I like the color." Charlotte gave an approving nod. "I like Lowa boots too."

Maybe they're not as isolated as I thought.

When she was a child, Mercy's parents had had little time or money for anything frivolous, which included fashion, hobbies, and entertainment. She and her sister Pearl had hidden magazines packed with clothing and celebrities and pored over them in secret at night, describing the shoes and hairstyles and jewelry in great detail to Rose, their blind sister. Mercy wondered if Charlotte had similar magazines.

The inside of the home was old and worn but immaculate. As she'd expected, Mercy didn't see a TV or computer. An old crank radio sat on a counter.

Somehow Charlotte has access to information like hiking-boot brands.

Mercy itched to check under the girl's mattress to see if she'd stashed an REI catalog there.

Truman opened cabinets in the kitchen area and looked in the fridge. All were well stocked with food. He walked to a window that faced a huge covered woodpile and nodded to himself. Mercy agreed; the children were well supplied and capable. The neat house and their healthy physical appearance were testimonies to that.

"Do you need anything?" she asked Theodore. The boy shrugged.

"No," stated Charlotte, crossing her arms, lifting her chin.

Tough little thing.

Mercy liked her.

Charlotte got four glasses, took a pitcher out of the fridge, and poured something. "Would you like to sit down?" she asked formally, indicating a small dining table and chairs.

Good manners from Charlotte too.

All of them sat, and Mercy sipped from the glass the girl had given her. It was lemonade—excellent lemonade. Truman drank deeply.

How do I tell them we can't leave them here alone?

If something happened to one of the kids, and Mercy had allowed them to stay after this visit, she'd be out of a job. And would never forgive herself.

"Did your mother ever talk about visiting your uncle before this?" asked Mercy.

"She never talked about him at all," said Theodore.

"Dad didn't let her," added Charlotte.

Mercy paused. "What do you mean 'didn't let her'?"

"It was a rule. They didn't talk about their relatives," Charlotte said matter-of-factly. "If I asked about grandparents, I got extra chores."

Mercy took a sip of lemonade as she gathered her thoughts. "Does that seem odd to you?" she asked carefully. "Or were there a few topics that were forbidden?"

"Grandparents, public school, vacations . . ." Charlotte wrinkled her nose as she thought.

"Motorcycles," added Theodore wistfully.

"You were homeschooled?" Mercy asked, already knowing the answer.

"Yes. Mom liked to teach," said Theodore. "She wanted to be a teacher when she was growing up. She went to a real school in Bend."

Mercy wondered how their mother had ended up in this isolated home without a phone.

For love?

"Truman told me your father died recently. I'm very sorry."

The children were silent for a long moment. "Thank you," Theodore finally said.

Mercy waited to see if the two would say anything else. They didn't. "Was he sick for very long?"

"Mom said it was a heart attack," said Theodore. "Died in his sleep." The boy's words were clipped as he stared at the table. Charlotte said nothing as she drew lines in the condensation on her glass.

I'll come back to the father topic.

"Can you show us your mother's room?" she asked. "And maybe the rest of your home?"

"Why?" asked Charlotte.

"Because Truman and I are trained to see things that many people don't," Mercy said gently. "We might see something that indicates where she went."

"She's at our uncle's," said Charlotte with a frown.

"But you don't know his name or where that is," said Mercy.

"True," said Charlotte.

"We might find something that can help us figure out who he is," said Truman.

Theodore stood. "This way." He set off down a narrow hall.

Mercy raised a brow at Truman, and they both pushed back their chairs.

The home was a single story. They'd had their lemonade in a large room with a kitchen, a woodstove, a dining table, and two well-worn sofas. Near the dining table was a tall bookcase packed with books. One shelf was all textbooks. Mercy spotted math, American history, and chemistry texts. The other shelves had volumes on gardening, livestock, first aid, and survival, reminding Mercy that their parents had been new to living off the grid.

Either way, they had raised competent children.

Down the hall were two bedrooms and a small bath. They passed a bedroom with neatly made bunk beds, and Mercy remembered the mess she'd seen in her niece Kaylie's room that morning. Clothes scattered across the floor and bedding piled in a lopsided lump. The other bedroom in the kids' isolated home was slightly larger, with a double bed—also perfectly made—and a crib. A small desk stood in one corner, stacked with books. Mercy picked up a battered algebra textbook with several dog-eared pages and thumbed through it.

"Hey!" said Theodore as Truman opened a drawer in the night-stand. "Stay out of her things."

14

"We're looking for a clue to where your uncle lives," said Mercy. "To do that we'll have to snoop a bit. I know it feels like a violation of her privacy, but she's been gone for weeks without a word, so I think she'd understand that we're trying to help."

The young teen looked away, frustration on his face. Truman watched him for a moment and then sifted through the contents of the drawer.

Mercy set aside her sympathy for the boy and continued her perusal of the desk contents. Everything seemed geared toward planning lessons for the two kids. A small calendar listed daily schoolwork, and Mercy noticed the detailed lesson plans had ended two days before.

Did Bridget plan to be gone this long?

Mercy knelt to look under the bed and was startled to find it was completely clear. In the small house, she'd expected the space to be used for storage. Truman was running his hands between the box spring and mattress, which left only the closet to be searched. Mercy opened the door, expecting a cramped space, and was pleasantly surprised by the large amount of room and neatly labeled bins.

Half the clothing was for an adult male. Three pairs of large, worn work boots were lined up on one side.

Her dead husband's clothes.

The usable clothing wouldn't have been donated; it would be saved for Theodore. Mercy wondered what the boy thought of one day wearing his dead father's clothing. She opened a bin labeled SWEATERS. She dug gently, determining that it contained exactly that: sweaters. More investigating indicated that the bins were full of clothing, exactly as labeled. She checked the pockets of the hanging coats and found four screws, a Leatherman tool, and a bandanna.

She stepped out of the large closet, ready to move on to the cabinets in the kitchen. The two children watched silently from the bedroom doorway as Truman flipped through a small stack of photos he'd pulled out of a large envelope.

"Where'd you find the photos?" Mercy asked.

"Under the mattress."

"That's so cliché," said Mercy. "That's one of the first places anyone looks." She joined him and studied the pictures. Charlotte chose that moment to vanish, and Mercy wondered if she was going to remove something from under her mattress.

Most of the pictures appeared to be from the 1990s, judging by the fashions and hair. They were family photos. Parents, daughter, son, and several dogs. Birthdays. Christmas. Vacations. Mercy thought the daughter in the photos resembled Charlotte, so she held out a picture to Theodore. "Is that your mother?"

He took the photo, his gaze stunned. "I've never seen this, but yes, I think that's her. She looks so young," he said in a dazed voice.

Mercy smiled. It was always hard to believe one's parents had ever been young.

"Can I see the rest?" he asked. Charlotte reappeared and took the photo from Theodore.

"Her hair was the same color as mine," she said in an awed tone. "It's so much darker now."

Truman handed the other six photos to the kids, who eagerly studied them.

Why would Bridget keep these from her children?

"We have grandparents," whispered Charlotte. "Do you think they're still alive?"

"I'll find out," Mercy promised.

If their mother is dead, would the grandparents take them in?

Mercy stopped the train of thought. There was no indication that Bridget Kerr was dead.

Maybe the grandparents or uncle were violent . . . Maybe Bridget cut off all contact for safety reasons.

"That must be the uncle your mother was going to see," Truman said.

Mercy moved closer to look over Charlotte's shoulder. The brother was much taller than Bridget as they stood in front of a Christmas tree.

She looked at the brother, wondering how they would locate him without a name.

Somehow we'll find him.

Something clicked in her brain.

"Charlotte, can I look closer at that Christmas photo?" Her hands were icy as she took the picture and studied the brother's features.

I'll be damned.

She showed the photo to Truman. "Recognize him?"

His forehead wrinkled. "No. Should I?"

"Yes. Imagine him with short hair and thirty more pounds of muscle."

Recognition flashed in his eyes. "That's Evan Bolton."

The Deschutes County sheriff's detective was their friend.

Mercy glanced at Theodore.

I knew I'd seen those old-soul eyes before.

4

Evan Bolton spotted Mercy and an ATV waiting on the side of the highway exactly where she'd said she'd be. Her phone call had been cryptic, assuring him that he would want the news she had to share and apologizing for the odd meeting location.

He pulled off the road, creating a plume of red powder from the cinders that lined the road. He let the dust settle and then lowered his window. Mercy was already covered in a fine layer of the dust, but her eyes sparkled. Even filthy from head to toe, he found her beautiful.

Nope.

She was married. When Evan had first met her on a case—also in the middle of nowhere—he'd been instantly attracted to the tall FBI agent, but he'd soon discovered she was involved with Truman Daly. Eventually Evan had grudgingly admitted the couple were perfect for each other. The three of them had become good friends, but Evan always felt like a third wheel when they hung out together.

"Why the mystery meeting, Mercy?" he asked in greeting. "Is my office bugged? Or yours?"

"Nice to see you too."

"You persuaded me to drive out here on my lunch. Tell me why."

"Do you have a sister, Evan?" Her gaze had turned serious.

His fingers went numb on the steering wheel.

What did Mercy find?

"Is she dead?" he whispered, images of Bethany flooding his thoughts.

"I don't know anything about a death," Mercy said quickly. "And we don't have evidence of a crime, but she's missing."

"Bethany's been missing for fourteen years." His voice cracked.

Mercy frowned. "Bethany? That's your sister's name?"

"Yes," he snapped. "Now tell me what the fuck is going on." His heart had beat in triple time since Mercy said the word *sister*.

Mercy pulled a photo from her knapsack. "Is this you? And Bethany?"

He took the picture and caught his breath. It was from a Christmas when he was a teenager. He greedily studied Bethany's face. He'd seen other photos from that holiday, but not this one. When he'd left for college, his sister had been a senior in high school.

Bethany had vanished a month before he moved back after his freshman year. He never saw her again.

"Where did you get this?" he croaked.

"Why did you say she's been missing for a long time? What happened?"

"Dammit, Mercy. *Where did you get this photo?*"

"From her home."

"You know where she lives?" His words sounded strangled.

Mercy gestured behind her at a narrow dirt road that led into the forest. "Evan . . . you really haven't had contact with her in fourteen years?"

"None. She ran off with a boyfriend when she was seventeen. My parents were livid. I was still at college, and none of us ever heard from her again." He swallowed hard.

"She goes by Bridget now," Mercy said. "Bridget Kerr."

"How do you know that?"

Mercy took a deep breath and told him a story about a boy who'd walked into an Eagle's Nest diner that morning. Evan listened. Dumbstruck.

I have a nephew and two nieces?

"She's been missing for two weeks? And no one reported it until now?" His brain spun with questions.

"I think you'll understand when you meet Theodore and Charlotte. They're very capable kids." Mercy paused. "She told the kids she was going to see you."

"I don't know anything about that. I haven't heard from her."

"Would she know how to find you?" Mercy asked.

He shrugged. "I live in my parents' old house. They're in Arizona now. And anyone running a Google search will figure out that I work for the sheriff's office."

Mercy looked doubtful. "The kids were raised off the grid. I don't know if they've ever used a computer."

"Are they *preppers*?"

"You say that like it's a dirty word."

"That's not what I meant. It's just that Bethany hated camping or roughing it." He slowly shook his head. "I can't believe what you're telling me."

Mercy pointed at the picture in his hand. "Both kids say that is their mother."

Evan stared at the photo.

What happened to you, Bethany?

"You better take me to them."

"That's why I had you come out here."

"Why are you on an ATV?"

She grinned. "Theodore didn't want us to know his home was accessible from this road. He guided us through some convoluted back way from the south that a truck couldn't travel. But the home is only a few minutes away from this spot." She got back on her quad and gestured for him to follow.

His SUV bounced down the rough, narrow lane through the woods. If Mercy hadn't been waiting for him at the side of the road, he would never have spotted it.

"Bethany's been living less than an hour away?" he muttered. He'd searched for her. When he joined the county sheriff's department, he'd tried everything possible to locate his sister, but he'd only found dead ends. He'd checked every year. Nothing. He'd hoped she wasn't dead. His father believed she was; his mother always held out hope.

At least his father always *said* he believed she was dead.

Bethany had run off in the middle of the night after numerous arguments about her boyfriend. His parents hadn't liked him. He was older. Their parents hadn't understood why a man in his twenties was interested in a seventeen-year-old.

Evan hadn't either.

His mother had thought the boyfriend was too controlling, and Evan agreed, since the man had convinced Bethany to leave her entire life behind. He'd never met Victor or known his last name. His parents hadn't known it either.

The lane took a sharp right, and his SUV jerked through the ruts. A moment later they reached a clearing. He passed a barn and two sheds before reaching the house.

He parked next to Mercy and opened his door. His hands slipped on the handle; they were wet with sweat.

Bethany is not here.

But her kids are.

He wasn't great with kids. He never knew what to say, and when kids learned he was in law enforcement, they always studied him as if he resembled a weird beetle.

He and Mercy walked toward the home. "They don't know you're coming. I wasn't sure how this would play out, and I didn't want to get their hopes up."

"What are their names again?" His brain was numb.

"Theodore and Charlotte. The baby is Molly."

"This is nuts. What am I supposed to say to them?"

Mercy halted and turned to him, surprise on her face. "You say hi."

"I haven't been around many kids," he muttered. "They don't seem to like me."

"Ollie and Kaylie like you."

"They're not kids. Aren't they about twenty-two?"

She gave him a withering look. "Kaylie just graduated high school."

"She seems older."

"Trust me, she's not." She tapped his chest with a finger. "I was clueless about teens, but I did very well when I met my teenage niece. I'm sure you can handle this."

"But you're a woman."

Both her brows shot up. "Do you really think *I* had any motherly experience when I took in Kaylie? I'd done nothing but work my butt off since college."

A thought hit him like a sledgehammer. "Am I supposed to take in *two kids*?"

"No one has said that."

"You implied it."

"I didn't mean to. I'm honestly not sure how to handle the situation yet."

"You need to call child services," Evan pointed out.

"I know, but I want to have a good option to present instead of CS swooping in and placing them in a strange foster home."

Evan sighed. He'd dated a woman with two small children once. It'd felt odd and made him question if he was meant to ever be a dad. That was the sum of his experience with kids—other than being one himself. He couldn't let Mercy talk him into anything that he might screw up.

She looked him up and down. "Breathe. You look as if I'm about to shove you off a cliff."

Aren't you?

She led him inside, where Truman was chatting animatedly about riding cows when he was younger. The young teen beside him was rapt with attention. On his other side, a blonde girl covered her mouth as she giggled at his story.

Bethany.

Charlotte took his breath away. It was as if he'd stepped back in time.

Her face was a slightly different shape, but she had Bethany's eyes and nose.

Truman described how he'd ended up facedown in the mud and cow pies, and Charlotte burst out laughing.

The sound ricocheted in Evan's brain; it was Bethany's laugh.

"Jesus," he muttered as he took a step back.

It's too much.

Mercy elbowed him. "Man up," she whispered. "You're a lot bigger than them."

It wasn't that. It was the assault of memories that he'd locked away, worried his sister was dead. In the last five minutes he'd learned she was alive, she'd had three kids, and now she and his other niece were missing.

Not an average Monday.

Charlotte noticed Evan first and went silent, her gaze locked on him. Truman and Theodore spotted him next.

"Bolton. Good to see you." Truman stood and crossed the room, holding out his hand. They shook.

"Day of surprises," Evan said to Truman in a low voice.

"Mostly good surprises," answered Truman. He turned to the kids, who were watching the exchange. "This is your mom's brother, Evan Bolton. He's a detective."

"She's not with you, sir?" asked Theodore. The teen's brown eyes looked way too old for his face.

Isn't that what people say about me?

"I'm sorry, Theodore. I haven't seen your mother in years."

The boy's face fell, and Evan's heart tumbled with it.

"I'll do everything I can to find her and Molly." He looked at Charlotte, including her in his answer. The girl was looking from Theodore to Evan and back.

"He looks like you, Theodore," she said, wrinkling her nose. "That's how you'll look when you're old."

Mercy coughed.

Theodore stood. "It's nice to meet you, sir." Charlotte jumped up and echoed her brother.

"Please don't call me sir," said Evan, struggling to find the right words. "I'm . . . Uncle Evan."

Did I just say that?

Charlotte beamed. "Uncle Evan," she said, appearing to test the title. Theodore nodded at him, hesitation in his gaze.

Evan took a deep breath. "How about we all sit down, and you kids catch me up on the last few years?" He headed for the spot Truman had vacated, between the two kids, and sat, determined to make it work. Theodore's disappointment and Charlotte's delight had struck a chord deep inside him. This was up to him to fix.

If I can interview a serial killer, I can talk to my niece and nephew.

5

"This can't be right, Ollie."

Ollie sighed as they trekked up the steep hill. He was tired of hearing Kaylie complain.

"Don't you think that there would be other treasure hunters here if we were in the right place?" she asked.

The thought had crossed Ollie's mind as he'd parked at Owlie Lake. For a summer day, the lake was quieter than usual. A couple of families ate picnics on the small rocky beach as little kids splashed in the ice-cold water.

"If you don't want anyone to know where you think the treasure is, would you let anyone see where you search for it?" Ollie asked. "They don't want to give their locations away." On the trail ahead of them, his dog, Shep, trotted and sniffed at every other tree, occasionally glancing back to make certain Ollie and Kaylie were keeping up.

"But we're not being sneaky," said Kaylie. "Your red truck is parked on the road for everyone to see. And it's not like we're trying to hide. Everyone at the lake saw us head this way."

She's right.

"We're being casual . . . like hiding in plain sight. No one knows we're looking for it."

Kaylie rolled her eyes.

Ollie had lost count of how many times she'd done that since he'd convinced her to join him in the treasure hunt. It'd been an easy decision to ask Kaylie to be his partner. If they found the treasure and split it, that meant it'd stay in the family. She wasn't his sister by genetics but was the sister of his heart.

When Truman and Mercy had married, it'd patched together a little family. Four people from separate walks of life. Ollie had been completely alone until he encountered Truman. They'd forged a bond, and then Truman had given him a place in his home and life. Kaylie's father had died almost two years ago, and she'd been taken in by her new-to-her aunt, Mercy.

The four of them were closer than families created by blood.

Unlike Ollie, Kaylie had grown up in the immediate area and was intimately familiar with the lands surrounding Eagle's Nest. After Ollie had pointed out that several words in the clues were homonyms, she'd suggested that the word *foul* in the term *foul water* in the eighth line could be a homonym for *fowl* and refer to the *owl* in Owlie Lake's name. But were the homonyms deliberate or accidental?

I have no idea what I'm looking for.

He assumed he'd know it when he saw it.

"I don't understand the clue about the wings," said Kaylie.

"'Where the brake would flatten her wings,'" quoted Ollie. "That's the next-to-last line. You're jumping ahead."

"But we need to look ahead. How else would we know what to look for next? Besides, nothing indicates that the lines are to be solved in order. I think we need to look at the whole thing as one big picture."

She had a point. But everyone who had a theory about the clues had a point. There were no rules from the treasure-hunt creator. Just a bunch of disjointed clues shaped into a brief essay. More like a bad poem.

In the Pines

Follow the bird that cried over the mountains of
    falling water
Far away there is a holy sea
There you must bow down to the rain
Yet your soul will grow weak
Take time to write where the butte is made of coal
Then seek the pears that overtook the plains
And meet the sun who led me to the high ridge
You must go past the foul water to discover what's
    hidden
Push hard to climb where the brake would flatten
    her wings
Where would it be?

It was a bunch of nonsense. But Ollie was hooked. He had as good a chance as anyone of solving it.

Shep froze next to him, his focus far ahead on the rough path. A low growl came from his throat, surprising Ollie.

"Did he growl?" whispered Kaylie, shock in her voice.

"Yeah." Ollie scanned the area. Shep rarely growled. Even when they'd encountered bobcats or found bear signs. The few times he'd growled, it'd been at people who were up to no good. "Let's get off the path."

"Barely a path," muttered Kaylie as she headed into the brush.

She was right. They had been following the faintest flattened trail, which appeared to be used more often by deer than by humans.

Because bears, cougars, and bobcats were common in the area, both Ollie and Kaylie were armed. Kaylie was a better shot. She'd been taught when she was young. Ollie had started much later but had worked hard to improve because he didn't like being shown up by her.

He grabbed Shep's collar. "Shhhhh," he told the dog, and he followed Kaylie.

They found a decent spot behind several pines that had grown close together. Shep was silent as Ollie listened hard, his gaze continually searching for movement in all directions. He didn't think Shep would growl at animals; he was nearly positive it was people.

It wasn't a crime to be in the woods. And most likely it was hikers ahead. But Shep's obvious dislike of whatever was up the path made Ollie extra cautious.

Seconds later they heard voices.

Kaylie met his gaze and gave a small nod. They would stay in place until the people passed.

Ollie heard two male voices, annoyance heavy in their tones.

". . . fucking waste of time," said the first man.

"Should we focus on someone else?" asked the second.

"No. I know these guys are serious hunters," answered the first. "They came all the way from Missouri."

The first voice made Ollie's skin crawl. Tim Giles.

Ollie had met Tim when they both worked in the warehouse at Lake Ski and Sports. Tim had offered to show him the ropes. The older man was in his late twenties, and Ollie had assumed he knew what was best. But Ollie saw him hide merchandise in his truck during lunch one day, and Tim caught him watching and promised he'd make Ollie's life miserable if he didn't keep his mouth shut.

Ollie had agreed and shrugged it off, telling the man he didn't care what he did.

Instead, he'd filmed Tim stealing a $300 backpack—a new style of pack that hadn't made it to the sales floor yet—and gone to the owner with the proof.

Tim was immediately fired, and Ollie discovered dog poop—he assumed it was dog—in the bed of his truck for several weeks. His driver's-side mirror was shattered, and the doors were keyed four times. He didn't tell Truman, but he did ask his boss if he could park adjacent to the warehouse entrance, a spot clearly in sight of at least one worker at all times. The manager eyed him during his request but didn't question it. Ollie suspected the manager knew the reason for it. Permission was granted, and the harassment stopped.

He'd encountered Tim twice since then. The man had slammed his shoulder as they passed at the hardware store and flipped him off in the grocery store parking lot.

A common bully.

"Did they know we were following?" asked the second voice.

"Probably," said Tim. "I'm gonna flatten their tire for leading us in circles." He laughed.

"I'd hoped we'd see them find it," the second said. "Then it'd be ours."

"We'd never have to work again," said Tim.

Ollie grimaced. Tim was a few beers short of a six-pack. All talk. The man would burn though the $2 million treasure in a year.

The voices passed and faded.

Kaylie poked him in the arm. "We need to tell Truman that someone is preying on the treasure hunters," she whispered.

"One of them was Tim Giles."

"The asshole you got fired?"

"He got himself fired by stealing."

"Hope he doesn't see your truck parked by the lake."

The thought had crossed Ollie's mind too. He stood and stretched his legs. "Ready to look a little more? If other treasure hunters are in the area, we might be onto something."

"Yeah, let's keep looking," said Kaylie. "I wonder which hunters gave them the slip."

"We need to be careful not to let people know we're looking," Ollie told her. "Don't talk about it with anyone."

Kaylie nodded and brushed a pine needle off her shoulder. "Those jerks might not be the only people trying to cheat their way to the prize. If they did catch someone who found it, what do you think they'd do?"

Ollie considered. "Tim is a lot of hot air, but if big money is involved, he might act."

"Act?"

Ollie touched the butt of his pistol.

"Holy shit! You think he'd shoot someone?"

"Maybe not him, but who knows how many other people are wandering around trying to find a shortcut to get rich? What if they're desperate?"

"They're not going to scare me off the hunt," said Kaylie, moving past him toward the trail. "Other hunters were here. That means that I might be right about Owlie Lake being the foul water."

Headstrong.

"Don't you have cats to feed?" he asked.

"Later."

Mercy had grumbled numerous times about her niece's tendency to do as she pleased and not consider all possible consequences.

He and Shep followed.

Someone has to keep Kaylie out of trouble.

6

By four o'clock Truman had the ATVs back in the department garage. He'd left Mercy and Evan at the Kerr home in the woods since Mercy seemed to have the investigation in hand, and Truman had received two texts from Lucas asking when he would return to town.

"Why?" Truman had asked when he called in.

"Ben had to break up a fistfight outside the diner, and we've had four complaints about trespassers looking for treasure."

"Ben okay?" The officer was in his seventies, had worked for the Eagle's Nest police department for over thirty years, and refused to retire. Which was a good thing because Truman depended on Ben's wealth of knowledge about the people in his town.

"Got scraped knuckles and a gleam in his eye," said Lucas.

"I guess that's good."

Truman was still chuckling about Ben when he entered the department and was surprised to see his three officers grouped in front of the large Deschutes County map on the wall. It was newly married officer Samuel Robb's day off, but he had come in to discuss search strategy with the other officers.

Lucas sat at his desk and grinned when he saw Truman's gaze land on the bickering officers.

"They've been doing that for an hour," Lucas whispered. "Earlier I had to forcefully peel Royce away to send him to check on Lucille Melton's chickens."

"What's wrong with the chickens?" asked Truman.

"She said someone's stealing eggs. Some mornings there's no eggs at all, and she was positive she saw a man in a baseball cap near her coop this afternoon."

"Don't chickens simply not lay eggs sometimes?" asked Truman.

Lucas lifted his hands. "It happens. But since she saw someone, I figured we should check." He glanced back at the three officers. "Royce didn't find anything wrong. He went and bought a padlock for Lucille to put on her coop's door. She seemed satisfied."

"Good."

Police calls about chickens, cows, and horses weren't uncommon. Sometimes residents simply needed a hand. The oddest animal call—so far—had come when the little Romero boy's frog had gotten on their roof. Mom had a bad leg and Dad was out of town. So Truman had grabbed a ladder out of the Romero shed and climbed up after the frog, who had been getting dehydrated in the sun.

Small-town life.

It wasn't for everyone, but he loved it. He didn't miss the pace of a big-city police department at all. He joined the three men arguing in front of the map.

"Did you figure out where the treasure is yet?" Truman asked, keeping a straight face.

"Lotta options," Ben said with a thoughtful look in his eye. "He was awfully vague in his clues."

The other two men nodded.

"It can't be too vague if dozens of treasure hunters have pinpointed Eagle's Nest."

"They're also gathering in Pigeon Forge, Tennessee," said Samuel. "We might be thousands of miles off."

"Well, I think Eagle's Nest is the right location," said Ben. "One of the first lines is 'Follow the bird that cried over the mountains of falling water.' I have no doubt that 'the mountains of falling water' refers to the Cascade mountain range. Eagle's Nest is the closest named town that fits. If the title 'In the Pines' doesn't describe our area, I don't know what does."

"But wouldn't a forge be hot and make a bird cry? Maybe Pigeon Forge is right," said Truman, half in jest.

"Big difference between a pigeon and an eagle," said Royce, his eyes serious. "We've been discussing what kind of bird would cry, but lots of birdcalls can be described as cries. So the clue is vague there, but we have to assume he used *cried* for a specific reason."

Why am I encouraging them?

"Royce, Lucas has a call for you to go on," said Truman, raising a brow at Lucas, who looked briefly confused.

"Um . . . yeah." Lucas grabbed a note off his desk. "Dixie Griffen spotted a suspicious man walking down Alder. When he saw her looking at him, he sped up."

The office went silent.

"That's it?" asked Royce. "She calls something in every other week."

"She lives alone and gets nervous," said Truman. "Nothing wrong with taking time to reassure her." He'd stopped by Dixie's home at least a dozen times in the past year. The other officers had done their share of stops too. "Swing by the Harris farm too. He's complained about trespassers. See if you can work something out to keep people from crossing his field."

"He put up a Trespassers will be shot sign," said Samuel.

"That didn't work?" asked Truman.

"Nope. He says people are taking selfies with the sign."

"Huh." Truman wished he could say he was surprised. "Stop by anyway. Maybe the two of you can come up with another idea." He looked to Ben. "Can I talk to you in my office for a minute?" The older man nodded and followed Truman down the hall.

Inside, Truman took off his hat and sat in his chair, tipping it back as far as it'd go.

"What's up, boss?" Ben asked, and he took a seat.

"You know Evan Bolton, the Deschutes County detective, right?"

"Yes, sir. Good man."

"Do you know his parents?"

Ben twisted his mouth as he thought. "Not sure . . . He's from Bend. I don't know as many families down that way."

"You ever hear about a sister of Bolton's that went missing?"

Ben's white brows jerked. "Sister?" He rubbed the back of his head, lost in thought. "Maybe. Did she run off with a boy? In high school or something?"

"Yes. Her name was Bethany Bolton."

"Rings a few bells. Seems like the young man involved was from around here. That might be why her name is familiar."

"His name was Victor Kerr."

Ben's eyes lit up. "Aha. The Kerrs. Shoulda known."

"Why?"

"I don't think I've heard the Kerr name in ten years. Before that seems like I'd stumble across one every month. Usually breaking up fistfights. There were quite a few men in the family . . . uncles, brothers, sons. I couldn't keep them straight."

"Do you remember a Victor?"

Ben thought hard. "Not really. The Kerrs I remember dealing with were in their forties and fifties a decade or two ago. Victor would be too young."

"They don't live around here anymore?" Truman asked.

"Nope. All gone. Some left and others are dead—the older generation anyway. I remember it was a big deal when two of the older crew died in the same accident. Joey and Josh. Drunk on the river."

"That's horrible." There'd been one boating accident in Eagle's Nest already that summer, and Truman knew there'd be more.

"One of the widows might still live in the area. I could check for you."

"Thanks. I'll look into it and let you know if I need an introduction," said Truman.

"Why the questions about the Kerrs?"

"Well, I started with questions about the Boltons. Bethany Bolton—now known as Bridget Kerr—is missing. She lives about a half hour from here, and her kids haven't heard from her in two weeks," said Truman. "When I contacted Evan, he told me she'd been missing for fourteen years. Ran off with a boyfriend. Evan said no one ever heard from her again."

"I'll be darned." Ben scratched his chin. "She never left the area?"

"Doesn't look like it. They've been living off the grid. The kids said they weren't allowed to talk about their extended family. They never knew they had an uncle until the mom said she was going to visit him."

"She went to Evan's?"

"Nope. She's vanished into thin air along with an eighteen-month-old."

Ben straightened in his chair. "A baby?"

"I notified Mercy since the FBI works closely with the National Center for Missing and Exploited Children. The more hands and experts on board with a case like this, the better."

Ben studied him for a long moment. "But you're not done with this case, are you?"

Truman shifted in his chair. The Kerr home was in the Deschutes County sheriff's jurisdiction, and with the FBI involved because of the missing baby, they had no need for a small-town police chief.

But Theodore Kerr had come to *him*.

Truman couldn't get the boy's serious gaze out of his mind.

I'm emotionally invested.

It wouldn't hurt to do a little legwork on the side and track down what was left of the Kerr family. He'd keep Mercy in the loop with what he found.

"No, I'm not done," he told Ben. "Where do you think the Kerr widow is living?" He grabbed a pencil and pulled out a notepad. "Who else in town should I ask about the Kerrs?"

"Hey, Chief!" Lucas yelled down the hall. "We've got a shooter at Walker's Lumberyard."

Truman was on his feet before Lucas finished yelling. Ben stepped out of his way as Truman strode out of his office and then immediately followed.

"I radioed Royce and sent him to the lumberyard," Lucas said.

"I'm on it too," said Samuel. "My gear is in my truck." He ran out the front door, slamming it behind him.

"What have you heard?" Truman asked Lucas as he set his cowboy hat on his head. His heart was pounding, but he was focused.

"Nick Walker called it in. Said two guys he didn't recognize had started arguing outside his business. He'd been keeping an eye on them when one pulled out a gun. The other darted into Nick's big warehouse as the first guy shot at him."

"Jesus," muttered Ben.

"Nick ordered all his employees into his office. Said he's heard two more shots. He thinks the second guy fired back."

"On our way."

"Truman, one more thing." Lucas paused.

"*What?*"

"Nick says Rose and baby Henry are on the property somewhere, but he can't find them."

Truman's heart stopped. Mercy's sister and nephew were precious to him. "What do you mean he can't find them?"

"Rose took Henry for a walk while waiting for Nick to finish with a customer."

Mercy's sister was blind. Rose was one of the most capable women he knew, but she had to be terrified by the shots.

"Nick is out looking for them?" asked Truman.

"Yes," said Lucas.

"Dammit! Tell Nick to get somewhere safe."

Lucas stared at him.

Ben shook his head. "You know Nick won't stop searching for his wife and son when there's a shooter around. Would you?"

No.

"Let's go." Truman headed out the door with Ben behind him.

7

Ben talked the entire time as he rode with Truman to the outskirts of Eagle's Nest. Truman tuned him out, his thoughts racing through different possibilities of what he might encounter at the lumberyard.

"Watch out!" Ben said as Truman sped around a curve.

Two pickups blocked the narrow road a hundred yards from the scene, their drivers crouched down behind the trucks, keeping an eye on the building. Samuel's truck was pulled off to the side. As Truman parked behind him, Samuel stepped out of the cab in shorts and a ballistic vest with POLICE in bright letters across the front and back.

"Who are the two men blocking the road?" Truman asked Ben.

"Lou and Phil," said Ben. "Nice of them to lend a hand and keep traffic away from the lumberyard."

Looking beyond the two trucks, Truman saw Royce's patrol vehicle far down the road, past the lumberyard, blocking the traffic from the south. The road was effectively closed from both directions to keep out passersby. Truman didn't see Royce.

"Tell them to leave," Truman ordered Ben. "Say thanks but to get the hell out of the area and that we can take it from here." Ben yanked the rifle from Truman's dash and left.

Walker's Lumberyard encompassed several acres. It had a huge yellow metal structure with three big sliding doors, and the grounds were stacked with dozens of piles of fresh lumber, creating a complicated maze.

"Royce," Truman said into the radio on his shoulder as Samuel joined him. "Where are you?"

"Inside the warehouse. Just to the left of the west door. I heard one more shot as I pulled up, but now they're just shouting."

"Did you see them?"

"No, but so far I've heard two voices."

"Have you seen Nick?" asked Truman as Ben returned. The two pickups pulled away, and the drivers each lifted a hand to Truman. He waved back.

"No. I saw three employees in the office as I passed the door. They're staying behind the counter."

"Samuel and I will come in through the east door, and I'll send Ben around to the rear."

"Got it," said Royce as Ben and Samuel nodded.

"Let's go."

Truman and his officers jogged along the road, staying low. Hyperalert but his breathing calm, Truman kept his eyes fixed on the building and listened hard for any sound. Lucas's voice sounded from his radio. "Nick says he's in the back of the warehouse. East corner. Says he saw two men. Both with handguns."

"Did he find Rose?" asked Truman.

"No."

"Tell him to stay put."

When the three of them reached the corner of the huge building, Ben split off as Truman and Samuel headed for the far door. Shouting voices sounded inside the warehouse. Truman eyed the stacks of lumber in the lot. Anyone hiding in them would be behind him and Samuel.

Are there more than two people involved?

"Royce, did you hear or see anyone outside in the stacks?"

"No."

He pressed his lips together. As much as he hated to not clear the stacks, his first priority was to get to the shooters and stop them. He and Samuel moved inside the big open door, each stepping to one side, their backs to the wall.

Shouts echoed off the high metal ceiling and walls.

"I saw you do it! Don't bullshit me!"

Truman spotted Royce. The officer was slowly making his way down the first long aisle of two-by-fours. Truman waved Samuel to the third row, and he took the second.

"No I didn't! I told you!"

"You're trying to steal from me!"

Truman pressed forward, his weapon leading. At the far end, a man darted across his aisle, a revolver in hand.

"Put away your fucking gun!" yelled one of the shooters.

The voices ricocheted in the warehouse; Truman couldn't pinpoint their locations.

"You stole my notes!"

Notes?

Truman briefly closed his eyes. *Are they treasure hunters?*

He sped to the end of his aisle and spotted a second man with a gun. "Eagle's Nest Police! Lower your weapon."

The second man turned, shock on his face, raising his arms in the air. His gun was still in his hand. Royce appeared at the gunman's four o'clock, his weapon aimed.

"Put down the gun," Truman said.

"It's not my fault," said the man. Truman estimated him to be in his early thirties. He wore jeans and a T-shirt with the brand name WRANGLER emblazoned across the front. His gaze held Truman's as he set the gun on the floor. "He stole something from me."

"Ben and I have the other guy," said Samuel through the radio.

"Good!" said Wrangler. "Arrest him for theft!"

"Take five big steps backward," ordered Royce, surprising Wrangler with the knowledge that someone was behind him. "And lay facedown."

Truman watched as Royce cuffed the man. "Who else is with you guys?" he asked Wrangler.

"It's just me and him."

"Who is he?" asked Truman.

"Dunno. Just caught him stealing stuff out of my car."

Samuel and Ben approached with the other suspect, and Nick Walker appeared from the back of the warehouse. His face was tense. "Did you see Rose?" he asked the officers.

All gave negative responses.

Samuel jerked the arm of his suspect. "You see a woman in here?"

"Nah."

"Me neither," said Truman's suspect.

"I'll help you look," Truman told Nick, holstering his weapon. "You got these two?" he asked his three officers.

They nodded, and Truman followed Nick toward the east entrance. The man's long legs quickly covered ground, making Truman break into a half jog to keep up.

"I've pretty much covered inside the warehouse," said Nick. "She's got to be outside somewhere." His voice was strained.

"I'm sure she's fine," said Truman. "They didn't even see her."

"Stray gunfire," stated Nick, walking faster as they left the building.

He has a point.

"I'll check this way," said Nick. Truman nodded and jogged to the other end of the big stacks of lumber.

Mercy had gone missing before. He understood Nick's anxiety.

Do I?

He didn't have a child. Nick's anxiety had to be double what Truman had ever experienced.

"Rose!" he shouted. He heard Nick do the same.

Barking came from the end of the lot.

Belle?

Nick's German shepherd was always at his side—or Rose's. Truman broke into a run. "Rose! Are you okay? It's safe to come out now!"

"I'm over here!"

Relief swept over him, and Truman followed Rose's voice. He spotted the dog next to two tall stacks of plywood. Nick appeared from the opposite direction as Rose cautiously stepped out from between the piles, Henry clutched to her chest.

Truman exhaled, and Nick pulled his wife and son into a giant hug. After a moment, Rose pulled back.

"What happened?" she asked. "Is everyone okay?"

"Two guys started shooting on the property," Nick told her. "No one is hurt, and the police have them."

Understanding crossed her face. "When I heard the shots, I stopped and got down as close as I could to one of the lumber piles. I didn't dare move. I actually felt the sound waves."

"You felt the gunshots?" Truman asked.

Rose nodded and touched one cheek. "A light pressure on my face and in my ears. I knew they weren't far away."

"The first two shots were outside, not far from the stacks," said Nick. "I'm glad you two are all right." He took Henry from her arms and kissed the boy on the cheek. Henry squirmed and reached for Rose.

"I'll check on my men," said Truman. He gave Belle a rough rub on her head. "Good dog."

The officers and the two cuffed men had just stepped out of the warehouse. The suspects were bickering.

"Shut. Up," Royce ordered the men, surprising Truman. The young cop was never rude.

"What's wrong?" asked Truman as he approached.

"I told you," said Wrangler. "This guy stole my stuff and won't say where it is."

"I done nothin'," said the second. He wore baggy cargo shorts and a sleeveless red shirt. His arms were covered in a dozen tattoos. Most were of dogs.

"I saw you!"

"I was picking up a nail next to your tire," said Dog Lover. "I wasn't in your car." He looked to Truman. "This guy shot at me right here in the parking lot. If someone shoots at me, I got the right to shoot back, right? The asshole was practically hunting me."

"Where's your car?" Truman asked Wrangler.

"The Honda over there," he said with a jerk of his chin.

Truman approached the red car and tried a door handle. It opened. "Where were these notes of yours?"

"Back seat in a notebook."

Truman opened a rear door and didn't see a notebook. He raised an eyebrow at Dog Lover.

"I got nothin' to do with it."

"He's from Ohio," said Ben, pointing at Wrangler. "This one's from Arizona."

Truman sighed. "Let me guess. You're both here hunting treasure."

The men were silent, shooting glares at one another.

Truman shut the car door and stepped back, studying the ground.

A flash of yellow under the car caught his attention. He knelt and pulled out a thin three-ring binder.

"That's mine!" Wrangler shrieked. "I told you he took it! He must have ditched it. I was protecting what's mine."

"And that justifies shooting at him?"

"I wasn't shooting *at* him. I was just trying to scare him a little."

Dog Lover spoke up. "I was only doing the same." He nodded emphatically.

"Do you hear yourselves?" Truman asked. "You two had a shoot-out in public over this binder. Doesn't that sound nuts to you?"

"I was careful," said Wrangler. "Made sure no one was in my line of fire."

Truman opened the binder, unable to listen anymore. It was packed with maps and printouts. Flipping through it, he found page after page of handwritten notes. They were written in perfect script. Handwriting an English teacher would be proud of. He eyed Wrangler's patchy beard and stained shirt. This wasn't a man with perfect handwriting or a man who had the intelligence to solve the clues.

"Don't look at those! That's my work!"

The binder still open in his hands, he looked at Wrangler. "You wrote this?"

"Of course. It's my binder."

"This is actually your handwriting?" Truman asked, fixing a stern eye on the man.

Wrangler shuffled his feet. "My sister's working with me. She's at home studying it some more while I physically look."

That makes a little more sense.

Truman took a closer look at a sketch of a map, also perfectly drawn and labeled.

"Close that! You're trying to steal what I figured out!"

Truman shut the binder with a snap. "You really think I care about this?"

"It's two million dollars!" Wrangler's eyes flashed with a touch of craziness.

"And you have the answer to finding that money in here?"

Wrangler clamped his mouth closed.

Dog Lover stared at the ground, guilt in his posture.

44

Truman looked from one to the other in disgust. The hunt had driven one man to steal and both to shoot. That was in addition to all the trespassing and traffic calls since Eagle's Nest had been in the spotlight.

I don't know how much more of this I can take.

The treasure hunt was upsetting the peace in his town.

What's next?

8

After Truman went back to town, Mercy watched Evan interact with his new niece and nephew. He'd been a deer in the headlights at first, but he was finally relaxing a bit. The kids were warming up to him. Theodore was quiet, but the sad look in his eyes had eased. Charlotte was talking up a storm.

Mercy's phone buzzed. A text from Eddie.

IS THIS A GOOD TIME TO TALK?

She headed out the back door of the house and called him. "What did you find?"

"Hi to you too," said Eddie.

"We already talked a few times today. Do you need a greeting every time?"

"Common courtesy. It's not like I'm asking for a bunch of small talk."

"Which you wouldn't get from me anyway."

Eddie sighed loudly in the phone. "I've been digging for information on the Kerr parents. After you told me her name had been Bethany Bolton, I found an expired driver's license. She never got one in her new name."

"Do you think she didn't drive?" Mercy wondered if her husband wouldn't let her. She was getting a sense of authoritarianism about

Victor Kerr that rubbed her the wrong way. The sad faces on the kids when they'd said they weren't allowed to discuss certain topics was still eating at her.

"Dunno. But the most recent license for Victor is over a decade old. Maybe he didn't drive either."

"Or had a license in a different name."

"For that matter, Bethany Bolton could have done the same."

"You're supposed to be answering questions for me, Eddie. Not creating new ones."

"I didn't find criminal records for either one of them, but I did find older records for a Joseph and Joshua Kerr in Deschutes County. Their ages would be about right for Victor Kerr's father or maybe an uncle. But the problem is Joseph and Joshua died several years ago. A boating accident."

"It's a dead end?" asked Mercy. "No pun intended. But what kind of criminal activity did you find?"

"Tax evasion. Rubber checks. Forged licenses. Joshua started a fire at a bank."

"You know what this sounds like to me?" asked Mercy.

"Yep. Sovereign citizens."

Mercy inwardly groaned. Sovereign citizens believed they were exempt from the laws of the United States. Mercy couldn't quite understand how they came to that conclusion, but it involved the end of the gold standard, admiralty laws, and secret Treasury accounts issued at birth. Most sovereign citizens were harmless; they fought the government with paperwork, tying up the courts with hundreds of pages of pseudolegal nonsense.

"Did you find an address for any Kerrs?"

"Extended family might be at this one address I found," said Eddie. "I see the names Christine Kerr and Linda Kerr associated with it. Maybe they were approached by Bethany." He paused. "They're way behind on property taxes."

"I'll take whatever I can get."

He read her the address, and she knew the location was about twenty miles from Eagle's Nest.

"I'll stop by there tomorrow morning and see if they've heard from Bethany. Let me know if you dig up anything else."

"I will."

"And Eddie . . . can you search for any unidentified female deaths in the area? Infants too—well, I guess the baby is a year and a half. To me that's not an infant." Baby Henry's smile popped into her head; he could almost walk. Her nephew was a little younger than the missing Molly Kerr.

"On it."

Mercy ended the call and spent a few moments outside the Kerr home, soaking in the quiet and sunshine. The area was silent and absolutely nothing moved. Even the firs and pines along the edge of the clearing stood absolutely still. No sounds of vehicles or people.

Perfect.

This was how she liked to live. She valued her privacy and quiet. After the wedding, she and Kaylie had moved into Truman's house in Eagle's Nest. The neighborhood felt like a typical suburb: cookie-cutter houses, close neighbors, and small lots. But they spent long weekends in her cabin hidden in the Cascade mountain range. They'd considered moving into the cabin, but it wasn't practical for their jobs or for the kids. She and Truman had discussed buying something closer to town on a few acres, but the perfect property hadn't come on the market yet.

Mercy pressed her ear to the door and heard Charlotte talking animatedly. Things seemed to be going well, and Mercy hated to interrupt. The large barn caught her attention, and she decided to check it out, along with the two outbuildings. She'd seen goats and heard chickens when they first arrived, but no other animals.

She slid open the heavy barn door and was greeted by the smell of hay. And manure. The goats had free access from their pen outdoors to a large stall inside. One baaed at her, and she scratched its head. A small tractor and attachments sat in one corner, covered with a light layer of dust. The walls were lined with an assortment of large cabinets. Some were wooden and homemade, while other plastic cabinets clearly came from a store. She peeked in one. Gardening tools. Another had feed for the goats and chickens. A third had neat rows of fruit and vegetables in glass canning jars.

Everything was very organized and tidy. Mercy approved.

She headed back to the house, noting the large propane tank at the back of the home and the solar panels on the roof.

This is a place someone could stay a long time.

Which was the goal of the prepper life. To live off the land and be prepared to isolate for extended periods. It took education and hard work to make it viable. The Kerrs appeared to have done that for their family.

Preppers came from all walks of life, and Central and Eastern Oregon provided the rural land and small towns to attract them. Here they lived in anonymity and privacy. The way Mercy had been raised.

When Mercy was young, she had been jealous of the town kids. They had the fashionable clothes, took vacations, and ate out in restaurants. It wasn't until she was older that she'd respected the skills and mindset her parents had taught. Mercy eventually moved to the big city but couldn't leave behind what had been hammered into her head for decades. Even though she owned a place in Portland, she bought a remote cabin and outfitted it for survival, doing maintenance there on the weekends, telling no one where she was or what she was doing.

Survival meant secrecy. If the world went to hell, you didn't want everyone to know where you'd set up your haven.

It'd felt like a dirty secret for years. Even her closest coworkers hadn't known about Mercy's hideaway.

Because of her upbringing, she had lived with a low-simmering anxiety, checking the national headlines every day, watching the international markets, searching for signs that indicated the start of TEOTWAWKI.

The end of the world as we know it.

The worry had driven her to prep and plan and never relax.

She'd changed when she met Truman and enfolded Kaylie and Ollie into her life. For years she'd believed it was best to live alone—fewer mouths to prep for. So she'd plunged forward, never looking up from her job and prepping her cabin. But the three of them had changed her, relaxed her, taught her that nonstop work was no way to live.

Being with the people you cared about was what a life should center around.

She learned balance.

Her cabin had burned to the ground over a year ago, but she and Truman had rebuilt on the same location. Now it was *theirs*.

And she was insanely happy.

She opened the door to the Kerr home and walked in on an intense discussion about Harry Potter. Theodore held a worn hardcover book in his lap. Both kids looked stunned.

Evan glanced at Mercy. "I just told them there are two more Harry Potter books beyond what they own."

"We *have* to read them," exclaimed Charlotte. "We thought the stories were over."

Theodore nodded, his eyes bright. "They're the best."

"I'll get them for you," promised Evan.

"Yeeeesss!" Charlotte punched a fist in the air as Theodore beamed. "When?" she demanded.

"Is tomorrow soon enough?" asked Evan.

Charlotte shook her head.

"Evan, can I talk with you outside a moment?" asked Mercy.

Both children glared at her for taking away their hero.

"It'll just be a minute," she promised.

The two of them stepped outside, and Evan exhaled heavily. "I think I won them over."

"Clearly. To Harry Potter fans, another book is like a gift of gold. Brilliant move."

"I asked what their favorite books were, and it went from there."

His grin hadn't left his face, pleasing Mercy. She'd honestly worried there would be no connection between him and the kids.

She cleared her throat. "I'm going to call child services and—"

"No."

"They can't stay here alone—even though they're clearly doing just fine."

"I'll stay the night," said Evan. "That's a better idea than taking the kids to my place."

Yes!

She'd hoped Evan would arrive at that conclusion. "You're sure about this?"

"Absolutely. It'll give me a good opportunity to talk with them about their parents and poke around a bit more. Maybe there is something here that indicates where Bethany went."

He looked content about his choice. Maybe even eager, which made Mercy positive that it'd been the right decision to bring him to the farm.

"Okay, but I'm still calling child services. They need to be informed. I'll give them your information."

Evan nodded.

"I'll do more digging on the family," Mercy continued. "I have a lead on some possible Kerr extended family. I'll check in with you tomorrow."

"I'm going to introduce them to bachelor mac and cheese tonight," said Evan. "I saw they had the sausage, bacon, and cornflakes I need for it."

Mercy's mouth watered. "Save me some."

"It's good served cold for breakfast too."

She wasn't so sure about that. "Good luck," she told him.

"I already got lucky today," he said with a tip of his head toward the home. "You use the luck to find Bethany."

"On it."

9

Ollie opened the box of fried rice, inhaled deeply, and immediately decided that Chinese takeout was one of his top-ten favorite things he'd discovered since Truman had brought him back into society.

I better make that top-ten favorite foods.

He'd discovered too many wonderful things to count. The internet. Cell phones. His truck. Girls. Food needed its own top-ten list.

He spooned out a huge serving and passed the box to Kaylie.

"Hungry?" she asked sarcastically as she glared at the rice level in the container.

"There's another container of fried rice," said Mercy.

Ollie took a big bite and grinned at Kaylie, making sure rice and beef showed in his teeth.

She rolled her eyes and dished up her own.

He looked around the table. Truman, Mercy, and Kaylie. They tried to eat dinner together several nights a week, and Ollie wondered if the others had any idea how much he enjoyed it. He'd eaten alone for too long after his grandfather died. Truman passed him another white box.

Szechuan chicken.

At Ollie's feet, Shep gave a soft whine as the smell reached him. The dog was partial to the spicy dish. Even the hot peppers. He had a stomach of iron. Ollie glanced up and caught Mercy watching him, a knowing look on her face. She didn't like any of the animals being fed from the table, so Ollie usually had to sneak him scraps.

"I met someone today who reminded me of you, Ollie," said Truman as Mercy nodded in agreement.

"Who?" asked Ollie after swallowing a big bite of chicken.

"His name is Theodore Kerr." Truman shared a story—with input from Mercy—about two children who had been living alone for the past two weeks.

"Is their mom alive?" Kaylie asked, her eyes sad.

"We'll find out," said Mercy.

Ollie's interest was piqued. He hadn't met anyone who'd lived in isolation as he had. Even though Theodore had a family, he'd still been cut off from the rest of the world for some reason.

"I'd like to meet him," Ollie told Truman, slightly surprised that he felt an affinity for someone he'd never met.

"We can make that happen." Truman then told them about the children's connection to Evan Bolton.

"I like Detective Bolton," announced Kaylie. "He tips well at the coffee shop. Aunt Pearl always tries to wait on him. She says she'd go for him if she wasn't married."

"Have you had any problems at the shop with the treasure hunters?" asked Mercy.

"It's been great for business," said Kaylie. "We're swamped," she added, pleasing Ollie. He wanted her store to be a success. Kaylie's father had left the coffee shop to her when he died. She now ran it with the help of her aunt Pearl.

"You're lucky there's been no problems," said Truman. "I've had complaints from several people in town about treasure hunters loitering or being obnoxious. And some of them can be dangerous. We had a shooting today."

Ollie had heard about the shots fired at the lumberyard. Something nudged his foot, and Kaylie made wide eyes at him.

She wants me to tell Truman about the guys at the lake.

He gave her an infinitesimal shake of his head. Tim Giles was a lot of hot air, and Ollie didn't want Truman involved unless Tim actually did something illegal. In the past Tim had harassed Ollie about having a police chief to hide behind even though Ollie had never gone to Truman about anything.

Tim was simply a jerk. And a bully.

Kaylie lowered her left shoulder in an odd way and focused on stabbing a shrimp with her fork.

She fed a cat something.

The cats, Dulce and Simon, were camped out under Kaylie's chair. They knew she was a rule breaker.

"I know you kids have been doing your own bit of treasure hunting," said Truman. "I want you to be careful around the town's newcomers. Apparently it can get violent when two million dollars is at stake."

"Do you think it's really worth two million?" asked Kaylie.

Truman shrugged. "It could be a big hoax. Who knows?"

Ollie had read everything he could find about Chester Rollins, the odd millionaire who'd hidden the treasure. The ninety-year-old had died a few weeks ago without any heirs, and his lawyer, who'd posted the hunt, had said Chester wanted it to be his legacy. The millionaire had a reputation for doing the opposite of what anyone told him and enjoyed ordering people around. From what he'd read, Ollie believed Chester would hide a treasure simply for the pleasure of making people scramble.

"I think he did it," said Ollie. "He seems the type. He liked to spend his money on weird things. I read he spent a hundred thousand dollars on ashtrays that belonged to Czar Nicholas the second."

"Well, I'll be glad when they leave town and I get some peace back," grumbled Truman, scooping up a piece of sweet-and-sour pork. "It's been ridiculous. Even the press is causing problems. They keep calling the station. After the shooting today, I swear Lucas was on the phone nonstop telling them it was none of their business."

"We had two news satellite trucks at the café this morning," added Kaylie. "They cleaned the shop out of lemon bars and tried to interview me. I wasn't interested in talking to them, but I saw them filming with Leighton Underwood."

Mercy laughed. "Leighton will give them an earful of nuttiness."

Ollie liked the tall old man. He had formal manners and always the oddest stories to tell. Leighton believed in aliens, a secret world government, and chemtrails that were dumbing down Americans.

The doorbell rang, and Kaylie jumped out of her chair. "That'll be the kittens!"

"More kittens?" asked Truman, shooting Mercy a stunned look.

"She didn't warn you?" Mercy asked.

Truman sighed, shook his head, and dug into his Chinese food. Ollie grinned. Kaylie had joined a cat rescue and had fostered two litters of kittens over the past several months. Apparently litter number three had just arrived. The last batch had been adopted a week ago, and Ollie missed seeing the little fur balls scamper around the house. Kaylie had converted an empty bedroom into a kitten room, but as the kittens got older, they had the run of the house.

Dulce and Simon were indifferent to the kittens and avoided them. Shep had earned the title of kitten uncle. He loved to snuggle with each litter and had surprised everyone by letting the kittens crawl all over him and chase his tail.

Kaylie reappeared, a large cat carrier in her hands. "There are five of them!"

"Sheesh," muttered Truman. But he was the first to stick a finger through the wire door of the carrier and scratch the head of a curious orange baby. "Great markings," he told Kaylie. "Look at all the multicolored spots on that one."

They all admired the babies, and Kaylie headed to the kitten room with her new charges.

"One of these days, she's going to find one that she can't let go," said Mercy.

"I don't think so," said Ollie. "By the time they've been here a month, she's tired of the vet visits and cleaning up after them. She's always happy to see them find good homes."

Ollie had become particularly attached to a little black tuxedo in the second litter. A family with two young boys had fallen in love with Tux and one of his siblings. Only the absolute adoration in the boys' eyes had made it bearable for Ollie to let the kitten go.

"I don't know how she finds time for everything," said Mercy. "She works more than forty hours a week. At least she won't have any college classes until the fall." She looked at Ollie. "How much time are you two spending searching for treasure?"

"Not much," said Ollie, his mouth full. Actually he was up late every night studying the various websites where people held discussions about the clues and hunt. He'd spent many hours fantasizing about how he would use the money. Kaylie had insisted a portion would go toward her kitten room to buy more supplies.

Ollie had his eye on a new truck. One with adaptive cruise control and a power outlet that worked like a generator. But he would always keep the old truck Truman had bought him because . . . well, because Truman had bought it for him.

The old truck was a sentimental symbol of his new life. It stood for inclusion and family.

"Think the treasure is actually somewhere near Eagle's Nest?" asked Mercy. She hadn't paid much attention to the hunt. Her job kept her busy. But she always listened and helped when Ollie had questions about the area. She'd lived in Eagle's Nest until she was eighteen. The town had changed since then, but according to Mercy, not by much.

"I'll let you know when I find it," said Ollie.

Truman set down his drink and took a hard look at Ollie. "You're really into this, aren't you?"

Ollie nodded, a little embarrassed that he was spending so much time on a long shot.

"Someone has to find it," said Truman. "Might as well be you. Just make sure you're keeping up at work."

"Of course." He loved his jobs at the sporting goods warehouse and the car dealership.

"And like I said, watch out for the other treasure hunters. Keep a low profile. Money makes people do stupid things."

"Yes, sir," said Ollie. He thought of Tim Giles's comments on the trail that morning and wondered if he should tell Truman.

Nah. Giles is just a bully.

He was almost certain.

10

The next morning, Truman was enjoying his first cup of coffee when Lucas appeared in his office doorway, looking pale.

"What is it?" Truman asked sharply.

"That shooter from the lumberyard that we processed last night." Lucas swallowed hard. "Samuel just called and said Sandy found him dead behind her bed-and-breakfast. He's been shot in the head."

"Which shooter?" asked Truman, standing and reaching for his hat.

"Billy Serrano."

Wrangler. The one who claimed his notebook was stolen.

Both men had been charged and released. Wrangler had gotten to keep his notebook.

Did we send him to his death?

"What the hell is going on with this treasure hunt?" asked Lucas. "Was he killed for his information?"

"Was he staying at Sandy's B and B?"

"Yeah. She said he stayed there the last two nights."

"She okay?"

"A little shook up. Samuel's taking care of her."

Truman nodded. The two were newlyweds, and he knew how protective Samuel could be even though Sandy was one of the most independent women in town. "Call county and tell them we need a detective and crime scene team. The medical examiner too," he said as

Lucas followed him down the hall. Truman didn't have the resources to process a murder with his tiny department. And the murder of a person he'd arrested and released the day before definitely required outside resources and support. "What local address did we get for the other shooter . . . Matt Stephens?"

"He gave a motel address in Bend."

"Send Royce over there."

Lucas nodded and headed back to his desk as Truman went out the front door.

Truman borrowed sheets from Sandy to hang to block the look-ie-loos trying to see the crime scene. The dumpster and fence were enough to block the view from three sides, but word had gotten out, and the locals were "casually" passing by, in addition to members of the press, who were more persistent and obvious about their desire for answers.

He fumed as he hung the sheets. Someone had tampered with the security cameras at the bed-and-breakfast. Cameras that he had bought and installed himself after Sandy had been a victim of vandalism. One had been set up to cover the area by the dumpsters. It had a perfect angle on the crime. He had checked the footage and cursed out loud as someone sprayed paint, blocking the view.

The medical examiner, Natasha Lockhart, had been examining the body for the last few minutes as Truman, Ben, and two crime scene techs watched. She carefully palpated the skull, and her gloved hands pressed and skimmed through the victim's hair. But when she moved to the facial bones, Truman focused on a wheel of the dumpster. Billy Serrano had a large exit wound that had obliterated one of his eyes. Looking at it was hard enough; watching someone touch it made him cringe.

"Entry wound at the base of his skull," Dr. Lockhart muttered to herself. "An upward angle to exit through the left orbit."

"Shot from the back." Ben shifted his weight, his hands resting on his duty belt, anger in his tone.

Truman said nothing. His mind was reviewing the interactions he'd seen between Billy and Matt Stephens the day before. He wouldn't have pegged Stephens as a murderer. A lazy thief, yes. But not a murderer. Royce had found Stephens at his hotel, and he'd agreed to return to the Eagle's Nest Police Department for questioning about the lumberyard incident the day before. Royce hadn't mentioned Billy Serrano's murder, and neither had Stephens.

Royce said Stephens had been a bit grumpy about being asked to return but hadn't balked. The two of them were already waiting at the station for Truman's questions.

It wasn't Stephens.

Any murderer with half a brain would have left town after killing someone he'd been accused of shooting at the day before. Instead, Stephens had answered the hotel door in his underwear and asked if he could finish his coffee before going with Royce.

So who did it?

The crime scene techs had found a nine-millimeter casing a few yards away and were still searching for the bullet. Drag marks and blood tracks indicated that Serrano had been pulled behind the dumpster after he was shot.

"How could no one hear anything?" asked Ben. "A suppressor on the weapon?"

"Probably," said Truman. Eagle's Nest was rural, but not rural enough for no one to report hearing a gunshot in the middle of town.

"It was planned," said Ben, his forehead wrinkling in thought.

"Yep."

Dr. Lockhart stood and removed her gloves, then set them on the body. She pulled out her phone, checked a weather app, and used her calculator. "Based on the temperatures overnight and his current body temperature, I'd estimate he died between midnight and three a.m. I'll verify it once I get him on my table and run some labs."

Truman was pleased with the relatively tight window of time. "The cameras were damaged at ten p.m. last night. Another indicator that it was planned."

"Need anything else, Chief?" Dr. Lockhart asked, sliding her phone in the back pocket of her jeans. She was petite with long, dark hair, and the kindest ME he'd ever met.

"A suspect."

"That's on you," she answered. She glanced behind him, and he sensed that the makeshift curtain of sheets had moved. "Actually, it appears to be on Evan."

"Truman. Natasha." Evan Bolton greeted them as Truman turned and held out a hand.

"This murder landed on your desk?" Truman asked. "What about Theodore and Charlotte?"

"When I got the call, I asked them how they felt about meeting Kaylie and Ollie and hanging out with them while I worked. They jumped at the opportunity." Evan's mouth flattened as his face went grim. "I don't think they've ever been to a suburban neighborhood."

"You're saying they're at my place?" Truman asked.

"Yep. Dropped them off a few minutes ago. I checked with Mercy first, and she thought it was a great idea. They don't need supervision, but I feel a little better, and I think the exposure will be good for them."

"You have kids now, Detective?" asked Dr. Lockhart, a sly grin on her face. "Congratulations. That was sudden."

Evan gave her a quick rundown of the previous day's events.

Dr. Lockhart pressed her lips together. "Two weeks ago I processed a Jane Doe in her thirties who was found in Jefferson County. I assume you've already checked?"

"Mercy and the FBI are handling that aspect," said Evan. "But I'll confirm that they've ruled it out." He paused. "Cause of death?"

"Strangulation. She was dumped off Highway 97."

Evan simply nodded, his eyes emotionless.

That Jane Doe could be his sister.

Truman felt for the detective.

Dr. Lockhart looked down at the body. "You've got a violent crime here, Chief."

"The town has been upside down since the treasure hunt made the national news, which is the only reason this guy was in town. I've had all sorts of problems with the hunters. It started as mostly trespassing, but it's escalated to fights and some shots fired."

"That's nuts," said Evan. "You already know this guy was involved?"

Truman updated him on the lumberyard shooting and told him the other shooter was waiting at the Eagle's Nest station for questioning.

Evan shook his head. "I'll search his room inside the B and B for the notebook and then go interview Matt Stephens. Money will make people do crazy things."

"I gotta tell you," Truman said. "I'm not feeling Stephens for this shooting. You'll see when you meet him."

"Noted," said Evan. "Sorry it's been so crazy for you. I thought it was a bigger crowd than usual hovering outside this scene. A lot of press too."

"Tell me about it. I want someone to find the treasure so the press and hunters will get out of my town." Truman glanced at the victim.

Will there be more deaths from the hunt?

11

Ollie tried not to grin. Charlotte couldn't take her gaze from the stud in Kaylie's nose.

He didn't notice Kaylie's piercing anymore, but he remembered how shocking the tiny glittering stone had seemed when they first met. Now it was simply part of her. The colors changed depending on her mood and clothes.

Before Evan dropped off the kids, Ollie and Kaylie had agreed on baking, video games, and kittens to entertain the kids for the day. Ollie remembered the first time he'd held a video game controller and was excited to see Theodore's reaction.

It wasn't going as planned.

Evan introduced the four of them and left, stating he was running late and that he'd check in later. Theodore had quietly taken a seat on the couch, eyeing a small bookcase crammed with novels. Charlotte had studied Kaylie from head to toe and gotten stuck on the nose piercing. "Can I see your closet?" she asked, still staring at the stud.

Kaylie paused for a long second. "I guess so. It's a bit of a mess."

Ollie coughed. Kaylie had as many clothes on her bedroom floor as in her closet.

"Can I see your shoes? And jewelry?" Charlotte asked, excitement growing in her voice.

"Charlotte!" said Theodore. "That's impolite."

"It's fine," said Kaylie, grinning at Charlotte. "I might even have some things I've outgrown that might fit you."

Charlotte clasped her hands together, a dreamy look in her eye. "Do you have any cocktail dresses?" she asked hopefully.

Kaylie blinked. "Ummm . . . no. Maybe some sundresses. Follow me. I'll show you the kitten room after that."

Ollie watched Charlotte eagerly trail after the teenager, leaving him alone with the silent boy. Sympathy filled Ollie. Theodore's mother had been missing for weeks. And now he'd been brought to a strange home with two teenagers.

"Do you want to see the kittens?" Ollie asked.

"We recently had a litter in our barn," said Theodore, who was still studying the books on the shelf.

I guess that's a no.

"Are you hungry?" Ollie asked, taking a seat on the ottoman and facing Theodore. "Did you eat breakfast?"

"Evan sort of rushed us out of the house this morning," said Theodore. "He said you'd have breakfast for us." The young teen squirmed and looked at his hands in his lap. "That felt kind of rude."

Ollie jumped to his feet. "Not at all. Kaylie brings home the leftovers from the café, and we've got some of her breakfast bars." A minute later he had Theodore seated at the kitchen counter with two of Kaylie's dark chocolate oatmeal bars. Theodore took a tentative bite and his face lit up. He took a second, more enthusiastic bite. Truman's black cat, Simon, hopped up on an adjacent stool and stared at Theodore, her yellow eyes asking him to share.

"Should I get Charlotte?" Ollie asked.

"Nah. Let her do her girly stuff." Theodore finished one bar and started on the other.

"Mercy said you like Harry Potter."

Theodore stopped midchew and straightened. "Do you have the two most recent books?" he asked around the food in his mouth.

"We do."

Theodore started to cram the rest of the second bar in his mouth.

"Slow down. I'll loan you the books, and you can take them home."

The boy slowed, nodded, and took a reasonable bite, but his eyes still glowed with excitement.

"Are you worried about your mom?" Ollie asked, pouring a glass of milk. Neither kid seemed concerned to him. He'd overheard Mercy mention the same thing to Truman the night before. It didn't seem right.

"I'm sure she's fine. She and my dad used to leave for two or three weeks at a time."

"They did?"

He doesn't mind talking about his father.

"Hunting trips or supply trips. So this isn't a big deal."

It seemed like a big deal to Ollie, and something must have worried Theodore if he'd contacted Truman. "Did they ever take you with them on those trips?" He set the glass in front of Theodore.

"No. We're not allowed to go to town, where there are unconstitutional laws. It's safer to stay at home." Theodore took a sip of milk and scowled. "The houses are really close together here."

Mercy had told Ollie she believed Theodore's father came from a family of sovereign citizens. Ollie had interacted with enough sovereign citizens to be familiar with their views, which were primarily that they weren't subject to any taxation or laws. No doubt Theodore was repeating what he'd heard from his father. Just like any population, the sovereigns had their bad apples. A group of which had murdered Ollie's grandfather.

Ollie suspected Theodore's parents simply wanted to live their lives, raising their family as they wished. The kids had perfect manners and were Harry Potter fans. Violence didn't hover around them.

But Ollie agreed with the observation about the houses. Their home was in a typical neighborhood with small fenced lots. He'd felt claustrophobic for his first few weeks in the home after living in the woods for years. "It takes getting used to. But the people who live around here are really nice. Most of the world is basically good," he told the boy. It'd taken Ollie a little time to learn that for himself.

Theodore shrugged as he drank more milk. "When I was little, my mom would leave me with the Taylors sometimes when she needed to go to town—they lived a few miles away. They were nice. Let me watch TV. We don't have one."

"What did you watch?"

Theodore screwed up his face in thought. "I remember a cartoon show where a boy named Ash had a pet Pikachu. It was yellow."

Ollie nodded. He was still a Pokémon fan.

"Sometimes the Taylors would watch a show where the people just sat behind desks and talked to you. It was boring."

News broadcasts?

"I couldn't tell my dad about the shows. He'd get mad."

"Why?"

"Said we shouldn't be watching them. They teach bad things." A wistful look crossed Theodore's eyes. "He told the Taylors to keep the TV off when we were there, but I think they forgot sometimes."

"Ta-da!" Charlotte swept into the kitchen, her hands in the air. She was wearing a yellow dress with a big daisy print and a purple sweater. On her feet were flip-flops with rhinestones and bows. She looked expectantly at Theodore.

"You look ridiculous," he told her.

"Hmph. Shows what you know." Charlotte pointed at the bar in his hand. "What's that?"

"I'll get some for you," Ollie told her. "Sit." He met Kaylie's gaze, and she jerked her head toward her bedroom. He gave Charlotte two bars, poured her milk, and followed Kaylie to her room. "What's the matter?" he asked.

"If my mother had been gone for weeks, I'd be freaking out," Kaylie whispered. "Even if I was raised in the middle of nowhere and used to being on my own. Charlotte doesn't seem concerned at all."

"I thought the same thing about Theodore, but he did make the long trek on foot to find police help. He's worried at some level."

"This isn't normal behavior."

"But maybe it's normal for them. When I came here, I thought and saw things differently. My thoughts weren't wrong—they were simply a reflection of how I had lived. If you were suddenly dropped in Charlotte and Theodore's environment, I'm sure they'd think some of your behaviors and thoughts were odd too."

"Is it possible they haven't told Truman and Mercy everything?" Kaylie put her hands on her hips, concern bringing her brows together.

"That's always possible," admitted Ollie. "But what could they be holding back?"

"Like they know exactly where their mom is. Or that she hasn't really been missing for weeks."

Ollie didn't see the logic. "Then why seek help from the police?"

"Kaylie?" Charlotte called from the other room.

"Something's not right with these kids," whispered Kaylie. "I'm going to figure it out." She nodded firmly. "Be right there," she called out as she left the room. Ollie followed.

"Can you give me the recipe for these?" asked Charlotte, holding up a half-eaten bar.

"Absolutely. I'll text it to—oh, let me write it down."

Ollie watched as Kaylie searched for a sheet of paper and then started to write. Nothing was written down anymore. Everything was emailed or texted. He'd never had a cell phone before he lived with Truman. It'd been strange the first week, a small constant weight in his pocket, but now he felt naked if he left the house without it.

Theodore had finished his bars. "Can I see the books now?" he asked Ollie. Ollie gestured for him to follow him to his room. Inside, he scanned his bookshelf for the most recent Harry Potters and handed them to Theodore, who accepted them as if they were made of gold.

"Do you want to try a video game?" asked Ollie.

"I'd like to read."

Theodore followed him back out to the family room, where Ollie pointed at a beanbag. "That's great for reading." Theodore immediately plopped onto the bag, and Simon came over to sniff at his shoes. After a moment, the cat decided Theodore was worthy and joined him on the bag, curling up at the boy's hip.

"Is that Harry Potter?" Charlotte exclaimed with her mouth full.

"Yes," said Ollie.

"You'll have to wait until I'm done," said Theodore. "I got it first."

"Not fair!" Charlotte looked from Ollie to Kaylie indignantly. "We should have flipped a coin to see who goes first." She looked ready to fight her brother for the book.

Uh-oh.

Ollie hadn't expected an issue. "Ummm . . ."

"You can read that vampire book you asked about in my room," said Kaylie. "Then switch."

Charlotte twisted her lips as she pondered Kaylie's words.

Kaylie leaned toward her and whispered loudly, "I promise you'll be hooked."

"I don't know if my mother will like me reading it."

Ollie grimaced, realizing which popular vampire book Kaylie was going to lend Charlotte. Romance and vampires didn't make sense to him.

Kaylie glanced at Ollie and then said to Theodore, "You don't seem too upset that your mother is missing."

Theodore looked up from his book. "I'm sure she's fine."

"Then why did you walk all the way into town to report she was missing?" asked Kaylie.

"Because she told me to."

"What?" asked Ollie. "When did she do that?"

"Before she left. She said to contact the police if she was gone for more than ten days, so I did." The young teen frowned. "Should I have not?" Listening closely, Charlotte looked from Kaylie to Ollie, mild curiosity in her gaze.

Ollie felt a need to reassure the kids. "You did the right thing."

"Okay." Theodore refocused on his book, and Charlotte took another bite of her bar.

That was easy.

Kaylie met Ollie's gaze and lifted one shoulder.

The kids' lack of worry was starting to bother him too.

12

Truman leaned against a wall at the Eagle's Nest police station while Evan Bolton talked with Matt Stephens. The dog lover from the lumberyard shooting the day before still didn't seem aware that Billy Serrano had been murdered. He wore the same cargo shorts but had swapped out his sleeveless T-shirt for a green one. Truman studied his dog tattoos, noticing most of them included dates. It appeared the man had documented on his skin the life of every dog he'd owned. And there'd been a lot of them.

Evan's search of Billy's room at the bed-and-breakfast hadn't turned up any sign of the treasure-hunt notebook. Billy's car had been empty too.

I still don't think Matt Stephens murdered Billy.

"When's the last time you saw Billy, Matt?" Evan asked.

"Yesterday. Right here when we were processed."

Evan made a note. "You haven't been to his hotel?"

Matt sat up straight. "Heck no. Did he say he saw me there? I don't even know where he's staying."

"You seemed very motivated by his notebook yesterday."

The dog lover looked away. "That was stupid. I know that now."

"Done anything else stupid lately?" asked Evan.

"Who's saying I did?" snapped Matt. "I ain't bothered no one since yesterday."

"And before that?"

Matt colored slightly and seemed to sink in his chair. "This treasure hunt ain't fair."

Truman fought to keep a straight face.

"Explain," said Evan.

"Well . . . everyone seems to know where to go. I read the clues and they don't make sense to me, but everyone else totally understands them." His forehead wrinkled in confusion.

"I've read them," said Evan. "They don't make sense to me either. Could mean a lot of things."

"Right? So I've been trying to listen when other people talk about them—follow their leads."

"Is that how you got interested in Billy's notebook?"

Matt ducked his head and looked to the side. "Yeah. I heard him talking on his cell phone in the coffee shop. He seemed confident. I snuck a peek at what he was studying, and it looked like he had good information there."

"You tried to steal the notebook."

"But I didn't steal it," he said earnestly, innocence on his face.

Truman couldn't stay quiet. "Only because you dropped it. What happened when you tried to take it again, Matt?"

"*I didn't.*" The man slapped one hand over his heart and held up the other like he was taking an oath. "I didn't try to steal his notebook again. I swear. And he's a lying piece of shit if he said I did."

"He didn't say you did," said Evan.

Matt slumped back in his chair. "See! I told you so. Sheesh." He wiped his forehead with a forearm. He'd been sweating profusely since he arrived, and his body odor filled the room. "Not my fault I don't got the clues figured out like everyone else."

"No one has found the treasure, so I don't think anyone has figured out the clues," Truman pointed out.

"Well, people sure act like they have."

"You steal anything else related to the hunt, Matt?"

"No." He squirmed in his seat. "I've followed a few people. Didn't bug them, though."

"And you haven't bugged Billy Serrano again."

"No." He slammed his hand on the table. "How many times do I have to say that?"

"Billy Serrano was shot and killed overnight, Matt. His notebook is missing," Evan said, his gaze locked on Matt.

Matt went very still, and the color drained from his face.

He's legitimately shocked.

Abruptly, Matt turned beet red. *"I didn't do it! That's why you brought me here!"* He turned toward Truman. "You gotta believe me! I ain't seen Billy since yesterday. I didn't shoot no one!"

"Where's your gun?" asked Evan.

"It's in my truck."

"Mind if we take a look at it?"

"Go right ahead."

Evan stood. "Back in a few minutes." He tilted his head for Truman to follow him as he left the room. They stopped halfway down the hallway. "You were right," Evan said to Truman. "I don't like him for the shooting either."

"Nope," said Truman. "Now what?"

"We hope the crime scene team finds some evidence."

"I feel Billy's death is related to the treasure hunt *somehow.* Especially since his notebook is missing," said Truman. "I thought it was bad enough that two people were shooting at each other, but now I've got a murder because of the treasure."

Evan nodded. "Money makes people stupid. Let's hope someone finds that jackpot soon."

13

Mercy admired the tall ponderosa pines that lined the drive of the Kerr home and ranch.

Eddie had dug for more information on Christine and Linda Kerr and briefed Mercy over the phone during her drive to meet with them. The women were sisters who had married brothers Joshua and Joseph Kerr more than fifty years ago in a joint ceremony. The two men had been dead well over a decade, their deaths the outcome of a boating accident. Neither woman had remarried, and the two had lived together ever since their husbands had died. There was one son who lived nearby.

Eddie had briefly spoken with Christine Kerr the day before to set up an appointment for Mercy and learned that Theodore's father, Victor, was the son of a third brother, Jack, who had also passed away.

Jack, Victor, Theodore. Grandfather, father, son.

Jack, Joshua, Joseph. Brothers. All dead.

Mercy had found it odd that so many men in the family had passed and said so to Eddie. He'd replied that Christine Kerr had been vague when he asked about Jack's death. She'd implied that it was an accident and then changed the subject.

It reminded Mercy of how Charlotte and Theodore hadn't said much about their father's death.

There are way too many dead men in this family.

Mercy parked next to a dusty Chevy pickup and horse trailer. The large white farmhouse appeared well maintained and had an inviting covered front porch with wicker furniture. Beyond the house were a half dozen large outbuildings. She saw a few horses in a far field but no other animals.

When Mercy learned that the Kerr ranch had once been a large sheep business, she'd suddenly realized these Kerrs were *the* Kerrs, as in Kerr Textiles. Mercy had a faint memory of her mother and father discussing the superior quality of their old Kerr blankets, and she could easily picture the Kerr label, a sheep's head with a haughty expression on a rich purple background. She'd always imagined the sheep was saying "Grrr" to rhyme with Kerr. The product line had died out decades ago. Mercy had never even seen it in a store.

I doubt Theodore and Charlotte know about this chapter of their history.

The children had been completely isolated from both sides of their family.

Footsteps sounded, and a tall woman walked around the corner of the covered porch. Her long graying hair was pulled back in a ponytail, and she wore jeans, creased tall boots, and a sleeveless plaid shirt. She was all sharp angles and corners, and Mercy instantly knew she was a horsewoman.

"You must be Agent Kilpatrick," the woman said, stopping and looking down at Mercy.

"I am." Mercy jogged up the stairs to the porch and held out her hand. "Mercy Kilpatrick."

"Linda Kerr." Her hands were leathery and her grip strong. Her eyes were an icy blue and heavily crinkled at the corners. Mercy liked her immediately. She knew Linda was in her early seventies, but the woman didn't have a grandmotherly vibe. She gave off a no-nonsense attitude that made Mercy picture her mucking stalls instead of cuddling grandchildren.

"Come in," said Linda, opening the screen door. "Chrissy!" she hollered into the house. "The FBI agent is here."

Mercy stepped into a time warp. Ornate, faded floral furniture. Knickknacks. Dark-green carpet. Patterned hardwood floors. Everything was immaculate, and she could faintly smell a pine-scented cleaner that her mother had always used.

Christine Kerr appeared.

There's the grandmother I expected.

Her smile was wide and her soft skin faintly pink, her white hair piled on top of her head. She was also tall and wore long khaki shorts with an oversize floral T-shirt. Where Linda made Mercy think of a rigid rectangle, Christine was a comfortable and inviting oval.

"So good to meet you, Special Agent Kilpatrick," said Christine. Her handshake was different from Linda's too. She took Mercy's hand with both of hers, giving it an affectionate squeeze.

I need to stop comparing them.

But the two sisters were a study in contrasts, and Mercy's interest was piqued.

Mercy was herded through the kitchen and out the back door to a large weathered deck. A wrought iron table and chairs sat below a large umbrella, and a pitcher of iced tea with sprigs of mint was waiting.

Along with cookies. Four different types of homemade cookies.

Mercy glanced at Christine. "Are you the baker?"

"Oh, no. That's Linda's passion. I'm a better cook, but her baking blows mine away."

"Damn right," agreed Linda, gesturing for Mercy to have a seat and pulling out her own chair.

Mercy sat and winced at a sharp poke from the hard iron seat.

"I may be the best baker, but Christine wins when it comes to martini making," said Linda.

"That's because you buy the cheap liquor."

"It's all just alcohol," said Linda.

"If that was so, then why are mine better?" Christine asked sharply. She shot Mercy a sheepish look. "Excuse us, Agent Kilpatrick. Sometimes we get a little snappish with each other."

"I have two sisters. I get it," said Mercy. "If we still lived together, we'd probably have murdered each other by now. And call me Mercy, please."

"Well, Linda does keep trying to murder me with those bees of hers," stated Christine.

Linda rolled her eyes. "You have an EpiPen in every room in the house." She looked at Mercy. "I raise bees. The honey makes a nice little income."

"At the risk of me dying," retorted Christine.

Linda passed Mercy the plate of cookies as Christine poured three glasses of tea. Mercy eyed the cookie choices, pondered for a split second, and then took one of each.

They're small. Well, two of them are small.

"I like you already, Agent Mercy," said Linda with a chortle.

"My niece is a baker. I don't hold back when there is serious cookie sampling to be done."

She bit into a piece of shortbread, and her taste buds rejoiced at the butter and sugar. "It's perfect," she told Linda.

"Wait until you try the chocolate chip," said Christine. "She rolls them in three types of chips."

"I've never seen a cookie quite like it." Mercy could barely see the dough of the cookie because of all the different-size chips in the way. She made a mental note to describe it to Kaylie. Taking a long swallow of her iced tea, she started to cough.

"Is that bourbon?" Mercy asked, blinking hard against the burn in her throat.

"Just a little," answered Christine. "Makes it go down easier."

Mercy didn't agree with either statement.

There's no way I can finish that glass and drive back to the office.

She took a bite of the chocolate chip cookie to get the flavor off her tongue. She'd never developed a taste for bourbon.

The cookie *was* excellent.

"The FBI agent who called me said you're looking for Bridget Kerr," Christine stated. "We haven't heard of or seen anyone with that name. I didn't know who she was until the agent said she'd married young Victor. I was sorry to hear of his passing."

"We haven't seen Victor in years," added Linda.

"He took off soon after his father, Jack, died—he must have been barely into his twenties," said Christine. "The boy was always a loose cannon. I asked my son Alex yesterday if he'd ever heard from Victor over the years, and he hasn't either. If anyone had heard from him, it would have been Alex. They were pretty tight, even though there was about ten years between their ages."

"Is Alex around?" asked Mercy. "I'd like to talk to him too."

"He's at work. I'll give you his phone number, and you can set something up."

"Victor's father, Jack, was the third of the three Kerr brothers, right?" Mercy asked as she pulled a small notebook out of her bag. "You were married to the other two?"

The women nodded.

"I'm very sorry for your loss." Mercy included both sisters with a look. "I understand your husbands died in a boating accident."

"It's been years ago now," said Christine.

"Was that before or after their brother Jack died?"

"About a year after. Jack was the baby of the family," said Christine. "He was killed in a car accident when he was around forty. It was very hard on Ethel, their mama."

"I can't imagine losing three sons within a year," said Mercy, making a note.

A boat and car accident within a year? Were they all adrenaline junkies?

It appeared Jack hadn't passed that gene to his grandson, Theodore. The young teenager was calm and collected.

"Ethel was a strong woman," said Christine as Linda nodded emphatically. "She built the Kerr textile brand, you know. It was her drive and creativity that put their woolen products on the map. After her husband died, she took over and pushed the company in directions her husband had never considered."

Mercy concentrated, trying to recall if Eddie had told her the name of the matriarch's husband. "What was his name?"

"Albert."

Her brain was happy to hear the non-*J* name. "I remember my parents had Kerr blankets," Mercy told them as she wrote down Albert's name with a huge *A*.

"Ethel designed all those patterns," said Linda. "And brought in different sheep to breed with the existing stock, trying to improve the wool. Albert hadn't wanted to do that; he liked things the way they were. But she had a magic touch, and every idea she implemented improved the products. It wasn't her fault the industry fell apart in the nineties. There was a dramatic shift. Globalization shook up the markets, and the need disappeared. Thousands of US sheep producers went out of business by the end of the century."

"And then the boys died in accidents not long after that," said Christine.

Mercy paused, trying to find a tactful way to ask about all the male deaths in the family tree. "There seems to be a lot of tragedy for the Kerr men."

Both women nodded. "A lot of fire in their blood," said Linda. "The Kerr men always had to be doing something risky, it seemed." She looked at her sister. "Although Albert died in his sleep."

"Remember when Ethel told you not to marry Joe?" Christine said. She looked to Mercy. "How many women tell a possible daughter-in-law their son isn't good enough for them?"

Linda laughed. "Her exact words were that he didn't have enough spine. I told her I was just fine with that because that meant he'd do what I told him to." The angular woman grinned. "Ethel thought that was the funniest thing she'd ever heard and told me it sounded like he'd found the right woman after all."

"She was protective of her sons," Mercy said.

"Especially Jack," Christine muttered.

Mercy's ears pricked up. "She played favorites?" She took a small polite sip of the spiked iced tea and a bite of the shortbread as a palate cleanser.

Christine exchanged a look with Linda. "Jack was definitely her favorite."

Linda said nothing.

The mood at the table had abruptly shifted. Mercy bit into the chocolate chip–covered lump as she debated pushing the subject. Anytime an interviewee suddenly clammed up about a topic, Mercy had discovered there was information that needed to come out.

Yep. Going for it.

"What did your husbands think about the youngest son being the favorite?" She glanced at her notes. "Looks like Jack was about fifteen years younger than them."

"Yes, they were teenagers when he was born. They didn't really grow up together." Christine had that look in her eye that said she wanted to talk but was holding back.

Mercy pressed again. "Why the big gap in their ages?"

Christine looked to Linda, who held up her hands in resignation. "Everyone knows," Linda told Christine. "It's not like it's a big secret."

Christine met Mercy's gaze. "Jack was illegitimate. Ethel had an affair, and Jack was clearly not Albert's son."

Now we're talking.

"He didn't look like Albert?" Mercy asked.

"That's correct, but anyone who can do math knew that Albert had been away in the military when Jack was conceived." She sat back in her chair and crossed her arms, relief on her face from getting the gossip off her chest.

Mercy wondered how that had affected the boy's life. "Was he treated differently?"

"No, of course not," the women said simultaneously, but their faces said otherwise.

"Ethel would tear the hide off anyone who said something," said Linda. "She was a mama bear when it came to that boy. She was a powerful woman at any time, but say anything the littlest bit rude about her Jack, and your ears would burn."

Christine nodded emphatically. "She raised him alone after Albert died, and men came out of the woodwork for years trying to meet her. Here was a strong, attractive woman with valuable property and a well-known business. Many of them thought she would be grateful for their offer of help around the ranch . . . or of marriage."

Linda snorted.

"She had different ideas," Christine continued. "She learned as much as she could from each man that came along and then sent them packing when she was done. Shocked a lot of them. They were used to being indispensable. They'd never met anyone like Ethel before."

"She sounds unique," said Mercy.

"She relished being an in-demand widow," said Linda. "She enjoyed the company of some very powerful men over the years." She looked at Christine. "Remember the one from France?"

"He was here to discuss sheep," said Christine. "He had massive sheep ranches in France. I never understood what he wanted with Ethel's smaller herds."

"It wasn't the herds that held his interest," Linda said dryly. "It was the owner."

"Good for her," said Mercy.

"That was all before the industry crashed." Linda sighed. "Nothing was ever the same after that. It was like something evil took root and didn't want to stop until everything with the Kerr name was gone. First the sheep industry and then the boys. And then Ethel."

"Jack's death really destroyed her," said Christine. "She stopped taking care of herself and let things go on the ranch. Joe and Joshua had to step up. And then they died a year later. It was simply too much for Ethel's heart. She didn't last long after that."

"And Victor? How was his life while growing up and then losing his father?"

The sisters looked at each other and shrugged. "Seemed okay," said Linda. "Never saw much of him, and then he simply left for good."

"Don't you find that strange? Did you wonder if he'd been hurt or killed?"

"He took all his stuff and his truck," said Linda. "He left on purpose. I've looked for him online but never found anything, so I assume he didn't want to have anything to do with us."

"Why would he feel that way?" Mercy asked, forcing mild curiosity into her tone when she really wanted to poke and pry into why Victor Kerr had abandoned this family.

Linda shifted in her seat. "Joe and Josh might have given Victor a hard time occasionally."

There it is.

"Because of his father, Jack?" asked Mercy. "Was Jack's parentage a problem between the three brothers?"

"I don't exactly know," said Linda, looking anywhere except at Mercy.

"It was," Christine said firmly. "Things came easy for Jack. Friends, looks, athleticism, smarts."

Christine is my gossip girl.

"He was much younger than the brothers you married," said Mercy, keeping her gaze on Christine. "Joe and Josh were jealous of a child?"

"Yes, and their mother was completely focused on him." She leaned closer to Mercy and lowered her voice. "And no one knows who Jack's father really is."

"I don't know why you're whispering," said Linda. "There's no one here but us."

Christine leaned back in her chair and took a long drink of her iced tea. "Habit when talking about Jack, I guess. Everyone in town still speculates about who got Ethel pregnant while Albert was out of the country."

Mercy doubted anyone still wondered except for the sisters. She looked at her notes. Five dead men in the Kerr family, including Charlotte and Theodore's father, Victor. Eddie had mentioned some distant cousins but hadn't mentioned whether they were alive or dead.

There's already too many dead.

Did someone pick off the Kerr men? Why?

She eyed Jack's name, wondering about his car accident. Getting the accident report and the medical examiner's report had been on Eddie's to-do list. Along with what information he could find on the boat accident that had killed Jack's brothers. Mercy looked up, studying the sisters across the table. They seemed content. Happy, even, as Christine poured them each a second glass of her special iced tea.

Their men have been gone for a long time.

They couldn't be expected to mourn forever. That'd be ridiculous.

Then why do I feel so judgy about their behavior?

Because of Theodore and Charlotte.

A feeling of protectiveness popped up every time Mercy thought of them. The two children were off to a rough start in life thanks to how their father had been treated by these women's dead husbands. She studied the women, wondering if they would accept a grandniece and grandnephew. They hadn't asked any questions about Bridget or Victor, which surprised Mercy a bit. At least one of them seemed interested in talking about the black sheep of the family.

She decided not to tell them about Theodore and Charlotte. For now. She didn't feel like fueling their gossip.

Her goal was to find Bridget and Molly. The children deserved their mother and sister back.

14

Mercy was late to the one o'clock briefing. Her boss, Jeff, along with Eddie and Darby, the office's intelligence analyst, were already seated at the table in the tiny conference room. The Bend FBI satellite office was small. Only five agents and a support staff.

"Nice you could make it," Eddie said as she arrived.

Mercy hadn't even stopped at her office to drop off her bag. She'd left the Kerr home with plenty of time to make the meeting, but the highway had been briefly closed in both directions while a county deputy and several locals tried to catch six horses that had escaped from a field and decided to dash back and forth across the road.

"Horses on the highway," she stated. The three others nodded in understanding.

It happened.

"What did you find out about the deaths of the Kerr men?" Mercy asked Eddie, eyeing the fresh sunburn on his forehead and nose. The young agent looked like a different person from the Portland hipster who'd transferred with her to the office more than a year and a half ago. Gone were the heavy black glasses, replaced by a pair of lightweight frames that would stay in place while he was active outdoors. His hair was shorter. Less likely to trap sweat and faster to dry. He'd eagerly embraced the active outdoor lifestyle that made people move to the high desert town, and Mercy had never seen him so happy, although she missed the nerdy glasses he'd constantly shoved back into place with one finger.

And apparently he still needed a mother to tell him to wear sunscreen.

"Jack Kerr, the grandfather of Charlotte and Theodore," Eddie announced as Mercy took her seat and opened her laptop. "Died in a single-car accident on Highway 20 about thirty miles east of Bend. State police responded to a passerby's call at about six a.m. The medical examiner's report puts his death closer to midnight, so the car was there for several hours before someone spotted it well off the highway."

"What happened?" asked Darby, rapidly typing notes. The intelligence analyst's long, loose braid hung over one shoulder, nearly touching her forearm. The die-hard marathoner was in her early forties and had one of the quickest brains Mercy had ever encountered. Jeff often joked that it was made by Intel.

"Alcohol level was three times the limit. He went off the road and hit a tree. Based on the skid marks, they suspect he braked and jerked the wheel because of an animal or something in the road. I printed these for you." Eddie shoved a few photographs across the table to Mercy.

She flipped through them. "Airbag wasn't sufficient?"

"Speed was estimated to be close to a hundred when he hit the brakes."

"Jesus," muttered Jeff.

"Anything else in the ME's report?" asked Mercy. She focused on a photo of Jack Kerr's profile, searching for a glimpse of his grandson, Theodore, in his features, but there was too much blood to see clearly.

"Severe trauma to the C1 and C2 vertebrae was the cause of death. Consistent with a crash."

"Horrible," said Darby, still typing.

"What about his brothers, Joshua and Joseph Kerr?" asked Mercy.

"Boating accident a year later," said Eddie. "Their boat was found drifting on Lake Billy Chinook. Joe's body was found four days later.

Again, evidence of high blood alcohol, but now add in methamphetamine. Joshua's body was never found."

The four of them shared a look.

"There's no way Joshua Kerr has been hiding out for that long," Mercy said slowly.

"Why not?" asked Darby. "By all accounts, Joe and Josh knew how to live off the grid. They both had criminal records."

"But the wives . . ." Mercy thought hard. "Which was married to Joshua?"

"Christine," said Eddie, checking his notes.

"Those two are the parents of Alex Kerr," said Mercy. "He was at work today but will stop here on his way home for a talk."

Mercy thought of Alex's mother, the smiling woman who liked spiked iced tea in the morning. Neither sister had mentioned that one brother's body had never been found.

Would they help one of their husbands hide for over a decade?

"If you accidentally caused your brother's death, would you come forward or take off?" asked Darby, still typing.

Mercy's stomach heaved.

My brother.

Levi had died while Mercy was untangling an old murder mystery. He'd been involved in the cover-up, and her investigation had brought the murderer out of hiding. Levi had literally stepped into the cross fire.

The room went silent as Darby abruptly stopped and looked up. "I'm sorry, Mercy. You know none of us feel you could have done anything to stop Levi's death. The blame is squarely on the man who shot him."

"I know," Mercy said. For a long time after Levi's death, she'd struggled with "What if." What if she had kept in touch with Levi? What if she hadn't left town when she was eighteen?

Would Kaylie still have a father?

Sometimes the guilt appeared out of nowhere and flooded her.

Like now.

"What did the medical examiner's report say about Joseph Kerr besides the blood alcohol and meth?" Mercy asked Eddie, yanking her focus back to the case in front of them.

"Water in the lungs. No physical trauma."

"So he actually drowned," said Jeff.

"Another reason for Joshua not to be hiding out—the death of his brother was most likely accidental," said Mercy.

"Short of Josh shoving Joe overboard, which can't be proven, I don't see anything in the ME report to say otherwise," said Eddie.

Mercy made a note to ask Christine and Linda about their husbands' alcohol and drug use around the time of their deaths. Nothing was raising big red flags, but she simply didn't like the quantity of dead Kerr men.

"What about the father—Albert Kerr?" she asked.

"No autopsy. Death was ruled natural. He had heart disease and just didn't wake up one morning."

"Is that normal? No autopsy?" Mercy looked around the table.

"They focus on suspicious deaths," said Darby. "An older man with heart disease and no outward signs of trauma would possibly not be autopsied. Especially back then in a rural area."

Mercy didn't like that answer, but she knew Darby was right. "Did you look into Ethel Kerr's death?" she asked Eddie.

"I didn't. I was focused on the men." He made a note. "I will. You said she died not long after her three sons died, right?"

"Yes." *Leaving everything to Christine and Linda.*
I assume.

"I'd also like to see her will," said Mercy. "And check if any of the men had wills."

"On it." Eddie cleared his throat. "And I can't find any sort of death record for Charlotte and Theodore's father, Victor."

Mercy let that fact process for a long moment. "Could his wife have handled everything herself? She and the kids simply buried him?"

"They could," said Darby. "You said they kept to themselves, right?"

"Somebody would have had to help," said Eddie. "Grave digging isn't easy."

Did Theodore have to dig his father's grave?

Mercy knew she needed to ask the boy about it. Kaylie had expressed concern that the kids hadn't said much about their dad's death. They probably didn't want to think about it anymore.

She made a mental note to have a discussion with Theodore while Evan was around.

"What about the Jane Doe in Jefferson County?" she asked. "The one from two weeks ago?"

"She was identified yesterday," said Eddie. "A missing woman from Idaho."

Mercy scratched that off her list. "Any other Jane Doe possibilities that could be Bridget Kerr?"

"Not in any Western states," said Darby. "I'm looking into some in the Midwest."

"Not feeling that," said Mercy, knowing she had no basis for the statement other than a gut feeling. Bridget Kerr had lived in the area all her life, and Mercy didn't think she would leave now.

Only if someone took her out of state.

"Where could she be?" she asked quietly. "How can a woman and baby disappear?"

"Did you get some photos of the two of them?" asked Darby.

"No," said Mercy. "Photos don't appear to exist. I had Evan ask Charlotte about it last night, and she told him they didn't have a camera."

"None?" asked Jeff. "Who doesn't have something to record their children? I mean, my sisters take photos and videos of their kids non-stop and also schedule professional photos at least once a year. And then there are the school photos." He shook his head. "I never know what to do with all the physical pictures they send me. I mean, I love my little nieces and nephews, but am I supposed to keep all of that stuff too?" He looked specifically to Mercy and Darby.

"I throw everything from my sister in a spare drawer," Darby said.

"Evan let them use his cell phone, and Charlotte promptly mastered the art of the selfie," said Mercy. She opened her phone to the pictures Evan had sent her and passed the phone to Jeff. Darby and Eddie leaned over to see.

"She's a ham," said Jeff, scrolling through the half dozen images of Charlotte sticking out her tongue. He stopped on one of Charlotte holding Theodore in a headlock. Theodore looked annoyed but tolerant of his energetic sister's antics. "And wow, Theodore does look like Evan. Exact same eyes."

Darby and Eddie murmured in agreement.

Mercy eyed the photo of the two siblings. "They're such good kids," she told the others, her heart contracting painfully at the sight of the happy young faces. "Would you purposefully leave these kids alone for weeks with no contact?"

"Hell no," stated Eddie as the other two shook their heads. "I know you've said they're competent and all, but I can't imagine their mom hasn't contacted them."

Jeff handed the phone back to Mercy and looked at Eddie. "Are you suggesting the kids have been contacted by their mom but purposefully not told us?"

"I'm not suggesting anything," said Eddie. "But I guess that is possible."

Mercy considered it. "Then why would Theodore walk into town to ask for help?"

"Good point," said Darby. "Could someone have sent him?"

Mercy shifted in her seat, not liking the sudden new possibilities the conversation was opening. "That would make these kids involved in something. I don't see that at all. They don't seem capable of pulling off a big lie about something like that. It wouldn't surprise me if they've held some things back, but I can't believe that they would be pawns in some bigger scheme. And to what end anyway?"

"Consider all possibilities," said Jeff.

"I know," replied Mercy. "I won't rule it out, but I can't give it much weight. It's more likely that their mom left them alone, intending to be gone for a short amount of time, but something has happened to her. Something not good."

I don't think this will have a happy ending.

15

Evan took a few seconds to admire the outside of the big Victorian home before taking the stairs. Earlier that morning, he'd barely glanced at the bed-and-breakfast. He'd been focused on the murder scene behind it. He'd driven past the historic Eagle's Nest home dozens of times but had never appreciated the work someone had done to restore it. The paint was fresh, and the gingerbread trim was in perfect condition.

He jogged up the steps and opened the front door with the large oval glass insert. The wood floor creaked as he crossed the foyer, the old home smelling of wood polish and fresh-baked bread. His stomach rumbled and he realized he had missed lunch. Again.

Later.

Sandy emerged through a swinging door, wiping her hands on her apron, her long red hair in a bun on top of her head. The B and B owner was tall, with warm brown eyes that were abruptly shadowed as she spotted Evan. "You're back." She used a cheerful tone, but her drawn face reflected the anxiety of having discovered a murdered man on her property.

"I am. How are you holding up?" Evan studied her carefully. He knew from conversations with her new husband, Samuel, that Sandy was tough as nails, having escaped an abusive ex and then carving out a new life in Eagle's Nest.

"Not bad. My current guests will have three different delicacies to choose from for tea because I'm baking to stay distracted. I guess you could call it stress baking." Her smile was weak. "What can I do for you?"

"I need to look at Billy Serrano's room again."

Sandy nodded and stepped behind the reception desk, then opened a locked drawer and removed a key. Evan wasn't surprised that she used real keys for her guest rooms. The old mansion was from a different era.

The door to Billy's room had been unlocked when Evan had visited it to do a cursory search for the precious notebook after examining the murder scene. He had no way of knowing if the killer had been in the room. Anyone could have entered it in the hours since Billy's death in the middle of the night. Or before.

If only they hadn't tampered with the cameras.

Evan acknowledged that if he were to plan a murder, he'd first take care of the cameras too. The only camera that hadn't been damaged was the sole indoor one that focused on the reception desk. It covered only part of the entry. It was simple to enter the B and B and not be on camera.

Sandy handed him the key. "It's been locked since your evidence team left this morning. I've accounted for all the keys except the one I gave Billy when he checked in."

"I saw it in his effects. I'll see that it gets back to you."

She grimaced. "That's not necessary. I'll have the lock changed." Sandy gestured toward the staircase. "You know where you're going."

He did. Evan thanked her and took the stairs two at a time. He stopped at the room at the end of the hallway and slipped on booties and gloves. The key slid into the lock, and he opened the door. After stepping inside, he closed the door and stood still, simply listening. The B and B was silent. There was no road noise in this room at the back of the house.

He took a deep breath and studied the small room, trying to look past the residual fingerprint powder left everywhere. Hundreds of guests had stayed in this room, and he had no doubt that Sandy had high cleaning standards, but the team would find dozens of prints.

If one turned out to match a suspect, it would help the case.

But first I need a suspect.

The room had high ceilings and a tall, narrow window. The decor was soothing and elegant, done in soft blues and greens. The furniture reminded him of his great-grandmother's house, and he wondered how much of it was original to the mansion.

Billy had been a slob. His clothes were on the floor where he'd shed them. Dirty jeans, T-shirts, and a pair of worn Nikes. Fast-food takeout bags had been crumpled and left on the nightstand.

A small bathroom and shower were attached, but the small sink was actually in the room outside the bathroom door. Toothpaste was smeared in it. The cap to the open tube lay beside it. Several towels had been left in a corner on the bathroom floor.

It appeared nothing had changed since his quick search that morning.

But now he was determined to do a more thorough look for the notebook. He hadn't fully appreciated that the notes could be a motive for murder. He did now. Truman had said his quick glance at the notebook's pages had indicated a well-researched plan for finding the location of Chester Rollins's treasure. And according to Truman, things were getting ugly among some of the competing treasure hunters.

Clearly, Billy Serrano's notes weren't perfect; the treasure was still missing.

Did someone want the notes badly enough to kill?

Evan started his search, determined to take his time and run his hands over every single thing in the room. He felt every inch of the mattress and box spring, checked every piece of furniture, and shook out every piece of clothing. His phone gave a quiet chime, and frustrated with his so-far-fruitless search, he checked his email and scanned the message. It confirmed what he'd already suspected: the shell casing found at Billy's murder could not have come from the gun in Matt Stephens's truck.

Matt could have used a different weapon, but Evan was 99 percent positive that Matt wasn't his suspect.

He slid his phone into a pocket and continued looking through the closet.

A knock sounded. "Evan, it's Sandy."

He opened the door and held up his palm. "Don't step in, okay?"

"Got it," she said. "I was just putting a guest's passport in my safe when I remembered that Billy Serrano had asked me to lock up something for him." She held out an oversize manila envelope. "I didn't know if it would be helpful or not."

Evan took the envelope and opened the flap. Inside was a thin three-ring binder.

Elation erupted inside him, but he nodded calmly at Sandy. "Yes, that might be helpful. Thank you so much."

"Sorry I didn't think of it earlier."

"You had a good reason to be distracted."

She grimaced. "How long does it take to get a sight like from this morning out of your head?"

It never leaves.

"Time will help." He hated the pain in her eyes. "I'll be done here in a minute. I'm sorry, but we need to keep the room as it is for a while."

"I have no problem with that," she told him. "I'm not looking forward to booking another guest in here very soon. When you're done, stop by the kitchen and I'll send a fresh loaf of cinnamon-raisin bread with you. And some pie."

"Thank you, I will."

She moved down the hall and Evan closed the door. He tipped the manila envelope, and the yellow notebook slid into his gloved hand.

He opened it and flipped through a few pages. The handwritten notes were neat, and there were several printed pages with maps and copies of online discussions. Everything was organized with dividers. He looked around the messy room, remembering that Truman had told him Billy Serrano had said his sister was the note maker.

Or did he steal it from someone else?

He had a phone number and address for Billy's sister, Meghan, in Athens, Ohio, but hadn't been able to find any other relatives. Evan had contacted the Athens Police Department to personally deliver the news of her brother's death, and they'd promised to send someone soon. In-person notification was always his goal. He hated the thought of that kind of news being delivered over the phone. He was still waiting on a confirmation that they'd spoken with Billy's sister. He wanted to ask her about the binder, but he'd wait to hear from the Athens police first.

He ran through a mental checklist. The crime scene team had collected evidence, but processing that evidence was going to take time. The medical examiner planned to do Billy's autopsy tomorrow morning. Evan needed to focus on where Billy had gone over the last few days and whom he had spoken with. Credit card statements showed he'd eaten at a few places in town, and Evan needed to visit and ask if anyone remembered if Billy had anyone with him. His only recent cell phone calls had been to his sister.

Evan checked the time and decided to wait until midafternoon to make his inquiries, when restaurant business was slower.

What I really want to do is look through Theodore and Charlotte's home while they're being entertained elsewhere by Kaylie and Ollie.

He stepped out of the room, made sure the door was locked, and pulled off his gloves and booties, determined to get out to the Kerr property before anyone needed him. He jogged down the stairs and was hit by the scents of Sandy's baking.

Pie first.

16

Evan looked around the silent Kerr living room, feeling a tiny bit guilty for tying up Kaylie's day off with Theodore and Charlotte. Especially since the two kids were so self-sufficient; they didn't need babysitters. But Evan felt they needed to be around other kids . . . adults . . . anyone.

I'm not their parent.

Who was he to make child-raising decisions regarding kids he'd known for twenty-four hours? But they currently had no parent. Did he have a moral obligation to take over?

Frustrated by the questions with ambiguous answers, he redirected his train of thought, debating whether he should recommend a crime scene team. But there was no evidence that a crime had taken place in the house. Yes, Bethany—Bridget—was missing, but she'd left of her own accord. Searching the home for an indicator of where she might have gone was his job.

No, it's Mercy's job.

Finding Bethany and Molly is not my case.

But he wanted answers.

Mercy had done a preliminary search of the home, and Evan had stayed overnight—and would continue to do so for several more nights. He'd assumed it would be an opportunity for him do a more thorough search, but the presence of the kids interfered. He couldn't dig through personal effects with the children watching, which was why he was here now. Last night Theodore or Charlotte had been his shadow the entire time. He'd never had anyone so focused on him. Theodore had peppered him with questions about his job, and they'd both asked hundreds of questions about their mother when she was younger.

Evan had dug deep to share memories with the kids, discovering he'd buried most of them in the years Bethany had been gone. As he shared, it had felt raw, but it had also felt cleansing and refreshing. He hadn't had anyone to talk with about Bethany for years. A couple of the guys at work knew his sister was missing, but they always discussed it from an investigative point of view. No one had ever asked him what her favorite fruit had been as a kid.

Until Charlotte had the night before.

He hadn't known the answer. But he had remembered picking strawberries with Bethany at a local farm on a blazing-hot day and had shared that memory, recounting a strawberry fight. The kids had been delighted to hear that their mother had shoved strawberries under Evan's shirt as he bent over a bush and then slapped her hands against his back, smashing them through his shirt.

They were in awe at the idea of Bethany as a feisty child.

Charlotte was similar in many ways. Bethany had also never feared giving an opinion or asking a question. His sister's eyes had widened in the same way Charlotte's did when she was amused. It was almost as if Evan had gone back in time as Charlotte sat beside him and talked nonstop through dinner.

I've forgotten so much.

The reminders of his sister were simultaneously torture and bliss.

Where are you, Bethany? Are you okay?

Evan turned and strode down the hall to Bethany's bedroom. A crib sat in one corner. He stared at it, wondering at what age children no longer used cribs. Molly was eighteen months old. That seemed old to be in a crib.

Or was it? He'd never been around babies.

Would Bethany purposefully leave Theodore and Charlotte alone for weeks? And never communicate?

A memory surged.

Bethany had been cradling a tiny tabby kitten that still had its eyes closed. She couldn't have been more than ten. They'd found the kitten alongside a country road. No other cats in sight.

"No, we can't leave it!" Bethany had told Evan. "Its mother is gone. It'll die!"

"I'm sure the mother will come back for it," Evan had said.

"You don't know that! It needs its mother!"

She had been so fierce, so protective. They'd taken the kitten to their parents, who'd arranged for a neighbor's cat with new kittens to take it on. Bethany had refused to leave until she'd seen for herself that the other mother would nurse the baby. It wasn't just kittens. She'd always had a protective mode that emerged, whether it was a bullied kid in her class or the homeless person on the corner. She always asked what she could do to help.

Why would Bethany leave her children?

A possible answer kept repeating in his mind.

She believed they were safer left behind.

His stomach churned. Something had happened. Something to drive her away. Evan didn't know if Bethany had truly planned to come find him or if that was a story she had told the kids. Surely she would have believed it safe to bring her children to him?

Why? She doesn't know me anymore.

Anger roiled through him. Bethany had been so close . . . and had never reached out to him or his parents. All of them had spent years worrying that the worst had happened. But she'd been just fine. Raising two awesome kids. Living what appeared to be a happy life.

Or was it? Maybe Victor wouldn't let her communicate with her family.

Victor was dead. She was free to contact Evan. But she hadn't.

Frustrated, he yanked open a drawer in the dresser and discovered men's socks. Black, brown, and white.

Her husband died months ago.

He frowned, wondering how long Bethany would have let her dead husband's things stay in her bedroom and again realizing it was a question to which he had no basis to formulate an answer. He didn't know the woman she'd become; he didn't know her relationship with her husband. No doubt some people quickly cleared things away when someone died, while others never did.

He moved over to the nightstand without the hand-lotion bottle on top and opened the drawer. Coins. A book of crossword puzzles. Masculine reading glasses. Keys. Loose nine-millimeter cartridges.

Should there be a handgun?

He'd seen three long guns on a wall rack behind the bedroom door. He did a quick search of the rest of the drawers in the room and the closet. He then checked the cupboards and drawers in the bathroom and kitchen.

No handgun.

He continued to poke around in the kitchen, his mind on fast-forward.

Did Bethany take it?

He could ask the kids.

I need to focus on finding leads to where Bethany went.

That was partially a lie. He was also searching for clues to who Bethany was. What her life was like. What kind of woman she'd become. Why she'd never contacted him.

All the questions that had haunted him for fourteen years.

A calendar hung on the inside door of one of the kitchen cabinets. Someone had turned it over to June. One of the kids must have done it, as Bethany had been gone since May.

He remembered how hot the middle of May had been instead of being at the usual pleasant temperatures. Evan recalled he'd left down his vehicle's windows to cool it off one afternoon and forgotten to lock it up before bed. The next morning he'd discovered some smartasses had left nine empty beer bottles and three McDonald's bags full of hamburger wrappers on his front seat.

But finding someone's garbage inside his vehicle beat having it stolen.

After the initial anger at himself for being careless, he'd found it pretty funny. He'd put the beer bottles in his recycling bin and tossed the McDonald's bags into the trash. And almost added a tiny beat-up white sandal.

So small.

Evan froze as he remembered how he'd spotted the sandal near one of his tires. He had frowned as he pictured the beer drinkers carrying around a baby during their late-night prank but had immediately decided that was ridiculous. At night, vehicles were usually tampered with by older teens and young adults. Not someone packing a baby. He'd then imagined a toddler flinging the sandal out of its stroller as the mother pushed past, the lost shoe unnoticed.

Instead of throwing away the shoe, Evan had set it near the sidewalk, hoping the owner would come looking for it.

It'd been gone when he returned from work.

But now he pictured Bethany in the dark outside his home, Molly in her arms.

Why would Bethany come and not knock?

He was jumping to conclusions. Big jumps. Huge. Ridiculously sized jumps.

He'd found a baby sandal. It could have come from anywhere.

Evan flipped the calendar back to May. The month was blank. So were the previous months. No notations to remind Bethany that she needed to leave her children alone for weeks.

Bethany had a well-used calendar on her desk for the lesson plans. What was the point of this one?

Maybe she just enjoyed the pictures.

The calendar featured photos of Oregon's natural beauty. The Painted Hills. Multnomah Falls. Crater Lake.

Evan closed the cupboard door. Bethany had loved to take landscape photos and had carried an ancient camera with her all the time. It made no sense that there were no photos of nature or of her children in the home. The absence of pictures didn't match the young woman he remembered.

Did Victor control her that much?

Bethany had been strong. Independent. Evan couldn't imagine her meekly doing things her husband wished that went against the person she had been.

But she'd been willing to leave home and never talk to her family again to be with this man.

Drugs?

It seemed the most likely thing that could drastically change a person's true self.

But the clean home and polite children didn't read *drug addict* to Evan. He'd seen the neat lesson book with the kids' homework written out month after month. *That* was definitely the Bethany he knew. A planner. An organizer.

His phone rang. The call was from a semifamiliar area code. *Ohio.*

"Detective Bolton."

"This is Sergeant Arterberry. We spoke this morning about the next-of-kin notification for your victim."

"Of course, Sergeant. Did you locate Meghan Serrano?"

"Officers stopped by her apartment twice today. No answer either time. Do you wish us to try again?"

Evan picked up the subtext: the Athens Police Department had made an effort, but it had regular duties to focus on. "I appreciate your help and time, Sergeant. I'll handle it from here with a phone call."

"Hate to have that sort of news delivered over the phone," Arterberry said, sympathy in his tone.

"Me too. But sometimes it's the only way." Evan thanked him again and ended the call. He blew out a deep breath and mentally ran through a speech to gently break to Meghan Serrano the news of her brother's death. His murder.

He entered her phone number, preferring to get it immediately out of the way. He hated this part of the job.

"Hello?" a female voice answered.

"This is Detective Evan Bolton of the Deschutes County Sheriff's Department in Oregon. Am I speaking to Meghan Serrano?"

There was a long silence.

"What happened? Is Billy okay?" she whispered.

"Is this Meghan?" Evan repeated.

"Yes." Her voice cracked on the single word.

"I'm very sorry, Meghan, but your brother, Billy, passed away this morning."

She inhaled sharply. "How? What happened? Was he in an accident?" Shock filled her tone as all the questions jumbled together.

Evan closed his eyes. *I hate this.* "No. He died from a gunshot. I'm in charge of the investigation into his death."

"Who shot him?"

"We don't know yet, and I will follow every lead until we find the person responsible. You knew he was in Oregon, right?"

"Yes. He's . . . working on a project out there."

"I assume you're referring to the treasure hunt."

Meghan was quiet for a moment. "Yes," she said resignedly. "I had paid for him to drive out there and look around."

"Had he talked to you recently about the hunt?"

"We talk—talked every day. I'm doing research back here while he's in the field. We catch up each evening." Meghan cleared her throat. "You don't have any idea of who did it?"

"Not at the moment," said Evan. "But we just found him this morning. Did you speak with him last night? Did he give an indication of any problems out here?"

"He told me someone had tried to steal his notes that day, but the police stepped in." She caught her breath. "Could it be that guy? Billy said he was an ass."

"Did he tell you anything else about that incident?"

"That's about it. He said the police questioned both of them."

Evan wondered why Billy hadn't told his sister that guns had been involved. Was the point not to worry her, or was it to hide something? "We know who that was and have questioned him. It's very unlikely that he was involved in Billy's death."

"How can you be sure?" she pleaded. "Our notes could be very valuable, and it makes sense that someone attacked Billy to get them. There's two million dollars at stake! We've worked hard to figure out where that treasure could be."

"I want to find the person who killed your brother, Meghan, and you need to know that I'm good at my job. You'll have to trust me when I say nothing indicates that man was involved."

"Does he have an alibi?"

"Billy was killed in the middle of the night. Ninety-nine percent of people won't have an alibi beyond 'I was sleeping at home.' We will be working off the evidence from the crime scene."

Hopefully the team finds some good leads from there.

"Where was Billy . . . shot?"

"He was found outside in back of the bed-and-breakfast he was staying at."

"Is it in a bad area?" she asked.

Evan paused, wondering how much research Meghan had actually done about the tiny community of Eagle's Nest for the treasure hunt. "Eagle's Nest doesn't have bad areas," he told her. "It's too small. I guess you could call the empty lot where people occasionally dump their garbage a bad area, but I assume you meant crime levels."

"I did." She let out a deep sigh. "I'll try to get a red-eye out there tonight. I'll book a flight as soon as we get off the phone."

"Is there anyone else I need to notify?"

"No. It's just been us for several years. He moved in with me a few months ago when he lost his job. When the clues for the treasure hunt were released, he was so excited. He thought that if he worked hard enough on it, he'd find it."

"A lot of people feel that way."

"Well, Billy had a *special* feeling. He was convinced he was destined to find it." She gave a soft sob. "I guess that was never true. Will they let me see him tomorrow?"

Evan pictured the huge exit wound that had eliminated Billy's eye. "Meghan, I recommend that you not see him. Again, you'll need to trust me on this."

"That bad?" she whispered.

"Yes."

"Can I have his things?"

"Some items will be held as evidence for a while. I'll figure out what you can take home."

"Do you have his treasure-hunt notebook?"

Evan hesitated. "I don't know. I've gone through his room, but I wasn't looking for that specifically."

Why didn't I tell her?

"If it's gone, that's your motive for his murder."

"I'll keep that in mind."

He answered a few more of her questions and ended the call, promising to meet with her when she arrived, and then stood for a long second trying to understand the instinct not to tell Meghan that he had the notebook.

Because right now everyone is a suspect.

17

Mercy looked up from her computer as Melissa rapped on the open office door. The office manager's cheerful face was glowing, and she had a glint in her eye.

"Alex Kerr is here to see you," Melissa said.

"Good!" Mercy quickly straightened her desk. There was no hiding the stacks of files and papers, but at least they could be in neat piles. She'd spent the afternoon reviewing the history of the Kerr family and verifying the information she'd gotten from the sisters. Everything they had told her checked out. Once she talked with Alex Kerr, she was headed home.

"He's cute," Melissa whispered. "Find out if he's available."

Mercy snorted. "I'm not your wingman. And I think he's twenty years older than you." Melissa was in her midtwenties.

"He doesn't look it at all." Melissa frowned. "Although he does use a cane. But it's sort of sexy."

"Melissa!" Mercy rolled her eyes. "Show him back, please." She sighed as the office manager vanished. Melissa's sunny personality attracted men in droves. Mercy suspected she'd dated most of the single men in Deschutes County but couldn't find someone she really liked. She often showed Mercy men's photos and bios on her dating app, wanting her opinion.

From what Mercy had seen, most male dating profiles weren't set up to attract women. Nearly every one had photos of the man holding dead fish or doing sweaty weight lifting. Things men liked.

A tall figure appeared in her doorway.

Melissa is right.

Alex Kerr was attractive. Dark hair, dark eyes, and an endearing half smile. He leaned on a cane.

Mercy stepped forward holding out her hand. "Mercy Kilpatrick. I'm glad we were able to finally connect."

He shook. "Nice to talk to you instead of your voice mail." They'd been playing phone tag throughout the day. Alex taught at the community college and had returned her calls between classes, and each time Mercy had been unavailable.

Alex took the chair she indicated. "My mother brought me up to speed," he told her. "I was shocked to hear of Victor's death."

Mercy sat and flipped over to a clean page on her notepad, writing his name at the top. "You were close to Victor?"

"Yes and no. I'm a good ten years older. That meant we ignored each other when we were five and fifteen, but when Victor hit his late teens, we hung out at family gatherings. Occasionally went hunting or fishing together. He always seemed older than his age."

"When did you last hear from him?"

"It wasn't long after his father's death. He called to tell me he was leaving town and didn't think he'd be back. I told him to keep in touch, but he never did."

"That's a two-way street," Mercy pointed out.

"I tried his phone number after a few months. It was disconnected. He wasn't on any social media sites, so I let it go, assuming he'd call when he felt like it. Mom said she never heard from him either, but that didn't surprise me."

"What do you mean?" asked Mercy, wanting Alex's view of the family dynamics.

He grimaced. "Victor and his dad, Jack, were always the black sheep of the family. They clashed with everyone else. Jack never got along with either of his brothers, and Victor continued that."

That lines up with what Christine and Linda told me.

"Why do you think that was?" she asked.

Alex glanced out her window before meeting her gaze, and regret flickered in his eyes. "My dad and Joe were assholes to them. They dragged me into it, but I was able to see past it by the time Victor was older. The two of us talked a lot about why the older brothers harassed his dad so much."

"What was the reason?" Mercy studied Alex. He seemed forthcoming. She could see a resemblance to Christine around his eyes. They crinkled in the same way when he smiled.

He gave a sheepish look. "It was stupid. Jack had a different father, and Grandma clearly favored him."

"I heard Ethel was a strong woman."

"Definitely. I was half-terrified of her growing up. She didn't take crap from anyone."

"But she allowed the bullying of her youngest?"

"She didn't. I heard her dress down my dad and Joe several times, but they continued with the passive crap, you know? She really fell apart when Jack died."

Mercy changed the subject. "I know you work at the community college. What do you do?"

"I teach driver's ed and motorcycle safety courses." He indicated his cane. "A bad motorcycle accident left my hip and knee a mess. It was my fault. I was young and dumb, so now I do what I can to pass on safe riding habits."

"Do you still ride?"

He grinned and his face lit up. "You better believe it."

No wonder Melissa was smitten.

"I assume Christine told you we're looking for Bridget Kerr, Victor's wife?"

"Yes. I was unaware Victor had married until she told me."

"She was Bethany Bolton before she married. Does that name seem familiar?"

He thought. "No. Does my mom know that? She didn't say anything about another name."

"I don't believe I mentioned it." Mercy hadn't thought it seemed relevant at the time. But with Alex's closer relationship with Victor, she'd hoped Victor had told him about a girlfriend. "Did Victor ever tell you about women he dated?"

"No. Our friendship didn't go that far." He paused. "My mom mentioned a baby," Alex said slowly, his eyes searching hers.

"Yes. We believe she has a toddler with her. Molly." Mercy had nearly said "had a toddler." She was determined not to speak of Bridget or Molly in the past tense.

"That's crazy. I hope you find them."

Mercy was tempted to mention Theodore and Charlotte, but similar to her interview with Christine and Linda, she held back. Alex seemed kinder than the older Kerr generation, but she knew anything she told him would most likely be repeated to his mother. The gossip queen.

She wasn't ready to expose Theodore and Charlotte to that.

"Your current address is the same as your mother's," Mercy said. "Before that you lived in Bend?"

"Before my divorce," he said curtly. "Now I live in a mobile home on the property. Divorce isn't cheap. Even when there are no kids involved." His face had gone blank, but resentment had flashed in his eyes before he controlled it.

"I'm sorry. Were you married long?"

"Eighteen years."

At least she could tell Melissa he was single, but she assumed he was carrying some baggage from the demise of the long marriage.

Melissa needs to stick to her own age group.

Mercy suddenly realized a person was missing from her investigation. "Alex, do you know Victor's mother's name?" She held her pencil ready. No one had brought up Jack Kerr's wife. Not Christine and Linda or even Darby and Eddie.

"Shannon Ayers. She passed away when he was six. Drug overdose. And no, Jack and Shannon weren't married." His expression was still blank.

"That's so sad," Mercy said, writing down the name.

Another grandparent Theodore and Charlotte will never know.

"Victor moved in with Jack after that?"

"Yes. He'd been living with Jack most of the time anyway. Shannon wasn't in any condition to be a parent. I'm surprised my mom didn't mention her. No one liked Shannon. Especially Ethel. Shannon wasn't nearly good enough for her favorite son. Why?"

"I'm just filling in the blanks," Mercy said, not surprised she'd found another family controversy.

And another early death . . .

Alex looked ready to leave. He shifted and winced, placing his hand on his cane, which he'd hooked on the armrest of the chair.

Mercy wondered if his hip or knee was giving him pain. Or if he simply didn't like the turn her questioning had taken. She'd exhausted her list of questions, so she stood, signaling the end of the interview. "I appreciate you stopping by on your way home. You've been very helpful."

Alex maneuvered himself out of the chair with his cane. "I don't see how. You're looking for a woman and baby. I've been no help with that."

"Just keep your ears and eyes open for them," Mercy said noncommittally. The Kerr family dynamics were odd, and she worried she wasn't going to learn something that would guide her to Bridget and Molly.

The whole family had been determined to make the lives of the black sheep miserable.

As far as she had seen, Bridget had no reason to approach this side of the family.

"I will." Alex shook her hand and left.

Mercy sat in her chair, thinking through the conversation. Alex had mostly confirmed what she'd learned from Christine and Linda. But she had gotten a new name to investigate: Shannon Ayers. She underlined the name on her notepad.

Mercy could easily imagine Ethel's disapproval of a drug addict dating her favorite son. And thereby giving Jack's siblings and their wives another reason to make his life miserable.

Hate gets passed from generation to generation.

Alex had said Shannon's name as if it were tainted. He would have been around sixteen when Victor's mother died. No doubt his memories of the woman had been enhanced by the scorn of his family looking down on a drug user.

Yet Joe Kerr's autopsy after he drowned had shown high levels of methamphetamine.

The pot calling the kettle black.

It's doubtful the family's drug history has anything to do with Bridget Kerr's disappearance.

Mercy needed to concentrate on the missing woman. The unusual family history was distracting her. None of them knew or had seen Bridget. Alex had a point when he'd said he'd been no help to her investigation since he hadn't encountered Bridget.

Why didn't he ask to see a picture of Bridget?

Her brain froze on the question. The Kerr sisters hadn't asked to see a photo either. But Mercy had essentially asked them if Bridget Kerr had knocked on their door and had assumed they knew who had been on their front porch lately.

And she'd only asked Alex if the names were familiar. He'd answered those questions.

But wouldn't someone ask to see a photo of the missing person?

The question ricocheted inside her skull, disrupting all other thoughts. Her brain coming up with a half dozen weak reasons no one had asked what Bridget Kerr looked like.

"If Bridget couldn't find Evan, there's no way she'd turn to this family," Mercy muttered to herself.

Mercy had no doubt that Victor had told Bridget multiple stories about the bullying of himself and his father at the hands of his family for years. Bridget wouldn't seek them out.

And the fact remained that Evan Bolton was easy to find. He lived in the same home where he'd grown up, and any internet search would place him with the Deschutes County sheriff's office. Bridget could have lied to her children about where she was going, but why bring up an uncle they'd never heard of? She must have had a reason for telling them that's where she was going.

But why didn't she tell them Evan's name?

18

Ollie parked his old truck behind the Lake Ski and Sports warehouse. He was about to start his usual six-hour shift, which finished up at midnight.

I'm already tired.

He hadn't known spending the day with Theodore and Charlotte would wear him down. Kaylie had also looked ready for a break when Evan picked up the kids at five. They were good kids, and Ollie liked them a lot. But Charlotte was always on. Always talking. Always moving. Full of questions and opinions. Her chatter wasn't pointless; she clearly had a sharp brain. But Ollie wanted to tell her it wasn't necessary to share every little thought she had.

Luckily she'd been mostly interested in Kaylie, leaving Ollie and Theodore together. Twice Theodore had told Charlotte not to talk so much, at which point she'd glared at him and proceeded to ask Kaylie more questions. Theodore had spent the entire morning with the Harry Potter book, his face intense as he read. Kaylie had asked him to stop reading for lunch, and the boy had begrudgingly set the book aside, his face surly.

Ollie understood. He didn't like to be interrupted in the middle of an engrossing book either.

After lunch, Kaylie and Charlotte had made plans to start the Kilpatrick coconut-cake recipe and discovered they needed powdered vanilla-pudding mix. Kaylie insisted they couldn't make the recipe without it, so Ollie recruited Theodore for a quick trip to the grocery store, happy to get out of the house. Theodore had left his book behind after ordering Charlotte not to touch it.

In the truck, Theodore had been quiet, his eyes scrutinizing every person and building they passed. Ollie had a flashback to his first truck rides with Truman. The man had often used the rides to find out what was on Ollie's mind. There was no better time to talk to a teenager than when they were trapped in a vehicle beside you.

As long as they didn't have headphones on.

Ollie had read the Harry Potter book three times, so he questioned Theodore about it. It was as if a mask had been removed. The intense, quiet child was suddenly animated and talkative. After a few enjoyable minutes, Ollie had changed the subject. "I'm really sorry about your dad, Theodore."

"It's okay." The young teen had turned his attention back out the window. "I really don't want to talk about it."

That was a quick shutdown.

He had wanted to get the boy to open up about his dad's death and his mother's disappearance because he had been surprised by how good it had eventually felt to discuss his parents' and grandparents' deaths with Truman.

Theodore just met me today. We won't immediately be best buds.

"My parents both died when I was three," Ollie had told him, keeping his gaze on the road. Out of the corner of his eye, he saw Theodore's head turn his way.

"I thought Truman and Mercy were your parents."

"Nope. Kaylie is Mercy's niece. Truman isn't related to any of us, but that doesn't matter. I consider him my dad now, and we made our own family." He'd glanced at the boy. "People don't have to be related to you to be your family."

Theodore's eyebrows came together as he pondered Ollie's words of wisdom.

Ollie went on. "I was raised by my grandparents, but they had both died by the time I was sixteen."

"What happened?" Theodore had blurted out.

Ollie had swallowed hard. "My parents died in a car accident. My grandmother got really sick a couple years later. It was just me and my grandfather for a long time until—" He stopped, questioning if it was appropriate to tell someone Theodore's age that his grandfather had been murdered.

His mother is possibly dead. The baby too.

"Did something bad happen to him?"

"Yes," Ollie had whispered. He'd loved his grandfather, the person he remembered the most. He'd learned how to survive on his own in the woods for two years thanks to what his grandfather had taught him. But he'd been lonely. "And I really don't want to talk about it either." He'd looked at Theodore. "I understand that you don't want to talk about your dad, but I wanted you to know that I'm a good listener when you're ready. Your uncle Evan is too."

The boy had been silent for a long moment as they drove through town.

"I can take care of Charlotte," he suddenly stated.

"I have no doubts about that at all," said Ollie. "But that doesn't mean you don't miss your mom and dad. And Molly."

"Do you think they're dead?"

Ollie had stiffened at the question, words deserting him. He could feel Theodore's gaze boring into the side of his skull. He finally glanced at the boy. "We have no reason to think that."

The boy had nodded and turned his head to look out the front of the truck. Ollie's brain had gone blank.

Why didn't I come up with something better to say?

For the rest of the day Ollie had regretted fumbling the important moment. He should have come up with something comforting and inspirational. Instead, they'd silently bought the pudding mix and driven home.

Now, in the Lake Ski and Sports parking lot, Ollie hopped out of his truck and slammed the door, still obsessing about what he could have said to Theodore.

"Hey, jungle boy!"

Shit.

Start walking.

"Yeah, *you*, ya shithead. Don't walk away from me."

Tim Giles. The bully he'd overheard at Owlie Lake yesterday, who had lost his job for stealing.

Every instinct told Ollie to keep moving into the safety of the warehouse, but he stopped and turned toward Tim.

The asshole sauntered his way as if he had nothing better to do than hang out in the parking lot of his former employer. Using his peripheral vision, Ollie didn't see any of Tim's cohorts or his black truck. He must have parked in the adjacent neighborhood.

Where none of the current employees would notice.

Was he waiting for me?

Tim's hands were empty, but the right leg of his cargo shorts swung as if there was something heavy in his lower pocket.

Not the best place to quickly reach a gun.

Ollie gripped his keys in one hand. He didn't trust the older man. Tim had been a pain in the ass to work with even before Ollie suspected him of stealing. Rude. Always late. Never pulled his own weight. He would have eventually been fired. Ollie's video of his theft simply sped up the process.

Tim stopped a few feet away and shoved his hands in his upper shorts pockets.

Ollie waited.

"Saw your truck at Owlie Lake yesterday."

Ollie said nothing.

"You huntin' the treasure?"

"I took Shep for a hike."

"While hunting treasure," Tim sneered.

Ollie kept his expression calm. "What do you want, Tim?"

"You know about that guy that got shot in town? The one that was looking for treasure?"

Ollie's fingers went icy. "Everyone's heard," he said with a casualness he didn't feel, remembering he'd told Kaylie he thought Tim was dumb enough to use violence to get at the treasure.

Did he shoot the treasure hunter?

"I heard that guy was getting close, so he got taken out." Tim's tone changed as if he was sharing a conspiratorial secret.

"Rumors." Ollie shrugged one shoulder. "We won't know if someone is getting close to the treasure until they reveal that they found it. And who knows? Maybe they'll keep it a secret."

He'd given a lot of thought to what he'd do if he found it. And not telling anyone outside of his immediate family seemed the smartest option. The press was poised to go nuts once it was found.

No thanks.

"They're saying that guy had done a ton of research . . . had a note-book packed with stuff." He looked expectantly at Ollie.

"And?"

"The police have it now."

"So?"

"That true?"

"I have no idea."

"Your uncle—or whatever the fuck the police chief is to you—must have the notes. He was there after they reported the body."

"Are you trying to make a point?" Ollie asked. "Because I'm going to be late for work unless you get to it. I like being on time."

"It's not fair that you have access to those notes. They should be made public for everyone."

Ollie stared at Tim.

Entitled much?

"I don't have access to anything," Ollie stated.

"Well, I bet the chief already read the notes. He'll probably tell you where to go look." He glared at Ollie. "That's not fair."

Is there any point in bringing up ethics with him?

It would be like arguing with a wall.

Frustration filled Tim's face. "The chief shouldn't be keeping the information for himself."

"I'm going inside." Ollie shoved the keys he'd been tightly gripping into his pocket. Tim wasn't violent; he was an ass. "You get another job yet?" Ollie casually asked as he passed the older man.

"Fuck you."

"Have a nice day," Ollie cheerily replied over his shoulder.

"I'm going to talk to the police about those notes. It's not fair."

"Good luck with that," Ollie said as he walked away.

"Your luck's going to run out one of these days!"

Ollie shook his head.

Tomorrow he would tell Truman what he and Kaylie had overheard at the lake and what Tim had said tonight about some treasure-hunting notebook.

Does it really exist?

He strode into the warehouse, wondering if Truman had taken a look at some notes.

Now Ollie wanted a look at this mythical notebook.

19

What kind of person would hide $2 million just to send people into a frenzy?

Before heading home, Truman scrolled through a Google search on Chester Rollins, the man behind the treasure hunt. He highly suspected that Billy Serrano's murder would turn out to be tied to his participation in the game. Truman wanted to know more about the man who'd set the wheels in motion that might have led to Serrano's death.

The only person responsible for Serrano's murder is the person who pulled the trigger.

But Truman was curious. The dozens and dozens of links he was sifting through were mostly to posts about the game. He wished he'd been able to research the man before the treasure hunt had hit the internet. He spotted a link with a date from ten years earlier and immediately clicked.

It was a good hit. An in-depth magazine interview with Rollins, complete with photos taken in his Idaho mansion. The lead photo was of Rollins sitting in an office that looked like a room from a British hunting lodge. Walls of huge stones, heavy ornate furniture, and animal heads on the walls.

Tons of heads. Dozens.

Truman had never understood the need to mount proof of a kill on a wall. Or understood how that was considered decor.

Chester Rollins seemed to believe that any empty wall space should be filled with a furry head.

Truman continued reading, already aware that Rollins had never been married but wondering if any of the women he'd been with had complained about the room. Sure enough, the interviewer asked Rollins how the past women in his life had felt about his hunting.

"Well, I'm still hunting, and none of the women are here. What do you think?"

Truman snorted.

The article went on to describe Rollins's hunts around the world. Truman skimmed, not interested in reading about how people with money to burn actually burned their money. Then the interviewer questioned Rollins about the women in his life, and Truman slowed down. With every name, Rollins gave a condescending description and a reason why the relationship had ended. Each breakup was because of the woman. Too demanding. Too needy. Too loose. Too insecure. Too much alcohol. Too much spending.

Yeah, right.

The common denominator was the man surrounded by animal heads.

Another photo showed Rollins on a gigantic chessboard that took up half a huge room. The pieces were the size of humans. Rollins stood in the place of the king, his arms crossed on his chest, giving a casual smirk for the camera. Rollins had been an active chess player, competing in many tournaments. He relished the game.

Truman studied the man's face, getting a sense that this was a man who thrived on controlling people. Someone who would create a nearly impossible treasure hunt for his own personal enjoyment of knowing it would make people scramble.

He knew from other articles that one of Rollins's attorneys had shared the clues, stating it was Rollins's wish. He'd left written instructions regarding the release of the clues after his death.

No one knew how much Chester Rollins had been worth when he died, but there had been a lot of public speculation. Truman had read estimates ranging from $10 million to $50 million. Rollins had no heirs, and except for the $2 million buried somewhere in the United States, the balance of his estate had been divided among a dozen charities. Truman had scanned the list. Most involved animals, and Truman wondered if in his old age, Rollins had experienced regret for all the hunting in his past.

Truman figured there were some disappointed second and third cousins somewhere. A few people had come forward, claiming that Rollins had been their father. Simple paternity tests had ruled them out as heirs.

What type of person believed they could simply claim someone was their parent? Had they never heard of science? Did they really think they'd walk away with some money and no questions? One woman had said she had been told all her life that Rollins was her father. She'd appeared to be genuinely shocked to learn her mother had lied. Or been mistaken.

Royce appeared in his doorway. "I know you're about to go home, Chief, but could you follow me out to the Wheelock farm first? Martin says he's got people camping illegally on his property. He's managed to chase off some of them, but he's got one guy refusing to leave. Martin threatened to shoot him, but that didn't work."

Truman closed the Chester Rollins search and pushed back from his desk. "Christ. Did he really say that to someone again?"

"I believe so. Lucas said Martin was so mad when he called in that he could barely talk. Says the trespassers are here for the treasure hunt."

Truman cursed under his breath.

Martin Wheelock was in his seventies, was the third generation of his family to own that farm, and took shit from no one. Truman wasn't surprised he'd threatened to shoot someone. He didn't believe Martin would actually do it, but the man was known to throw out threats right and left. No doubt strangers on his property had set him off in a big way. Truman would have been annoyed too.

After grabbing his cowboy hat, Truman followed Royce in his SUV and arrived at the Wheelock farm ten minutes later. Royce turned into the property and drove past the farmhouse, taking a dirt road toward the southeast section of the property. A minute later Truman spotted three pickup trucks, and a little farther away was a small Toyota sedan. Martin stood near the tailgate of one of the trucks with two other locals whom Truman recognized from neighboring farms.

Martin called in some support.

All three had rifles slung over their shoulders and cross looks on their faces, and Truman was thankful that someone had decided to call his office before any guns went off. The Toyota sedan was parked next to a small grove of trees that sheltered a single blue tent. Truman didn't see anyone near the tent.

Truman parked and approached the group with Royce at his side. "How you doin', Martin?" he asked as all the men shook hands.

"Sorry you had to come out, Chief," answered Martin with a glare at the tent twenty yards away. Martin Wheelock wasn't a tall man, and Truman doubted his weight crossed one hundred pounds, but the man emitted the energy and authority of someone three times his size. Strangers had a tendency to underestimate him, and Truman suspected that might have happened with the camper who refused to leave.

"There were four tents pitched out here when I spotted them an hour ago," Martin said. "I kindly let them know this wasn't public land and that they needed to leave." He worked his lips, turned his head, and spit into the dirt.

Truman suspected the words had been polite—but backed up by the rifle hanging on Martin's back.

"Don't know why people think they can just pitch a tent anywhere," said Martin. "Where they gonna do their business?"

"Business?" asked Royce, a puzzled look on his face.

"Pee," answered Truman. "And more."

"Ohhh." The young police officer nodded emphatically.

"I got the others to leave. They were assholes about it," said Martin. "But at least they left. This last guy is actually the politest one in the bunch, but he's dug his heels in and won't budge."

"Did he say why?" Truman asked.

Martin looked at him in surprise. "Does it matter? He's trespassing."

"Did you see any weapons?" Truman asked.

"Nope. He gave us shit about us being armed. Probably one of those anti-carry folks."

Truman wasn't about to assume the man was unarmed. "Is he in the tent?"

"Yep."

"What's his name?"

"How the hell would I know?" Martin looked bewildered.

Truman was a firm believer in people skills. Especially in law enforcement. He'd been lucky that his training officer in San Jose had been a master at them. Truman gestured for Royce to follow him and headed to the tent, noting it was zipped shut.

"Hello, the tent," Truman said as he approached. "I'm Eagle's Nest police chief Truman Daly. Can you come out so we can discuss a different location where you can pitch your tent for tonight?" He stopped a dozen feet from the tent door, and Royce moved to a position a few yards away from the tent's side to keep Truman out of his line of fire—if necessary.

The zipper on the tent lowered six inches, and Truman could just make out an eye. Truman rested his lower arms on his utility belt, his hands free and near his center. A nonthreatening pose.

But one in which he could quickly reach his weapon.

"Officer Gibson is on your left. There's just the two of us," Truman told the eyeball. "Come on out and let's talk."

The eye vanished and the zipper fully opened. The man who emerged appeared to be in his early twenties. Jeans. Black T-shirt. Bare feet. Scraggly beard. He looked clean, but Truman smelled a sharp scent of sweat the moment he stepped out of the tent.

Having three men with guns confront you could do that.

"What's your name?" Truman asked. The camper looked nervous, but he held strong eye contact and kept his chin up.

"Isaac." He glanced back at Royce, who was just far enough behind him that Isaac couldn't see him and Truman at the same time.

"Where are you from, Isaac?"

"Coos Bay."

Truman was familiar with the town on the southern Oregon coast. "Why are you camping on private land? There are plenty of campgrounds nearby."

Isaac's chin rose a fraction. "They're full. All of them. Believe me, I checked."

Truman nodded. "Sorry about that. I know that's probably not what you expected to find, but there are a lot of people visiting the area right now."

"I noticed."

"Let's figure out a solution. I know the hotels close by are full. Maybe we can find you something in Bend."

Isaac looked at his feet and swallowed. "I don't have the money for a hotel right now. I was planning to camp."

Truman noticed the wedding band on Isaac's left hand. "You here for the treasure hunt?"

His gaze went back to Truman's. "Yes, sir. We could really use the money—that is, my wife and I. She stayed home because she needs to work. But I . . ." He looked at his feet again.

. . . don't have a job at the moment.

Hotels weren't cheap. And Truman suspected the rates in the area had gone up as treasure hunters filled the rooms. That left campgrounds and private home rentals.

"Is that why you didn't leave when Martin asked?"

Isaac looked past Truman to where Martin and his backup were waiting. "I wouldn't say he asked. He pointed his gun at us and told us to fucking leave."

"And you stayed because?"

Frustration crossed Isaac's face, and he scratched his beard. "I didn't like the way he was telling us what to do. He didn't have to be an ass about it."

Muttering came from the direction of Martin and his cronies. Truman didn't care to know what they were saying.

Isaac appeared to be aware he should leave, but some stubborn streak had made him stay. And the fact that he didn't know where else to go.

"Well, let's get you packed up and off Martin's land; then we'll figure out a place for you tonight." Truman had no idea what that place would be, but he wanted Isaac away from Martin before the man lost his temper again. "Royce will help you break down your tent." He jerked his head at Royce, and the officer immediately stepped forward.

As Truman turned away, he heard Royce strike up a conversation with Isaac about one of the clues. Truman headed back to the surly threesome. "You all got smartphones on you?" he asked the three. Each one nodded. "Okay. Here's your first law enforcement assignment. Start calling hotels. Maybe start up in Redmond and Madras. Something out of the way a bit where the treasure hunters haven't completely taken over all the rooms. Tell them you're calling for the Eagle's Nest Police Department and that we need a room tonight."

"Why should we? He said he didn't have money for a hotel," argued Martin.

Truman held his gaze. "I'll cover one night. And you guys will help me out by making a few phone calls. I think you can handle it."

"And what happens tomorrow night when he comes back, expecting to get another free room?" snapped one of the other men.

"Not going to happen," Truman said evenly.

"You don't know that," said Martin.

"Trust me. Now start calling. I want a room lined up before he has his car packed. Or are you too busy standing around to make a few calls?"

Martin was the last to pull out his phone. Truman turned away and walked back to where Royce and Isaac nearly had the tent finished. They were in deep discussion about a certain clue. Something about pears and planes. Truman shook his head.

No wonder no one has found it.

The two men shoved the tent into the trunk of the Toyota, still comparing theories, identical expressions of fascination on their faces.

"I told Isaac he's welcome to pitch his tent near my shop," Royce told Truman. "It's got a half bath and an old shower in it." He looked at Isaac. "I'm warning you, it's not great. Lotta rust, and it's pretty creaky, but it's better than nothing."

Truman narrowed his gaze at Royce. The officer and his wife lived on a few acres. The shop was an ancient building about fifty yards from his home. "You sure about this? You better run it by your wife." Truman's plan to help Isaac didn't include inviting a stranger to live with one of his officers.

"We figured out our wives went to the same high school in Cottage Grove," Royce said with a grin. "One year apart. I bet they know each other."

"You figured that out while I talked with Martin for thirty seconds?" Maybe Truman needed to take people-skills lessons from Royce. The young officer did talk too much, and often his naivete made him blunder, but maybe it had worked for the best here. He studied Isaac.

The stress was gone from the young man's face, replaced by a lively interest. His eyes reflected the simple kindness Truman had always seen in Royce's.

Two peas in a pod.

His gut told him Isaac was a decent man. Just down on his luck. And stubborn.

"Call her now," he ordered Royce. The officer nodded and pulled out his phone.

Truman held Isaac's gaze. "Don't fuck up this offer. Be respectful of my man's property and sometimes overly friendly nature."

"Chief!" Royce's face turned red.

Isaac nodded. "Not a problem."

"Good. Let me see your driver's license."

The man promptly handed it over. Truman snapped a photo of it and the license plate of the Toyota, then gave it back. He didn't plan to do anything with the information; he was sending a message that he knew who Isaac was.

"You good?" he asked Royce, who immediately nodded. "Then I'm headed home," Truman told him. He walked back to the three men, who were all on their phones. "You can cancel the hotel search. Isaac's got a place for the night."

"Good. Because we're not finding shit," said Martin. "Hotels within fifty miles are full."

Truman grimaced. "Hopefully this will be over soon." He touched his hat to the three men, got in his vehicle, and let out a deep sigh.

I'm so over this treasure hunt.

20

The next morning in her office, Mercy sipped on her coffee with heavy cream and listened to Darby. The data analyst sat across Mercy's desk, a slightly disappointed look on her face.

"If there are legal wills out there," said Darby, "I can't find a record of them for any of the Kerrs who have passed. From what I know of Joe and Josh Kerr, I'm not surprised. But I expected more of Ethel Kerr. This was a woman of business with a keen brain."

Mercy agreed.

"What about title transfers of the Kerr property? Is that a path to trace?"

"I looked into that. Ethel had created a transfer-on-death deed which named Christine and Linda as beneficiaries. It was legally recorded after the deaths of all her sons."

Mercy ran a finger over her coffee lid. "After?"

"Maybe she realized after her boys died that she needed to make some sort of arrangement."

"Christine and Linda said Ethel wasn't the same after Jack died. They made it sound like she'd given up on life. Is that a person who has the presence of mind to make legal arrangements?"

"Maybe the women prodded her to do something. Maybe the deaths of the boys were a wake-up call." Darby looked at her notes. "She really should have created a trust to handle all her assets."

"Were there a lot?"

"I don't know. Obviously the Kerr brand fell off the face of the earth and eliminated any income. Debts from a failing business could have cost her even more. It happened so long ago, I can't find good records."

"Let me talk to the women again. See if they know about a will."

Darby stood. "I prefer physical sources to human-memory sources."

Mercy snorted. "Don't we all. Let me rephrase that: we all should. But I'll take what I can get. Something will lead us to a possible place that Bridget and Molly Kerr could have gone."

"It's been weeks," Darby said quietly.

"I know." Mercy's heart saddened. "My gut on this isn't good."

"Let me know what you find." Darby left her office.

Mercy debated which sister to call and went with Linda. Christine might be her gossip girl, but Linda was frank and straightforward. She answered immediately.

"It's Mercy Kilpatrick, Linda."

"Good morning, Mercy," said the woman. "What can I do for you?"

"I have some follow-up questions from yesterday."

"Go right ahead."

Mercy liked that she didn't force small talk first. Mercy rarely had patience or time for that.

"Did your husbands have wills? My staff has been looking for legal documents and haven't found any."

"No," Linda said promptly. "Neither Joe nor Joshua bothered with that. They, of course, thought they'd live forever. Wills were something they'd do when they were old. But early on, Ethel was very insistent that Christine and I be joint owners on everything with our husbands, thank goodness. It made it much easier after they died. Things simply stayed in our names, and theirs were removed. It took longer for Christine since Joshua's body was never found. She had to wait for the state to declare he was dead."

"What about Ethel? Did she have a will?"

"Ethel did. She wrote it up herself."

"That's not the smartest thing to do," said Mercy. "Being a sharp businesswoman, I'm surprised that's what she did."

"We were surprised too," said Linda. "Everything had to go through probate because she did it that way. But at least she kept it simple. She said everything was to be divided into thirds and go to the three boys. But since they had died just before she did, and she didn't change it, things eventually worked their way to Christine and me. I have a copy of it if you'd like. It was found in a safety-deposit box after her death."

"But what about Victor?" asked Mercy. "Wouldn't he have been entitled to Jack's third of the estate after Ethel died?"

There was a long silence.

Linda finally spoke. "There really wasn't much left after Ethel died. A little savings. She'd lost almost everything in the nineties. The land was the main asset—which we now have to come up with the property taxes for each year. We talk about selling all the time. It's worth a good chunk of money."

"So if you sell, one-third of that would go to Victor's wife, Bridget."

Linda was silent again.

"Who is now missing after the death of her husband," Mercy continued. Subtle alarms rang in her head, and she wondered if Linda and Christine had made any effort to find Victor after Ethel's death.

Linda told me she'd looked online a bit.

That wasn't enough effort in Mercy's eyes. But what motivation would the women have to find someone who was owed part of their inheritance?

With the death of Ethel, Victor would be legally entitled to his father's share. And then Bridget. And if Bridget was never found, then Charlotte and Theodore should get it.

It would be a messy legal fight, but doable and worth it if the Kerr property sold for a lot of money. Mercy scribbled a note to check the tax-appraisal value on record with the county office. It wasn't a reflection of the market value, but it was a place to start.

"I assume there's been no progress on finding Bridget and her child?" Linda asked.

"We're following some leads," Mercy said noncommittally, instinctively keeping Charlotte's and Theodore's existence to herself again.

If Bridget is dead, do these women have a legal right to guardianship of Theodore and Charlotte?

Mercy knew nothing about the laws.

Evan is a much closer blood relative. An uncle versus two great-aunts.

Would a guardianship also control the kids' inheritance?

Questions for Darby to research.

She thanked Linda for her time and ended the call. Mercy sat for a few moments, her brain processing the call. Linda and Christine had a possible financial motive to keep Bridget out of the picture.

Could the two women be involved in Bridget's disappearance?

Bridget might have left her home on her own, but if she had knocked on Christine and Linda's door, would they feel threatened to learn their dead brother-in-law, Jack, had surviving heirs?

Mercy didn't want to believe it.

But I can't rule out the possibility. Yet.

21

Truman had just placed his hand on the knob of his front door, ready to leave for work, when Ollie said his name. He turned and was instantly amused by Ollie's serious bedhead. Ollie was usually sound asleep at this hour. The teen yawned and tugged at the hem of the T-shirt he'd slept in. Shep was at his feet and gave a full-body stretch, a canine image of the downward-dog yoga position.

"Whatcha need, son?"

"I ran into Tim Giles at work last night." Ollie rubbed one eye.

Truman pondered the name. "Didn't he get fired?"

"Yeah. He was waiting in the parking lot for me when I got there."

Anger unfurled in Truman's chest. "What'd he do?"

"He didn't *do* anything. He's all talk," Ollie stated quickly, his eyes widening as he looked at Truman. "Don't get heated."

"You tell me some asshole you got fired is waiting for you in a parking lot? You bet I'm going to get heated."

"He just wanted to talk," Ollie told him. "Well . . . and try to scare me a bit. I hadn't told you yet that Kaylie and I saw him out at Owlie Lake when we were treasure hunting."

More treasure-hunting problems.

"They didn't see us. We heard them coming and hid, but he and his friends were talking about stealing the treasure from some other hunters they had followed."

"What?"

Ollie winced. "No one has found it, obviously, but Tim and his friends are tailing hunters they think are close to finding it."

Truman closed his eyes for a long moment.

Just what I need.

"And what would they do to the hunters who actually found it?" he asked Ollie.

The teen shrugged. "Dunno. I first wondered if they'd . . . kill . . . someone for it, but I can't see Tim doing that. He's a big bully and a jerk, but I don't think he'd go that far."

"Money makes people do things they never dreamed of."

"Yeah. But anyway, last night he wanted to know if I'd seen some notebook that belonged to the guy who was killed at Sandy's B and B."

The hair on Truman's neck rose. "How'd he know about it?"

Ollie's eyebrows shot up. "So it does exist?"

"What have you heard?" Truman hadn't considered that other hunters would have gossiped about Billy Serrano's notebook. No doubt the description had grown with each rumor, and the book was now a legend that contained a magic map to the treasure.

"Tim implied that it was really good research and that the guy had been murdered for it. Is that true?"

"We don't know why he was murdered."

"Tim says it's unfair that you have the notebook now and that you and I will use it to find the treasure. He's pretty worked up about it. Kept saying it wasn't fair and that the notes should be shared with everyone."

Truman couldn't speak. *A bully who is worried about fairness?*

"I know," said Ollie. "The guy is an idiot. He expected me to share police evidence with him. But once I realized that's the only reason he confronted me, I walked away." He paused and scratched Shep's ear. "So this notebook is real?" he casually asked.

Truman sighed. "Yes, the victim had a notebook related to the treasure hunt. Just like a lot of the hunters do. I seriously doubt the notebook leads the way to the treasure any more than anyone else's notes. Although since Billy Serrano was killed, no doubt the rumor mill is working overtime and claiming that the notebook was the motive."

Ollie nodded, his focus on his dog.

He won't look at me. He's dying to go through that notebook.

Truman wanted to laugh, but the damage the treasure hunt had caused, possibly including a death, was all too real. "Let me know if he harasses you again."

"I can handle him."

"Well, keep me informed."

"Will do."

"Go back to bed. See if you can get another hour's sleep before you get ready for work."

"On it." Ollie yawned again and headed for the hallway, his dog at his heels.

Shep slept on Ollie's bed every night. He was a good dog. Intelligent and quiet, and even the cats liked him.

Truman watched the dog's tail vanish around the corner and promised himself that he would *not* pay Tim Giles a visit and warn him to stay away from Ollie. He needed to let Ollie handle it.

Get to work. Forget about the bully.

Truman had backed out of the driveway when Lucas called.

"What's up, Lucas?"

"I just walked into the office. Someone broke a window here last night. The west-side one near the coffee maker."

Truman's day wasn't off to a great start.

"Does it look like someone got in?" Truman asked. "How come the alarm didn't send me a notification?"

"No one got in. The reinforced glass held, but it's all cracked now. Definitely needs to be replaced. As for the alarm, it didn't get set last night." Annoyance filled Lucas's tone. The office manager ran a tight ship and took it personally when standards weren't upheld.

"Who was it?"

"Ben and Samuel closed up last night. They each probably thought the other person set the alarm. This isn't the first time I've arrived and found it off."

"You need to tell me when that happens."

"I tell whoever fucked up. Trust me, they get a taste of my displeasure."

"Did we catch the culprit on camera?"

"I'm getting ready to check."

"I'll be there in ten minutes."

Truman strode in the department door and hung his hat on the nearby hooks. No other officers had arrived yet, but Lucas was at his desk, scowling at his monitor.

"What'd you find?" Truman asked as he went to look over Lucas's shoulder. His big, wide shoulder. The department office manager had the physique of a defensive tackle for a pro football team.

"This happened around two a.m." Lucas hit PLAY on the recorded camera feed on his screen.

It was a view from the front of the police department. Truman watched the gray, grainy image as a truck drove through, and then Lucas switched to the camera on the west side of the building.

"That truck was the only vehicle to drive past within thirty minutes of someone trying to break in. Five minutes after it passed, the west camera recorded this."

Mounted under the eaves, the camera captured the entire side of the building and the shrubs that grew alongside it. Truman studied the motionless image for a long moment. The clock ticking off the seconds in the corner was the only indicator that it wasn't a photo. The camera at Sandy's B and B had been tampered with before Billy Serrano's murder. He was glad the department cameras had been left alone.

"There he is," Lucas grumbled.

Truman didn't see anything until the man rose out of one of the bushes. "Is that a baseball bat in his hand?"

"Yep."

"Who doesn't consider that a police department would have cameras?"

"An idiot."

The shadow peeked through each of the west-side windows and then returned to the smallest. He lifted the bat as if waiting for a pitch and swung it at the window. He flinched and paused after the hit, looking over his shoulder and all around.

"Waiting for an alarm to go off," muttered Truman.

A second later he confidently aimed a series of hits at the window. Truman studied the figure. He seemed of an average size and wore a ball cap. So far there had been no clear views of his face. He wore jeans and a long-sleeve T-shirt. "Can you make out the design on the back of his shirt?" Truman asked.

"No. I isolated it and enlarged it right before you got here, but it's too grainy. It's something big and round."

After two more swings, the figure stepped back, his shoulders heaving. And then he kicked the side of the building in what Truman assumed was frustration.

Lucas snorted. "See? Idiot." The man darted off-screen, and Lucas ended the video. "I scanned the next thirty minutes. No vehicles drive by. I'll keep scanning the rest of the views to see if he returned for any reason." He turned to look at Truman. "Think he was drunk?"

"A good possibility. Go back and freeze the truck that drives by."

Lucas pulled up a still image of the vehicle, enlarging and shrinking it to try to get a better view. "I can't tell what the make is. It's a huge truck. I suspect it's a Ford. My best guess on color is black, but it could be navy or dark gray."

Truman agreed. "Call someone to repair that window."

"Already done."

Truman clapped him on the shoulder. "That's why you're the boss."

"Damn right. You gonna talk to Samuel and Ben about the alarm, or do you want me to?"

"I'll handle it." Truman strode down the hall to his office, pulling out his cell phone and hitting Ollie's number.

"Yeah?" The teen sounded as if he'd fallen back to sleep.

"Do you know what Tim Giles drives?" Truman asked.

"Why? I'd really prefer you left it alone." Ollie suddenly sounded more awake. "I can handle Tim."

"This is for something else."

"What?"

"Can't tell you right now. Do you know or not?"

"A Ford. A black F-350," Ollie reluctantly said.

"Thanks, Ollie."

"Now can you tell me why?"

"No. But don't worry. This has nothing to do with you seeing him last night."

"Okay." The teen didn't sound very certain.

Truman ended the call and woke up his computer monitor, wanting to take a second look at what Lucas had found and pondering a discussion with Tim Giles. He could show the man an image of the truck and ask if it was his—of course there was no direct proof that the driver was the man with the baseball bat. But he could check Tim's truck for a baseball bat.

It appeared that Tim—if he was the one in the truck—wasn't the sharpest tool in the shed and would possibly admit to the vandalism if shown photos from the night before. Truman wondered if the man would continue to try to get the notebook and cause more damage. The best way to prevent additional damage to Truman's police station would be to let the man know the county sheriff, not the Eagle's Nest police, had the notebook in evidence.

Should Tim be a suspect in Billy Serrano's murder?

That wasn't Truman's decision. It was Evan Bolton's, which meant Truman needed to send Evan the videos from the previous night and tell him about Ollie's encounter and conversation with the man. Two encounters, counting the one at Owlie Lake.

Truman's responsibility was the damage to his building, not Serrano's murder.

But he continued to think about it. A clear image of the exit wound on Serrano's face was burned into Truman's brain.

Maybe Evan should take me with him to talk to Tim Giles.

22

Is this how it feels to be a parent?

For the fifth time that morning, Evan checked his phone to see if he'd missed a call. He'd bought a cheap cell phone for Theodore and Charlotte to use to call him in case of an emergency. The two kids had immediately argued over who got to carry the phone, making Evan wonder if he had been shortsighted in not buying two. Instead, he told them to leave it on the kitchen counter. Seeing their clear disappointment, he said they could each use it for five minutes every hour if they wanted to take pictures and videos.

I'm glad I didn't buy a smartphone.

He didn't envy parents who had to manage kids and cell phones.

It had been hard enough for him to leave the kids alone that morning, even knowing they'd been competent on their own during the last couple of weeks. Kaylie was going to spend this afternoon at the kids' house after finishing a morning shift at her coffee shop. Ollie couldn't stay with them because he had a full day of work.

While Evan was still staring at his blank phone screen, a call came through. Not recognizing the number, he answered.

"It's Meghan Serrano. I got in late last night. Can we meet sometime this morning?"

Billy Serrano's sister. She sounded tired.

"Good morning, Meghan. I hope your flight was good."

"It was okay, but I barely slept last night thinking about what happened, and I've considered what you said about not viewing Billy." She swallowed audibly. "You're probably right."

"I'm glad you agree. I can fit you in anytime this morning at my office."

"Is now a good time?"

"Yep. You can find me at the Deschutes County Sheriff's Department. Check in at the front desk and they'll let me know you're here."

"Looks like I can be there in about ten minutes. I appreciate your time, Detective." Meghan paused. "Do you have any updates on a suspect?" she asked hopefully.

"We're still sorting through leads," Evan told her. "We'll find him."

"Okay." Her tone was flat, sounding as if she understood that nothing had panned out so far.

Evan ended the call and sighed. The crime scene team hadn't turned up any leads, but it still had more evidence to examine and testing to do. It could be a very long process.

Truman had called earlier with an odd story about a man who had threatened Ollie about Billy Serrano's treasure-hunting notebook. Ollie had also overheard the man threaten to harm other hunters in his effort to get the treasure, and Truman suspected he'd tried to break into the police station overnight to find the notebook. He'd agreed to meet Truman at noon at Tim Giles's apartment for questioning.

The hunt had brought out the ugly in people.

Evan opened a file on his computer. He'd photographed every page of Billy Serrano's notebook before handing it over to evidence. There were twenty-six pages of notes and maps, most of it in perfect handwriting, which he'd been told was probably Meghan's. The other handwriting in the book was barely legible. Most likely Billy's.

Billy's notations were written in the margins. They were records of what he'd physically found when he'd followed Meghan's suggestions about clues.

In Billy's notebook each poem line had its own page—some several pages—and references to possible landmarks that the clue might indicate. Evan read for a few minutes. He found himself following the logic Meghan and Billy had created among most of the clues and locations. But some of the correlations made no sense at all to Evan. How did they decide "A holy sea" could mean a viewpoint? Why did they suggest part of the next line, "bow down to the rain," referred to the King of Apples Orchards?

No one knows what they're doing with these clues.

Chester Rollins is probably rolling over in his grave with laughter at the craziness he's created.

Evan's phone vibrated again, and Mercy's name appeared on his screen.

Did she find Bethany?

Tension tightened his jaw. "Bolton," he answered.

"It's Mercy. I wanted to update you on my visit with the Kerr sisters yesterday."

"Is there any news of Bethany?"

She paused. "No."

Mercy knew better than to give him a mitigated answer like the one he'd given Meghan Serrano a few minutes before. "What did you find out?" he asked. His tension evaporated a bit. She hadn't called to tell him she'd found Bethany's remains.

No news can be good news.

But he hoped more than anything that he'd get to see his sister again. It'd become a permanent ache in his chest. One that painfully flared every time he looked at Charlotte. For years he'd buried it—it was the only way he'd been able to move on—but the ache and emptiness were back, and stronger than ever.

Mercy told him about Ethel Kerr's will and how Theodore and Charlotte might be entitled to inherit a large amount of money if the Kerr property was sold. "Even though a third of Ethel's assets were left to the kids' grandfather, I don't think there's much currently left other than the property. I doubt it's worth suing over at the moment."

Evan weighed her words. The last thing he wanted to do was start a legal battle that could cost more than he had. But a third of the proceeds from the sale of the property could possibly set up the kids for life.

Which they might need if their mother was gone.

A thought struck him. "Are you implying that the kids could be in danger from the Kerr family? Because of this money?"

She sighed. "It's crossed my mind."

Evan's brain continued down that path. "And maybe Bethany is missing because of it? Jesus Christ, Mercy. Do you really think those women are capable of that?"

"It doesn't matter what I think," said Mercy. "We have to consider that possibility. And I'm not sure how relevant this is, but I don't think the Kerr sisters know about Theodore and Charlotte. I've never mentioned that Bethany had kids other than Molly, and the sisters have never said anything about them either."

"Okay," Evan said, his brain still racing. A surge of protectiveness had filled him. He'd first experienced it after he had met Theodore and Charlotte, but in the last two minutes, it had exploded almost painfully. An urge to get the children in his sight. And not let them out.

"I don't know how I feel about this," Evan lied, attempting to get the unsettling rush of emotion under control. "Anything else?"

"So far nothing unusual has turned up other than Joshua Kerr's body was never found."

Evan was silent for a long moment, analyzing that fact from every angle.

Could be nothing.

"I know what you're thinking," Mercy said into the silence. "His disappearance makes my mind race too." She paused. "I had an uncle who everyone—nearly everyone—believed was dead for nearly forty years when he wasn't. So it can happen."

"It's pretty rare," said Evan.

"Definitely. But back to Bethany and Molly. We've got the Center for Missing and Exploited Children involved, although they really want some pictures of Molly. I can't believe none exist."

Evan thought of the tiny baby shoe he'd discovered weeks before.

It was probably a neighbor's.

"I'd really like to see pictures too," said Evan. He and Mercy talked for another minute, and then he said goodbye after a deputy stuck his head in Evan's office to tell him he had a visitor. Evan stood and straightened his collar and noticed the deputy giving him an odd look.

"What is it?"

"She's got a dog with her."

"So?"

"Just making sure you're not allergic or something. It's pretty cute."

"Nope." Evan followed the deputy out front.

Meghan was the only person in the waiting area, and sure enough she had a small dog in a tote bag on her lap. The black-and-white puffball peeking out of the bag *was* cute. Meghan stood as Evan walked over, and she smiled hesitantly, her eyes red and puffy. She was tiny, with short blonde curls, and didn't resemble Billy Serrano at all.

The dog's owner is cute too.

Evan introduced himself and shook her hand.

"This is Oreo," she said as Evan held out his hand for the dog to sniff. "He likes everyone. I don't go anywhere without him." Meghan followed Evan to his office and took the seat he indicated. Only the dog's head was visible over the edge of the tote, and its gaze locked on Evan as he sat down.

"I'm very sorry for your loss, Meghan," Evan said, dragging his feet about starting his interview questions. It was hard to question relatives. The polite move would be to give them several days to grieve, but it was crucial to get as much information as possible at the beginning of an investigation. He'd learned to be as gentle as he could.

"Thank you, Detective." She stroked Oreo's ears, and the little dog turned to lick her hand.

"I'm sorry, but I'm going to jump right into the questions I have for you."

"That's okay. I know it's your job, and I want to help find who shot my brother." She shrugged. "Not that I know anything."

"You never know what little thing could help."

She nodded but didn't look convinced.

"I know you had talked with Billy every day he was here," Evan began. "And he told you about an incident with the man who tried to steal his notebook, but did he specifically mention any other hunters? Maybe someone he met while getting dinner . . . maybe someone he met at the bed-and-breakfast?"

Meghan frowned as she continued to pet the dog. "He'd said the town was full of people looking for treasure. I can't think of a single person he mentioned specifically except for the one questioned by the police. Billy tried to keep to himself. He wanted to keep a low profile and not be noticed by other hunters."

"Why didn't he want to be noticed? Did he say that specifically?"

"Yes, he did. He was suspicious of everyone, even back home. Refused to talk to people. Here, I know he was worried that someone would steal our work—which I guess someone tried to do."

"Doesn't that attitude seem a *little* over the top to you?"

She shrugged. "Billy had a strong paranoid streak. He always has. He told me someone spread bad rumors about him at work and that's why he lost his job. Said he'd caught someone looking in the windows of his apartment a few months ago and was convinced they were going to come back and break in. He's told me stuff like that all his life."

"The comment about the apartment windows was before the hunt started?"

"Yes, a few months ago. So I wasn't surprised when he said he was being super careful here." She sucked in a shuddering breath. "For all the good *that* did him." She lifted the dog out of the tote, gave him a hug, and settled him on her lap. Two round black eyes continued to stare at Evan.

"Meghan," Evan said carefully, "did you know he was armed?"

"Yes. Of course he was." She looked puzzled.

"Did you know he shot at someone he believed was trying to take his notebook?"

She gasped softly. "No!"

"That was the incident he told you about, but he left out the part about shooting at the man, who also returned fire. Luckily no one was hurt."

Shock filled her face. "I had no idea." She frowned. "But you don't believe that is the man who later shot him?"

"We don't."

Meghan's brows narrowed as she thought. "He did tell me about being chased out of someone's sheep pasture. Said two other hunters were also there, and the owner threatened to send his dog after them if they didn't leave. The other hunters dragged their feet about leaving, but Billy got right out of the pasture. He's scared of dogs—got bit real bad when he was younger. He doesn't even like Oreo." She gave the dog a kiss on the top of its head.

"Was he close to the treasure at that sheep pasture?"

Meghan gave him a half smile. "Who knows? He swore he wasn't going back, and so we moved on to the next clue. I think we got as far as that clue was going to take us."

"Where was that?"

She said nothing and kept her gaze on her dog.

She doesn't want to give away any of the clues.

Evan pressed his lips together. "Are you planning to continue the hunt where Billy left off?"

Meghan finally looked at him. "I think we were very close. I also believe that's why Billy was killed."

"How are you going to do it without his notebook?" Evan had yet to tell her the notebook had been located.

"I have copies of all the pages he had. I'm the one who wrote them up."

"If you think he was killed for it, are you sure you want to jump into this game?"

She gave him a fixed look, determination in her eyes. "I'm already in this *game*. I'm the one who figured out every clue that Billy followed. I had to stay behind because *one* of us had to work to pay the rent. Billy could never keep a job."

Evan blinked. The tiny grieving woman in front of him had suddenly turned into a resentful sister.

People show grief in different ways.

"We did find his notebook," Evan told her. "It turned up in the safe of the bed-and-breakfast he was staying at."

"Good. At least he listened when I told him to lock it up. When can I get it?"

"It's being examined in our lab." Seeing the frustration on her face, he quickly added, "But you have a copy of everything, right? So it's okay if you don't get it for a few days?"

"It's not okay," she told him. "I know Billy was writing his own notes in it. I don't have those."

Evan thought for a long moment. The notebook was evidence. But was the actual evidence the written information or the physical notebook itself? Meghan already had most of the information, so would it matter if she had the rest?

He made a decision. "How about if I have the lab copy the pages for you?"

She relaxed. "That's acceptable. When can I get them?"

"I'll send a request as soon as we're done here. I believe you'll have them by tonight." He stood. "I'll walk you out."

Why don't I copy it for her before she leaves?

Because Meghan's desire for the book was making him cautious. She'd appeared more interested in the notebook than in her brother's death.

It wouldn't hurt to make her wait for the information.

And give me time to look into her.

23

Truman trudged up the outdoor stairs to Tim Giles's apartment with Evan Bolton close behind him. The detective had agreed he should talk to Tim after he heard Ollie's story that Tim had threatened to harm other treasure hunters.

Truman was there to question the jerk about the damage to his window. Deep down he was furious with the man for harassing Ollie and would love to go toe-to-toe with the bully, but he had to let Ollie fight his own battles. He wasn't a child.

Ollie had a strong sense of integrity and honor, and Truman was proud of him. He'd taken to referring to the teen as his son. It wasn't biologically accurate, but it was emotionally accurate. Kaylie had also sneaked into his heart, and he thought of her as a daughter. He might never have biological children of his own, and he was okay with that.

"Gonna be another nice one," Evan commented as he and Truman reached the top of the stairs and turned to check the view. The sky was a perfect blue.

"Just like always," added Truman. He believed Central Oregon had some of the best weather in the world. Little rain and changing seasons. Warm summers and chilly winters. Snow but not too much snow. And tons of sun no matter the time of year.

Truman walked past three apartments and stopped at Tim Giles's. He rapped on the door, and he and Evan stood to the sides. He listened hard but could only hear the traffic from a highway two blocks away. He knocked again.

From the corner of his eye, he caught a movement on the ground level. A man had just come out of a door below the other set of stairs, a basket heaped with laundry in his arms. He froze as Truman made eye contact. Then he yelped, dropped his laundry, and ran.

"That's him!" Truman said as he turned to dart for the stairs. He'd recognized Tim from the driver's license picture he had printed out.

He and Evan thundered down the stairs as Evan shouted, "Stop! Deschutes County sheriff!" They reached the bottom and sprinted in the direction in which Tim had disappeared. They turned at the end of the building in time to see Tim vanish around a corner to the back. Truman turned up his speed, following a concrete path that led to the rear. Farther ahead and across a parking lot was another building in the apartment complex.

Truman turned the corner and spotted Tim running through the pool area. People on loungers idly watched him pass, as if a man sprinted by in jeans and a T-shirt every day at the pool. When Truman and Evan approached at full speed, a few of them sat up, finally realizing that something was up.

"Stop! Deschutes County sheriff!" Evan hollered again.

"Get the asshole!" a woman in a red bathing suit yelled as they passed her. She stood in the shallow end of the pool, holding hands with two kids.

Sounds like Tim isn't popular in his complex.

Tim glanced back at them without breaking stride and continued around the second building. Truman pushed harder, glad he hadn't worn cowboy boots that day. Instead, he'd worn a heavy work shoe with great traction. A little bulky for his sprint, but every stride felt stable.

Behind the second building, a steep embankment dropped twenty feet to a creek.

Creek was a generous description. It was a wide, dry bed with a narrow rivulet of mud down the center.

Tim had almost reached the bottom of the bank when Truman and Evan started down. The slope was steep, but the dirt was firm. The officers did a hopping sideways-shuffle step down the embankment, their arms wide for balance. Truman covered the last six feet in one giant leap, feeling the impact travel up his legs and spine. With Evan on his heels, Truman tore after Tim, who was running along the thin river of mud. The distance between them had narrowed considerably.

Tim glanced back, his eyes wide.

And promptly tripped over his own feet and went flying. He landed in the mud on his hands and knees and scrambled to get to his feet. He'd taken two stumbling running steps when Truman tackled him, taking him back into the sludge.

"Oooof!" Truman landed hard on the man's back and let his weight pin the smaller man.

"Get off me!" Tim shouted, twisting and trying to throw Truman off.

"No."

Evan knelt beside them and grabbed one of Tim's arms, twisting it back and slapping a cuff on one wrist. Truman lifted up to plant one knee in the center of Tim's back and grab the other arm. Evan cuffed it, and Truman pushed himself off Tim's back onto the muddy ground beside him. He sat there for a moment, his heart trying to pound its way out of his chest and his lungs heaving from the long sprint.

Evan slapped him on the shoulder. "Nice tackle."

Truman nodded, not having the breath to speak.

"Let me up!" Tim tried to sit up. A difficult task with his hands cuffed behind him. He succeeded only in digging his shoulder and the side of his face deeper into the mud.

"In a minute," Truman managed to say. He wiped sweat off his forehead, which coated it with mud. "Shit." He was covered in dirt below his knees and up both arms. He looked at Evan, who only had muddy feet and hands. His eyes were lit up from the chase, and Truman suspected his own looked the same. "I haven't been this muddy since I played high school football," he said.

"Me neither," said Evan, studying Tim, who'd finally stopped wiggling. "How come you ran from us, Tim?"

"I only did what anyone else would do," Tim answered sullenly. "You're cops, so I ran."

"Most people would ask how they could help if they saw us knocking on their door," said Truman.

"Bullshit."

"Not bullshit," said Evan. "And we're not wearing uniforms. What made you decide we were law enforcement?"

Tim was silent, and Truman watched him mentally struggle to come up with an answer that didn't make him look bad. He nudged Tim with a filthy shoe. "Detective Bolton asked you a question."

The muddy man's eyes widened at Evan's title.

He knows he's in trouble.

"Can you sit me up?" Tim asked. "So I can talk without getting more mud in my mouth?"

Truman stood, and he and Evan each grabbed Tim under an armpit and hauled him into a sitting position in the deepest part of the muck. Tim glared at the dirt and then at each man in turn.

"Now," said Truman, "why did you think we're law enforcement?"

"You're both wearing badges."

True. Both men had badges on their belts.

"You couldn't see that from where you were standing downstairs," Truman pointed out. "Try again."

Tim grimaced. "I recognized you." He tipped his head toward Truman. "You're the police chief."

"You're not a resident of Eagle's Nest. How would you know that?"

Exasperation crossed Tim's face. "You're Ollie's uncle or dad or whatever."

Satisfaction filled Truman. "That's right. I'm his whatever. So I know you saw him last night."

Tim stared at his muddy feet, avoiding Truman's gaze.

Truman saw Evan was trying to hold back a laugh.

"I also know that your black F-350 and you were at my police station around two a.m.," Truman said, stretching the truth. "I've got a couple of nice angles on video."

Tim's shoulders sank.

"What were you thinking, using a baseball bat on a reinforced window? With cameras watching?" Truman asked.

"I was drunk," Tim muttered.

"So you were also drinking and driving?" asked Evan. "Man, when you screw up, you like to do it in a big way."

"Being drunk is a poor defense for the damage you did," said Truman, not surprised at how easily Tim had essentially confessed. He'd heard "I was drunk" as an excuse for every stupid action imaginable and was sick of it. "And another thing. I don't have the treasure-hunt notebook you were trying to steal from my police station. It's not my evidence. It's part of a Deschutes County sheriff's investigation."

Evan raised his hand. "That'd be me."

Tim groaned and shut his eyes, tilting his head back.

"Yeah, you screwed up."

"Well, you probably copied the notebook first," Tim said to Truman. "That's not fair. It's information that should be released to the public."

"It's private property," said Evan. "Why in the world should it be available to you?"

"The guy who had it is dead. So that doesn't matter anymore." Tim scowled.

Truman threw up his hands. Tim was an ass. "He's all yours," he told Evan.

"I'm not sure I want him," retorted Evan.

"Why should I have to go with him?" muttered Tim. "I didn't do nothin' to his place."

"That's correct," said Evan. "But I would like to have a few words with you about where you were two nights ago."

"What happened two nights—" Tim blanched as he connected the dots. "Hey! I ain't got nothing to do with that! I didn't kill no one!"

"Double negative," murmured Truman.

"What?" Tim stared at him, his eyes wide in shock.

"If you didn't have anything to do with the murder of Billy Serrano, then you shouldn't mind me asking a few questions about it." Evan looked at his own muddy hands. "But I'd like to clean up. Let's head back to the sheriff's department, and we can talk there." He bent over and grabbed an armpit, and Truman followed his lead, both of them lifting Tim to his feet.

"I don't need to go there," said Tim.

"I bet I can get you a shower and some clean clothes," said Evan. "You don't mind wearing orange, do you?"

Truman bit the inside of his cheek, knowing Evan was giving the man a hard time. The two of them led Tim to the steep embankment and started up, each keeping a hand on one of his arms to balance him.

"You can't arrest me! I've done nothin'!"

"A minute ago you confessed to driving drunk and trying to break into the Eagle's Nest police station," said Evan. "That doesn't sound like *nothin'* to me."

"I didn't kill no one!"

"I'm glad to hear it," said Evan. "You can tell me all about it in town." He hauled on Tim's arm as the man tried to plant his feet.

"Wait, wait! I want to make a deal!"

"Uh-huh," said Truman, also giving a solid pull as the man tried to stop again.

"I might know something."

Truman and Evan exchanged a resigned look.

"What *might* you know?" asked Evan.

"I know who might have done it."

"Done what?" asked Truman.

"Killed that guy," Tim said in a quiet whisper, his panicked gaze going from one man to the other.

Truman and Evan stopped halfway up the bank. Truman lifted one shoulder in a shrug.

Tim's a bottom-feeder. But sometimes they find stuff.

"We're listening," said Evan.

"There's been this dude hanging around. I've seen him talking to other treasure hunters. Most people don't seem to like him. I saw him talking with the guy who got shot the day before he died."

"What's *this dude* look like?" asked Evan.

"He's got a beard."

"And?" asked Truman. "How old?"

Isaac, the stubborn trespasser, has a beard.

"Dunno. Not old. Not young."

I'd consider Isaac young. But maybe Tim would not.

"Yet this guy you can't describe you recognized as the same person you'd seen in town," said Truman.

"Well, I mighta followed him at one point."

"You might have?" Evan asked.

"Yeah. I thought he was onto something, so I followed him to the diner to listen to him talk." Annoyance crossed his face. "Couldn't hear nothing."

"Anything else?" asked Truman.

"That's it."

Truman looked at Evan. "That solve your murder?"

"Nope," said Evan. "We're still going in."

The two men continued to haul Tim up the slope.

24

Mercy was driving back to her office in Bend after a late lunch when she got a call from Kaylie. She grinned, wondering if Charlotte was already wearing on Kaylie's nerves. The teenager had been exhausted the night before after spending the day with the high-energy, inquisitive girl.

Mercy touched a button on her steering wheel to answer.

"Hey, Kaylie. How are the kids?"

"I want you to know that everyone is okay," Kaylie whispered. "We're hiding behind the barn."

The hairs rose on Mercy's arms. "What happened?" She slowed and pulled to the side of the road, her entire focus on Kaylie's name across her dashboard's screen.

"There's someone in their house. We were outside when we heard a car coming, and the kids instantly went to hide—"

"They automatically hide when someone comes?"

"That's what they told me," she continued in a whisper. "Anyway, this man walked right into their house. No knocking or anything. The kids say they don't know who he is."

Mercy pulled a U-turn. "Stay put. I'll be there in twenty minutes."

Twenty minutes is too long.

"Kaylie, I'm going to hang up and call the Eagle's Nest police station. They're the closest to you, and I'll have them send someone right away. I'll call you right back. Put your phone on silent," she ordered.

"I just did. Hurry, Mercy."

"Are you armed?"

"No," Kaylie whispered.

"That's okay. Stay hidden."

Mercy ended the call, hit the speed dial for the station, and interrupted Lucas's greeting.

"Lucas. It's Mercy Kilpatrick. I need you to immediately send someone to—shit!"

She didn't have an address. All she had was a mental image of where to turn off the country road.

"What's wrong, Mercy?" Lucas asked sharply.

"There's a prowler or someone at Theodore and Charlotte's home. Kaylie is there with the kids, and I'm too far away. *And I don't know the damned address.*" Her mind raced. "Is Truman there? He knows where it is."

"No, he's out."

"I'll call him. Can you send someone to run lights and sirens on Jasper Creek Road? The home is near that road about five miles from where it leaves Highway 97. Maybe the sirens will scare them off."

"On it. Sending Ben."

"Have him keep an eye out for me or Truman."

"Copy."

Mercy ended the call and immediately dialed Truman. It went to voice mail. "Dammit!"

She called again. Voice mail. But this time she left a message for him to get out to the kids' house and call her ASAP.

She called Kaylie back. "I'm coming as fast as I can," she told the girl. "Ben is heading over. You should hear his sirens in no more than ten minutes running up and down Jasper Creek Road. I didn't know how to tell them to get there, Kaylie. I don't know the address."

"I asked Theodore. He says there is no address. They pick up mail once a week somewhere else."

"Is the man still in the house?"

"Yes."

"The kids okay?"

"Yes. We're all good. Trust me, these two know where to hide on this property."

"I don't know whether to be relieved or saddened by that fact," Mercy said. She heard Charlotte say something in the background.

"He's coming out!" Kaylie hissed almost silently. "And walking this way."

Mercy clenched her steering wheel, floored the gas pedal, and pulled into the oncoming traffic lane to pass a pickup. She didn't have lights or sirens and for the first time fervently wished she did.

"We're leaving the barn," Kaylie whispered. "We're going into the woods."

"Be careful!"

"We are."

"Give me a description of the vehicle. And the man."

"It's a brown Chevy pickup. Not old . . . but not new." Kaylie spoke calmly. "I only got a glimpse of the man . . . I can try—"

"No," ordered Mercy. "Don't go back. Keep going into the woods."

"He's wearing boots and jeans and a white short-sleeved T-shirt. Brown beard and short hair."

For someone who'd only gotten a glimpse, Kaylie gave a solid description.

"He's opening the barn door on the other side."

"Did you see any weapons?"

Mercy heard Kaylie ask the kids the same question.

"No."

"That doesn't mean there aren't any," Mercy told her.

"I know."

"Can you think of anything in the house that would indicate to him that you're on the property?" Mercy asked.

"There are cookies in the oven," Kaylie said grimly. "And my car is parked here."

"Okay. Don't worry about it. Stay out of sight. You gave me enough description." A beep pulled her attention. "Truman's calling me. I left him a voice mail to head your way. I'll call you right back."

"Mercy?" Kaylie asked.

"Yeah?"

"We're going to be okay. Don't worry about us."

"Impossible." Tears threatened at her niece's levelheadedness. "Love you."

"Love you too."

Mercy switched over to Truman's call. "Are you headed over there?" she asked, skipping a greeting.

"I am. I was headed back to the office, so I'm only a few minutes away. What's going on?"

"Turn on your lights and sirens," Mercy said. "A man showed up at the farm and walked right into the house without knocking. The kids don't know who he is. Luckily they were outside when they heard him coming and hid."

"*What?*" Truman's siren sounded through the call. "Are they okay?" he asked loudly.

"Yes. They were hiding behind the barn, but he's checking the barn now, so they moved to the woods. Kaylie said the kids know how to hide."

"Why am I not surprised," said Truman.

"I'm headed over there, and your office sent Ben, but it sounds like you're the closest. Brown Chevy pickup. Jeans and white T-shirt. Brown hair and beard."

"Copy."

Mercy's system beeped again. "Kaylie's calling."

"Take it." He disconnected.

She pressed the button. "Kaylie?"

"Mercy, smoke's coming out of the windows of the house! He set a fire!" Her voice cracked.

Mercy gasped as she straightened in her seat. *A fire?*

"No! I said to stay put!" Kaylie ordered, her voice away from the phone. "Sit down! You can't do anything! Theodore!"

Mercy imagined the boy struggling with Kaylie to get to his home. "Is the man still there?"

"He's in the barn. I can hear him breaking things. Glass keeps shattering," she hissed. "I had to grab Theodore's arm to keep him from dashing back."

"Truman will be there first. You should hear him coming any second," Mercy told her. "I'm going to hang up and call 911 for the fire. *Keep those kids away.*"

She ended the call and dialed 911. Her mind was clear, but her heart was trying to hammer its way up her throat. She briefly slowed for a four-way stop, looked both ways, and floored it through the intersection. One good thing about rural country roads was that the traffic was usually light.

"911, what is your emergency?"

"There's a house fire off Jasper Creek Road about five miles east of Highway 97. I don't have the address, but they should be able to see the smoke." Mercy leaned forward, studying the sky over the trees ahead, seeing nothing. But she was still miles away.

Her system beeped at her. Truman was calling.

He'll have to wait.

"What's your name, ma'am?"

"I'm Special Agent Kilpatrick from the Bend FBI office. There is an intruder on the property, and three children are hiding nearby in the woods," she said in a rush as Truman's call beeped again. "Eagle's Nest police and myself are both on the way."

The dispatcher's keyboard clacked in the background. "Activating fire and police response."

Mercy exhaled, relieved that the dispatcher had not asked more questions before acting.

"Can you stay on the line, Agent Kilpatrick?"

"No. I need to call the kids back, and the police chief is trying to reach me."

"Is this the best number to call you?"

"Yes. Gotta go." She hit two buttons, and Truman's siren filled her vehicle. "Truman?"

"I'm almost there. Mercy, I see smoke. I don't know if—"

"It's their house. The man set a fire."

"Shit! Damn him!"

"Fire is on their way."

"A brown truck just pulled onto the highway, I—"

"That's him!"

"But he didn't drive out from their property. I'm still a half mile away." Frustration filled his voice.

"Keep going, then. I'm going to call Kaylie." She ended the call, sped past another car on the two-lane highway, and dialed. The phone rang and rang.

"Come on, Kaylie!" She waited, holding her breath, willing the girl to answer the phone.

Voice mail.

"Dammit!" She waited for Kaylie's cheery message to end. "Call me!" She hung up and dialed again.

Voice mail.

She drove on in silence, her mind racing.

Truman can handle it. The kids are competent.

She blew out a breath. Five more miles.

Who would set the home on fire? Why?

"At least the kids were out," she muttered to herself. "What if he had come in the middle of the night? Thank goodness Evan would have been—oh, crap!"

Evan doesn't know this is happening.

She made another call.

25

One hour later

"Everyone is safe," Mercy repeated to herself again, keeping one arm around Kaylie. She'd barely let go of her niece since she arrived. Adrenaline was still pumping through her system. Less than a year ago, Kaylie had nearly died from a gunshot. Mercy had heard the shot and been at her niece's side within seconds.

They both still had nightmares about it.

Mercy had driven the long dirt road to the children's house, flashbacks of Kaylie's shooting haunting her, and had arrived to see Truman and Theodore coming out of the house, hoses in their hands. Ben, Kaylie, and Charlotte had been examining damage in the barn, and Mercy had almost fallen apart at the sight of her niece standing healthy and tall, her hands on her hips.

There had been no sign of a brown truck.

The truck had been gone when Truman arrived, and Mercy knew he was still a bit angry with himself for not following the brown vehicle he'd seen on Jasper Creek Road. The driver had run for his truck just after the kids had first heard Ben's siren. Theodore had told them the truck had driven west off the property, not down the driveway, so it had made its own road back to the rural highway.

Part of the house had bad smoke damage, and the living room furniture was destroyed. The fire department had arrived to find the fire out, but it had pulled out two still-smoking, large sofas and then thoroughly checked over the house. The home would have fully caught fire if Truman and Theodore hadn't used the hoses when they did.

"It reeks of gasoline inside," Truman had told Mercy. "I think he soaked the furniture and then lit it."

The furniture was the only thing that had actually burned.

And Kaylie's cookies.

Smoke continued to hover over the house and clearing. Mercy had smelled it all the way out on the road. It floated through the tall pines, blending into their branches.

Evan had clasped Charlotte's hand since he had arrived. Fury would cross his face every few minutes, but he held his temper. He'd arrived twenty minutes after Mercy, and she'd fielded his phone calls for his entire drive, assuring him that the kids were fine and giving him descriptions of the truck and driver so he could call in a BOLO for Deschutes County.

The intruder had made a mess of some of the home-canned goods stored in the barn, smashing the glass jars on the concrete. Charlotte and Theodore were angry about the destruction of their mother's work. The rows of canned fruit represented hours of effort, and breaking them was a careless ruin of preparation for future problems.

Mercy understood their frustration.

Preparing for the future was deep in her blood.

"The kids will stay in my house from now on," Evan announced for the third time. Guilt warred with the occasional anger in his expression. After becoming a guardian two days ago, he had been experiencing unfamiliar parental emotions. Mercy sympathized. She'd been thrust unexpectedly into the parental role too.

Parenting wasn't for cowards.

When the safety and well-being of another person depended on you, it changed the way you looked at everything.

"Is it safe to get our stuff out of the house?" asked Charlotte.

"The house is fine," said Mercy. "We'll have the water and smoke damage in the living room cleaned up, but not today. Ben and Kaylie will go inside with you. Don't touch anything but the items you'll need for a long stay with your uncle," said Mercy. "Your clothes are going to smell of smoke, but they can be washed."

"The books are ruined," Theodore said in a low voice. The boy had been very quiet since the fire. His somber eyes had been taking in everything, processing.

"We'll buy more," promised Evan. "Today on the way home."

Theodore nodded and followed Charlotte, Ben, and Kaylie into the house.

Evan turned to Mercy and Truman. "Nothing on the BOLO so far."

"I should have followed that truck," said Truman.

"I don't want to hear you say that again," said Mercy. "There were three scared kids waiting for you here."

He grimaced. "I know. I don't think I'd call them scared, though. They were mad about their house being set on fire, but not scared. When I arrived Kaylie practically had Theodore in a headlock to keep him from rushing into the house."

Which was why she hadn't answered Mercy's calls. Her silent phone had been in the back pocket of her jeans.

"Who would do this?" Evan wondered out loud. "I've questioned Kaylie and the kids. They all say this man moved with confidence when he walked in the home. No hesitation at all. As if he knew exactly where he was going." He looked at Mercy. "You talked to Linda Kerr this morning, and then this happened. Coincidence?"

"I don't know," said Mercy. "If the incidents *are* related, that means the Kerr sisters—or at least one of them—already knew where Victor and Bethany lived. The sisters are awfully good liars if that's so. From our first contact, they've claimed to not know about Bethany and to have no idea of Victor's whereabouts."

"Maybe after your interview yesterday, they set some wheels in motion to try to find out where Victor and Bethany lived," said Truman. "You told them Victor was dead and Bethany was missing . . . maybe they expected the house to be abandoned. But in that case they still wouldn't know about the kids."

"Whoever was inside knows about the kids now," Evan said grimly. "It's pretty clear from the interior of the home that multiple children live there."

"But why burn down the house?" asked Mercy.

"There's something inside they didn't want anyone to see or to find?" Evan suggested.

The three of them were simply tossing out ideas and questions, exploring every possibility, seeing where it would lead.

"All of us have gone through that house," said Mercy. "If someone was intent on destroying something important so we wouldn't see it, I don't know what it was."

"And did the fire destroy whatever it was?" added Truman, looking back at the smoking furniture. "Is it still in there? Or did he take it with him and then set the fire to cover his tracks?"

The three of them eyed each other, thoughts racing in their heads.

"I'm nearly certain this has to do with the disappearance of Bethany and Molly," Mercy said quietly, glancing at Evan. "Did we miss something important inside?"

"What could it be that would drive someone to burn down a home?" asked Evan, looking past Mercy at the house. "And what's with breaking jars of peaches in the barn? That sounds like someone who was angry. That's childish shit after the gutsy move of burning down a house. I wouldn't have believed that the two things were related if the kids hadn't seen it."

"Are they sure only one person was here?" asked Truman. "I'm certain I saw one person in the truck I passed on the road."

Mercy pondered that for a moment. "We can ask Kaylie again, but unless someone was hiding with their head down in the truck when they arrived and left—which makes no sense—I believe it was only one man."

"Do you think someone was here because Bethany is missing or because they were looking for the kids?" asked Evan.

"I don't know," said Mercy. "Both answers could be correct."

"Here they come," said Evan, his face brightening as he watched Theodore and Charlotte come out of the house with their arms full.

Does he know he loves them already?

Evan left to intercept them and took a bag from Kaylie. He directed the children to his vehicle and started to load their belongings inside with Ben's help. Kaylie approached Truman and Mercy, a frown on her face.

"Something's up with those kids," Kaylie told them in a serious tone.

"Were they upset by the damage inside?" asked Mercy. "I'm sure that was traumatizing to see."

"They were very quiet as they studied the living room and kitchen," said Kaylie. "Do you know how eerie it is to hear nothing but silence from Charlotte? Ben and I didn't let them touch anything in the main living space, and their bedroom wasn't too smoky because their door was shut. I helped Charlotte pack, but she kept going with Theodore into the bathroom. I could hear them arguing."

Mercy listened, wondering if she hadn't searched the home thoroughly enough.

What could the children be hiding?

"Did you question her about it?" she asked.

"I did, and her answer was, 'It's stupid stuff,' which is what she's told me a few times before when she and Theodore quarrel." Kaylie paused. "But this time she wouldn't look me in the eye and kept her head down, focusing on packing her clothes. Usually she's full of eye rolls and drama when talking about her brother."

"They just went through a dreadful experience," said Truman. "I wouldn't expect them to act normal. Did Ben overhear them say anything?"

"I asked and he said no," answered Kaylie.

"I'll ask Evan to thoroughly examine what each kid packed," said Mercy.

"Do you think they knew what the intruder was looking for?" asked Kaylie. "Theodore fought hard to get away from me when the house was set on fire."

"Sounds like he wanted to protect something," said Truman. "But for all we know that could have been the Harry Potter books."

"I don't think Theodore would risk running into a fire for books," said Mercy.

"Maybe they'd respond better if you or Truman asked them what's going on," said Kaylie. "You're more authoritative."

Mercy eyed the children heading their way, Evan between them with a hand on each one's shoulders. Theodore carried himself the same way Evan did, his head slightly tilted to the left, his shoulders straight. Truman mumbled something about strong genes under his breath.

"We're going to head out," Evan said as he reached the group. "Ben said to tell you he's going back to town," he told Truman. "Something about a neighbor's pigs in someone's garden."

"That'd be the Blanchards' garden," said Truman. "Their neighbor is going to end up with an unexpected gift of bacon if he doesn't figure out how to keep his pigs on his own property."

Evan and the two kids turned to leave.

"Wait," said Mercy. She couldn't get Kaylie's concern about the kids out of her brain. She looked from Theodore to Charlotte. "Is there something you need to tell us? You are arguing more than usual. Is there something that law enforcement should hear from you two?"

Charlotte's eyes widened.

Bingo.

"Mercy," Evan began.

She raised a hand at him. "I think Charlotte has something to say."

Evan frowned and glanced down at the girl, who was exchanging fierce looks with her brother. "What's going on?"

"No, Charlotte," Theodore ordered her. "You know better."

"I think we should—" she started.

"It's not safe!" Theodore hissed at her.

"Whoa," said Evan at the same time that Truman asked, "What's not safe?"

Mercy sighed, disappointment filling her gut. The two kids *had* been keeping secrets.

Hopefully it's not important.

26

Every cell in Evan's body had gone on high alert when Theodore told Charlotte, "It's not safe."

I thought they trusted me.

Discouragement crept up his spine. Perhaps he'd expected too much too fast. After all, they had only met two days ago. No doubt it took time for kids to learn to depend on someone.

But I would do anything to protect them.

The realization took Evan's breath away. He'd never experienced that feeling. He struggled to speak. "What isn't safe?" he managed to ask Theodore in a firm voice, hoping the boy hadn't noticed his floundering moment.

"Nothing." Theodore wouldn't look at him.

Charlotte stamped a foot, and her brother shot her a glance that could kill. "Tell them or I will," she stated.

"It's not our secret to tell!" Theodore wrenched his shoulder out from under Evan's hand and made a beeline for the barn, his legs and arms pumping hard.

Evan took one step after him and stopped, looking to Mercy and Truman in confusion.

"Let him go," advised Truman as Mercy nodded. "Give the boy a moment."

"But . . ." Evan watched Theodore vanish into the barn.

"He's mad," announced Charlotte.

"We can see that," said Mercy. "Would you tell us why, please? I understand Theodore is concerned about safety, but honestly the best thing you can do is tell us. We're law enforcement, Charlotte. Safety is our job. No one can protect you and Theodore better than the three of us."

"She's right," said Kaylie. "You and Theodore have been whispering about something since we met, and I think you need to share."

Evan watched Charlotte study Kaylie's face and then glance at Mercy and Truman. "You won't get mad?" she asked, looking at Evan.

"Charlotte, I can't think of a single thing in the world you could tell me that would make me mad," Evan told her, feeling the truth of his words as he spoke. "What's wrong?"

Charlotte's gaze went to the barn. "Our parents made us swear not to tell. They said it would be dangerous if anyone knew," she said in the softest voice that Evan had ever heard her use. Kaylie's brows shot up at the quiet tone, and concern flared in her eyes.

"It's okay, Charlotte." Evan placed both hands on her shoulders. "Look at me." It took a moment, but the girl raised her gaze. The agony in her eyes made him want to hurt someone. "You're safe with me. I won't let anything happen to you or Theodore."

"It's not just us," Charlotte blurted, dropping her gaze.

Evan was stumped. "What happened?"

The little girl sucked in a deep breath and looked at Kaylie from the corner of her eye. The teenager nodded encouragingly.

"Our daddy didn't die," Charlotte whispered.

Evan struggled to keep a neutral expression as shock flashed through his limbs. "Why did you tell us he did?"

Charlotte's shoulders slumped. "He and Mommy made us swear not to tell *anyone* he was alive. It was for our safety and his." She looked at the smoking house and wiped at one eye. "This fire proves he was right. I told Theodore that we should tell you now, but he got angry. He said we were to take the secret to our graves to protect our daddy."

"Your graves?" Bile rose in Evan's throat.

What kind of promise is that?

"Not really," Charlotte said, with a one-shoulder shrug. "That's just him being dramatic. We only had to keep the secret until our daddy came back."

Evan looked to Mercy and Truman. They appeared as shocked as he.

"Charlotte," said Mercy kindly, "where's your dad?"

"I don't know. Mommy went to find him. She said he'd been gone too long."

A faint ringing started in Evan's ears. "She was coming to me for help to find your dad?"

"Yes."

And she never made it.

The white baby shoe rose from his memory again, making his stomach churn.

"But Charlotte, why tell people he was dead?" asked Truman. "Couldn't you say he was out of town?"

"Because," she said firmly, her little face serious.

Evan waited for her to finish the sentence. When she didn't continue, he prompted, "Because . . . why?"

She frowned. "To keep him safe. And us safe. I already said that."

"Yes, you did," said Mercy faintly. "They didn't tell you why he had to go somewhere?"

"To keep all of us safe."

"Safe from what or from who?" Kaylie beat Evan to the question.

Charlotte tipped her head to the side the smallest bit, confusion in her eyes. "I don't know. I asked that too. Mommy wouldn't tell me. She said to always say he'd died no matter what."

Evan's mind spun, trying to understand why his brother-in-law would fake his death. One answer kept rising to the surface.

Because someone was trying to kill him.

"I think I better go talk to Theodore," Evan said. "Stay here," he told Charlotte. Mercy moved a half step closer to the girl and nodded at Evan.

He couldn't stop the flood of questions in his head as his boots crunched on the gravel between the house and barn.

Who set the fire?

What did they want?

Where did Victor and Bethany go?

Why would parents make their kids keep a secret that big?

He entered the barn, careful not to step in the sticky liquid still covering the concrete floor. The glass was gone, cleaned up by Kaylie and Ben, but the syrup from the home-canned goods needed to be hosed off. The barn was long and narrow and smelled of smoke and peaches. He strode past storage cabinets and the goats.

"Theodore?" he called.

No answer. Evan scanned the dark nooks and crannies as he walked toward the large sliding door at the far end. He didn't think the boy would hide in a corner; he wasn't the type. He'd reacted out of anger and confusion. Evan ached for Theodore, understanding the conflict that must be warring in his heart.

Should Theodore keep his parents' secret or confide in other adults?

Evan had learned that Theodore took pride in following rules. And when to break those rules was a tough lesson for someone like Theodore to learn.

He's feeling alone. And betrayed.

"Theodore?"

Evan slid open the back door and stepped out. Ahead was a deep woods that Evan knew went on for acres. A mix of ponderosa and lodgepole pines. Because of the pines' lack of low branches, he had a good view far into the woods. He scanned the area under the trees, seeking a glimpse of Theodore's red shirt among the sagebrush and big rocks.

"Theodore!" he shouted. Evan waited a long moment, hoping for a reply.

He'll come back when he's ready.

Disappointed, Evan walked around the corner of the barn instead of back inside, continuing to glance over his shoulder at the woods, hoping for a flash of red. He rejoined the group and gave a small shake of his head at their inquiring glances. Charlotte's eyes were bloodshot and her cheeks damp. She held tight to Kaylie's hand.

"I'm sorry, Uncle Evan," she said in a tiny voice. "We should have told you earlier." She moved toward him and wrapped her arms around his middle, burying her face in his shirt. He hugged her back, stunned by the warmth and affection filling him.

"It's okay. You did what your parents told you to do. But now it's time to let us shoulder that burden and figure out where your parents are." His tongue stumbled over "parents." It hadn't fully sunk in that Victor was alive.

Hopefully alive. And hopefully Bethany and Molly too.

It's been weeks since they left.

And longer for Victor.

"I didn't see Theodore," Evan told her. "Do you know where he'd go?"

Charlotte pulled back and sniffed, rubbing the back of her hand under her nose. "No, but he'll be back. He does that sometimes—disappears into the woods. He's bragged that he's got a good hiding spot. One time he stayed there overnight because he was upset about something. Mommy and Daddy were so mad about that."

"I bet," said Evan. He looked to Mercy and Truman. "I guess I'm not leaving right away."

"Maybe you should go," said Kaylie. "I bet Theodore is watching us right now. If you and Charlotte leave, that will take the wind out of his sails. He's upset at Charlotte. If she's gone, maybe he'll come back sooner."

Evan saw her point. "But I can't leave while he's missing."

Mercy glanced at Charlotte. "I suspect these two know how to handle a few hours in the woods on their own."

Charlotte nodded emphatically. "He's fine. He'll come back when he's not mad at me anymore."

"I don't think he's mad at you, Charlotte," began Evan.

"Yes, he is. I told the secret. He's told me twenty times in the last two days that I shouldn't tell."

"You did the right thing," said Truman. "Knowing that your dad is alive will help us figure out how to search for your mom and sister."

Could the three of them be together?

But why haven't they contacted the kids?

"When did your dad leave?" Evan asked.

"He'd been gone a week when Mommy decided to go look for him."

Mercy stepped away from the group and made a call. Evan heard her relay the information about Victor Kerr to someone in her office.

"Charlotte, is there anything in the house that your parents would want to keep hidden?" Truman asked. "Something that man would be hunting for?"

The girl scrunched up her face as she thought. "I don't know."

"Would Theodore know?" asked Evan.

She answered with a shrug.

Evan met Kaylie's eyes and gave a small jerk with his head.

"Charlotte, let's get in the car," said Kaylie. "I think we're leaving soon." She took the girl's hand and led her away.

Evan lowered his voice as he spoke to Truman. "I'll come back in a couple hours and look for Theodore. It'll be light until almost nine."

"How about I ask Ollie to look for him?" asked Truman. "He's got a personal connection with the boy, and he knows how to track in the woods. Plus, Theodore might be more likely to approach him."

Evan wanted to do the search and nearly turned down the offer. But he saw the logic in Truman's suggestion. "Okay. But I want to know the minute he finds him."

"Of course," agreed Truman as Mercy returned.

"I've set the wheels in motion to look for Victor Kerr," she told Evan and Truman. She raised a brow at Evan. "I don't like the timeline. It's been too long since he vanished."

"You're not the only one who doesn't like it," said Evan as dread crept along his nerves.

What happened to this family?

27

Ollie stared at the blackened furniture left in front of the Kerr home.

Beside him, Shep flared his nostrils several times.

"Yeah, it smells bad here," Ollie agreed. He walked to the front door and gave the handle a cautious tug. Locked. He stepped to one side and peered in the window. The ceiling in the living area was black, and filthy streaks trailed across the floor where the furniture had been dragged to the door. Puddles of murky water covered the hardwood.

Those poor kids.

Truman said the kids had gone inside to pack their things to take to Detective Bolton's home. Now Ollie put himself in Theodore's shoes, viewing the intentional destruction through the boy's eyes. Theodore was stoic. Ollie knew he'd simply take it all in, figuring out what would need to be done to fix it.

First his parents and little sister went missing, and now this.

But Theodore would be hurting deep inside. Stoic or not.

His vanishing into the woods was sufficient evidence that the boy was torn up inside.

I'll find him.

Truman's request that Ollie be the one to search for Theodore made him proud. It was a vote of confidence from the man Ollie admired more than anyone else. Except maybe his grandfather, who had passed nearly four years before. The more Ollie learned about the outside world, the more he was impressed that his grandfather had left it all behind and raised him.

"Let's go, Shep." Ollie pointed toward the barn, and the dog set off, darting across the gravel and then waiting at the barn door for Ollie to catch up. Ollie did a quick search in the barn. No Theodore. He exited out the back door and stood for a long minute, breathing deep and letting his gaze take in his surroundings. The scent of dry, dusty dirt reached him, along with the slightest whiff of crisp, cooling air. *The creek?* He had the two hours until sunset to search for Theodore, but because of the acres of tall pines, it'd get darker earlier than that.

Looking down, he saw a definitive set of tracks that had walked forward from his position, paced a bit, and then walked back around the barn.

Detective Bolton.

Ollie slowly moved forward, his gaze sweeping the ground rapidly, waiting for something to snag his sight. Shep stayed at his side as if he knew not to run ahead and mark up any existing tracks that could be Theodore's. Ollie's gaze suddenly shot back to an imprint in the powdery fine dirt, and he spotted the next one farther beyond than he had expected.

Theodore ran.

Ollie set off in that direction, letting his instinct guide him through the pines, looking for the most logical path among the sagebrush and trees. For twenty minutes he walked, spotting a faint boot impression here and there to guide him. Three times he had to double back and do a wider sweep to pick up the tracks when Theodore had taken an odd turn.

Ollie sympathized with the boy, wondering how hard it had been to keep the secret when Ollie had questioned him about his dad's death. Now Ollie knew it'd all been a big lie.

Shep suddenly lunged to Ollie's left, leaped over a low bush, and darted to a tree trunk, his paws scraping at the thick bark as he tried his best to climb after a striped chipmunk. Ollie grinned. His dog had tried unsuccessfully for years to catch one. Shep finally sat, staring mournfully at the chipmunk in full sight on a high branch.

"Let's go, boy. You can try another day."

Shep gave a disgusted huff at the chipmunk and returned to Ollie, who scratched his ears. "We've got work to do." Ollie looked at the lowering sun.

Plenty of time.

They continued, and a moment later Ollie spotted older tennis shoe prints that went in the same direction as Theodore's boots. "Charlotte said he had a hiding spot. Looks like he regularly came this way," he told Shep, who acknowledged his words with a flick of an ear.

As Ollie moved deeper into the woods, numerous pine cones and pine needles covering the forest floor made him alter his tracking technique a bit. Now he also looked for disruptions of the needles and the light trails left by kicked pine cones.

The forest suddenly opened, and Ollie found himself in a clearing with blackened, branchless tree trunks, remnants of an old forest fire. Apparently it had happened long ago, since thorny shrubs and grasses now thoroughly covered the ground, instead of being sparse and interspersed, as they were under the live trees. Ollie paused, looking for a sign that Theodore had pushed his way through the brush.

A shadow passed over the brush, and Ollie looked up to see the white underside and long crooked wings of a circling osprey. Shep whined, eyeing the bird.

"He's not interested in you," Ollie told his dog. "Come on." He'd spotted a heel print far to his right. Theodore had turned instead of walking between the dead trees. After a few minutes he saw a low hill, its sides covered with gigantic boulders.

That's where I'd hang out.

The footprints led toward the hill.

A desire to climb and crawl and explore every nook and cranny of the rocky hill swept through him, and he wondered if Theodore had experienced the same feeling the first time he saw it. As he got closer, he cupped his hands around his mouth. "Theodore! It's Ollie!"

He slowly worked his way around one side of the hill, his gut telling him he was in the right place. Shep's ears suddenly perked up, and he lifted his nose. Ollie followed his line of sight.

Theodore was calmly sitting near the top of the hill on a boulder. His legs were pulled to his chest, his arms wrapped around them. He was too far away for eye contact, but Ollie knew he was watching them. He raised a hand at the boy, who did nothing.

Theodore could have hid instead of letting me spot him. He's ready to be found.

He thought about asking Theodore to come down but decided to go up instead. He worked his way around some of the boulders and then climbed over another—after checking for rattlesnakes, which would love the warm rocks. He used his hands to balance as he shuffled his way up the side of the hill, dodging crooked tiny trees that seemed to grow out of nothing. He finally reached Theodore and took a seat beside him with a sigh. Shep had beaten Ollie to the top and proudly sat next to Theodore, the boy's hand stroking his head.

Theodore wouldn't look Ollie in the eye, his focus on Shep.

"You okay?" Ollie asked, not knowing how to start.

Theodore nodded.

"Is it true your dad didn't die?" Ollie asked.

Now Theodore looked at him. "Yes. I only lied about it because we were supposed to." Guilt flashed on his face, and he looked miserable.

"You know, when I was younger I used to pretend all the time that my parents hadn't died. I imagined that they were traveling and would eventually come see me."

"He's alive," Theodore said forcefully. "Charlotte didn't make it up. It's true." He scowled. "I hate her."

179

"Because she told the truth to responsible adults? After your parents have been missing for weeks? I don't think it's fair to hate her for that."

"She's a pain. Always talking when she shouldn't be." Theodore scooped up a handful of rocks and threw one as hard as he could. Shep tracked the rock, his ears forward, but he kept his seat.

"Kaylie and I butt heads all the time," Ollie told Theodore. "She's always talking and telling me what to do. Drives me crazy sometimes. Wait until Charlotte starts dating. I swear girls pick the dumbest guys and don't listen when we tell them the guys are idiots. Sisters are frustrating."

Theodore's scowl deepened. "No one will date Charlotte. She's too bossy." He threw another rock.

"Well, your secret is out now, so you might as well let it go. I know Mercy, Truman, and Detective Bolton are already trying to track down where your dad might have gone. Truman said that Charlotte only knew that your dad left to keep everyone safe. Do you know more about where he went or why he left? How would that keep you safe?"

Theodore was silent for a long moment.

"Don't keep any more secrets, Theodore," Ollie said. "It's been too long. Your dad might need help. And maybe you know something that's important—but you don't realize it's important. So you need to tell them everything you can remember."

"He said some people might be looking for him," Theodore stated as he let the rest of the rocks fall out of his hand. "He said he'd leave so they wouldn't find us."

"That sounds pretty important," said Ollie, keeping his tone even. Unease had shot through him at the boy's words. He'd imagined a bird pretending to have a broken wing to lead predators away from her nest.

Were the people looking for his dad dangerous?

"Theodore . . . it sounds like he thought you could be in danger?" Ollie asked hesitantly.

"I don't think he would have left us alone if we were."

Ollie pondered that logic as he took out his cell phone. He'd promised Detective Bolton he'd let him know when he found Theodore.

No service.

Unsurprised, he slid the phone back in a pocket. "Charlotte said you stay here overnight sometimes."

Theodore laughed. "Once. I nearly froze—but don't tell her that. I won't do it again without a sleeping bag. There's a good rock overhang for protection on the other side, but it gets too cold at night."

Ollie had noticed the temperature had dropped in the forty-five minutes since he'd left the cabin. And that was with the sun still shining. "In that case, let's get going." He stood and held out a hand for Theodore. The boy took it and got to his feet.

"Can I stay at your place tonight?" Theodore asked hopefully.

"No. Detective Bolton is expecting us."

"I don't want to deal with Charlotte. She'll make fun of me for leaving."

"Just ignore her."

"That's what I usually do, but she doesn't shut up."

"Try this." Ollie looked the boy in the eyes for several long seconds.

"Jeez. What are you doing?" Theodore looked away. "That's creepy!"

"I read about it. You hold eye contact with someone who is annoying you and imagine slicing the skin off their face with a razor blade."

"*What?*"

"It's an acting technique. It makes your stare really intense. Kaylie hates when I do it to her."

Theodore's expression turned thoughtful. "I'll try it. Now I want to get back and freak her out with that."

Pleased he'd helped, Ollie gestured down the hill. "Lead the way."

28

The next morning Truman slid into a booth at the diner and flipped over the mug on the table. Two seconds later, Sara filled it with coffee.

"The usual this morning, Chief?"

"Actually, I'm in a hurry. I'll have a toasted bagel with cream cheese."

"Want to try the Hawaiian bagel? It's a little bit sweet, with tiny chunks of pineapple. We just got some in yesterday."

Truman had already tried the Hawaiian bagel. Dozens of them over the past three weeks as Kaylie worked to perfect the recipe in their kitchen at home. He never wanted to see a pineapple again. "I'll have the cranberry and walnut bagel."

The diner ordered many of its specialty breads and sweets from Kaylie's shop. Bagels were a new item at the Coffee Café and had instantly become bestsellers. Truman had yet to tire of the cranberry bagel.

"You got it." Sara turned away and topped off more cups of coffee on her way back to the kitchen. Truman took a sip of his coffee and then raised it in salute to the three old-timers sitting at the counter, who each lifted a hand in greeting.

For once the restaurant wasn't crowded with treasure hunters. But it was just after six, and Truman was eating breakfast a little earlier than usual. The current diners were ranchers grabbing a bite and sharing local gossip before they started their day. The sun had been up for a good half hour, and Truman was surprised some were still lingering over their coffees. He craned his neck to see the booths around the far side of the counter and made eye contact with Ina Smythe.

Startled that she was out and about so early, he grabbed his coffee and went to join her. He'd known Ina since he was a teenager spending summers in Eagle's Nest. A good friend of his uncle's, Ina had recommended him for the chief's job when it had opened up. Looking back now, Truman had a clearer understanding of her "friendship" with his uncle. He'd been a bit blind as a teenager and oblivious to the not-so-secret relationship between them, but he remembered being puzzled by the hunger in his uncle's eyes when he looked at Ina. She'd sat at the front desk at the police station for decades before retiring in her seventies and appointing her grandson Lucas as her successor.

She'd always been like an aunt to Truman. A nosy, bossy aunt.

He sat across from her, taking care not to knock over her cane, which she'd hooked on the end of the table. "You're up early, Ina."

"Good morning to you too, Chief." Her dark eyes crinkled in pleasure. Even though she moved slower than she used to, she was still a powerhouse in the town. People listened when she gave her opinion. And she gave it often.

Truman grinned. "Good morning. I'm happy I get to enjoy your company with my breakfast."

"Flirt." She huffed but appeared pleased by his answer.

"What brings you into town this time of day?" he asked.

"I've been waiting for you."

He didn't understand. "Why didn't you call me?"

She waved a hand. "Didn't want to bother you while you were working."

He doubted that. Ina Smythe had no problem bothering anyone.

"Well, now you've got me. What's up?"

"I don't like all the outsiders in town. I want them to leave," she said firmly.

"You and everyone else," said Truman. "Not much I can do except try to keep them out of trouble. Do you have a suggestion to clear them out?"

Ina lowered her gaze and toyed with the tea bag in her cup.

Surprise shot through Truman.

She's hesitant to tell me something.

He'd never seen her waver over anything. And he didn't like it. He leaned over the table. "What's wrong?" he asked in a low voice.

Her gaze shot to his. "Nothing's wrong. Just trying to gather my thoughts and figure out the best way to tell you my story."

He relaxed a bit. "Maybe start at the beginning."

She flashed him a sharp look that said she didn't appreciate him stating the obvious. "I wasn't always this old, you know."

Truman took a sip of his coffee. "Me neither."

"Don't be flip. You wait until you're in your seventies and see how your knees feel."

My left one already aches every morning.

She went on. "What I meant was that when I was in my twenties, I was quite the hottie."

"You're still a hottie, Ina. I know that several men have proposed to you in the last five years."

She snorted. "I've outlasted enough husbands, thank you very much. These men are just looking for a caretaker and cook."

Truman scratched his chin. Ina's cooking had a lousy reputation, so that didn't carry weight as a reason.

"Anyway, when I was young, I had my choice of men. It was the sixties . . . people were starting to take a little more time before they got married. Not marrying the first person they met right out of high school."

Ina was a wild one.

Sara set his bagel on the table. "Need anything else, Chief? Ina?"

"I'm good," said Truman.

"No, thank you," replied Ina. She waited until the waitress was out of earshot before continuing. "I met a man one evening. I was at a bar in Bend with some of my girlfriends. He was quite a bit older than me but oh so charming. A real smooth talker."

"Ina, are you sure you want to tell me this?" Truman wanted to squirm. It was as if his mother were sharing details about her dating life before she'd met his dad.

"I'm getting to the point."

Good.

"We hit it off. He was in town for a long weekend, and I spent almost every minute with him. I even called in sick to work one day so we could go white water rafting."

Truman took a large bite of his bagel and tried to picture a young Ina in a raft. He couldn't do it.

"I called him Rolly. He was fun and told me I was beautiful. It was an amazing few days."

Her wistful smile made Truman's heart squeeze.

"I never heard from him again after he left. He had my phone number, but I moved soon after and changed my number. I'd think about him occasionally."

"Have you looked him up? What's his last name?" Truman instantly regretted his questions as he remembered she'd said he was much older. The man might be dead.

"He's passed. It was all over the news not long ago. It was Chester Rollins."

It took Truman a long second to process that Ina Smythe had had an affair with the playboy millionaire who'd created the treasure hunt. "You're kidding me," was all he could say.

"Nope." Her eyes gleamed. "Told you I was something to look at back then."

Truman grinned. "Good for you. With him constantly in the news the past few months, it must have brought back a lot of memories."

"Definitely. But here's the reason I'm telling you this." She paused. "All the news outlets are saying that Rolly doesn't have any heirs. I happen to know that's not true."

"Are you sure?"

"Yes. He has a daughter. He showed me a baby picture back then. The baby was only a few months old."

Truman took another bite of bagel as he thought. "Maybe she didn't survive . . . she could have passed away at some point."

"But then the news would say that he had a daughter who died. They haven't said that. I think no one knows about her. Maybe she doesn't even know herself."

"Did he say anything about her mother?"

"Not a word. I remember when he brought up his daughter that I was instantly jealous of the connection the woman had with Rolly. He didn't tell me anything about her, and I didn't ask. He was fascinated by this baby. He claimed it changed the way he looked at the world. Told me he'd never been married, didn't plan to, and never thought he'd have a child."

"Then how can that fact have stayed a secret? If he talked to you about it, he must have told other people."

"You would think so," said Ina with a shrug. "It was pillow talk, you know. Sometimes you say more than you expect because you feel close to the person at the time. I don't know why other women haven't come forward saying he told them he has a kid." She frowned. "There was the drinking, though . . . we drank almost nonstop during our three days together. He loved champagne and always had a bottle open. I look back now and cringe when I realize we went rafting drunk and he must have driven around drunk—not that we left his hotel that much."

Truman held up a hand. "I don't need to hear that part."

"I read online that he'd been sober for decades. He must have decided to stop drinking soon after I was with him. Maybe he was better at keeping his secrets to himself when he was sober."

"Even if there is an heir, I don't see how that fact can stop treasure hunters from coming to Eagle's Nest."

"I'll guess this person doesn't know Rolly is their father. But if they did, don't you think she'd have a strong claim on any prize that turned up? I'd contact a lawyer right away if I knew part of my inheritance was being given away."

"I'm sure Chester Rollins had a proper will or trust or whatever it is that rich people have written up to dole out their money after death. I doubt someone popping up out of the woodwork is going to stop the treasure hunt. A few people have, and a simple paternity test has destroyed their claims."

"But this person truly is related," Ina argued.

"Only if the mother wasn't lying or mistaken when she told Chester Rollins the baby was his. One of the people who came forward had been told all her life that Rollins was her father. She was shocked to find out he wasn't. Maybe that was her."

"I read that story," said Ina. "She was way too young to have been born in the sixties. You're looking for someone in their late fifties or so."

"I'm looking?"

Ina beamed. "Yes, you. I know you can find her. You and Mercy can, with all the computer resources she has. If you find the heir and tell her, she can start some legal business and let these treasure hunters know that they might not get to keep any treasure they find. Don't you think that would stop them?"

"Well, if I was a hunter, I'd simply not tell anyone I found it. For all we know that has already happened, and the people in town are wasting their time."

Ina frowned and tapped her fingers on the table as she thought. "Either way, I still think this daughter of his should be told who her real father is. It could be life changing for her."

Truman imagined the media circus that would crop up if a legitimate Rollins heir was found. "Life changing is right. She'd never have another moment's peace." He grinned and leaned forward, speaking in a quiet voice. "I bet you could cash in on a story about your time with *Rolly*."

"Oh, hush! I'd never do such a thing." Disgust made her crinkle her nose in a way that Truman found delightful. "I don't want any limelight. That was private."

"Why was he in Bend back then? He lived in Idaho, right?"

Ina sipped her tea, concentration in her eyes. "Some sort of conference or convention . . . something to do with ranching, I think. Lots of ranchers from out of state were in town. After Rolly met me, he didn't attend any more of that conference. I remember urging him to go, and he just laughed it off."

What if . . .

"Ina, do you remember the places you went with him? Did you take him anywhere near Eagle's Nest?"

She thought hard for a moment. "We did a number of hikes, and I drove him through town, but we didn't actually stop at any of the businesses here. We tried to be discreet about where we went, so people didn't see us together. That was for my benefit because we both knew we'd only be together for a few days. I didn't need tongues wagging about my reputation in town."

"I assumed the gossip train was as strong back then as it is now."

"Stronger," said Ina. "People have more distractions these days. Rolly and I did a lot of outdoor activities where we wouldn't run into people." She winked. "When we weren't busy with *indoor* activities."

"Stop," Truman ordered, trying not to laugh. "You're making me uncomfortable. I don't want to think about that. The reason I asked is because maybe while he was here, he found a place where he later decided to hide the treasure. He was from out of state, and who knows if he ever came back to the area. The two of you might have visited a place that later inspired him. Can you remember exactly where you went?"

Ina snorted. "Now you're getting caught up in the hunt? And you think something in my memory will help?" She rolled her eyes. "I swear half my brain emptied out when I turned seventy."

His curiosity had been piqued. "Think about it. Try to remember where the two of you went. Maybe this will help the treasure get found and get all those people out of our town," he added, appealing to her original desire.

She nodded thoughtfully. "You have a point." She grimaced. "But my memory isn't what it used to be. I mostly remember how I felt when I was with him—not where we were."

"Spend some time on it," said Truman. "Take a look at a map. Maybe a map of hiking trails around here, and see if it prods any memories."

"I'll do that." Her gaze was distant as she went back in time.

"I'm headed to work." He pulled some bills out of his wallet, set them on the table, and then stood and grabbed the last half of the bagel to take with him. "Let me know what you come up with."

"So you can pass it on to your men?" She raised a brow. "Lucas has told me how your officers are caught up in the hunt. He says they spend every spare minute discussing the clues."

"If you think of a location that might be a possibility, I'll follow your wishes on how you want it handled," he promised. "Have a good day, Ina."

He strode out of the diner as he took a bite of bagel.

Could the key to the treasure hunt be in Ina's memory bank?

Truman didn't care. He just wanted his town back to normal.

29

Evan started his third cup of coffee as he blearily stared at his department computer monitor. He'd had a hell of a time falling asleep the night before. An intruder at the kids' home and Theodore's vanishing act had set his nerves on edge for hours, making sleep impossible even after Theodore was home and safe. Evan had gotten up three times in the middle of the night to check on the kids as they slept. He'd stood in their doorways listening and watching, feeling like a trespasser. But also feeling the heavy responsibility of two young lives.

Parenting took an iron gut.

This morning he'd hated to leave his house, even though Ollie had shown up as planned to spend the morning with the kids. Kaylie would take over around noon. Evan had thanked Ollie again for finding Theodore, and the young man had brushed aside his thanks. "He was ready to be found," Ollie had said. "I happened to be there when it happened."

Evan was certain Ollie had done more than that.

He refocused on his in-box, scrolling through the sixty emails that had arrived overnight, and noted that Tim Giles had been released late the previous evening. He'd been charged with property damage to the Eagle's Nest police station. His weak claim that he might know who had shot Billy Serrano had been a desperate Hail Mary to get on Evan's good side.

His phone rang. "Bolton," he answered, his gaze still on his emails.

"Evan, it's Mercy."

He froze. "Are the kids all right?"

"Yes! They're fine! I'm sorry I startled you. I should have known your brain would immediately go there with a call from me."

His lungs relaxed. "My fault. I'm still a little on edge from yesterday. I slept like crap."

"I'm not surprised. I can still smell smoke on myself, and I've showered twice since then."

Evan had noticed the same thing while driving to work. "What can I do for you, Mercy?"

"It's what I can do for you. You asked me about the airlines, remember?"

"That's right. I forgot. Been a bit distracted." He'd been looking into Meghan Serrano's background. He'd been uneasy after his interview with her, disturbed by her focus on the treasure-hunt notes. To establish Meghan's movements for the last several days, he'd emailed Mercy the morning before, asking for her help in finding out which flight she had taken to Oregon. Evan could have asked Meghan, but he wanted the information from the source. The FBI had easier and quicker access to airline information than he did.

"Meghan Serrano didn't fly in on Wednesday or even Tuesday night," Mercy told him. "She arrived on Monday."

Evan didn't understand. "That can't be right. I informed her of her brother's death on Tuesday."

Her brother, who was killed in Tuesday's early-morning hours.

"Mercy . . ." Evan's brain sped ahead.

"But doesn't it make sense that she'd be here helping her brother with the treasure hunt?" Mercy asked. "Why wouldn't she be in town?"

"Because when I called to inform her, she told me she would catch a flight here that day," said Evan. "And when I talked to her yesterday morning, she told me she'd flown overnight. If she was in town already, she deliberately hid it from me."

Mercy was silent for a long moment. "You think one sibling decided they were getting close to the treasure and wanted it for themselves?"

"I don't know," said Evan. "Something felt off about her during our interview." The fact that she had been in town when her brother was murdered now crossed and crisscrossed and ricocheted at all speeds through his mind. "The ME said the bullet entered at an upward angle," he told Mercy. "I met Meghan. She's short."

"But to kill her brother for a treasure that hasn't been found yet?" Mercy asked. "That takes a special person."

"*Special* is one word for it," Evan said grimly. "Thanks for the info. Now I have some other angles to investigate."

"And I'll keep you updated with whatever I find on your sister and Molly, Evan. I appreciate you giving us room to work."

He snorted. "I fight to keep from calling you every hour. You have no idea how often my mind shifts to Bethany. Part of me is glad I've got this case to distract me . . . the other part wants to shadow you all day."

"I'm lighting fires under people left and right. We'll find them." Mercy ended the call.

Evan sat very still, his mind still spinning as he brought his focus back to Meghan Serrano. He looked up the phone number for the hotel where Meghan was staying. He checked the time and crossed his fingers.

A young-sounding man answered. "Deschutes Hotel."

"Nadine Powers, please."

"One moment. I'll see if she's in."

Evan had known Nadine for years. Her brother had been one of his closest friends in college.

"This is Nadine," she answered.

"Nadine, it's Evan Bolton."

"Evan, nice to hear from you. How are things?"

"Good. I only have a moment, Nadine, but could you check something for me?"

She sighed. "You're not asking me to break the rules again, are you?"

"Just bend them a little for law enforcement. And for your brother's buddy."

"What is it?"

"I need a check-in date for Meghan Serrano. She's currently staying in your hotel."

Computer keys clicked. "She got here Monday. Two p.m."

"Perfect. Thank you. Just what I needed."

"Is she going to be trouble?" asked Nadine.

"Nothing like that," said Evan. *I hope.* "I was simply confirming when she got here."

"Uh-huh." Nadine didn't sound convinced.

Feeling guilty about using Nadine for information, he asked for an update on her kids and then ended the call a minute later.

He leaned back in his chair, tapping his fingers on his desk. So far the only thing Meghan was guilty of was telling lies. Not a reason to lock her up. But a good reason for paying her a visit.

Evan could only think of one reason Meghan would not have told him that she had been in town since Monday. And so far the evidence found at the murder scene had given no leads.

Wait.

Evan learned forward and searched his computer for a piece of evidence he'd reviewed the day before. It was the video from another business down the block from the bed-and-breakfast. The camera at the B and B had been damaged around 10:00 p.m., so when he'd sent deputies to nearby businesses to check for video of the street and sidewalks, he'd included that time in his request.

A church and the feed store had shared their videos. The church's angle had shown the street behind the bed-and-breakfast. When Evan had viewed it the day before, he'd been looking for Tim Giles or his big truck, neither of which had appeared. Now he wanted to check for another vehicle.

He found the clip he wanted and sped through the hour before ten o'clock, stopping whenever a vehicle or person came into view. He stopped the video as a little Toyota sedan came on the screen. The view didn't show the license plate or get a good image of the driver, but Evan had seen a Toyota exactly like it when he walked Meghan to the front door after her interview the day before and watched her get in a sedan.

I need to pay Meghan a visit.

30

Mercy drove to her office, her morning coffee in hand, thinking about the revelation at the Kerr home the day before.

Victor Kerr was alive.

Last night she and Eddie had dug deeper into Victor's past and found very little. Like Bridget, Victor Kerr had vanished off the grid fourteen years earlier. She suspected he used an alias when he needed to, one his kids weren't aware of. A property search listed the land as belonging to Jack Karr. Victor's father's first name and what Mercy assumed was a deliberate misspelling of Kerr. Just enough to stay under the radar if someone was searching for him but close enough to blame a clerical error if needed.

A search for anything else related to Jack Karr went nowhere.

Her mind kept circling back to one question: *What would keep Victor and Bridget Kerr away from their other children?*

She had no good answers.

The fire the day before had made her more determined to find the Kerr adults and little Molly. She strongly suspected the fire had been set to destroy something, possibly something related to the location of the missing Kerrs. Theodore and Charlotte claimed they rarely had visitors and that only a few neighbors knew where they lived. But neither had recognized the man nor the vehicle from the previous day. The man had seemed very confident about where he was going.

Her phone rang. "Special Agent Kilpatrick."

"Mercy, it's Natasha Lockhart. Do you have a minute?"

Mercy's hands tightened on the wheel. Understandable when one received a call from the medical examiner. "What can I do for you, Dr. Lockhart?"

"I'm at a murder scene near Owlie Lake." The ME hesitated. "I know you're looking for a woman in her thirties with blonde hair. This one has no identification on her."

"Is there any sign of a toddler?" Mercy asked in a rush. "She might have an eighteen-month-old with her."

"Not that I'm aware of." The doctor's voice was quieter as she asked a question in the background. "The sheriff's department hasn't found anything that indicates a toddler was here."

"Tell them to expand the search area," Mercy directed. "I'm on my way."

"Park at the south trailhead. Prepare for a mile hike."

"I'll be there in fifteen minutes." Mercy ended the call and blew out a deep breath.

Is it Evan's sister?

It took at least fifteen minutes of mostly uphill hiking for Mercy to reach the scene after she had parked at the trailhead at the lake. She had counted five Deschutes County sheriffs' vehicles in addition to the medical examiner's van in the lot, and then frowned as she spotted a television-news satellite truck at the far end of the lot.

Another dozen regular vehicles had been there, along with several hikers milling around, unable to pass the deputy guarding the trailhead. The news crew had been interviewing two of them.

In a clearing a dozen feet off the main trail, Dr. Lockhart stood up and stretched her back as Mercy approached the scene, her gaze locked on the blonde hair of the motionless woman on the ground. The deputies had cordoned off a large area around the body. Mercy spotted several Deschutes County officers walking a grid farther into the woods, their focus on the forest floor, their flashlights scanning back and forth as they slowly searched.

Will they find Molly?

Her gut churned at the thought of discovering the young girl's body.

She took a deep breath and focused on the adult victim before her. The woman was lying on her stomach and wore tennis shoes, yoga pants, and a heavy sweatshirt. Exactly what was needed for a hike during June's chilly mornings. Next to her shoulder was a tote bag. The hair covering most of her face was shoulder length and curly.

"A hiker found her a couple of hours ago," Dr. Lockhart told Mercy. "I think the hiker was actually a treasure hunter, but he claimed he was just hiking. One of the deputies took him down to the station for a report."

"I need to see her face," Mercy said, staring at the blonde hair.

Will I know Bridget Kerr when I see her?

Mercy had only seen old photos. And Charlotte. Evan had said Charlotte looked almost identical to his sister when she was that age.

I'll know.

"Come around." Dr. Lockhart pointed to where she wanted Mercy to stand. Mercy reached the spot and crouched, her gaze locked on the part of the woman's chin that showed below her hair. Dr. Lockhart lifted the victim's shoulder and rolled her back, exposing the full face. Part of her face was splotchy with the dark purple of livor mortis.

Not her.

Mercy stared for several long seconds. Her immediate gut instinct when she saw the face had said it wasn't Bridget, so now she searched the woman's features for the reasons behind that reaction. The eyes were too far apart, her nose delicate and short, the face round instead of an oval. She'd been an attractive woman, and inside, Mercy raged at whoever had taken her life.

"Mercy?" Dr. Lockhart asked.

"I don't think it's her."

"Think?"

"I'm ninety percent positive it's not her."

The doctor frowned. "That's not enough—"

"Mercy?" Evan Bolton's voice made Mercy stand and turn. The detective was signing the scene log, his startled gaze on her.

"I called him," Dr. Lockhart said quietly behind her. "He'll know if it's his sister."

Mercy understood.

How did it feel to get that phone call?

"I don't think it's your sister, Evan. But you can confirm," Mercy told him.

Evan's face was drawn, his eyes looking even older than usual as he walked around to Mercy's side. He crouched down as Mercy had, and Dr. Lockhart lifted the body again. His eyebrows shot up, and his mouth opened the slightest bit.

He knows her.

"That's Meghan Serrano," Evan told Dr. Lockhart and Mercy. "Her brother was the murder victim behind the bed-and-breakfast."

Relief swept through Mercy that it wasn't his sister, but her anger about the woman's life being cut short still simmered.

Dr. Lockhart laid the woman back down. "The treasure hunter."

"Yes," said Evan. "Meghan was his partner. I interviewed her in person on Wednesday." He shook his head. "This morning I went to her hotel to speak with her again, but she wasn't there. How'd it happen?"

"So far everything is indicating she was strangled," answered Dr. Lockhart. "And it was recent. Between three and seven a.m."

"Who goes hiking at three a.m.?" asked Mercy.

"Maybe she was brought here or was asked to meet someone here," said Evan. "She's a treasure hunter. I hate to admit it, but I think she and her brother were getting close to solving the hunt. It's at the top of my motivation list for Billy Serrano's murder."

"She might have been murdered for that?" asked Mercy. "That would make two deaths because of this damned greedy hunt. It's getting more out of hand every day."

Truman is going to be furious.

"It's possible," said Evan. "She was very protective of her brother's treasure-hunting notebook. We sent her copies of his pages last night. Was anything found with her? Notes?"

"Not so far," said Dr. Lockhart. "Her bag was empty. No wallet or anything. They started a wider sweep of the area a half hour ago, looking . . ." Her voice trailed off. "Nothing has turned up yet," she finished.

Looking for little Molly.

Evan stood and rubbed his hand across his face. Mercy sympathized. He had to be relieved that the dead woman wasn't his sister, but there was still the big question of what had happened to Bridget. Not knowing a loved one's fate was hell; Mercy knew.

Evan had been Mercy's rock when Truman had vanished for weeks, kidnapped by revenge-seeking sovereign citizens. Not knowing if Truman was dead or alive had nearly broken her, and Evan had helped keep her head above water. "I'm sorry, Evan."

"What the fuck is going on, Mercy?" he muttered. "This hunt . . . it's killing people."

He hadn't stated the other aspect she knew was weighing on him: What the fuck was going on with his sister?

Mercy looked at the woman on the ground, her heart aching as she thought of Meghan's last moments, knowing someone was choking the life out of her.

Did Bridget suffer a similar fate?

"Wait." Evan suddenly spun around, scanning the area. "Her bag was empty?"

"What's wrong?" Mercy asked.

"Where's her dog? She carries a little black-and-white dog in that bag."

"That explains these tiny prints." Dr. Lockhart gestured at the ground around the woman. "Forensics got plenty of pictures before I tromped over them. I had assumed an animal had been attracted to the body."

Mercy studied the ground. "They look like little dog prints to me." Her heart broke at the thought of the dog next to its dead owner.

"Oreo. The dog's name was Oreo," said Evan. "It's friendly. Well, it was friendly while she was holding it in my office." He cupped his hands around his mouth. *"Oreo! Here, boy!"* He continued to circle the area, staring into the brush. "I think it's a boy."

Mercy tried to find a set of tracks to follow, but it appeared the dog had gone back and forth between the brush and its owner multiple times.

Such tiny little paws.

"Surely it would have come out when we arrived if it was friendly," Dr. Lockhart said, also trying to make sense of the tracks. "The searchers are still working the ground to the west. They haven't gone east yet."

Unless a predator got it.

Mercy moved into the brush, gently calling the dog's name. She dug in her pocket for the jerky-and-cheese snack she'd packed that morning, slid it out of the plastic, and waved it around.

What dog won't come out for cheese?

Evan paced fifteen feet to her left. "Should we be spending time on this?" he asked in a low voice.

Mercy understood. A woman had been murdered, and now they were searching for a dog. They should be focused on their investigation.

"I think Meghan would have wanted us to find her dog. It seems the right thing to do for her. We won't spend too long."

"You're right."

The forest floor didn't offer many places to hide. The brush was scrubby, mostly leafless. A thick layer of pine needles covered the ground, crunching as they walked and hiding any tiny paw tracks. Mercy stepped over the rotting trunk of a fallen pine and then followed the dead tree to the root end. She bent over to look inside, and a perfect triangle of two shiny black eyes and a little nose stared back at her. "Hello there, Oreo," she said softly.

He looks terrified.

Mercy squatted and held out the cheese and jerky. The nose quivered, and the dog stepped out of the log. "Evan," she projected in a calm voice toward the detective searching a few yards away, "I have him. He's scared." She broke off a tiny piece of cheese, and Oreo took it from her fingers. "Good boy. I bet you're hungry." He took another piece and didn't flinch as Mercy scooped him up. All his focus was on the cheese.

"That's him," Evan said as he reached them. "Hey, Oreo." The dog sniffed his hand and turned back to Mercy for more cheese. "Now what?" he asked. "We call animal control?"

"Do we really need animal control for a four-pound dog?" asked Mercy. The two of them headed back to the scene.

"Can you take him home for a bit?" Evan asked. "You've already got a house full of pets. One more wouldn't matter."

"I could put him in the kitten room, and no one would even notice," said Mercy. "There are three black-and-white kittens in the current litter." She studied Evan's face for a moment, noting the kindness in his eyes as he petted the dog. "But they're currently being quarantined," Mercy quickly added. "And I don't know how Dulce and Simon would take to a new dog. But I bet Charlotte and Theodore would appreciate having a dog to play with while they're at your house. You can figure out what to do with him later."

Indecision flickered across his face.

"I bet he'd keep Charlotte occupied." Mercy twisted the knife.

"That's a good point." Evan sighed. "I'll take him temporarily and let my boss know. Meghan told me it was just her and Billy in their family. If there are any distant relatives, they're back in Ohio."

Mercy doubted anyone would demand the dog. She handed the puff to Evan, who scratched the dog's chin.

"I think you might have been generous when you said four pounds," he stated, settling the dog into one arm.

"It was your turn to take the orphaned pet anyway," said Mercy. "Remember when we found Dulce at a crime scene? You made me take her home."

"As I remember, it didn't take much convincing. And now she lives happily ever after," said Evan.

He had a point. Dulce had a life of leisure. She and Kaylie were inseparable, and it had started Kaylie's obsession with fostering kittens.

How did I go from no pets to currently having eight?

Mercy smiled. She'd also gone from living alone to having an instant family.

She wouldn't trade her full house for anything.

31

Truman shut the station door behind him and nodded at Lucas, who was on the phone. Truman had just returned from a call to Tom Ellery's home. Tom had called about a suspicious car driving erratically up and down his street a dozen times. Normally a citizen would approach the car to see what was going on, but Tom was in a wheelchair, and his home sat far back from the street. His niece, who checked on him each day, wouldn't be by for another hour.

Convinced he would find a treasure hunter or a drunk, Truman had driven to the neighborhood. Instead, he'd found a frazzled mother teaching her fifteen-year-old daughter to drive. They'd picked the wide dead-end street to practice on because no cars ever parked along it. Truman had agreed with their selection and then knocked on Tom's door to explain why the car had been on his street. Then he'd spent twenty minutes mounting a blind that had fallen in the living room window and had been too heavy for Tom's niece to handle.

Truman stopped in the department's break room, set down the coffee cake Tom had insisted he accept as a thank-you, and poured a cup of coffee.

Royce suddenly appeared in the doorway, a hopeful look on his face. A normal occurrence within ten seconds of baked goods arriving in the break room. "Whatcha got?"

"Coffee cake."

"Is it good?"

"Haven't had a chance to take the foil off," Truman said dryly.

"I'll do it." The young officer eagerly removed the foil and cut himself a piece while Truman watched. He'd taken three big bites when he noticed Truman's gaze on him. "Can I get you a piece, Chief?" he asked with his mouth full of cake.

Ben stepped into the break room. "I smell cinnamon." He spotted the cake and picked up the knife.

"Cut the chief a piece," said Royce. His last bite vanished. "I'll take another too."

"It'll be almost gone then," Ben grumbled. "Kaylie hardly has any day-old products to drop off these days with all the treasure hunters stopping at her coffee place." He took a bite. "We need our daily baked-goods fix."

"That reminds me." Royce looked to Truman. "Remember Isaac? The treasure hunter I said could camp on my property two nights ago?"

"Yes. How's that going?" asked Truman, accepting a piece of cake from Ben.

"Good. He's a nice guy. But he's thinking about heading home. He says looking for the treasure feels too dangerous now that two people have been killed."

A couple of hours earlier, the Eagle's Nest Police Department had been informed of Meghan Serrano's murder, but Truman hadn't realized the information had made it to the public too. "He heard about that? Or did you tell him?"

"Isaac said everyone was talking about it this morning. He's not the only treasure hunter thinking of packing it up," said Royce. "Everyone is pointing fingers at each other. He said it's not as fun as it was."

"Could be the answer to our problem," said Ben. "Can't say I considered scaring people out of town."

"Isaac's idea of fun was being kicked off Martin Wheelock's farm practically at gunpoint?" asked Truman.

"Well," said Royce, "besides that incident." His expression grew serious. "Isaac says several people have mentioned one guy in particular that gives them the creeps. Gives off a bad vibe. Isaac came across him while exploring around that cinder cone off the Crooked River and has seen him in town too."

"Sorry, but a bad vibe isn't worth passing on to the detective who's working the two murders," said Truman.

"He often wears a Seahawks cap," Royce added helpfully.

"I know there's a lot of competition between the hunters," Truman said. "I have a hard time accepting tips from them unless they have a damned good reason . . . like someone had been shot at."

"Like at the lumberyard," added Ben.

"I don't think that's happened again yet," said Royce. "But Isaac said he'd let me know if he saw him. It does make sense that the killer would be a hunter, though. Everyone talks about Billy Serrano being quite the clue finder. Isaac says his reputation has really grown since he died."

"Rumors," stated Truman. "They always get bigger after someone passes."

"Maybe that's what led the killer to his sister," said Royce.

"Evan Bolton is on top of it," said Truman. "But do let me know if you hear something credible—not gossip." He left the men to their coffee cake and went to his office, closing the door behind him. He sat down at his desk, thought for a long moment, and then called Evan.

"Bolton." The detective was curt.

"It's Truman."

"Hey, Truman." Evan's tone lightened. "What can I do for you?"

"Mercy told me about Meghan Serrano."

"Yeah, I didn't see that coming. I feel like I should have been more aware."

"Any leads?"

"Not yet. Dr. Lockhart is doing the autopsy this afternoon. Meghan's hotel said she left at three in the morning. They have video of her leaving her room alone, and their parking-lot video shows her driving away by herself. Her car was parked at the trailhead where her body was found. Forensics went through it and then had it towed in just before lunch. I'm waiting on their report and her cell phone records. The hotel told me no one called her room."

"You've gone through the hotel room?"

"Yes. Me and a team. Nothing seemed unusual."

"Had you given her Billy Serrano's notebook?" asked Truman.

"No. It's still in evidence. But I did have it scanned and emailed to her." Evan cleared his throat. "She used the hotel business center to do some printing last night, which I assume was for the notebook's pages. If she did, the pages are missing. Not in her car or her room."

"Shit," said Truman.

"My thoughts exactly. I think the motivation for her murder is pretty clear. And yes, I already checked with the hotel to see if she put anything in its safe. The one in her room hadn't been used."

"What would make her leave her room at that time of night?" asked Truman.

"I think either she got a phone call or had a prearranged meeting," said Evan. "I doubt she decided to suddenly go hiking at that time of night."

"The treasure hunters in town are a gossipy bunch," said Truman. "Maybe someone will talk."

"We've had two dozen tips about Meghan come in already."

"Anything helpful?"

"Not yet. Still checking into a few. But I get the feeling they are hunters turning in other hunters to slow them down."

"Royce told me that a lot of hunters are talking about one guy in particular, but all he could say is that the guy gives people the creeps."

"Not helpful," said Evan.

"Agreed. What about Matt Stephens? Is he still in town?"

"I checked on him first thing this morning because he and Billy had that dispute at the lumberyard. He's still at the same hotel. I woke him up, and according to the hotel door logs, his room's door hasn't opened since eight p.m. last night."

"Someone's killed two people," said Truman.

"Or two people have killed two people," said Evan. "Before Meghan was killed, I was about to take a hard look at her for her brother's death. She deliberately lied to me about being in town during the time period he was killed."

Truman was speechless, thinking of his own sister.

I can't fathom that.

"Who knows what goes on in families," said Evan after a few seconds. "I can't make the assumption they were killed by the same person. Two very different methods were used."

"Did you go through the notebook?"

"Briefly. It seems organized and deeply researched, but big parts of it make no sense to me. I haven't paid enough attention to the locations that hunters are zeroing in on."

"I glanced at it too. Royce also told me that since Billy Serrano was murdered, his reputation for being sharp and close to finding the treasure has become quite the legend among the other hunters."

"Not surprised. I'd like to do a deeper dive into the notebook. If there is an indication where Billy was going to search next, and Meghan's killer now has the same notes, he could turn up there at some point."

"I don't know if the notes are that precise," said Truman. "Maybe you need to enlist someone who's been dissecting clues for a while to take a look at it."

"I had the same thought."

Truman realized he was overstepping investigation boundaries. *Not my case.* And he changed the subject. "How are the kids?"

"Good. Upset about the damage to their home, but they were both happy to see Ollie when he showed up this morning. I can't thank him and Kaylie enough for helping me out."

"That asshole who set the fire yesterday was up to no good. I don't want to think what could have happened if he had run into the kids."

"Trust me, that thought kept me up half the night. I hope they weren't the target."

"Someone knows what happened to their mom and dad. And the baby. I have a bad feeling about it," Truman said grimly. He hated to talk about Evan's sister like that, but he knew Evan was feeling the same way. "The same someone could be looking for the kids."

"And was that the person who set the fire yesterday?" asked Evan quietly.

"Most likely," said Truman, again regretting that he hadn't followed the brown truck. "Mercy is determined to find your sister."

Evan was silent for a long second.

"She's good, Evan," Truman said into the silence. "I can't think of anyone else I'd want working on my case."

"I know she is," agreed Evan. "But you have no idea how hard it is for me to step back and let Mercy and the FBI take the reins. I feel like this is the closest I've been to finding my sister in years." He paused. "But a part of me is anxious about what Mercy will find," he said in a low voice. "I just discovered Bethany has been alive all these years. It'll rip me up to find out—find out I'm too late."

"I hear you," said Truman, his words filled with feeling. He wouldn't give the detective any platitudes about his sister still being alive.

Both men knew the odds were getting worse every day.

32

It was late afternoon when Evan walked across the parking lot, trying to block out the scene he'd just witnessed.

Meghan Serrano's autopsy.

Images of the young woman sitting in his office for her interview had flooded his mind throughout the entire disturbing procedure. He couldn't equate the charming, petite blonde with the cold body that he'd just watched be cut open.

Will my sister be next?

Thoughts of his sister had spun through his thoughts as he watched Meghan's autopsy, and it'd taken physical effort to keep his mind from leaping ahead. It always followed a negative path, wanting to assume the worst.

I'm scared to hope she's alive. If she isn't, the truth might destroy me.

During the autopsy, Dr. Lockhart's strangulation suspicions had grown stronger; Meghan's hyoid bone had been broken.

The rest of her autopsy hadn't turned up anything of significance. Preliminary blood screens were clear. No other bruising or trauma. Evan had to look away from the tattoo on her forearm. It was of Oreo. A perfect replica of the dog's markings and facial expression.

Evan had driven Oreo home after he left the crime scene. The dog had sat silently on the seat next to him, his eyes locked on Evan the entire time. Guilt had radiated through Evan every time he met the dog's gaze and imagined its confusion.

He'd also felt like a thief, but assuaged this feeling by telling himself that he was keeping the dog from an overcrowded county kennel for who knew how long. His supervisor had been silent for a long moment while Evan explained what he'd done, and then he'd ordered him to thoroughly document the temporary decision.

"Temporary," his boss had emphasized.

"Absolutely," Evan had answered.

But then he'd passed the dog into Charlotte's eager hands. Both she and Theodore had been instantly charmed by the tiny animal. Evan hadn't told them the full story of the dog. Only that it'd been left behind at a crime scene and he was keeping it *temporarily* until the rightful owners could claim it.

He didn't believe the kids had heard a word of his explanation.

Evan got into his vehicle and sat, staring at the medical examiner's building, his mind a jumbled mess of Meghan's crime scene, her interview, her dog, and her autopsy.

How does Dr. Lockhart do that every day?

People asked Evan the same question about his job. He loved his job. Each day was different, and he genuinely believed he was making a difference in people's lives. But some days majorly sucked. Like today.

Over the years, his job had left him with a mental file of horrific images permanently burned into his brain. It took effort to keep them from invading his daily thoughts. Or his dreams at night.

But he wouldn't trade his job for any other.

Evan started his vehicle. He had work to do.

The clock in the corner of Evan's computer indicated it was nearly time for him to head home. In the past he would have worked as late as he wanted, but now he had two kids waiting. Even though Kaylie would stay until he got there, Evan didn't want to take advantage of her kindness. Ever since the break-in and fire at their home, he wanted an adult with Charlotte and Theodore at all times. Preferably himself, but he couldn't avoid his work, and Kaylie had proved herself more than capable of handling an emergency with the kids.

But in the last twenty-four hours, his worry about their safety had escalated.

No one knows they're staying in my house.

But supposedly no one had known where the kids' home was either. That had been proved wrong.

Were the kids the target? And then the fire set in anger like the jars were broken in the barn?

Why would someone want to hurt these children?

He scowled. He'd seen children hurt over and over in his job. The why never made sense.

Evan wasn't taking any chances. The kids weren't to be left alone.

He checked his email for the last time, and his gaze locked on a message from a friend he'd contacted that morning. Evan had asked him to enhance the video of the sedan driving near the bed-and-breakfast the night Billy Serrano was killed. The county forensics department also had the video, but Evan knew county might not get to it for weeks.

This particular friend owed him a favor due to bets lost on the golf course. Evan had learned long before to play for favors, not money. His friend had formerly been with the state crime lab but opened his own private lab several years earlier. Ninety-nine percent of his work was contracts from local law enforcement. Police departments sometimes decided the high cost of a private lab was worth the speed in an investigation.

Evan scanned the email and then opened the enhanced video.

The license plate was clearly visible in the video, along with the profile of a blonde female driver. He cross-checked the license plate. The car was Meghan's rental.

His golf bets had paid off.

Evan sucked in a deep breath and leaned back in his chair, his mind racing.

This doesn't mean she killed her brother.

He picked up his desk phone and called the sheriff's lot where her car was being held. He asked if the vehicle had been processed, and after a long hold was connected to a tech.

"We took an inventory," Tyler the tech told him. "It's also been vacuumed and dusted, but that evidence hasn't been sent to the lab yet."

Frustration filled Evan. It could take weeks for the evidence to be examined.

"Can you email me the inventory?" he asked, desperate to get a start on anything. "Any weapons? Did you find a stack of printed pages or a notebook?"

"Nothing like that," said Tyler. "But I'll send you the list of what we found."

Evan rattled off his email, and the tech promised to send it immediately. Evan hung up, disappointed.

Did I really expect her to have a gun in her car?

So far there'd been no leads on the weapon used to shoot Billy Serrano. Eagle's Nest dumpsters and garbage cans near the bed-and-breakfast had been searched. Evan had felt a little bad for the teenage explorers used for that particular activity, but the kids were in the explorer program to get a taste of police work, and sometimes that meant digging through garbage. They'd also combed yards and bushes for several blocks around the crime scene.

He refreshed his email. Nothing from the vehicle tech.

He stood and started to pick up his desk and pack his bag to head home. Then he used the bathroom and checked his email again.

There it is.

He opened the inventory list in the department's secured database and started reading. A rental agreement, a raised dog seat, dog-poop baggies, a collapsible dog water dish, a container of kibble, one opened water bottle, Starbucks napkins and straw covers, two suspense novels, a drugstore receipt, and a hardware-store receipt.

Nothing that said, "I murdered my brother."

Evan opened the photos of the items and quickly scrolled through each one, noting he'd read one of the novels a year ago. The drugstore receipt was for a candy bar and Benadryl. She'd paid with a debit card. The local hardware receipt was for one can of spray paint. She'd paid with cash, and it had Monday's date. The day before Billy's death.

"Bingo."

Evan tamped down his excitement as he studied the black-spray-paint receipt. The same color as the paint used to damage the camera overlooking the bed-and-breakfast parking lot.

Why pay cash to cover your tracks and not throw out the receipt?

Someone else could have put it in her car.

He called the phone number at the top of the hardware-store receipt and asked for the manager.

A young woman came on the line, and Evan identified himself. "How long do you keep security video?" he immediately asked. "I'm interested in the one that covers the check stands."

"We only have one check stand," she replied. "We store three months' worth of video. It's digital."

"Three months?" He was surprised.

"Cloud-based storage. Three months is nothing these days."

"If I swing by, can you show me Monday's video from around seven p.m.?"

The manager was silent for several seconds. "I probably should call the district manager first. Don't you need a warrant or something?"

"Don't you review video sometimes during your shift? It'll be like that, but I'll be looking over your shoulder," Evan said smoothly. "If I see something I need a copy of, I'll get you all the paperwork you need."

"Okay," she said, reluctance in her voice.

"I'll be there in ten minutes."

An hour later, Evan pulled into his home driveway.

The hardware-store manager had had the video feed for the date and time ready when Evan had walked in the store. Within two minutes he'd watched Meghan Serrano pay for a can of spray paint while Oreo peeked out of her bag. Additional video showed her getting into her car and driving off alone. The manager had been the one to ring up the purchase of paint. "I remember the dog," she'd told Evan. "I'd thought it was a stuffed animal at first."

Evan headed up the walk to his front door, convinced Meghan had been involved in killing her brother. If she hadn't actually pulled the trigger, she'd known who had.

That knowledge might be why she'd been strangled.

He opened his front door and was immediately rushed by Charlotte. Her face was wet and her eyes red with tears. She wrapped her arms around him and cried into his shirt.

Stunned, he looked to Kaylie, who stood watching the scene, her hands on her hips. "What happened?" he asked.

"She's upset," Kaylie said.

"I can see that." He untangled Charlotte's arms to get her to look him in the face. "What's wrong? Did something happen?"

"Do you think they're *dead*?" The words burst out of her mouth, fear and despair in her eyes.

God, she looks like Bethany.

He didn't need to ask whom she meant. For days everyone had wondered why the kids weren't more upset by their parents' absence. That time was over.

Something had hit home with Charlotte.

"I don't know," he told her, deciding to be as honest as possible. Charlotte and Theodore were sharp; they'd pick up on lies or false hope. "But we've found nothing that indicates that at all."

"But you can't find them! They've been gone for weeks."

He looked at Kaylie again, lifting a brow in a silent question. Until this evening, Charlotte and Theodore had seemed fine. What happened?

"She overheard Ollie and me talking," Kaylie said quietly, anguish on her face. "We didn't say anything bad . . . we were just voicing questions about the fire."

Clearly it was bad in Charlotte's mind.

Theodore appeared in the foyer, Oreo in one arm. "What's going on?"

At least Theodore doesn't appear upset.

"Can I have the dog?" Evan asked, holding out his hands. Theodore handed over Oreo and Evan gave him to Charlotte, who embraced him with a shuddering sigh and immediately buried her face in the dog's fur. Evan remembered how Meghan had used the animal for comfort during her interview. Oreo helped Charlotte too.

"Let's sit down," he said to Charlotte, leading her to the family room. "You too, Theodore."

"I need to go," said Kaylie, grabbing her purse. "You good?" she asked Evan, hesitation in her eyes.

"Yes," he said, feeling surprised. He truly was confident he could handle Charlotte and give whatever she needed at that moment.

Last week he would have been frozen with insecurity.

Kaylie said goodbye to the kids and left.

The three of them sat on the sofa, Charlotte still nuzzling the dog. Theodore had a look of mild confusion on his face.

"Is there word on our parents?" he asked.

"Not that I'm aware of," Evan told him. "I'm sure I'll get an update from Mercy tonight. But she would have called me immediately if she had important news."

The boy pressed his lips together and nodded.

"Everyone kept asking me if I was worried about my mom and Molly," Charlotte said. She wiped her face and swallowed several times, trying to compose herself. "I wasn't. Mom said she'd be gone for a while, and I knew my dad was taking care of whatever he was worried about, but now everyone is super worried because of the fire yesterday—and I am too."

Her earnest gaze broke Evan's heart.

Her sense of safety is gone. Her confidence shattered.

He'd never seen Charlotte like this. Over their few days together, she'd always been outgoing and confident. Never this cowering little girl.

"The fire was scary," Evan said, validating her feelings. "I can understand why you feel alarmed now."

"I miss my mom and dad," she whispered. "And Molly. She's just a *baby*! What if something horrible happened to *her*?"

Beside her, Theodore paled and dug his fingers into his thighs, his knuckles whitening. He said nothing, but his eyes were wide.

He keeps things inside. Charlotte is the vocal one.

Evan knew the boy was hurting as much as his sister.

They need to feel safe.

Evan couldn't tell them what had happened to their parents, but he could assure them they were secure.

"You are safe with me," he told her, pulling Charlotte tight to him on the sofa. "Both of you. Nothing is going to happen to you two as long as you're here with me."

"And if they never return?" Theodore finally spoke, his words slow and quiet.

Evan met his gaze and studied those old-soul eyes so like his own. "Then you have a place with me permanently. I'd consider it an honor."

Something flickered in Theodore's gaze and then vanished, but the boy nodded.

Charlotte tightened her arms around Evan. "I love you, Uncle Evan."

Shock went through him at her heartfelt words, making his eyes burn. He couldn't breathe, and a subtle vertigo rocked him. His brain struggled to identify what had just happened.

I didn't expect that.

"I love you too, Charlotte. Both of you," he said, still holding Theodore's gaze. He repeated his earlier offer. "You'll always have a home with me when you need it."

Truth.

A promise he felt in every cell of his body.

33

I have nothing.

Frustration filled Mercy as she stared at her office computer. She and Darby had been working all afternoon to see what they could dig up on Victor Kerr, searching for a clue as to where he might have gone. Darby had left two hours ago, and the time was staring Mercy in the face. She needed to go home and start fresh tomorrow.

It was as if Victor Kerr had been wiped from existence in his early twenties. Everything Mercy found was more than a decade old. He'd thoroughly vanished. It felt like more than the usual prepper falling off the radar. Victor had erased his tracks as if he didn't want to be followed.

Did he go into hiding?

He had told the children he was leaving to keep them safe. Had the danger started earlier than just this spring?

Mercy thought about how Charlotte and Theodore weren't allowed to talk about their grandparents or other relatives. How the Kerr sisters and Alex Kerr had lost all contact with Victor—their own flesh and blood.

Is Victor hiding from his relatives?

It wasn't too hard to avoid people. Victor Kerr could have simply circumvented his father's family. He could have moved to a new city to get away from them. Instead, he'd stayed in the general area and didn't tell his kids about his or Bridget's family.

Online he was a ghost.

It feels paranoid.

Victor's uncles, Joe and Joshua, had considered themselves sovereign citizens. Theirs was a lifestyle rooted in paranoia and a firm desire to never be told what to do. Victor could have been the same. Mercy had inferred from the children that he was controlling. There were taboo topics. He kept them away from other people. They couldn't watch TV or have internet access.

That was control.

And somehow Victor had persuaded Bridget to leave her own family behind to go with him. Had he used fear? Threats?

A subtle chill crept up Mercy's spine. Controlling spouses. Boyfriends. Always the first people looked at when women disappeared.

Was he controlling enough to hurt Bridget? And Molly?

But Victor had left first. Then Bridget had followed. Had they gone somewhere so dangerous that they'd believed it was safer to leave the two children behind?

Then why take Molly?

Mercy figured Bridget hadn't been ready to be separated from the toddler. Or she'd been told to bring Molly.

Someone who had the need to control his family wouldn't let Theodore and Charlotte escape his net for long.

Someone came looking for them yesterday.

Mercy studied Victor's old driver's license photo on her computer screen and wished she had an updated picture. Any picture. This photo was over fifteen years old. He had brown hair and eyes, just like Theodore. She could see the resemblance between father and son, but the shape of Theodore's old-soul eyes definitely came from his mother's side of the family.

Victor couldn't have been the man who'd come to the house the day before. Both Charlotte and Theodore would have recognized their father, even in a fleeting glimpse. The most likely scenario was that

Victor had sent someone to get his children. Mercy could understand setting the fire to possibly destroy some sort of evidence, but breaking the glass canning jars made no sense.

So much anger there.

She leaned back in her chair, her nerves jangling. Someone had been upset about not finding what they wanted at the Kerr farm. And it was most likely the children. Mercy grabbed her phone and looked up Kaylie's location. Her niece was at home, not at Evan's. That meant Evan was with the children. Mercy's nerves settled a bit. Evan would protect those children with his life.

Truman and Ollie were at home too.

The four of them had agreed to use their phones to track one another. Mercy felt peace of mind from seeing her loved ones' locations. Both she and Truman had gone missing in the past. The phones wouldn't have made a difference either time, but they might if it happened again. It was reason enough for the four of them to tolerate the lack of privacy.

Mercy checked her notes. She'd searched every database she could think of to find current information for Victor Kerr. Her gaze caught on Shannon Ayers's name. Victor's mother. The woman had been dead for almost thirty years.

Mercy typed her name into the first database anyway.

Over the next few minutes, she checked the usual sites. Death records, tax records, credit reports, arrest records.

Most of the information was minimal. Shannon Ayers had passed away before a lot of things were online. Most of what Mercy found was the bare bones of records that had been scanned or manually entered years later. Her death lined up with the time period Alex Kerr had given. An old driver's license photo appeared. Shannon had the big hair of the eighties in the photo. She was a pretty girl with a narrow face and heavy eyeliner. The photo had been taken four years before her death.

Was she a drug user at this point?

The address on the license caught Mercy's eye, startling her. Shannon Ayers had lived within a couple of miles of Mercy's cabin in the Cascade Range foothills, a fortified and well-stocked haven she'd created in case society suddenly went to shit.

Now the cabin was more of a weekend getaway. She and Truman often went to get some private time away from the kids and do upkeep. For a place that was rarely lived in, the cabin took quite a bit of maintenance. Mercy insisted that everything always be in perfect working order and the supplies frequently refreshed. The need was deep in her blood.

I never know when we'll need it.

The cabin had been her security blanket for years. The result of a compulsion she couldn't leave behind when she moved to Portland. She had needed the safety net it provided. The knowledge that she had a place to survive had allowed her to function in the normal world. It'd been the most important thing in her life for years.

Now, not so much.

Truman, Kaylie, and Ollie occupied her brain's space. Yes, the cabin was a safety net for them too, but she didn't obsess about it the way she used to. It wasn't her waking thought every morning. Truman said she was less uptight than when they'd first met.

Mercy snorted. She had been uptight. Everything in her life had centered around future safety. It wasn't until she'd met Truman and reconnected with her family that she'd learned to live in the moment.

She wondered if Victor had the same fears and uncertainty. It was common for preppers to focus their life's energy on being ready.

Did he leave to do something for his family's future?

Mercy didn't know. She eyed Shannon Ayers's address again and typed it into a title search. The property was now owned by the county. She checked the history. The property had gone back to the bank when the mortgage stopped being paid and then eventually ended up with the county because of unpaid property taxes. Mercy assumed it'd gone to auction—probably multiple times—and wondered why no one had bought it.

She pulled up an aerial view of the property and liked what she saw. Thick woods along the road, a stream to the east, and the remains of what had once been a double-wide mobile home. She liked the acreage's layout better than her own cabin property's.

Could Victor be hiding out on his mother's old property?

It was hard to see clearly, but the mobile home didn't look habitable from the aerial view, and Mercy figured that after thirty years of neglect, it was crumbling to the ground. The property would be a good place to hide out; everyone seemed to have forgotten about it. The bank. The county.

She went back to the databases, searching for any sort of connection between Shannon and Jack Kerr. A shared address or shared utilities. But it was as if they had never crossed paths, which Mercy found odd, considering they'd had a child together.

Mercy compiled what little she'd found and sent it in an email to Darby, knowing the analyst would dig deeper.

She returned to the aerial view of the property. She and Truman had been looking for a place close to town but not actually in town for their daily residence. Their current home was in a cookie-cutter subdivision, and they wanted more space. Her cabin wasn't an option because it was too far out of town, and Shannon Ayers's old property was the same.

But the hidden aspect of it spoke to her. It was exactly what a prepper looked for in a hideaway. Maybe her sister Pearl would be interested. She and her husband, Rick, currently had a farm, but it was in clear view of the highway and multiple neighbors. Mercy knew they actively prepped. They would appreciate this property.

Mercy decided she'd kill two birds with one stone tomorrow and check the property for any sign that Victor Kerr had been there, and also to scout it for Pearl and Rick.

Who am I fooling? I want to look at it for myself.

She sighed and logged out of her computer, feeling as if she'd accomplished nothing that day.

I rescued a dog.

That had to count for something. No doubt Charlotte and Theodore had been excited, even if Evan was not. She pictured the three of them on the sofa with the dog, watching TV in domestic bliss.

Mercy abruptly put the image out of her mind. The three of them weren't a family. Those kids had parents, and Mercy was acting as if they'd simply live with Evan for the rest of their lives.

I've got to find the rest of their family.

34

Mercy drove past the driveway to her cabin in the forest. It wasn't really a driveway. It was more of a packed dirt track that was nearly impossible to spot from the rural main road. Only someone who knew it was there and was looking for it would be likely to spot it. Anyone who drove down it would trigger her alarm system, and she'd get a notification on her phone.

It felt odd to not stop, and she decided to make a quick check of the property after she went to Shannon Ayers's old place. She continued for a few more miles. The winding road was gravel and rutted, and she spotted the occasional Forest Service signage nailed to a pine. She checked her GPS and slowed, scanning the side of the road for any hint of an entry to the old Ayers property. A minute later she turned around and drove the stretch again, scanning every bush and tree.

There it is.

A thin stretch of cleared dirt angled away from the road, nearly hidden by wild rhododendrons. Mercy studied the opening and then decided to park on the main road and enter on foot. She stepped out of her Tahoe and stood silently, listening. The forest was silent. No birds. No engines. She hadn't seen another vehicle in twenty minutes and doubted anyone would pass while she checked out the property. She headed for the dirt path and halted as she spotted a tire track in the powdery dirt.

When was the last rainfall?

She couldn't remember. Probably two weeks. Maybe more. The tracks could be weeks old.

Or they could be from yesterday.

Someone could be camping on the property. Or could have checked it out for a purchase. Or the tracks could be from high school kids looking for a place to drink. Either way, she was glad she was armed. She was standing in the type of area where people shot first and asked questions later, but she didn't feel a need to call for backup. She knew this side of the Cascade Range and its people.

My people.

She headed down the path, following the tracks. She didn't know much about tire tracks, but they were wide with deep treads, giving her the impression they were from a large truck or SUV. The trees were densely packed, just as she'd noticed on the aerial view, but ahead they thinned out, and she could see more of the blue sky. After several more yards, the property opened up, and she spotted the crumbling mobile home in the southeast corner of the acreage. The roof had caved in at one end, and the walls had collapsed inward. Graffiti dotted one of the walls.

No vehicles were visible.

Mercy relaxed a bit and continued to follow the tracks, which led toward the home. The land was lightly sloped and overrun with dried tall grass that poked up among the large volcanic rocks. She didn't like the rocks. It would require a bulldozer to move them to make the property more useful. It was a common sight in parts of Central Oregon: remains of explosions from ancient volcanoes scattered across fields.

The property was extremely rocky, and Mercy realized that was the reason it hadn't sold. It also explained why the home was tucked away in an odd corner of the property. It was the only place clear enough that no rocks needed to be moved. She climbed up on the nearest big boulder and surveyed the area, disappointed that it wouldn't be an ideal place for her sister to build. Mercy's property had some of the volcanic rocks but wasn't covered like this one.

She hopped down and continued to the house, growing confident it was too decrepit for Victor Kerr to use as a hiding place. The tire tracks went around to the back of the house, but first she stopped and studied the warped walls and moldering roof. She tried to read the graffiti but could make out only a letter here and there. It appeared a few people had sprayed their personal illegible tags, letting everyone know that they had been immature enough to mark property that didn't belong to them.

There had once been a small set of wooden stairs and a porch at the front door, but these were now a pile of rotten boards. The door was gone, and she could see the sky through the opening. Linoleum flooring had curled, uncovering swollen particleboard below.

At one point someone had nailed a lattice around the base of the home, but it had fallen apart, leaving small pieces of wood dangling from the bottom of the home and exposing the concrete foundation. Stepping into the home would mean risking a leg going through the floor. Saddened by the neglect, Mercy sighed and followed the tracks.

Whoever was here recently didn't use the house.

The tread marks weren't as obvious near the house. The dirt was firmer and mixed with packed gravel. She rounded the back corner of the house and realized the tracks simply made a loop around the home. Essentially they led nowhere.

But someone has been here more often than it takes to spray graffiti.

The rough track to the home should be overgrown with weeds and grass if no one had lived here in thirty years. At the back of the house, she stared in surprise at an extension ladder that had been left lying on the ground close to the house. It hadn't been there for thirty years; its shiny metal told her that someone had brought it not too long ago. She instinctively looked up at the collapsing roof, wondering if someone had used the ladder to access it.

But why?

Casting one last glance at the mystery ladder, she left the packed dirt and wandered away from the back of the home through tall grass toward a large group of lava rocks, expecting to find a cache of empty beer cans left by teenagers. She climbed up on one of the shorter rocks and was surprised by a deep hole on the other side.

A lava tube.

Something moved at the bottom.

35

It's a human.

Mercy could see a hand and arm. Which moved again. Barely.

Her first instinct was to back away and not let the person see she was "spying" on them.

Her second instinct was an overwhelming need to help.

She dropped to her knees, peering into the darkness. The lava-tube opening was about a dozen feet wide, and the person lay at the bottom of the deep, dark hole, almost hidden, but visible enough for Mercy to sense that something was very wrong.

"Hey!" she said loudly. "Are you okay?"

Nothing moved.

Clearly they're not okay.

People don't choose to nap in the bottoms of isolated lava tubes.

They must have fallen and been badly injured. The walls of the tube were rough and jagged but were angled, making them impossible to climb. If they'd hit their head when they fell, they would be in a serious condition.

As her eyes adjusted, she made out the profile of a face and dark hair. She yelled again and shone her phone's flashlight into the tube—which did nothing to penetrate the deep darkness. The lava tube had to be fifteen to twenty feet deep.

"Shit." She looked around and spotted a long length of rotting rope in a pile on the other side of the opening.

Absolutely not.

Her gaze fell on the ladder.

That's why there is a ladder in the middle of nowhere. Someone used it to put them in there.

Her lungs seized when she realized the person in the hole had been deliberately left. It was doubtful they had fallen. But they weren't dead; she was almost positive of that fact. Mercy hadn't imagined the movement of their arm. She'd seen it twice.

Is it Victor?

"Victor?" she asked, raising her voice to carry to the bottom. Her heart pounded. She might have found exactly whom she'd come looking for. Her gut told her it was a man, but she wasn't sure.

Nothing moved.

She stood, her mind racing, wanting to grab the ladder and get him out, but it was clear he was in no condition to climb a ladder, and she couldn't carry him out. She needed help. And an ambulance. Mercy checked her phone. No service.

Just like at her cabin. Her best bet was to head north on the road for a few minutes. She'd found service there before.

"Hey!" she yelled at the person. "I have to leave to call for help. I'll be right back. I won't be gone more than ten minutes, and then we'll get you out of there."

Nothing moved.

Shit.

Mercy jumped off the rocks and sprinted toward the road. She always had a well-stocked first aid kit in the back of her Tahoe—it was more of a mini emergency room kit. Supplies for gunshot wounds, scalpels, splints, tourniquets, sutures, and an analgesic inhaler that wasn't approved for use in the US. It wasn't a wimpy kit of Band-Aids and adhesive tape. She'd saved lives with her kit before, including Kaylie's and Eddie's. But before starting anything, she needed to call for help. Panting, she climbed in her Tahoe and sped down the road.

Ten minutes later, Mercy came racing back, a thick cloud of dust in her wake. She'd given the 911 operator a detailed description of how to find the property and advised her that getting the person out of the hole wouldn't be simple.

Her tires slid in the gravel as she skidded to a stop at the driveway and threw the vehicle into park. She jumped out and dashed to the back of the vehicle as her door alarm beeped, and then dug through a supply bag in her cargo space until she found what she wanted. She turned on the battery-operated flares and tossed three into the road, leaving the emergency responders an obvious sign of the location of the driveway. She leaped back into her seat and cranked the wheel to turn down the rutted road to the property. She was jostled and tossed from side to side in her seat as she focused.

Help summoned.

Now I do what I can until rescue arrives.

She parked behind the house, her attention on the ladder. It was a lightweight aluminum extension ladder, and she easily carried it. She leaned it against a tall rock and scrambled back to the location where she'd originally spotted the person. She knelt and shone a powerful flashlight from her emergency pack into the hole. It definitely was a man. "I'm back! I'm coming down, and then we're gonna get you out."

Nothing moved.

Shit.

In the bright light she saw that his face was crusted with dried blood. A dark blanket covered most of his body. Three full water bottles lay beside him.

Why didn't he drink the water?

Mercy hauled the ladder up her rock, extended it as far as she could, and guided the bottom into the hole. She struggled for several moments, trying to find a decent place for the feet of the ladder. The bottom of the hole was rock. Lots of jagged, uneven rock. She finally found a reasonably stable location, but the ladder still jerked around.

If I fall, at least help is on the way.

She shoved the flashlight into a pocket of the medical duffel bag and put her arms through the straps to wear it like a backpack. Mercy took a deep breath and turned to step down the ladder and into the hole.

Two steps down, the ladder lurched, and she grabbed at the rough wall, slicing two fingers.

I should have worn gloves.

She steadied and slowly moved down the ladder, keeping her weight close to the frame. The temperature dropped as she went lower, and the walls sloped away. The lava tube was much wider at the bottom than the top. There was no way to climb out unless a person was part spider. She reached the bottom and turned in a circle with her flashlight. The tube continued to her left, forming a narrowing crawl space that would give claustrophobic Truman nightmares.

I wonder how many teenagers have explored this tube?

Based on the rotting rope near the entrance, she knew someone had checked it out in the past.

It was a dangerous lava tube. A person could easily become trapped. Like the person lying before her.

She ran her light over the man she suspected was Victor Kerr.

He's been gone three weeks. Has he been in here the entire time?

His hair was overgrown, and he had a short, scraggly growth of beard. His face was thin and drawn, his eyes closed. The hand and arm outside the blanket were also crusted with blood. She focused the flashlight on his hand. His fingers were bloody and mangled, several of his fingernails missing.

Did he try to crawl up the walls?

Mercy squatted beside him and gently touched below his jaw as she watched for his chest to rise and lower.

Thank God.

His pulse felt strong but slow. He breathed, but it sounded rough. Either his lungs were congested or his airway was swollen.

"Victor," she said. *"Victor."*

He didn't respond. She shook his shoulder, and his body stiffened as if in pain, but his eyes stayed closed. She carefully lifted the thin blanket, noting it was damp. His other hand looked worse than the first one. Mercy pinched the skin on his arm. It took several seconds to flatten back into place.

He was dehydrated. But three full water bottles lay nearby. And several empty ones were tossed to the side.

Maybe he couldn't open the bottles with his battered hands?

She opened a bottle, set it aside, and tried to lift his head into a position from which he could drink.

The man screamed, the whites of his eyes showing.

Mercy nearly yanked her hands away but instead eased his head back to the ground with shaking hands as his scream echoed in the cavern. Her lift had hurt him horribly, but now his eyes closed again, and his mouth sagged.

Moving him when he might have a back or spine injury wasn't my smartest idea.

She picked up her flashlight and shone it on his face. He was severely bruised and swollen under the crusted blood, and his open mouth had shifted crookedly to one side.

Is his jaw broken?

Another reason he wouldn't have drunk from the water bottles.

Tears burned behind her eyes as she imagined his thirst, knowing that water was available, but being unable to drink.

She had to get fluids in him. Now. There was one other option.

Mercy turned to her kit and removed a bag of IV fluids. She put a tourniquet on his arm and ripped open an alcohol wipe. She watched his face as she cleaned the skin over a vein.

Get fluids going, then assess the rest of him.

Dehydration was deadly. But so simple to address.

Mercy had placed an IV port only once before, but she'd watched it done dozens of times on YouTube. She'd added a number of medical procedures to her survivalist repertoire to use her custom emergency kit to its fullest potential. She found a good place to set her flashlight and illuminate the area.

Mercy wrapped the tourniquet around his arm as tightly as she could to force blood through his veins, knowing that starting an IV on a dehydrated person was a challenge even for professionals. A glance at her medical kit told her she had three chances to get it right or risk causing an infection. This wasn't a clean doctor's office. This was field-work, where speed took priority over perfection.

She gloved up and cradled his elbow in search of a vein. It wasn't great, but it was there. She took a deep breath and was pleased to see her fingers didn't shake as the needle pierced his skin. Blood immediately flowed to the chamber, and she exhaled.

Got it.

She pulled back the needle a little and advanced the cannula into place. She removed the needle and finished with the catheter. She flushed the line and hooked everything up, only to realize she'd forgotten to remove the tourniquet. The stretchy band was removed, and she peered at her work, pleased to see fluids were moving.

There was nothing to hook the bag on, so she held it as she did a quick check of the rest of her patient. He wore a sweatshirt, jeans, and boots. All of which were filthy. She checked his pockets for identification but found nothing. She quickly palpated his limbs but didn't find any obvious injuries or active bleeding. Most of the damage appeared to be to his face and hands. His wounds were dry and crusted. Several fingers appeared broken, and she was concerned about his head injuries.

He didn't respond as she spoke to him.

She was glad he'd screamed. It told her his brain was still functioning on some level.

She sat and waited, holding the bag and studying his face. His jaw was definitely crooked and swollen. Either broken or out of joint.

It's Victor.

Even through the beard and grime, she saw a resemblance to Theodore.

Relief flooded her. The kids would have their dad back.

But Bridget and Molly were still missing. Mercy scanned the cavern, ridiculously hoping to see them alive and well in a corner.

At least she didn't see two bodies in a corner.

Mercy had dozens of questions for Victor. Especially about his wife and toddler.

What if he's been here the whole time and has no idea they're missing?

She wanted to shake him awake and make him answer her questions. But she doubted he'd be able to speak, even if he were conscious. So she waited, adrenaline still bubbling through her veins. She exhaled, trying to shake off the stress of the last hour. Looking up, she fought off a sensation of being trapped in the cavern. The ladder was still in place, and she'd made the right decision to call for help first. Carrying Victor up the ladder would have been impossible. She kept one hand on his wrist, drawing comfort from the steady pulse beneath her fingertips. The minutes slowly ticked by.

The faint wail of a siren reached her ears.

He's going to make it.

36

Evan spotted Mercy and Truman sitting in the hospital's waiting area and strode in their direction. Truman had his arm around Mercy as she leaned into him, her eyes closed. Truman's gaze met Evan's, and he said something to Mercy, who lifted her head and spotted Evan.

I can't believe she found Victor.

In a hole.

Mercy had called him as she drove to the hospital, but kept it short, needing to make other calls. Evan knew only basic details. His first instinct had been to call Theodore and Charlotte to let them know their father had been found, but Mercy's mention of head and possible spinal injuries made him wait. At the moment, Victor was in surgery.

I'll tell them when I know his condition.

The kids didn't need to sit in a hospital waiting room, waiting to hear if their dad was going to survive.

Mercy and Truman stood to greet him. Her jeans were dirty, and one hand was bandaged. She followed his gaze to her hand. "I sliced it going into the tube. It's nothing."

"You're amazing," said Evan. Emotion made his voice crack.

The fate of a man I've never met is messing with my head.

"You would have done the same," Mercy answered.

"I wouldn't have found him in the first place. I'm still fuzzy on what exactly led you there."

Mercy gave him a quick rundown of her discovery of Victor Kerr's mother's old address. She described her search of the property, which had been mostly motivated by curiosity once she realized the building was uninhabitable and unlikely to house her missing persons.

"How did they get him out of the cavern?" Evan asked.

"They strapped him into a rescue board and used a system of pulleys to raise him out. I was impressed with the responders' calm as they came up with a solution. They had no doubts they could get him out. It was just a matter of adapting their equipment to the rocks surrounding the lava-tube entrance."

"You mentioned head injuries," said Evan. "How bad is it?"

Mercy grimaced. "I don't know. The EMTs said he never woke up during transport. In the cavern I saw a number of wounds to his head—older wounds—scabbed over but still swollen. They were worried about pressure on his brain, which is why they took him immediately to surgery. His jaw is broken or out of socket, and his hands are a disaster."

"How did—"

"Are you Victor Kerr's family?" A man in scrubs looked at the three of them, the only people in the waiting area.

"Yes," said Evan, stepping forward.

"You're family?" the man asked, stressing the word *family*.

The three of them pulled out their law enforcement IDs at the same time. "I'm his brother-in-law," said Evan. "Current guardian of his children."

"Special Agent Mercy Kilpatrick," said Mercy. "I'm investigating Victor's disappearance."

The doctor looked to Truman, who said, "I'm with her," gesturing at Mercy.

His explanation seemed sufficient. "Mr. Kerr is out of surgery and in recovery," said the doctor. "We relieved the pressure on his brain with a cranial flap. He had two subdermal hematomas. We also put his jaw back into place and wired it shut to stabilize the break. His fingers are splinted for now. They will require surgery in the future."

"Cranial flap?" asked Evan.

"We removed a piece of his skull. Also called a craniotomy."

Evan didn't care for the visual his brain presented.

"Agent Kilpatrick." The doctor paused. "I believe this man was tortured. And not just once but over a period of time. He has bruises all over his body in various states of healing. I know there was a question of whether or not a high fall into lava rock could cause his injuries, and I see little evidence of that. His injuries don't indicate one place of impact."

"Could it have caused the head wounds?" asked Mercy.

"In theory it could have caused one of them, but I did a close examination and took a number of photos before the surgery, and my impression is that the head wounds were all caused by the same object. I'm no forensic investigator, but I know what a blow with a hammer to the skull looks like. I've seen several," he stated grimly.

"Jesus," muttered Evan. "And the hand injuries?"

"The way several of the knuckles have been crushed into almost a pulp, I would consider a hammer did that too. Then there's the fingernails that have been ripped away. I don't want to sound like I see too many movies, but that says deliberate torture to me." He looked at the three of them one after another. "Why was he tortured?"

"We don't know," said Mercy. "I need to question him."

The doctor shook his head. "Good luck. He's not going to be able to speak or write for a while. And we can't guess what he'll be like when he wakes up. Brain damage is impossible to predict. He may never be the same, or he may heal up with no changes at all. You might be able to get some yes-or-no questions answered . . . at some point."

Evan turned away and ran a hand over his face. Victor could be severely affected for the rest of his life.

How am I going to tell Theodore and Charlotte?

A hand touched his arm. It was Mercy. "He's alive," she said, her firm gaze holding his. "We'll all get through this one day at a time. The kids will learn and eventually understand."

Evan nodded. "I can't tell them he was tortured," he whispered.

"I don't believe they need to know that right away. 'Injured in a fall' is a sufficient explanation for now."

Evan looked back at the doctor. "Is it possible he won't wake up?"

"It's possible."

Those kids.

"I need to call them now," said Evan.

"You can't tell them by phone," Mercy said.

Evan stared at her, understanding her point.

"But they should be told ASAP," said Truman. "Even though I assume the doctor won't let him have visitors for a while," he said in a questioning tone, with a look toward the surgeon, who nodded.

"I still think they should be told in person," said Mercy.

"I'll FaceTime them on Ollie's phone," Evan said. "Does that work?"

Mercy and Truman nodded, agreement on their faces.

"I'll be back. Text Ollie that I'm about to call," Evan told them before heading down the long hall. He needed to be outdoors. The antiseptic smell of the hospital was suddenly nauseating him. He pushed through the outer doors and breathed deep in the sunshine. The noon sun was bright, and the sky a cloudless blue.

A perfect day.

He FaceTimed Ollie's phone without preparing what to say.

Just tell them.

"Uncle Evan?" asked Theodore, his serious face appearing on Evan's screen.

"Hey, Theodore. Is Charlotte there too?"

"Yeah. Ollie said you wanted to FaceTime us."

"Did Kaylie get there yet?" Evan had left the kids with Ollie supervising, but Kaylie was due to take over after her lunch rush.

"They're both here. We're all playing Scrabble," said Theodore.

"Hi, Uncle Evan," Charlotte piped up, and her face popped into view.

"Hi, Charlotte. I hope you're destroying them at the game." She often beat both Evan and Theodore. The phone was suddenly turned so he could see Charlotte, Ollie, and Kaylie at the table with the game.

"Kaylie is winning so far," said Charlotte, disappointment in her face. "I'll catch up."

"Say . . . kids." Evan scrambled for the right words. "I have some good news. Your dad was found this morning, but he's injured and in the hospital," he quickly added.

"Is he going to be okay?" asked Theodore as the other three simultaneously turned to face the phone.

"He had surgery this morning," said Evan. "He has head injuries and hurt his hands. He can't talk for a while because they wired his jaw shut. It was broken."

"What happened?" asked Ollie.

"We're not sure. He was found in a remote area in a deep cavern. He may have fallen in." Evan flinched at the deliberate vagueness of his statement.

It was silent for a long moment, and Evan was glad both Kaylie and Ollie were there. Charlotte shifted closer to Kaylie, and the teenager put her arm around the girl.

"When can we see him?" Charlotte asked in a small voice.

"I don't know the answer to that yet," said Evan. "He's going to be unconscious for a while because of the surgery."

"I'd still like to see him," said Charlotte. "Even if he can't see or hear me."

Evan vacillated.

Will that be good for her? Or traumatizing?

"Me too," said Theodore, turning the phone so Evan could see his face.

"Okay," said Evan, making what he hoped was the right decision. "I'll find out when he can have visitors. Don't be disappointed if it's not until tomorrow."

He had assumed it would be better to keep the kids away until Victor was interactive, but he'd had a crushing thought as he spoke to Charlotte: What if Victor passed away from his injuries, and his kids hadn't been able to see him?

Evan would never forgive himself.

It was the deciding factor in his decision.

"What about our mom?" asked Theodore. "And Molly? Were they there? Did Dad tell you where they were?"

"They weren't there. We still don't know where they went." Evan paused. "Your dad wasn't able to communicate in any way because of his injuries," he said delicately.

"Oh." Theodore's disappointment was heavy in the single word.

"The FBI is still looking," said Evan. "They won't give up until they find your mom and Molly."

"It's okay, honey," Kaylie said in a soft voice, and Evan heard sniffles.

It broke his heart to hear Charlotte cry. And then Theodore turned the phone, and he could see her buried in Kaylie's arms for comfort.

"I'm just so worried." Charlotte's words were halting, spoken around sobs.

"We're all worried," Evan admitted. "It's normal to feel that way. But we'll find them." He worried that his sister might be in as bad shape as Victor.

Someone had tortured Victor, and there would be hell to pay.

If they'd done the same to his sister, Evan would come at them with worse.

"I'll head home after I find out when your dad can have visitors. Probably within the hour. Ollie, how long can you stay today?"

"I'm off today, so whenever."

"Okay. If you could hang around until I get there, I have some things related to the treasure hunt I'd like your and Kaylie's opinion on."

"No problem."

Evan ended the call. He had decided to take Truman's advice to have another hunter look at Billy Serrano's notebook. He knew Kaylie and especially Ollie had spent many hours dissecting the clues. He hoped one of them could offer some helpful insight about the notes. Something to point him toward whoever had murdered Billy and Meghan.

Evan fought to change gears back to his own case. He'd been caught up in the discovery of Victor Kerr and then worried about whether his sister was safe and how the kids would react to the news about their battered father. Seeing Victor's injuries had made Evan stress about what might have been done to his sister.

What if she's hurt in the same way?

But Evan was responsible for finding out who'd killed Billy and Meghan Serrano. He stared up at the sky, struggling to calm the bubbling anxiety in his chest. Seeing Victor had suddenly made his sister very real. He'd had to compartmentalize her disappearance so it wouldn't affect him every day. For too long, she'd simply been a question in his mind, an emptiness. He'd always wondered if she was okay, but now her well-being dominated his thoughts.

Billy and Meghan are already dead.

It was urgent that their killers be found, but finding Bethany before she ended up like Victor—or worse—was a priority.

It might be too late.

Theodore and Charlotte entered his mind. Their dad was back—for now. They deserved to have their mother and sister back too.

I need to put this family back together.

37

Ollie jumped when he heard Evan unlock the front door.

Truman had called and confided in him that the children's father had been brutally beaten. He'd wanted Ollie and Kaylie on alert for anything odd as they stayed with Theodore and Charlotte.

Evan's eyes were grimmer than usual. He handed Kaylie a thick manila envelope and then led the kids into the living room. Ollie eyed the envelope.

The Serranos' clue research.

Charlotte carried Oreo like a baby. She'd been inseparable from the dog. As Ollie and Kaylie settled at the kitchen table and took a stack of papers from the envelope, Evan spoke to the kids. "The doctors think tomorrow is the earliest that your dad can have visitors," he said.

"Why?" Charlotte asked.

"Because his brain is injured and swollen. They're keeping him in a deep sleep to let it heal."

Ollie strained his ears to hear anything from Theodore, but the stoic boy was silent.

"They allowed me in his room for a minute," Evan said. "I'm not sure he heard me, but I told him the two of you were staying with me and that you were safe."

Charlotte questioned the logic of Evan being able to speak to her unconscious father while the children were not allowed to do so. Evan calmly handled her questions, and Ollie tuned them out to focus on the pages of clues. He was excited to finally see the infamous notebook, but his elation was dampened by the condition of the kids' father. After several minutes, Evan distracted Charlotte with a teenage-musical movie, and he and Theodore came to sit at the kitchen table, where Ollie and Kaylie had divided up the pages.

Ollie turned another page, fascinated by the perfect handwriting and complex notes.

He had been aware of the murders of Billy and his sister, Meghan, but hadn't known how deeply they'd been invested in the treasure hunt.

They were die-hard hunters.

"What do you think?" asked Evan.

"I think someone put a *lot* of work into this," murmured Kaylie. "These people were serious hunters. I can't imagine the time it took to put this together."

Ollie nodded, focused on a hand-drawn map. It looked like an illustration from a novel. He pushed the page across the table to Kaylie. "Do you recognize the landmarks on this? I'm not familiar with them."

She frowned as she studied the map. "I think this is north of Owlie Lake. I've hiked a cliff in the area that zigzags like is drawn here."

Ollie skimmed through his stack of pages, wanting an overall feel for the Serranos' process, and then switched with Kaylie and did the same with her pile. A growing sense of validation made it difficult to sit still in his seat. "Are you seeing what I am?" he asked Kaylie.

She nodded. "They were trying out the theory based on language, just like we kept discussing. They went a lot deeper, though."

"What theory?" asked Evan.

"Well," said Ollie, "first you have to understand the type of person Chester Rollins was. We all know he's into games, which is obvious because he created the hunt, and he'd done similar things on a much smaller scale when he had guests at his ranch. The more interviews I read or watched with him, the more I noticed he never gave straight answers to anything."

"That's right," said Kaylie. "He annoyed a lot of journalists."

"But he was answering their questions," said Ollie. "He did it in a way that was open to multiple interpretations. It was a matter of figuring out which was right."

"I saw an interview where he seemed to talk in circles," said Evan. "People afterward said he was losing it. The start of dementia. I've even read this treasure hunt is impossible. That it was created by someone who'd lost the ability to think rationally."

Ollie glanced at Theodore, who was listening intently, soaking it all in. He knew the young teen was very sharp. He had a knack for seeing straight to the core of issues and solving them.

"I don't think it was dementia," said Ollie. "I think he knew exactly what he was saying all the time. And I think the lines of 'In the Pines' are the same. They seem random and disjointed, but I think he was playing with language. Kaylie showed me that many of the words he uses are common homonyms. And from what I'm reading here, the Serranos were basing a lot of their interpretation of the clues on the same theory."

Evan understood. "So that would explain why they suggested the line 'a holy sea' could reference a viewpoint—because homonyms could change the meaning to 'wholly see.'"

"Exactly," said Kaylie.

"Now to figure out which meaning each word actually has," said Evan.

"Rollins didn't write directions on how to interpret the clues," said Ollie. "This little essay is essentially a poem, and to me, very little can make sense in a poem. It's all about the reader's interpretation."

"That's right," said Kaylie. "I believed I was seeing a pattern in the last few lines, but then it didn't fit at all when I went back to the beginning. For example, the final line is 'Where would it be?' At first glance it seems like a simple ending for the poem—one that simply wraps things up in general terms. But he uses three homonyms. *Where/wear*, *would/wood*, and *be/bee*. That's a lot packed into a four-word sentence."

"Wear a wood bee?" asked Evan, a skeptical look on his face.

"Who knows?" said Kaylie. "Perhaps the wood bee is the relevant part . . . or perhaps it's a combination of the homonyms actually in the clue and the ones that aren't."

"This is why we looked around Owlie Lake," said Ollie. "The one line says, 'Go past the foul water,' and we were seeing if he meant *fowl* instead of *foul*." He pointed to the zigzag path on the map. "It appears the Serranos had the same thoughts about the name of the lake because this shows that Billy went looking in that area."

That last line about the bee was one of Ollie's favorite clues. It was short and appeared superfluous. Which made him believe it was very important. Exactly something Chester Rollins would do.

"Is Eagle's Nest even the right place to start?" asked Evan.

"We think so," said Kaylie. "The first clue includes a bird that cried. A lot of people agree that *cried* is a synonym for *bawled* which is a homonym for *bald*—as in no hair."

"A bald eagle," said Theodore. "Therefore, Eagle's Nest."

"Let's read slowly from the beginning and see how the Serranos interpreted things," said Ollie. "The problem is they appear to have been stumped on a few clues. Some of them have virtually no notes. Like this clue that says, 'The pears that overtook the plains.' Kaylie and I haven't figured out that one either. Does he mean *pairs* as in a duo or the fruit? And does *plains* actually mean plateaus or large fields? Or actual flying planes, which could refer to an airport?"

Evan's brain hurt.

"I'll let you guys focus your brains on this gibberish," said Evan, pushing back his chair. "I need to get back to work. I should be home around dinnertime." He tousled Theodore's hair and went to say goodbye to Charlotte.

Ollie sifted through the pages until he found the first clue. It had two pages of notes, many of which cross-referenced other notes on other clues. He took a deep breath, excitement building in his stomach.

A fresh pair of eyes can make all the difference.

"I'll grab some lemon bars," said Kaylie. "I need more sugar to think."

"Ollie, tell me your thoughts as you read," said Theodore. "Sometimes saying them out loud can help."

Charlotte wandered over. "I want to listen too." In her arms, Oreo's nose twitched, his focus on the plate in Kaylie's hand as she came toward them.

Kaylie set down a plate heaped with lemon bars. "Let's get to work."

Ollie grabbed a bar and began.

38

"Uncle Evan."

The voice was young. Evan opened his eyes and was confused by the dark room. He blinked and saw a black silhouette standing at his bedside. Adrenaline flashed through his veins, and his heart skipped two beats. Then he recognized Theodore.

"What is it?" Evan struggled to sound awake and calm even though his heart was walloping its way out of his chest and deep sleep fogged his brain.

"There's someone in the house," Theodore said in a whisper.

The brain fog lifted. Evan sat up and put his feet on the floor, and Theodore stepped back from the bedside.

"You sure?" Evan asked. A stupid question. Theodore didn't over-react. If he had seen someone, someone was there.

"I heard something outside, so I got up and saw someone walking close to the house in the backyard. I think there are two people. When I went toward the family room, I heard someone in the kitchen. I know the sound of that creaky spot near the dishwasher."

Evan knew it too. He opened the drawer to his nightstand. "Where's Charlotte?"

"She's still asleep. Oreo is awake but on her bed."

"Not much of a watchdog," Evan commented as he touched the fingerprint lock on his small gun safe.

"He's watching over Charlotte."

Evan chose the Glock over the SIG Sauer and grabbed an extra magazine.

Is this necessary?

The house fire two days ago flashed in his mind. Evan suspected someone had wanted to hurt the kids.

The gun was necessary.

"I want you to go into Charlotte's room and shut the door. If you hear anything, wake her, and both of you get in the closet and be silent." Evan unplugged his phone from the charger and tucked it in the waistband of his pajamas.

"I don't need to hide. I can shoot," whispered Theodore.

"I want you to keep your sister in her room. I know you can shoot, but the goal here is to not need to shoot. If I make some noise, they'll probably leave."

But first I want to see their faces.

If one was the person who had set fire to the kids' home, Evan wanted a good look at him.

This house didn't have an alarm. Evan lived in a sleepy neighborhood of well-maintained old homes. He had never felt the need for or even thought much about an alarm. Until tonight. Now he cared because he had two kids under his roof.

"But—" started Theodore.

"Do it."

"Yes, sir."

"Where's your cell phone?" Evan asked.

"Right here." Theodore had it in his hand.

"Call 911. Tell them there's someone in the house and someone outside. Also let them know I work for the sheriff's office, and I'm armed."

"Yes, sir." He dialed as he followed Evan down the hallway to Charlotte's room. Evan could barely make out her head against the pillow, but two black doggy eyes shone from the middle of the bed.

"Good dog," Evan whispered. Theodore entered the room, reluctance in his posture. Evan heard him speak softly to the dispatcher as he closed the door.

Okay. Where are you?

Evan padded silently down the stairs, straining to hear any odd noise. The kitchen was at the back of the house between a formal dining room and the family room. At the bottom of the stairs, turning right or left would eventually lead him to the kitchen. Evan moved toward the family room. He stopped every few feet and listened but heard no sounds coming from the kitchen.

Theodore had heard someone there; the creak was distinctive.

Evan rounded the corner from the hall and slipped into the family room. A few more steps and he'd have a view of the galley kitchen.

Silence.

Keeping against the far wall of the dark family room, Evan moved to see into the kitchen.

Empty. He had a clear view to the dining room beyond.

He must have gone back outside.

Evan continued along the far wall until he could see out the sliding glass door. He kept to the side of the door in the shadows, where he could see all of the patio and a good portion of the yard. The door's latch caught his eye. Unlocked. He was positive he'd locked it before bed.

Oreo.

The dog frequently needed to pee outside. One of the kids must have brought the dog down after Evan was asleep.

Little dog, little bladder.

He knew how someone had gotten in; now he wanted to know why.

From his hidden vantage point, he stared hard into the backyard. It was dark, with only the faintest light spilling from the streetlight at the front of the house into a small section of grass.

Something moved in the far corner of the yard. A dark figure against the pale wood of his fence. Definitely human.

They're outside.

But why back in that corner?

There was nothing in that part of the fenced yard.

Power cable.

Evan flipped the light switch to turn on the patio lights, and nothing happened.

Shit.

Evan locked the door and moved to the kitchen, tension ratcheting, checking the yard from each window, staring hard for another glimpse of the shadow or its companion. They'd vanished.

Could it be treasure hunters?

He had a copy of the notebook that was rapidly growing famous among the hunters.

But who knows I have it?

No matter the motivation, whoever was outside had signaled bad intentions by tampering with the power to Evan's home.

Who would do that to a law enforcement officer's house?

Someone desperate.

The sounds of far-off sirens reached Evan's ears. Relief swept over him, but he was frustrated he hadn't seen anyone's face. No doubt the two had started running the second they heard the sirens too. The police would have to search the neighborhood in the dark, and Evan had low expectations for their success.

BOOM!

An explosion sounded from upstairs, and Evan tore out of the family room back to the foyer.

A second explosion.

Gunshots.

Charlotte screamed as Oreo barked frantically.

"Kids!" Evan shouted. He rounded the corner into the foyer and had darted up two steps when a huge man leaped from the top of the stairs, his arms and legs spread wide.

He's flying. At me.

Evan raised the Glock and squeezed twice before the man crashed into him and slammed Evan backward onto the foyer floor. Evan's head hit the wood floor, and the man's impact on his chest knocked the wind out of him. He gasped for air as the man rolled off him, his hand on Evan's Glock. The intruder yanked.

Evan fired directly at the man's chest, and the man fell back, shrieking in pain. And then he went silent and limp.

His gun still pointed at the intruder, Evan rolled to his side and sat up. Something wet was on his face and he wiped his cheek, smelling the metallic scent of blood. The man didn't move. He was spread-eagled on his back. Evan crawled away, keeping his gun trained on the body, and then sat heavily on the stairs, fighting to catch his breath.

He was inside the entire time.

He went upstairs after the kids.

"Kids! You okay?" Evan yelled, not taking his gaze from the man.

The sirens were loud, and lights flashed from the front of Evan's home, highlighting the body with blue-and-red flickers. Evan stared at his face, unable to see clearly in the dark with the pulsating lights.

Why don't they answer?

Images of Charlotte limp and bleeding made him want to vomit.

"Kids?" he shouted again.

"Is he dead?" shouted Charlotte from the second story.

"Are you and Theodore okay?" Evan yelled back. "Is anyone else up there?"

"No, and we're fine. Theodore is talking to the police on the phone."

"Stay upstairs. Tell the police that the intruder is down right behind the front door, but there is still another outside. I don't know where."

The sirens suddenly stopped. The lights continued. Evan risked a glance up the stairs and saw the kids peeking around a corner, Charlotte clinging to the dog, and Theodore beside her with the cell phone to his ear.

"Tell them we need an ambulance," said Evan. Blood glistened on his hand, and he patted his chest and legs, searching for a wound. His adrenaline still pumping, he could be injured and not know it.

I don't think it's my blood.

"Tell the police I'm opening the front door," Evan said. "I'm not putting down my gun until someone else can come cover him." He waited until he heard Theodore repeat his words and then pushed to his feet. He shuffled across the foyer, never looking away from the intruder on the floor. He threw the locks and swung the door open. He was immediately hit with spotlights.

"I'm Detective Bolton!" he shouted, wincing at the light but keeping his attention on the immobile man. "One of the intruders is down. He's right here."

He waited for the officers to recognize him. He'd met most of the Bend police force at least once. He sensed two uniforms approaching but kept his gaze glued to the man, his gun pointed at his chest.

"Evan," said one of the officers, caution in his tone, "it's Steve Westcott. My partner and I are coming in."

Evan knew Sergeant Westcott from softball. "I haven't searched him, Steve. *Christ.* I haven't cleared the house either. Two kids upstairs." Proper police procedure had been the last thing on his mind.

"I see the kids," said Westcott, stepping in the door. He turned and yelled for more officers to come in. "Kids, you can come down now. I want both of you to walk straight out the door and to one of our cars."

"If you've got him covered, Detective, we'll start clearing the upper floor," said the second officer as more entered the home.

"I got him," said Evan, knowing the house needed to be checked for other suspects before they could attend to the man on the floor.

Two officers started to pass Theodore and Charlotte on the stairs. "Hang on, son. Whatcha got there?" asked one of the officers.

Evan glanced away from the body on the floor in time to see Theodore hand the officer Evan's SIG Sauer. "Theodore! I told you not to—" Evan froze as the kids approached, a realization hitting him. "Theodore, *did you fire that gun?*"

"Yeah. The intruder came into Charlotte's room. I'd already put her and Oreo in the closet."

Dizziness swamped Evan.

"You were supposed to be in the closet too," Evan muttered, knowing there was no point in lecturing the boy. The two kids gave the man on the floor a wide berth.

"He dropped a gun upstairs," said Theodore. "It's in the hallway."

"Did he fire?"

"No."

He brought a gun into my home.

"I'll take care of it in a minute," said Sergeant Westcott.

Charlotte paused in the doorway and looked back at Evan.

"Did he hurt you, Uncle Evan? There's blood on your shirt," she said.

"I'm fine. It's not my blood. Go outside." A quick glance out the door showed at least a half dozen patrol units lighting up his neighborhood. The kids left.

Westcott eyed the blood on Evan's shirt. "You sure?"

"Pretty sure."

"I'll search the suspect." Westcott gave Evan another once-over. "Then I want a medic to check you out."

Evan nodded. His head had stopped spinning, but he couldn't take a deep breath.

The sergeant crouched by the body and felt under his jaw. "He's got a pulse. Unconscious, though."

A weight lifted off Evan's shoulders.

I didn't kill him.

The sergeant started to check the man for weapons. "He's wearing a vest!"

"You're joking." Evan was stunned. No wonder the man hadn't stopped after he shot him while he leaped through the air.

"Nope. I can see three holes in his shirt. That from you or the boy?"

Evan tried to remember. "I got off two shots when he lunged at me off the stairs. And then another when he tried to take my gun. I heard two shots upstairs. Theodore didn't say if his shots hit him or not."

"His arm's bleeding. One of you got him outside the vest. Or he hurt himself. I'm not finding any weapons currently on him." Westcott rolled the man to his side and cuffed him.

Evan's arms were stiff as he lowered his gun. He stepped closer to the man and bent over to study his face in the flashing lights. Dark hair. Thirties or forties. And a beard.

Did he burn the kids' home?

"Know him?"

"No. But he fits the description of the man that tried to set fire to the kids' house the day before yesterday."

"I heard about that. Your niece and nephew, right? Their parents are missing."

"Found the dad. He's in the hospital."

"Good to hear."

Officers came down the stairs as two more entered the foyer from the family room. "House is clear, Sergeant."

"Good. Go check in with the neighborhood search for the other suspect. We've got a K9 unit coming," said Westcott. The men nodded and left.

Two EMTs entered, briefly blocking the lights. One knelt by the man and opened his kit as the other stopped and pointed at Evan's shirt. "You hurt?"

Evan was tired of the question. "No."

"Take off your shirt," ordered the EMT.

Evan slipped the T-shirt over his head and turned in a circle as the EMT shone a flashlight on his torso.

"Okay." The EMT joined his partner at the man on the floor. "Wait. This one of you? He's got on a vest." He glanced back at Evan and Westcott.

"Definitely not," said Evan.

"Looks like it saved his life," said the other EMT.

"He came prepared," said Westcott. "He must have known you would be armed. Risky. Why the hell would someone take such a chance? What did he want?"

"It has something to do with the kids . . . or their family. I don't know what." Evan was almost positive the man was the fire setter, which meant it had nothing to do with the Serranos' treasure-hunt notebook.

"What the hell?" muttered one of the EMTs as they worked on the man.

"Take it off," said the other.

"What is it?" asked Evan, trying to see over an EMT's shoulder.

"He's wearing a fake beard."

39

Mercy sipped her coffee, appreciating the heavy cream, as she watched Victor Kerr sleep.

Sleep? What is it called when they're in an induced coma?

She'd stopped for coffee before visiting Victor's hospital room. Mercy had been up half the night after hearing what had happened at Evan's home, unable to go back to sleep. An early-morning phone call to the hospital had told her Victor's condition was unchanged, but Mercy had come and sat by his bedside anyway. If the doctors decided to wake him, she wanted to be there.

She had questions.

So many questions.

Which he probably can't answer.

Evan was on his way over with the kids so they could see their father for the first time in weeks. Mercy studied Victor's face, trying to view it through the eyes of his children. His entire scalp was covered in bandages. His eyes were black and blue, his face covered with cuts and bruises. A half dozen tubes and wires connected him to machines. At least his jaw was in the right place now, but his mouth was wired shut.

Evan had prepared the kids. They knew what to expect.

It would still be a shock.

Doctors were guarded about Victor's prognosis. He would have more tests this morning to check the swelling on his brain. One doctor told her that the fact that Victor had made it through the night was a good sign.

Congrats. You didn't die overnight.

Mercy stood as Evan, Theodore, and Charlotte entered. They all had dark areas under their eyes, and Theodore had forgotten to comb his hair. The kids' gazes locked on their dad, and Charlotte froze, her hand tight in Evan's. Theodore thrust his hands into his front pockets and blinked hard as he stared at his father in the hospital bed. Mercy's eyes met Evan's and she saw doubt. He was questioning if he'd done the right thing in letting the kids see their father in this condition. Mercy knew it was right. Victor could die, so his kids deserved to see him.

"It's okay," Mercy told them. "You can get closer." She moved to stand near Victor's head and gestured at Charlotte. "Come talk to him." Charlotte dropped Evan's hand and approached. She was solemn, her eyes wide. She wore a sparkly mini backpack that Mercy recognized as a cast-off of Kaylie's. The eleven-year-old loved girly things.

She needs her mother.

They both do.

Charlotte tentatively laid a hand on Victor's upper arm. One of the few areas not covered in bandages. "Daddy? It's Charlotte." She leaned close to his ear and spoke clearly. Theodore had hesitated but now went to his father's other side. He made to touch his father's arm but pulled back, his gaze scanning his father's face.

"Tell him what—" Mercy stopped. She'd nearly suggested the kids tell their father what they'd been up to, but the recollection of their burning furniture and the attack in Evan's home made her stop. "Tell him you've missed him."

Theodore swallowed. "I've missed you, Dad." He glanced at Mercy, and she nodded encouragingly. "It's really sucked since you've been gone."

Truth.

"I'm glad you're back," Theodore said.

"Me too," echoed Charlotte. "Uncle Evan found a dog, and we've been taking care of it. His name is Oreo, and he sleeps on my bed at night. He's really tiny, so I think it'd be okay if we brought him home when you're better."

Mercy caught Evan's eye and he shrugged. She knew his attempts to reach any Serrano relatives about the dog had turned up empty. If the kids wanted the dog, they could probably keep it. Charlotte continued to talk about the dog, and Theodore gently set his hand on his father's arm, listening to his sister but intently watching his father's face.

Evan tipped his head at the door, and Mercy followed him out of the room. "I think they handled it well," he said with a questioning glance at Mercy. He needed confirmation.

"I agree. But watch them. They might have strong reactions later. It can't be easy for them to see him like this."

"I've never met the man, and it's tough to see," said Evan.

"How are the kids after last night?"

"They're holding up better than I expected. Both were impressed with the hotel's buffet breakfast, and I thought Charlotte would get sick from so many waffles. They haven't slept. Been awake since two a.m., so they'll crash this afternoon. I'm taking the day off."

"Understandable."

"Not letting them out of my sight until we find whoever was outside my house last night."

"Your suspect hasn't said anything?" Mercy asked.

"Nope. He came to while the EMTs were transporting him to the hospital, but he won't say one word. Not even *lawyer*. He's going to be released from the hospital in a couple of hours. He's got some broken ribs, and a bullet went through his arm, but they say he doesn't need to stay overnight for that. They were worried about a head injury, but tests ruled it out. He'll go straight to the county jail from here, and I hope fingerprints will tell us who he is. I've started to wonder if I'm jumping to conclusions and possibly the fire setter was a different guy."

"Logic says it's the same guy," said Mercy. "The kids are the common denominator in both crimes. He went to their bedrooms. Clearly he was interested in the children, not you. But it's not certain."

"I've considered that he was interested in the treasure-hunter notes, but I think you're right about it being the kids." He rubbed his forehead. "I'm exhausted and thinking in circles. The kids aren't the only ones who will nap later."

"Did you figure out which shot missed your intruder's vest and wounded him?"

Evan grimaced. "I'm not positive, but I think Theodore's did. He told me he fired one shot over the guy's head and then fired directly at him when the first shot didn't make him leave. I got off three shots that I thought were directly at his chest, but there's a bullet hole in my foyer's ceiling, so I suspect I missed one of the first ones. It's a blur. He was coming right at me from above. If my weapon hadn't already been out, I wouldn't have had time to draw it."

"Good shooting for Theodore. That's hard to do in a stressful situation," said Mercy.

"Tell me about it."

"Any word on the second person who was there?"

"No. The K9 followed a scent to a street a block away and then couldn't pick it up again. Most likely the person got in a vehicle. They're checking video from nearby home security systems to see if one caught the car or suspect."

"Hopefully the guy you caught will talk and give him up."

"He *will* talk," Evan said firmly.

"Will you ask the kids to look at him and to see if they agree he was the man who set the fire at their house?" questioned Mercy.

"I think I'll show them some pictures instead. I don't want them around him."

"Or Kaylie could take a look. She saw him."

"Pictures will have to do for her too. You heard about the fake beard he wore last night, right?"

"Yes," said Mercy. "I'd like to hear his reasons for that."

Evan glanced at his watch. "Can you stay with the kids for a few minutes? I want to see him to take photos before they transport him to the jail."

Mercy checked on the kids. They'd both pulled up chairs to their father's bedside, and Charlotte was still talking. "I'd like to come with you. Maybe an FBI badge will encourage him to talk." She gestured to a nurse headed their way. "We'll be back in five minutes," she told the nurse. "Is it okay to leave the kids with their dad for a bit?"

"I'm about to take his vitals and change some bandages, so I'll be in there. I'll stick around until you come back."

"Perfect. We'll hurry." Mercy led Evan away before he could change his mind about letting the kids out of his sight. They took the elevator. "This guy went after the kids, and there's a good chance he's the man that set the fire," she said. "To me that means he *might* be involved in their parents' disappearances too, so I want to talk to him." She frowned. "I wonder if he knows that Victor isn't in that pit any longer."

"Now you're jumping to conclusions. There's nothing concrete linking him to Victor," said Evan. "I'm only operating with half a brain this morning, but even I can see that."

"No conclusions," said Mercy. "I'm thinking out loud." They exited on a different floor, and she followed Evan down a hall. The mystery man's room was obvious because of the police officer in a chair beside the door. He spotted them immediately and stood.

"Detective," he greeted Evan.

Mercy showed him her ID. He did a surprised double take at it and then looked at her face, making her wonder if he'd heard stories about her. She'd had a few notorious cases since joining the Bend FBI a few years ago.

Evan opened the door, and she followed him into the small room. The patient was watching TV and ignored them.

Mercy stared, confusion ricocheting through her brain.

"Hello, Alex. Funny seeing you here," she managed to say.

Alex's gaze whipped from the TV to her face. Surprise and then anger flashed in his eyes.

"You know him?" asked Evan.

"That is Alex Kerr," Mercy said, keeping her tone level. "He's Victor's cousin. I interviewed him a few days ago about the missing Kerrs."

"But . . ." Evan blinked hard, words apparently escaping him. He shook his head as if to loosen the cobwebs.

Mercy felt the same way.

Alex came after Theodore and Charlotte with a gun. And possibly set a fire in their home.

Why?

She thought through her meeting with Alex.

Wait . . .

"Was his cane found at the scene?" she asked Evan.

"Cane? Not that I'm aware of."

Mercy turned a thoughtful gaze on the man in the hospital bed. "A fake beard and a fake cane? I assume the limp isn't real either. Does it depend on who you want to be that day? Or who you're trying to mislead?"

Alex said nothing and turned his attention back to the TV.

"Outside," Mercy told Evan. If she stayed in the room, she might blurt out a dozen questions that should be handled in an interview room. Evan didn't move, his gaze still locked on Alex Kerr, dozens of different emotions flickering through his eyes. Mercy took his arm and pulled him out.

"Victor's cousin broke into my house?" Evan muttered in the hallway. He looked dumbstruck.

"I intend to find out what else he's done," said Mercy. "I want to officially interview him. He might be involved with Bridget and Molly's disappearance."

At the mention of his sister, Evan appeared to pull himself together. "I'll set it up right away."

Mercy pulled out her phone. "I'll get the ball rolling on a warrant to search his home." Her hands shook from the adrenaline that had been dumped in her system thirty seconds ago. Finding the kids' mom and little sister suddenly felt closer than at any previous point in her investigation.

This may be the break I need.

40

Truman parked in front of the Eagle's Nest police station and sighed as he saw who was pacing on the sidewalk. The man spotted Truman and halted, watching expectantly as Truman turned off his vehicle and sat there, taking a long sip from the coffee he'd just bought after his lunch. Truman wanted to back out and leave.

He wasn't in the mood for a Tim Giles conversation.

But Truman got out of the vehicle and approached Tim. The man looked as if he was fighting the urge to run—as he'd done when he'd spotted Truman and Evan at his apartment door. But he stood his ground and even made eye contact.

"Morning, Chief," said Tim, shifting from one foot to the other.

Mildly shocked at the greeting, Truman stopped, wondering what was making Tim simultaneously squirm and be polite. "What can I do for you, Tim?"

The man cast a quick glance around the area. "Can we talk inside? This is private."

Truman took a deliberate look at the deserted street and then headed for the door, motioning for Tim to follow. Inside, he greeted Lucas, who raised a questioning brow as he spotted Tim. Truman gave a minuscule one-shoulder shrug.

He had no idea what the man wanted.

Truman strode down the hall to his office, wondering what would motivate Tim Giles to approach him. He sat in his chair and pointed at another across the desk from him. Tim tentatively perched on the edge of the chair and gripped his hands in his lap. And then moved them to the chair arms. And then back to his lap as he looked around at the photos on Truman's walls.

Truman waited a few seconds to see if Tim would speak first. He didn't. "This is private," Truman told the nervous man.

"I see that." Tim cleared his throat and focused on Truman, looking ready to speak. "I got a buddy who works at the hospital in Bend."

"He's a doctor?"

"No. He's sort of an orderly. Does whatever's needed. Mostly pushing people around in wheelchairs and stocking and running errands."

"Is your friend in trouble?" asked Truman.

"Oh, no. That's not it at all." Tim shifted his hands back to the chair arms. "Remember I told you about a man I'd seen near the bed-and-breakfast where that guy was killed?"

"Billy Serrano is the name of the man who was killed," stated Truman. "Yeah, you told Detective Bolton and me that the guy you saw there was a treasure hunter. You tried to spy on him."

Tim didn't even look abashed at Truman's last comment. "That's the one. The other hunters didn't like him. No one likes him. Works alone and won't talk to anyone. Well, my buddy at the hospital is also deep into the treasure hunt, and says this guy was admitted overnight with a gunshot wound."

Truman went still, knowing about the shooting at Evan's home. "How'd he get shot?" he asked.

He can't be talking about the same guy.

"A cop shot him. The guy broke into his house." Tim shook his head. "Now *that's* stupid—breaking into a cop's house."

"No more stupid than trying to break into a police station."

Tim slouched, his gaze on the floor. "You know I was drunk. Anyway, my buddy is positive the guy in the hospital is the guy I saw near the B and B."

"But *you* haven't seen the patient yet. How would your friend recognize someone you saw?"

"Because he was with me when I followed him one time, trying to get a leg up on the clues. All the hunters have seen that guy. Everyone thinks he's an asshole."

"Okay." Truman leaned back in his chair, considering Tim's story. The man felt strongly enough about it to face Truman. Or mislead him. "The other day you mentioned he had a beard."

"He had one. Dave said he shaved it off."

"But he still recognized him without it."

"Yup."

Truman was silent, watching Tim continue to squirm. The man couldn't sit still. "Anything else?"

"Nope."

"I'll pass on your story to Detective Bolton." He stood to let Tim know the session was over. But Tim didn't move.

"Ummm." He fidgeted like a kindergartner. "Any chance there's ummm . . . you know . . . a reward if that's the guy who killed Serrano?"

"Not that I'm aware of."

Tim deflated but stood. "Okay. Hope it helps."

Truman watched him leave and then called Evan.

"I've got an interesting theory for you. Remember Tim Giles?" Truman asked.

"How could I forget?" said Evan.

"He believes your intruder is the man he saw near Sandy's B and B talking to Billy Serrano. He's got a buddy in the hospital who is positive about it."

"You know the intruder has been identified, right?" asked Evan.

"No. I hadn't heard."

"When did you last talk to Mercy?"

"Early this morning. Right before she headed to the hospital."

"She's the one who ID'd him," said Evan. "His name is Alex Kerr. He's Victor Kerr's cousin."

Truman tried to fit the pieces together. "Charlotte and Theodore's relative broke into your house? With a gun?"

"Exactly. And now you're saying he could be a suspect in my Billy Serrano case."

"Tim Giles is saying it, and believe it or not, he felt credible to me. Or at least he truly believes what he's saying."

"Alex Kerr refuses to speak. I don't think he'll admit to shooting Billy Serrano—wait."

Truman waited.

"Kerr dropped a weapon at my house." Excitement rang in Evan's voice. "I'll have forensics compare it to the bullet and casing from the Serrano scene."

"How long will that take?"

"Shit. Too long."

"What about a private lab?"

"I'll run it by my boss. I've got no suspects on either Billy's or Meghan's death, so I think he'll authorize it. I'd like to find out if Alex Kerr is involved while we still have him in custody."

"I'm struggling to believe that the person who murdered the treasure hunters could be the same one who terrorized your niece and nephew. How do those crimes connect?" asked Truman.

"To make it more complicated, Mercy suggested a third link," said Evan. "She thinks if Alex Kerr went after Theodore and Charlotte twice that he may be involved in their parents' disappearances."

Truman's brain spun.

"Victor can't talk or write, so even if he was awake, he can't tell us who beat the crap out of him," said Evan. "But the doctors are going to ease off some of the medications keeping him sedated to see if he'll come around. If he's lucid enough, I might be able to get a nod or shake of the head if I present him with a name. They ran some scans on his head this morning and are very pleased with the results."

"That's fantastic."

"I'm going to stick around, see how he does. Mercy took off a while ago. She's waiting on a search warrant for Alex Kerr's home, but she wanted to be ready to go with an evidence team the second it was approved."

"I assume she's looking for something to lead to your sister and Molly," said Truman.

"Yes. Or that indicates Alex was involved in Victor Kerr's injuries." Evan paused. "I'm trying not to get my hopes up about my sister," he said in a quiet voice. "But damn, I hope this is the key."

"I'm pulling for you," said Truman. "And for those kids."

"Thanks," said Evan.

The call ended, and Truman sat for a long moment, tapping a pen on his desk as he tried to process what they'd learned in the last twenty-four hours.

Someone had severely beaten Victor Kerr and presumably left him to die.

The man who'd broken into Evan's home and gone into Charlotte's bedroom with a gun was a relative, Alex Kerr.

Alex Kerr may have tried to burn down their home.

Alex Kerr might be a treasure hunter who had killed Billy Serrano. And therefore possibly Meghan Serrano.

Since Alex Kerr had used violence to get to the children, he might be involved in their parents' disappearances.

It appeared Alex Kerr could be a one-man crime spree.

But there was a second person at Evan's last night. Who?

Truman thought about how Tim Giles had nervously sat in his office and pointed at Alex Kerr for the murder of Billy Serrano.

The three of them were treasure hunters. In a cutthroat game that promised millions.

Some hunters had already proved they'd do *anything* to win.

Would one rat out a treasure-hunting partner to get them out of the way to the prize?

Truman stood and grabbed his hat.

I already know where Tim Giles lives.

41

Mercy sat on the bumper of her SUV tapping her fingers against the vehicle, energy simmering under her skin. She'd pulled off the rural highway three miles from the Kerr ranch and parked, waiting for her warrant to search Alex Kerr's home to be approved and signed by the judge. Eddie would email her a copy the minute it was signed and then bring the original to the ranch. A team of crime scene techs was on standby. But Mercy wanted to be there first.

The day was warm and blue, with a mild breeze that felt cheerful. It was the wrong weather for the job she was about to do. It should be overcast and gray. Depressing. Ominous.

Please be the link to Bridget and Molly.

She stood and walked through the gravel, kicking at bigger rocks. A pickup slowed as the driver assessed her situation. Mercy shook her head at him, smiled, and waved him on. He waved back and sped up.

Two people had already stopped to see if she needed help.

Country life.

She walked around her SUV, imagining all the different ways the search could go. Some good. Some bad. The layout of the property was fixed in her brain. The big farmhouse. Barn. Outbuildings. Alex's mobile home.

Alex's home wasn't in sight of the main house, where Christine and Linda lived. It was at the back of the property, as if it had been added as an afterthought. She recalled how his demeanor had tightened as he mentioned his divorce. It'd been a brief flash of anger but had shown that his anger could rise quickly, almost instantaneously.

Who else has seen that anger?

Possibly Victor. Alex's actions toward Victor's children could indicate anger at the parents. Making him her first suspect in Victor's disappearance.

But why is he angry?

Victor's father, Jack, had been the first black sheep of the family, harassed by his brothers, who were jealous of their mother's attention and Jack's natural abilities.

Would that hate carry down to the sons?

Alex and Victor were first cousins. Alex had claimed they'd been friends as they grew older but had then grown apart. Alex had also said he hadn't seen Victor in forever.

Mercy believed that was a lie.

It was a feeling in her gut. The moment she'd made eye contact with Alex in his hospital bed and he'd refused to speak, she'd known he'd tortured Victor.

Please let Bridget and Molly be safe.

Most likely, Christine and Linda didn't know that Alex was in the hospital. He'd spoken to no one and hadn't requested a phone call since he'd been caught. His silence spoke volumes about his crime the night before.

Does Christine know her son has been stalking Theodore and Charlotte?

Alex must have been aware of the children's existence as he sat in Mercy's office and never said a word about them, so it was possible Christine and Linda knew about them too. And also never mentioned them during their conversations with Mercy.

Or they knew nothing.

And then there was the touchy subject of the one-third of Ethel Kerr's estate that should have gone to her third son, Jack, or his heirs: Victor, Theodore, Charlotte, and Molly.

"I can't rule out money," mumbled Mercy. She'd found that money, power, and sex were usually the motivations for crimes.

She checked for any missed phone calls.

How much longer for the warrant?

Mercy got back in her vehicle and turned on the music, searching for a distraction. She pulled a file folder out of her bag and opened it to look at a photo of Bridget Kerr. The image was grainy, taken from a DMV record of her driver's license photo back when she was still Bethany Bolton.

She recalled that neither Christine nor Linda had asked to see a photo of the missing Bridget. Nor had Alex.

Mercy had assumed they'd tell her if any strange women had knocked on their door.

Never assume.

"Shit." Mercy started her vehicle. She wanted Linda and Christine to see the photo even if it was old and grainy. They didn't need to know she was about to search Alex's home for evidence to connect him to Victor Kerr's torture. And for the missing Bridget and Molly.

"Follow-up visit and questions," she said to her reflection in the rearview mirror, practicing a casual smile. She wouldn't call ahead. She wanted the women surprised, not prepared.

Does that mean no cookies?

A few minutes later, she parked in front of the big farmhouse. With the picture in her bag, she climbed the steps to the covered porch and rang the doorbell. A minute later she rang it again and knocked loudly.

Dammit.

Mercy headed back down the steps and decided to walk around to the back of the house. There was the deck with the table and umbrella where she had shared cookies and spiked iced tea with the women. Taking a faint path toward one of the outbuildings, she spotted Linda Kerr riding in an arena. The tall woman sat perfectly straight in a Western saddle as the large pinto moved at an impossibly slow jog. It wasn't a lazy trot; it was a slow, precise movement, the horse's head and neck in a perfect position.

Mercy recognized the skill. She'd attended enough horse shows in her past.

Linda spotted her and immediately turned the horse in her direction, holding one hand to shade her eyes. A second later she waved. "Hello, Agent Mercy!"

Mercy returned the greeting and stopped at the arena fence. The scents of horse and dry dirt reached her. Good scents. Ones that reminded her of her parents' farm and all the time she'd spent with the horses as a kid. The pinto approached and exhaled through his nose at her, his ears forward, an interested look in his eyes. She petted the velvety nose, wishing she could reach far enough through the boards to run a hand along his beautiful neck.

"What brings you out today?" Linda asked. She dismounted and led the horse along the fence toward the small stable. Mercy followed on the other side.

"Just some follow-up questions. I rang the bell at the house, but no one answered. Is Christine around too?"

"Yes, she should be at the house. What time is it?"

"Almost one."

"She's probably napping, then, but I bet the doorbell woke her. Give her ten minutes and she'll be functional," Linda said with a grin. Inside the stable, she slid a halter over the horse's bridle and grabbed the crosstie on each side of the aisle, hooking them on the halter. The horse secure, she turned to Mercy. "What are your questions?"

Mercy pulled the low-quality photo out of her bag. "I primarily wanted you to look at this. I forgot to show you a picture of Bridget Kerr last time I was here."

Linda took the paper, and Mercy studied her face.

The woman considered the photo for a long moment and then shook her head. "I'm sorry. She doesn't look familiar to me." She handed the photo back to Mercy. "Is that an old picture?"

"Yes, but it's all we have."

"I'll call Chrissy and make sure she's up," said Linda, removing her phone from her shirt pocket. "If she is, you can show it to her." She touched the screen and held the phone to her ear.

Mercy decided to indulge herself and pet the horse's neck. Warm animal. Smooth hair.

I miss horses.

"You up?" Linda asked into the phone. "Yes, that was the FBI agent, Mercy. She's here in the stable with me." A pause. "She's got a photo for you to look at." She gave Mercy a small nod. "I'll send her up. Put out that new batch from yesterday." She ended the call, slid the phone back in her pocket, and turned her attention to a buckle on the bridle. "Go ahead. I'll come up as soon as I put Picasso away. I've got cookies from a new recipe for your professional taste buds to sample."

"I'm not the pro." Mercy laughed. "I'd be happy with those chocolate chip ones again."

"Still have those too."

Mercy strode out of the stable and back to the big house, noticing that her hand carried the scent of horse on it. More memories emerged. She and Rose on horseback in the woods. As long as her horse had another to follow, Rose could ride anywhere and through anything.

More kids should grow up with horses.

She checked her phone for a message from Eddie about the warrant. Nothing. A few minutes later she knocked on the front door to the big house. It was opened almost instantly by Christine.

"Come in! Come in! I'm sorry I was asleep."

"And I'm sorry I woke you," said Mercy, trailing the smiley woman through the house to the kitchen.

"Linda wanted you to try these." Christine grabbed a plastic food storage container off the counter and handed it to Mercy. "Will you carry this for me? I put some iced tea outside, and I'm sure Linda won't be long." She opened a cupboard and grabbed tiny floral plates and some napkins. "Linda made black-and-white cookies. It's her first time. I think the white icing isn't quite right, but she disagrees."

Mercy glanced out the window and saw a pitcher and glasses on the wrought iron table. Staying for cookies hadn't been on her agenda, but her last visit had been enlightening. This was a good opportunity to gently prod them for more information about Alex. She studied Christine and decided she didn't know her son had been arrested and was currently in the hospital. She was her chipper self, her smile in full force. Although she had a bit of bedhead going on and her eyes looked as if she hadn't quite woken up all the way.

Christine ushered her out to the deck and poured a tall glass of iced tea for each of them. Mercy eyed the glass, wondering how much bourbon it held. She took a careful sip.

Way too strong.

"Christine, do you mind if I get a glass of water? I want to be able to drive back to town."

Christine was setting out the plates and folding the napkins into intricate shapes. "Go right ahead. I won't take it personally." She laughed. "The glasses are in the cupboard next to the sink."

Mercy reentered the house. The kitchen was dated but immaculately clean. The refrigerator and dishwasher looked new, but the range was an avocado-colored relic. Mercy opened the cupboard by the sink, grabbed a glass, and used the water tap on the fridge. She watched her glass fill.

Wait.

What did I just see?

She set her half-filled glass on the counter and opened the cupboard again. On the second shelf, above the regular glasses, were two sippy cups. One with Big Bird and one with Elmo.

Mercy stared.

Neither woman has grandkids. The cups are right in front. Not pushed to the back or on a top shelf as if rarely used.

Molly.

Mercy shut the cupboard and stood motionless for a long second, her mind processing what she'd seen.

Go. Get backup. Now.

She went to the sliding glass door. "Christine? I'm sorry, but I got a text and need to get back to the office."

"Oh! I'm sorry too. Let me send some cookies with you." Christine dumped several cookies onto a plate and carried it toward the door.

Mercy stepped aside to allow the woman to pass and surveyed the kitchen and dining room, searching for other hints that the two women weren't living alone.

"I'll put them in a baggie, and you can be on your way."

As Christine bustled around in the kitchen, Mercy slowly backed away to where she had a line of sight to the front door.

"Here you go." The woman gave her a big smile. "Let Linda know what you think."

Mercy took the baggie, thanked her, and passed through the living room toward the front door.

The floor creaked behind her, and a blow to the back of her head felt as if it cracked her skull. Mercy dropped to her knees, her vision tunneled, and she dropped the cookies as she reached for her weapon.

Another blow and then stars flashed in her sight.

And then nothing.

42

Truman was halfway to Tim Giles's home when Ina Smythe called. He pressed a button on his steering wheel.

"Hello, Ina. How are you doing?" he answered.

"Good, good. My back's bothering me, but that's nothing new."

He was pleased that her voice was chipper. He knew she had good days and bad with her back, hips, and knees. Today appeared to be one of the good ones. "What can I do for you?"

"You told me to look at forestry and trail maps of the areas I went with Rolly."

Their conversation of two days ago popped back into Truman's head. "Did any of the location names seem familiar?" He'd nearly forgotten he'd asked her to pinpoint any areas that might have special meaning to Chester Rollins.

"Oh, they're all familiar. When you live in the same place all your life, you encounter everything at least once."

"That is true."

"But one did jump out. I've spent the last day and a half stretching this old memory of mine to determine why it caught my eye."

"And?"

"I went online to find pictures of the location, and sure enough I'm positive I went there with Rolly at least twice. It looks different now. The trail's been improved and railings were added. Even has a bathroom at the trailhead. But I know we were there, and I remember how Rolly loved the viewpoint."

"That's great." Truman turned off the rural highway. "Where?"

"The viewpoint is called Angel's Rest. It rang a bell as soon as I saw the name. Rolly said it was named after me." She chuckled. "He was always calling me his angel. I have to say, this search has brought back a lot of memories. One time up there we found a wide, flat rock that was far off the trail. We knew no one would come across us, so—"

"Ina . . . is this a detail I need to hear?" Truman twitched his shoulders, not caring for the mental image the grandmotherly woman was creating.

She chortled. "I guess not. But I remember Angel's Rest made an impression on him."

"Anywhere else?"

"I'm still going through the maps. I'll let you know if there is more."

"Great. I really appreciate it and—"

"One other thing. I misremembered about his baby. I had it mixed up."

"He didn't have a child with someone?" Truman asked.

"Oh, he did. But it was a boy, not a girl. Another friend had a baby girl around the same time."

"You're positive?"

"Yep. Swear on my grave. I gotta go now. Company is at the door."

"Thanks, Ina." Truman ended the call and had five seconds to process Ina's information before a call from Eddie, Mercy's FBI cohort, lit up his screen.

"Hey, Eddie," he answered.

"Any chance Mercy is with you?" asked Eddie.

"No, I think she's at the hospital."

"She's not answering her phone. I got the warrant she wanted. She'd texted me about it a half dozen times, asking if it was ready, and now I'm at the site. The search is underway, and I still can't reach her."

"Warrant for what?" asked Truman.

"Search warrant for Alex Kerr's home and vehicles."

"I heard about that. I haven't talked to her, but Evan Bolton told me she ID'd him this morning."

"My calls are going straight to voice mail."

"Sounds like she's out of cell range."

"For as impatient as she was to get this warrant, I don't think she'd spend that much time in an area where I couldn't reach her to say it was ready."

Truman agreed. He knew the cellular dead spots in his county. Everyone did.

"Hang on," he told Eddie as he pulled to the side of the road. He shifted into park and grabbed his phone to open the app that tracked his family.

Ollie and Kaylie popped up within ten seconds. Kaylie was at the coffee shop, and Ollie was at Burger King. Mercy's locator flashed her position of two hours ago and then went blank. Her little icon spun, stating NO LOCATION FOUND. Over and over and over. Truman refreshed the screen three times.

NO LOCATION FOUND.

What did it say before it vanished?

Truman closed his eyes, concentrating on what he'd seen.

Abbotswell Road. It was far out of town.

"She's not showing on my locator," he told Eddie.

"I know that happens sometimes and usually isn't a big deal, but that doesn't mean I like it," said Eddie, his voice hard.

Eddie was like a brother to Mercy. He'd been crushed when she vanished the year before.

"Before it updated to 'No location found,' it briefly showed her on Abbotswell Road."

"That's about a mile from here. She must have been on the way at that time."

"She wouldn't have gone before getting the warrant," said Truman.

"Not into the home, but she would go and pace around outside since Alex is in the hospital. I don't understand why she's not here. What would make her go somewhere else?"

"Good question. I hope she soon realizes she's out of cellular range."

"We'll probably be done here in the next couple hours. I can't believe she's missing this."

"I'm sure she'll show up. I'll head over so I'm there when she arrives," said Truman as he made a U-turn. Uncertainty itched under his skin.

This isn't like Mercy.

Tim Giles can wait.

43

"What the hell were you *thinking*?"

"What was I *supposed* to do?"

"You should have used your brain! Look what you've gotten us into!"

Footsteps passed by Mercy's head, making the floor quiver as she fought to clear the cobwebs in her brain. She was on her belly, her hands tied behind her back. She opened one eye a sliver and saw dark-green carpet.

The back of her head throbbed.

Christine.

The woman had hit her. Twice.

Mercy was in the Kerrs' living room, her cheek pressed into the rug and her shoulders aching from the position of her hands.

Christine was arguing with Linda.

"I'm positive she saw the sippy cups. I had to do something to keep her from leaving. I'm not letting all Alex's work go to waste. This family comes first."

I was right.

"We need that money. We *deserve* it," Christine told Linda. "Jack's antisocial son doesn't deserve it."

Victor.

"That loser left society. Wanted to be on his own and live off the land. He doesn't need the money."

This must be about Ethel's will.

Mercy had been right. The women didn't want to give Jack Kerr's third of the inheritance to his descendants.

"My Alex risked everything last night, and I don't know if he's alive or dead! I've been combing social media and calling news stations trying to find out what happened. No one will say anything!"

Mercy kept her eyes closed, surprised that Christine hadn't heard that Alex was alive and in the hospital. And in a lot of hot water.

"Well, either he's *dead* or he's hurt," said Linda, making Christine wail. "I appreciate what you two tried to do, but you've fucked up on a massive scale."

"We were doing what's best for the family. The motto has always been to protect the family at *all costs*. If Alex is hurt, I know he'd never say a word against us. He'd take our secrets to the grave."

In this case, that's not an admirable quality.

Rug fibers tickled her nose, and she imperceptibly shifted to relieve it.

Just how many secrets do these women need taken to the grave?

"Well, then *where is he?*" asked Linda. "We can't do this on our own." She sighed, and a boot nudged Mercy's thigh. "What the fuck did you think we could do with an *FBI agent?*"

"I *had* to stop her."

"I get that."

"Then why are you talking to me like that?" Christine's voice was full of tears. "I didn't know what else to do."

Someone kicked her ribs, and Mercy grunted.

"I thought you were awake," said Linda, crouching near Mercy's head, a rifle in her hands. "You've caused a big complication."

"Someone will be looking for me soon. They know where I am," Mercy said, half into the carpet. Speaking made small flashes appear on the backs of her eyelids. It was tough to enunciate, and every inch of her head ached.

"I don't believe you," said Linda. "If they were on their way, you wouldn't say that, hoping they'll surprise us."

She's right.

"Why are you here?" Linda asked.

"To show the picture," Mercy mumbled, trying to move her mouth as little as possible to keep pain from shooting through her brain.

"Bullshit. What happened to Alex?" asked Linda.

"Dunno."

"What are we going to do with her?" whispered Christine.

"We?" asked Linda. "*You* created this problem! You and that hothead son of yours."

"We did it for all of us!"

"Shut up and let me think!" Linda paced in a small circle.

Christine went quiet.

"Right now it doesn't matter what your intentions were. You've got an FBI agent who knows you hit her in the head and tied her up." Linda stopped and glared at her sister. "You think that'll just go away?"

"No," Christine said softly.

"Damn right. Let's get her downstairs for now, and we'll figure it out later. I'll move her vehicle. At least you did one thing right by taking a hammer to her phone. Grab a shoulder."

The women grabbed her under her armpits and dragged her across the carpet. Mercy thrashed, determined to fight. These women would go to far lengths to protect themselves, and that meant nothing good for her.

"Hold still!" Christine lost her grip on Mercy's shoulder, and Linda pulled up harder on the other shoulder. Mercy flailed about, getting her knees underneath her. She tried to pull a foot forward and push to her feet but fell back to her knees.

I need to headbutt. Bite. Knock them over. Do something.

Something slammed into the back of her head, and explosions went off behind her eyes.

Then dark again.

44

Someone was singing.

Hush, little baby, don't say a word . . .

Her eyes closed, Mercy relaxed, willing her excruciating headache to go away. Her pillow was hard and bulky. No wonder her head hurt.

They hit me.

Her eyes flew open and met the kind gaze of a young woman. She sat on the floor in the small room, a toddler on her lap. Mercy abruptly pushed herself up, ignoring the pain shooting through her brain, unable to look away.

"You're Bethany Bolton." The words spilled out of her mouth.

She's alive.

Shock made the woman's eyes widen. "I was. Now I'm Bridget Kerr. How did you know that? Who are you?"

Overwhelming relief made Mercy's arms weak, and she lay back down on the floor. "I've been looking for you; everyone's been looking for you." Her sentences ran together. "We didn't know if you were dead or hiding or what."

"Who are you?" Bridget's voice shot up an octave.

"FBI," Mercy said, closing her eyes as the room started to slowly spin. "My name's Mercy and—oh! Your kids are fine! They're staying with Evan." She blinked and refocused on the woman, seeing hints of

Charlotte in her face. The blonde toddler simply stared at Mercy, her expression blank.

"Evan? My brother? He's with Charlotte and Theodore?" Bridget's voice cracked. "What about Victor? *Where's Victor?* Alex wouldn't tell me what he did with him."

"Your husband is in the hospital. He's been roughed up."

"You saw him?" Tears streamed down Bridget's face. "What happened? What did Alex do to him?"

"Alex Kerr is responsible?" asked Mercy. Her brain was slow, trying to put the pieces together. "I'd suspected that, but I wasn't sure. Victor's got some broken fingers. And a broken jaw. I'll be honest with you. He has a head injury, and I don't know how serious it is. I do know Alex left him to die. He was found in the bottom of a lava tube, dehydrated and unconscious, but he's getting the best care now."

Bridget rested her lips on top of Molly's head and squeezed the little girl until she squirmed in protest. Soft sobs came from the mother. Molly turned, looking up at Bridget's face, and set a small hand against her wet cheek. "I'm okay, honey," Bridget whispered. "Everyone is okay. Charlotte and Theodore and your daddy. We're going to get out of here."

"How long have you been here?" Mercy asked. The spinning had subsided, and she pushed up to a sitting position. She checked for her phone and weapon. Both were gone. So were her shoes. She was in a room the size of a small bedroom without any windows or chairs or a bed. A few small, thin cushions were spread on the concrete floor, and Mercy stared at the odd cushions, a memory prickling. They were covered in faded fabric with palm trees and parrots.

Cushions for deck chairs.

Mercy had sat on the hard metal chairs as she ate cookies.

While Bridget and Molly were kept prisoner.

They were locked in the basement while the sisters entertained me upstairs.

284

Mercy's stomach churned. She'd been so close.

"Depends what day it is," Bridget said with a harsh laugh. "It feels like I've been here for months."

"According to your kids, it's been almost three weeks since you left."

"I've been here that entire time," Bridget said. "These fucking people are crazy. Victor had always said they were selfish, violent bastards, but I'd assumed he was a bit biased. Instead, he was absolutely right."

"You're talking about Christine and Linda?" Mercy asked.

"And Alex. The whole family is rotten to the core. It was bred into them." Hate and anger infused her tone, her words clipped. "I was so naive."

Mercy continued to take stock of the room. A mini fridge sat in a corner, boxes of crackers and cereal on top. A large heap of colorful toys were piled in another. Several children's books, the kind with hard pages, ideal for toddlers, were stacked on top of a box of diapers.

She's been locked in this room with Molly for weeks?

Mercy shuddered. The lack of windows was disorienting. She had no idea of the time or how long she'd been unconscious. She recalled Linda had mentioned a downstairs. No wonder she felt as if they were buried. Mercy sniffed. The room smelled of dirty diapers. She glanced back and saw a limp garbage bag on the floor with several small bulges that must be the used diapers. Next to it was a large bucket with a lid.

Is that her toilet?

She looked back to Bridget, who nodded. "Yes, that's what you're thinking it is. And I'm sorry if it smells bad in here. I've gotten used to it. They usually wait about five days before swapping out the bucket, but I think it's gone longer this time."

Mercy's bladder abruptly woke up.

I can't. Not yet anyway.

"Baby wipes have been my salvation," Bridget said. "I've kept both of us pretty clean with those, but my hair feels disgusting." She touched her scalp.

"Do they feed you?" Mercy asked.

"Yes. They're pretty good about making sure we have plenty of food. I take that as a sign that they'll eventually let us go."

Mercy thought of Victor in the bottom of the lava tube. No one had let him go.

"The hard part is entertaining her." Bridget bounced Molly on her lap, the child's expression still somber. "I read books over and over. We sing songs, do yoga and as much physical activity as we can." She lowered her voice. "But she's stopped talking. She didn't have a lot of words . . . maybe twenty or so, but she'd at least prattle. She doesn't even do that now." Bridget wiped a tear from her cheek. "I don't know how much longer we can do this. They've told me they'll give us some of the money if I don't tell anyone or the police that they've held me here. They believe it will keep me quiet. That's bullshit. I will do everything I can to put them in prison for this. So I lie and tell them I will keep silent for the money."

Ethel's estate. A third of that belongs to Victor anyway.

"How generous of them," Mercy said dryly. "How did you connect with the women in the first place?"

"I knocked on their door." Bridget grimaced. "But I went to Evan's first—"

"*What?* Evan said he hasn't seen you in fourteen years!"

"That's true. All I did was leave a note—I wasn't sure how he felt about me for leaving and never getting in touch."

Mercy stared. "Where did you leave a note?"

"On his vehicle in his driveway."

"He never found it. It must have blown away."

"I pinned it with a windshield wiper. There's no way it could have blown off." Bridget's face crumpled. "Assuming he'd found that note was the one thing that was keeping me sane in here. I'd hoped he'd try to find Victor for me."

"You didn't know where Victor went? Why did you instruct your kids to tell people he'd died? They felt very guilty for sharing that secret with us. Theodore was furious with Charlotte for telling—but she did it at the right time. We needed to know."

Bridget covered her eyes with one hand. "Bless them. They're such good kids. I feel horrible that we put that burden on them."

"They *are* good kids. I agree completely. And they've formed a tight bond with Evan."

Bridget cried again. "I'm so glad. It's been so hard for me to stay away all these years. I loved my brother dearly. Still do."

"You'll have to tell me why you never contacted your family, but first I want to know why you couldn't find Victor."

"I wasn't positive where he went. After a week went by, I started to worry. I couldn't sit home and do nothing."

"This is where cell phones would be handy," Mercy said.

"I know. Victor and I discussed them dozens of times, but we're committed to living and raising our children a certain way. Cell phones are convenient but not a necessity."

Mercy hoped Charlotte wasn't addicted to the cheap phone Evan had bought for the kids.

"I still don't understand why Victor had left and why you'd prepped the kids to say he had died."

She sighed. "It's complicated. Victor didn't fully trust Alex and—"

"Wait." Mercy straightened and her head instantly throbbed. She felt more stable, but sudden movements hurt. "Alex said he hadn't heard from Victor since he left town over a decade ago."

"That's a bunch of bull." Bridget stroked Molly's hair. The toddler had curled up against her mother's chest, supported by one of Bridget's arms. The way an infant would be held. "Victor ran into Alex in town a few years ago, and after that, they'd meet up occasionally for a beer. They'd been close at one time, but Victor said he'd never felt fully comfortable around the man. Alex only cared about himself. After they reconnected, Victor didn't tell him about me or the kids. He wouldn't tell him where he lived either. Part of the reason we've had no contact with my family is Victor was afraid the Kerrs would find us through them. He had no trust in the older members of that family." Her face dropped. "I thought he was exaggerating a little. He wasn't. He thought it was safe to see Alex occasionally, but he was wrong."

"I went a long time without speaking to my family," Mercy slowly admitted. "But I felt pushed away . . . abandoned. I'm struggling to understand how you stayed away from what sound like good people for so long." She paused, remembering how the kids couldn't speak about taboo subjects. "Bridget, do you feel that Victor is too controlling? Of you and the kids?"

Bridget's gaze grew distant. "I can see how it looks that way to an outsider. But we agreed to all things as a couple. I came up with many of the restrictions we put on the kids. They weren't solely his ideas. We decided our kids didn't need to know about our lives before we met. It made things easier to have a rule not to discuss it. We also wanted a simple life. One away from society's consumerism and growing crime. Living off the land was a dream for both of us and made sense with our goals of avoiding the other Kerrs. You have to understand how much Victor didn't trust Christine and Linda. He believed they'd do anything to keep people out of their way."

"He was right," said Mercy. She still felt Victor had an unhealthy level of control over his family.

"I'll do anything for Victor," said Bridget as a half smile lifted her lips. "When we met, it was like my soul had been waiting for him. We both knew instantly ours was a special love . . . a big love, a fervent love. A follow-him-to-the-end-of-the-world love. And having the kids only made it stronger. It's never weakened in all the years we've been married. We're a true partnership. I think few people have that."

I have that.

Her chest suddenly tightened with a physical ache for Truman.

I understand that fervent love.

"So I knocked on the front door here," said Bridget. "I wasn't certain who would be living in the old Kerr home, but Victor had said that Alex still lived on the property. I knew about his aunts. According to Victor, they'd never accepted him or his father as part of the family." She pressed her lips together, a speculative look in her eye. "Victor always suspected the women were behind their husbands' boating accident."

Mercy wished she could say she was surprised. "Did he have proof? If you knew that, then why did you come here?"

"I didn't know where else to go. I knew he sometimes connected with Alex, so it seemed a logical place to start. As for proof, Victor researched the boating investigation but was never quite satisfied it was an accident, considering what he'd heard about the women and his grandmother Ethel."

Mercy was fascinated. "What did he hear about Ethel?"

"Supposedly she poisoned her husband. I can't remember his name."

"Albert," Mercy offered. "You're suggesting the Kerr women are black widows."

Hesitancy crossed Bridget's face. "Again, there's no proof. Just talk. But Victor felt strongly about their husbands' deaths."

"They had a lot of drugs and alcohol in their systems—well, one of them did. They never found the second." Mercy still half expected Joshua Kerr to come out of the woodwork somehow. She'd learned not to believe someone was dead until she'd seen the body.

"It was enough to make Victor suspect that they poisoned Ethel. He said she went downhill rapidly. I know that happens sometimes, but the timing was too convenient."

I was right to wonder about all the deaths in this family.

Christine and Linda might be more than black widows.

"That makes me even more surprised that you came here," said Mercy.

"At the worst, I thought they'd be rude and send me away. I had no idea they'd do this to me. I'm essentially a stranger."

"What happened when you got here?" Mercy asked.

"They invited me in. Oohed and aahed that I was married to Victor and went on about how they hadn't heard from him in years. Before they told me that they had baby pictures of Victor in a box in the basement—that's how they got me down here—they gave me tea and cookies as if I was a welcome guest. Christine took to Molly right away, playing peekaboo and finding a stuffed animal for her to hold."

"Did they buy the books and toys?" Mercy gestured to the piles.

"Yes. They're all brand new. I saw the hunger in Christine's eyes when she brought them down. She can't look away from Molly. I suspect she desperately wants grandkids. Linda teased her about it." Her gaze dropped. "I've let Christine take Molly upstairs."

Mercy blinked.

"Even though I know they're evil people, I honestly believed Christine wouldn't do anything to her, and being locked up down here isn't healthy for Molly. Upstairs, Christine would take her to see the horses and walk around outside." Bridget winced. "It gave me a break too." She met Mercy's eyes, guilt on her face. "I'm a horrible mother," she whispered.

"That's not true at all," said Mercy. "You're in a horrible situation. You did what you believed was best for you and Molly. And I think you did the right thing." Mercy couldn't imagine how stressed and exhausted Bridget must have been to allow her captor to play with her daughter. "It probably helped them trust you and gave more credence to the fact that you agreed to not tell anyone what they'd done for part of the money."

Bridget nodded but didn't look convinced. Then her expression grew serious. "When Chester died, Victor got a letter from him that—"

"Chester who?"

Bridget frowned. "Chester Rollins."

"The millionaire? What did he have to do with Victor?"

Bridget's jaw dropped open a little, surprise in her eyes. "I assumed you knew. You talked about the money."

Mercy was lost. "Ethel's estate? Victor has a right to his father's third of the estate. Isn't that why Alex nearly killed Victor?"

"No. Not at all." She vehemently shook her head. "Chester Rollins is Victor's grandfather. He left him an inheritance."

"Victor is heir to the Rollins fortune?" Mercy squeaked.

"Well, sort of. It's more complicated than that."

Mercy struggled to put the pieces together. "Christine told me it was a mystery who fathered Jack. She said Ethel's husband had been away when Jack was conceived. You believe it was Chester Rollins?"

"I *know* it was Chester Rollins. He got in contact with Victor a few years ago and told him. He constantly pressured Victor to allow him to name him as his heir, but Victor didn't want it."

Mercy was dumbstruck.

Who turns down millions and millions of dollars?

A guy who lives off the grid and refuses to carry a cell phone.

"Victor hated everything about Chester. He felt he abandoned his father, Jack, to those wolves that are the Kerrs. Victor was also sickened by his displays of trophy hunting and his public life as a playboy. He didn't want the man's money; he didn't want any sort of connection. Another reason we told the kids to say Victor had died was if Chester's lawyers or reporters came snooping around. Victor had a hunch that things would publicly explode after Chester died."

"So Chester died, and Victor got a letter that said what?" Mercy—like the rest of the country—knew Chester Rollins had left all his money to charities except for the $2 million in the treasure hunt.

"You have to know Chester," said Bridget. "He's a bit odd. He likes puzzles, notoriety, and anything different from the norm."

"I've read about it."

"The letter gave directions to the treasure."

Mercy was stunned. "Did Chester think Victor would accept a two-million-dollar treasure when he'd already turned down an inheritance?"

"The letter said that this way the money would be private. No one has to know who finds the treasure . . . or even if it's found at all. Victor had a big fear that we would be mobbed by the press if he was outed as Chester's heir. He values privacy above almost everything else. Our lives would have been turned upside down if we accepted any money."

"Then why didn't Chester just give it to Victor anonymously? No one had to know."

"Victor was convinced someone would figure it out. And Chester got a lot of pleasure out of creating the clues for that hunt. He has a flamboyance about him and loves people talking about him. Even if Victor never got the treasure, Chester was satisfied that he'd created an infamous legacy with it."

"His treasure hunt has gotten people killed," said Mercy. "A brother and sister have been murdered, and there've been other close calls. Eagle's Nest has dealt with overcrowding and trespassing and people setting up camp wherever they please. The hunters are a determined bunch."

"I had no idea it was that out of control," said Bridget. "I'd seen an article about the interest in the hunt during the week Victor was gone, but I didn't know it'd come to that. Victor's plan was to get the treasure and not tell a soul."

"If Victor didn't want the money, why did he leave to get the treasure?" asked Mercy.

Guilt flashed on Bridget's face. "I convinced him. I told him we should hold it for the kids. A fund if something happened to one of us. A safety net. He wasn't happy with the idea, but he finally agreed to go look for it. But somehow Victor crossed paths with Alex. Alex told me Victor came to him for help in locating the treasure in exchange for part of it, but I don't believe that. I suspect he accidentally ran into Alex in town."

"You've seen Alex?"

"Oh, yes. He's been here several times. He's been unable to locate the treasure and is convinced that I know where it is. He said Victor was holding out on him. He took pictures of Molly and me down here to threaten Victor. I assume he told Victor he'd hurt us if he didn't lead him to the treasure."

"You're lucky Alex believes you know something. That might be the only reason you're still alive." Mercy thought of Victor's damaged hands and the blows to his head. Alex had tortured him for more information to find the treasure. "But I thought Alex didn't know about you and the kids."

"I don't think he did until I knocked on his mother's door." Bridget shuddered. "After that he forced Victor to tell him where we lived. I can't imagine what Alex did to get that information out of him." She pressed her cheek against Molly's. "I've been so worried about Charlotte and Theodore since I found out he knows where we live."

"I think he went there," said Mercy. "The kids were hiding and saw a man go into the house and—everything is okay, but he set some of your furniture on fire. He was very angry and intent on causing damage."

"That sounds right. I think he believed the kids might know something that would tell him where the treasure was. Or he was planning to use them to threaten Victor more."

"I thought the letter had the directions."

"Alex claims it's incomplete. He thinks there's a second letter. He's furious about it. I'm sure he tried to get Victor to fill in the holes, but how could Victor tell him something he didn't know?"

"You didn't get a second letter?"

"No."

It was starting to make sense. Alex must have worn the beard to stay incognito while hunting for the treasure. It didn't explain the cane he'd brought to her office, but she suspected that had been to give her a view of him as unthreatening, less likely to ever be a suspect if something came up. He had gone to Victor and Bridget's home, searching for the kids and an answer. When he didn't find it, he became angry and destructive, starting the fire and breaking things in the barn. After striking out there, he'd broken into Evan's.

If he hadn't been caught, Mercy would not have considered a man who leaned heavily on a cane as a suspect in those two physical crimes.

"The police have Alex, but he's refusing to speak to them," Mercy told her, deliberately holding back how close he'd come to getting Bridget's children. This mom had enough on her mind.

What would he have done to those kids?

"Thank God he was caught," said Bridget.

"No one knows how to find the treasure?" Mercy asked.

"From what Alex told me, I think that's true. He's threatened me several times, believing I know the answer, but I don't. I barely looked at the letter Victor got from Chester. I was more caught up in what the treasure could mean to our family—good or bad." Bridget leaned back against the wall with a sigh, Molly asleep in her arms. "I guess it was bad." Her eyelids slowly closed.

Mercy lay back down on the cushions, her mind processing what Bridget had revealed.

Greed. Money.

Alex had upended several lives in his pursuit of money.

And Christine and Linda appeared to be willing partners.

Mercy had to get Bridget and Molly away from the women. With Alex arrested, the women might resort to violence—or worse—when it came to covering their tracks.

"What exactly happens when they bring you food or remove the bucket?" Mercy asked.

"Both of them used to come," Bridget said, her eyes still closed. "I was to go to the corner and sit with my back to them. Linda would stand at the door with a cattle prod while Christine brought in food or replaced the bucket. Now it's just Christine. She doesn't make me turn around as long as I stay in the corner. She carries the cattle prod in one hand and the food in the other." Bridget yawned. "I bet they'll both come down since you're here now."

"We need a plan," Mercy said.

Bridget's eyes flew open. "You heard me say 'cattle prod,' right?"

"I'm not going to sit here and wait for someone to come find me," said Mercy. "They're two women in their seventies. Even a cattle prod can't even the odds if you and I work together." She touched the back of her head and winced, feeling sticky and crusted blood. She stared at her fingers, trying to calm the nausea that roiled in her gut again, and blinked away a bout of dizziness.

Maybe the odds aren't as even as I hope.

Her gaze roamed the room and settled on the door.

One way out.

45

Truman spotted Eddie right away.

The FBI agent stepped out of Alex Kerr's double-wide mobile home as Truman pulled in. Several other federal government–looking American vehicles parked along the narrow driveway, which forked. One fork led to the house and the other to a large stand-alone garage. The garage's roller door was open, and he saw two techs examining a half dozen motorcycles. Truman parked behind a Ford Explorer, and his heart sank.

Mercy's Tahoe wasn't there.

He checked the app. NO LOCATION FOUND.

The sight of the spiraling icon made him want to throw his phone. *Shit.*

Eddie met him halfway up the drive. "No word?" he asked. "When I heard your tires on the gravel, I hoped it was her."

"I still can't find her." Truman had called her six times on his way. Each call had gone directly to voice mail.

Eddie rubbed the back of his neck, his forehead wrinkled with concern. "I don't like it."

"Me neither, but I'm sure she's fine."

Am I trying to convince him or me?

"I'm not surprised we're uptight after what happened last time," Truman said. Mercy had gone missing for weeks last winter. Truman silently held Eddie's gaze, not wanting to overreact. But he didn't want to underreact either. "It's only been a few hours."

"Did you check with Ollie or Kaylie?"

"I almost did. I can't figure out how to ask without alarming them. Look how you and I are reacting. Those kids don't need to go through this."

Eddie nodded but didn't look convinced. "But she might have told one of them where she went."

"Then she's fine, and we'll hear from her when she's back in range."

A muscle in Eddie's cheek tightened several times as he considered Truman's words. "Then we'll wait. You want to take a look?" He gestured at the home.

"Sure. If it's okay." Anything to distract him from thinking about Mercy.

"They're almost done inside. Never hurts to have another pair of eyes, though." The two men headed to the home and went up the small set of wooden stairs.

"Anything interesting?" asked Truman.

"They've removed his laptop and desktop," said Eddie. "And towed away his pickup for processing. I took a look before they left. The man keeps a surprisingly clean vehicle."

"Or he just cleaned it," Truman pointed out. "You're looking for anything that ties him to Victor Kerr's torture, correct?" Truman refused to pull punches on what had happened to Victor Kerr. He wouldn't use the word *injuries*. The man had been tortured.

"And for any sign that connects him to Bridget and Molly Kerr."

"Cell phone?"

"Haven't found one. He didn't have one on him last night either."

"It's got to be somewhere."

"We have discovered that Alex was interested in the treasure hunt. He's got maps and several pages of handwritten notes. I bet there's more on his computers."

"That lines up with what I learned this morning. I talked to Evan Bolton about it, but you haven't heard." He updated Eddie on his conversation with Tim Giles that indicated Alex could be involved in the shooting of Billy Serrano.

"Wasn't his sister murdered too?" asked Eddie.

"Yes. Meghan Serrano. Strangulation."

Eddie stopped. "You're suggesting that those two treasure-hunt murders are connected to Bethany and Molly Kerr's missing persons cases."

"I think Alex Kerr is in the middle of both."

Eddie frowned, and Truman could almost hear the gears spinning in his brain. "The warrant includes any weapons we find. We've removed two long guns but no handguns."

"According to Evan Bolton, Alex dropped a handgun in his home last night. Bolton is comparing it to the bullet found at Billy Serrano's murder scene."

"Do you know if there've been any leads on the second person who was at Bolton's break-in last night?" asked Eddie.

"Not that I'm aware of. But I think you're standing in the right place to find those leads. I'd been on my way to question Tim Giles about his location last night. I'd wondered if he and Alex had formed some sort of treasure-hunting alliance."

"Isn't he sort of an idiot?" asked Eddie. "Alex doesn't seem the type to befriend someone like that."

"I agree. Maybe something in Alex's home will point to last night's cohort."

A crime scene tech came around a corner in the home, two paper bags in his hands. Eddie and Truman stepped out of his way. "Did you finish the bedroom?" asked Eddie.

"Yes," said the tech. "You can go anywhere except the smaller bathroom. We'll finish that and be done."

"Come this way." Eddie gestured to Truman and led him down a narrow hall to a bedroom in use as an office. A large desk stood in the middle of the room. A spot absent of dust in its center indicated where the desktop computer had been removed. Two tall bookcases were packed with books, binders, trophies, and boxes. Several enlarged photos hung on the walls. Most were of Alex with various motorcycles. The trophies were associated with dirt bikes and motorcycles too. All were more than two decades old.

"What did the techs find?" Truman asked.

"They cleaned out the drains, looking for any hair samples that could belong to Bridget. I sent a team to get hair from her brush at home. They cut out a stained piece of master-bedroom carpet that tested positive for blood. The stain was small. Only two inches in diameter. They've vacuumed the furniture and carpeting. Lifted a few prints. But we haven't found anything yet that directly indicates any of the missing Kerrs were here."

"The computers might provide your best leads," said Truman.

"My thoughts exactly."

"This is the treasure-hunt stuff?" Truman gestured at the notepads and maps on the desk.

"Yes. I've followed the hunt a little bit and am familiar with a lot of the poem, but what I see here is that Alex is only concentrating on the last few lines. I don't see any references to the earlier ones."

"He jumped ahead?" Truman asked. "Maybe he used someone else's research to get to this point. I know Meghan Serrano's research is missing. She had copies of her brother's work from Evan Bolton. He believes she printed them out right before she was killed."

Eddie nodded. "That would explain why he's so focused on only a few clues. But everything here is in his handwriting, and I haven't seen photocopies of other research."

"Maybe he scanned and saved them on one of his computers. That would help tie him to Meghan's murder."

"I'll tell the computer forensic guys to check for that. We've been focused on finding something to link him to Victor or Bridget."

"Alex could definitely be the center of multiple investigations," said Truman. "Have you talked with his mother or aunt yet? I know they live nearby."

"They're in the big white house on the east side of the property. I'll swing by there next. I'm surprised they haven't popped in to see what's happening here."

"Is their home visible from here?" asked Truman.

"No, but you'd think they'd notice the dust we stirred up on the gravel roads."

"Mercy told me the Kerrs' unusual history," said Truman. "The men in the family don't seem to live as long as the women."

Eddie snorted. "Yes, that's been discussed in our meetings. The family has had more than its share of tragedy. Darby looked into most of the deaths. All were accidental, as far as we can tell."

"Mercy liked the two sisters she interviewed. She said they were colorful characters, but I know she wondered if the matriarch's estate had been handled correctly. Are you going there soon?"

"That's the plan," said Eddie. "I need to tell them what went on here today and ask a few questions."

"I'll go with you."

46

Rap, rap, rap.

Mercy had heard footsteps coming down the stairs and moved into position before the sharp knocks on the door.

"Bridget!" Christine's voice came through the door. "You know what to do. Get the agent into the corner with you."

She called me "the agent," not Mercy. Not a good sign.

Christine had impersonalized her. A behavior associated with violence. An attempt to emotionally detach from a victim.

"I can't move her," Bridget called back. She'd scooted into her corner and set Molly behind her, distracting the toddler with a spinning toy.

"Make her move herself!"

"She's still out. Whatever you drugged her with hasn't worn off yet," Bridget lied. They had decided to imply that Bridget believed Mercy had been drugged. Thinking Mercy was still unconscious would hopefully lower the sisters' defenses and make them curious about her physical condition.

Silence from outside the door.

Good. She's surprised that I'm still unconscious.

"Whatever it was, she threw up some of it," Bridget lied again. "Maybe that will help it wear off faster."

Things could go two ways at the moment. Christine would open the door as usual, or she would go get Linda. Mercy had a plan if both women came, but it was less likely to be successful than the plan for a single woman.

"She vomited?" Christine asked.

"Yeah. She choked on it a bit, and I cleaned it up, but she's breathing fine now. How long will the drug last?"

More silence.

Don't go back upstairs.

Mercy was counting on Christine's curiosity.

Fumbling and clicking came from the door.

Yes!

Mercy tensed, visualizing her next move. She lay on her side, her back to the door, holding tight to her stomach two plastic glasses that would be out of Christine's line of sight if she entered. A toddler's book was casually propped up and opened to a page with a poor-quality mirror—"Say hi to the baby!"—giving Mercy a grainy view behind her.

She tamped down a retch, breathing through her mouth, avoiding the putrid smells. Bridget's gaze met hers, and she gave a small nod. Their plan was in play.

A distorted image of Christine appeared in the mirror, and she cautiously moved toward Mercy. "Stay there," she ordered Bridget.

"Of course," Bridget said.

"*My God*, it stinks in here," Christine muttered, taking another step toward Mercy. "I'll bring another bucket."

Mercy twisted onto her back and hurled the contents of the glasses at Christine.

The woman shrieked as urine and shit hit her in the face. Mercy launched herself off the ground and tackled the screaming woman onto her back. She slapped a hand over Christine's mouth and yelled at Bridget, "*Go, go, go!*"

Bridget was already in motion, Molly under one arm. She leaped over Mercy and Christine and yanked the long cattle prod out of the woman's grip.

Mercy's front was wet with piss, and her shit-covered hand slid off Christine's mouth. The woman's shrieks echoed off the walls of the small room. Mercy covered Christine's mouth again, fighting back nausea, refusing to think about the brown substance coating her fingers. As soon as Bridget was out the door, Mercy rolled off, pushed to her feet, and lunged toward the stairs. She slammed the heavy door behind her and threw the locks.

"We did it!" Bridget said in a hoarse whisper as Mercy grabbed the long cattle prod.

"Stay here until I say it's clear," she ordered the woman.

Christine started to pound on the door and shriek for Linda, but the sounds were surprisingly quiet. Mercy glanced at the door and saw that it had been reinforced with layers of padding and wood. If Bridget had screamed during Mercy's tea with the sisters, she would have never heard her.

Mercy wiped her hands on her pants and crept up the stairs toward the door at the top.

So gross.

She clenched the cattle prod's handle. To use it, she'd need to be within a few feet of a person. Not the best weapon, but she couldn't be picky.

I've got to find my gun. And phone.

No. Christine destroyed it.

Dammit.

She reviewed the layout of the home in her head. She was pretty certain the door at the top of the stairs was just off the far end of the kitchen. To get out, she could go through the kitchen and nook to reach the back door to the deck. If she turned the other way, she believed it would take her through another sitting room and then to the foyer and front door.

But she wasn't positive.

When she'd been invited into the home, she'd entered and been led to the right, past the living room. At the time she'd noticed french doors on the left side of the foyer, and through them caught a glimpse of a very formal sofa and old-fashioned desk.

Mercy gripped the knob of the door at the top of the stairs, hating that it would swing out. She wouldn't be able to see into the kitchen. Glancing behind her, she saw Bridget on the first stair near the bottom, Molly on her hip. They both stared at her with wide eyes. Mercy put a finger to her lips, and Bridget quietly said, "Good luck."

She silently turned the knob, listening hard for any sound beyond the door. She opened it a few inches, and the half-inch opening near the hinges gave her a narrow peek into the kitchen, where sunlight streamed in.

All quiet.

Mercy opened the door farther, holding her breath, thankful for nonsqueaking hinges. The cattle prod at her side, she slipped through the opening and closed the door behind her. She took a few cautious steps into the kitchen.

Where would they put my gun?

No time to search. Get Bridget and get out of the house.

The plan was that when one or both of them escaped the house, they'd run up the long drive to the road to flag down help.

The house was quiet, so she returned to the door to signal for Bridget to come out.

"Agent Mercy."

Linda stood near the door to the deck with a shotgun aimed at Mercy.

Mercy's vision narrowed, seeing only the opening of the barrel.

I screwed up.

Lead her away from Bridget and Molly.

Mercy lunged in the opposite direction, scrambling to keep her feet beneath her, wishing she wore shoes, not her slick socks. She slipped and landed on her hands, crushing one finger with the cattle prod handle.

BOOM!

Drywall exploded where she'd stood a split second before, creating a shower of chunks, dust, and bird shot.

Her shoulder lit up with pain, but she burst forward, aiming to get around the corner ten feet away, into the formal sitting room, and then out the front door. She flung herself around the corner, not caring that she'd dropped the cattle prod. It was useless against a shotgun.

Mercy froze.

She wasn't in a sitting room. She'd entered a large butler's pantry. There was no access to any other room on the first floor.

Shit.

To her right, a narrow, ancient-looking, steep set of stairs led upward.

Servants' stairs.

BOOM!

The corner behind her blew up, and she dashed up the stairs, heart and feet pounding. She tripped on the uneven boards and speed-crawled up the steps on her hands and feet, expecting the next shot to hit her from behind.

Screams filled the stairs.

"Mercy! Come back!" Bridget shouted over the screams.

The screams didn't stop as Mercy reached the top, her shoulder on fire.

"Mercy!"

Bridget shouted her name again, but someone else was screaming. Linda.

The cattle prod.

Mercy pounded back down the stairs and found Linda writhing on the floor as Bridget pressed the cattle prod into her back.

Bridget came up behind Linda with the prod as she was chasing me.

Crackling sounded as Bridget shocked her over and over. Bridget's angry eyes met Mercy's. "Get the gun!" she shouted over Linda's screams.

The shotgun was on the floor inches from Linda's hand. Mercy grabbed it, pumped another shell, and pointed it at Linda.

"Don't move!" she shouted at Linda.

Bridget stepped back with the cattle prod still in hand, panting hard, and Linda went limp on the floor, crying. Mercy didn't know if her tears were from the constant shocks or the knowledge that her life had just gone to hell.

"Where's Molly?" she asked Bridget.

"At the bottom of the stairs. I'll get her." The woman vanished, and Mercy heard her steps going down to the basement.

"Police!" A crashing sound came from the living room.

Mercy knew that voice.

"Truman!" she shouted. "I've got her covered. The house is clear, and we're next to the kitchen."

Bridget emerged from the basement with Molly in her arms, and then Truman's big form stepped into the room. He lowered his weapon as he took in the sight of Linda on the floor and Mercy pointing a shotgun at her.

"Mercy?" Eddie showed up behind Truman. "Oh, thank God." He pushed past Truman and knelt with a knee in Linda's back as he pulled out handcuffs. "We heard the gunshots."

Mercy lowered her shotgun and stepped out of the way. "Christine Kerr is in the basement." Her shoulder was on fire, but she only had eyes for Truman and locked on to his gaze as if it were a lifeline. It sure felt like one.

It's over.

A second later he had her enveloped in his arms. His chest felt like a rock. A safe and solid rock. "You okay?" he asked, burying his lips in her hair.

"I am now." Exhaustion suddenly hit, and her knees went liquid.

"You're bleeding!" He spun her around to look at her back. "You're not okay!"

"I caught some bird shot. It's not bad." She had no idea if it was bad or not, but she wanted his arms around her again. She tried to turn back into him, but he held her still, examining her back.

"What's that smell?" he asked, an odd tone in his voice.

"You don't want to know." An urgent need to wash her hands sent her out of his grip and to the kitchen sink.

Truman looked at Bridget. "You're Bridget. And Molly."

Bridget nodded as Molly buried her face in her mother's shoulder.

"Your husband and kids are going to be happy to see you," said Truman.

"Not as happy as I am."

47

As he got out of his truck in the hospital lot with Theodore and Charlotte, Evan watched Truman's SUV stop at the emergency room entrance. He'd had a brief call with Truman a half hour ago. Bridget and Molly were fine and being brought to the hospital for a reunion with the other kids and Victor.

I'm about to see my sister.

Emotions ricocheted through him. Excitement. Caution. Worry.

What if she doesn't want to see me?

Fourteen years was a long time to stay out of contact. He was concerned she'd want to continue that silence. The thought of never seeing Charlotte and Theodore burned like acid in his stomach.

As he and the kids crossed the lot, Mercy stiffly stepped down out of the SUV.

Something's not right.

The back passenger door opened, and a woman and toddler got out.

Bethany.

No, I need to call her Bridget now.

"*Mom! Mom!*" Theodore took off in a sprint. He reached his mother first and threw his arms around her, tears streaming down his face. Charlotte was a split second behind him and nearly knocked all of them over with her energetic hug.

Evan jogged after them, his gaze locked on Bridget's face. She looked the same, but she didn't look the same. Somehow she'd grown older while she was away.

I have too.

It was odd to see her as a mother. But it also felt right.

The kids love her desperately.

"Yet!" Molly thrashed in her mother's arms. "Yet!"

"What's Molly saying?" Evan asked Mercy as he stopped beside her. She watched the reunion, her eyes suspiciously wet.

"I think that's short for Charlotte."

Molly rapidly jabbered as Charlotte took the little girl from her mom and spun her around in a hug. Molly shrieked with laughter.

"Oh, thank God," Mercy said quietly. "Molly stopped talking while they were locked up in the basement. She's looked numb since I met her."

Bridget looked up from her embrace with Theodore and met Evan's gaze. "Evan," she whispered, her voice cracking.

Evan took two steps and wrapped his arms around his little sister. She was still petite, barely reaching his shoulder. But she was no longer a teenager. She'd built a life and had amazing kids.

She's alive.

"I can't believe it," he said over and over.

"I'm so sorry," Bridget said. "I'm sorry I didn't contact you all these years. I've missed you so much." She pulled back and looked at him, apprehension in her face. "Mom and Dad?"

"Living the good life in Arizona. They'll be ecstatic to know you're okay."

Relief filled her face, and she sagged against him. "I'm so sorry," she repeated again.

"You're all right?" he asked.

"I'm fine." Bridget looked at Molly, who'd moved to Theodore's arms. He grinned at his little sister, teasing and tickling the side of her neck, making her chortle in glee.

Bridget closed her eyes. "I never thought I'd hear her laugh again."

"I'm sorry you went through that," Evan told her.

"It could have been much worse." She smiled at Mercy, who was standing a few feet away, leaning on Truman. "Mercy was determined to get us out."

"Everything okay?" Evan asked Mercy. She wore a windbreaker zipped to her neck in the warm afternoon. Pain hovered around her.

"I'll be fine. Might need a few stitches." She shrugged and winced.

Evan raised a brow at Truman, who nodded. "She's promised to let an ER doctor take a look at her."

"Let's go see Victor," Evan said to Bridget. "The docs told me he's sort of awake." He looked around and sniffed, wrinkling his nose. "What's that smell?"

Two hours later, Mercy was bird shot–free and on her way with Truman to Victor Kerr's hospital room. There were odd numb spots in her shoulder and back where the ER doctor had injected lidocaine before removing the shot. Thirteen little metal balls had been embedded under her skin. The doctor had exclaimed, "Look at that!" with every tiny piece he dug out.

Mercy had had no desire to look.

She'd cleaned up as best she could in the ER. There had been spare clothing in her GOOD (get out of Dodge) bag in her Tahoe, which Linda had hidden behind a barn. She'd washed her hair in a hospital sink, having borrowed some shampoo that made her hair feel like straw. A shower was her priority once she saw Bridget together with her entire family.

Truman opened the hospital room door, and Mercy was thrilled to see that Victor's eyes were open. Molly sat on his stomach, and the other two kids were on one side, as close as possible to him. Bridget sat on his other side, her gaze never leaving her husband's face.

Charlotte was showing him pictures of Oreo on her cell phone.

"Hey," said Evan as she and Truman joined him. He smiled at her, and Mercy did a double take. His eyes were full of life. He'd always appeared so serious, as if he carried a great burden.

He was burdened. His sister had vanished.

"How's it going?" Mercy asked.

"Good. Victor can sort of speak without opening his mouth. I can't really understand him, but Betha—Bridget has no problem." The smile disappeared. "Victor confirmed that it was Alex who tortured him."

"So horrible," said Mercy. "And all for money."

"I heard from Eddie. Christine and Linda Kerr have been arrested. They're both talking up a storm, pointing fingers at each other and Alex."

Mercy snorted. "What happened to 'Protect the family at all costs'? I guess staring at a prison sentence puts a new perspective on things."

"The Kerrs didn't know Jack's father was Chester Rollins. That was something Alex got out of Victor when he found out about the letter that supposedly gave the location of the treasure."

"I'm not surprised. According to Bridget, Victor just found out a few years ago."

"Two more things," said Evan. "The women say Alex shot Billy Serrano and also murdered his sister, Meghan. They claim the sister was in on her brother's murder, and then Alex killed her later. I guess he charmed her at first, convincing her that her brother shouldn't take half the treasure, and then did away with her when her notes didn't lead him straight to it."

"What a horrible man," muttered Mercy. "What's the second thing?"

"Christine was the other person at the break-in at my home last night," said Evan. "The one that got away."

"She was going to harm those kids?" asked Truman.

"She claims that wasn't the plan."

"Like Bridget and Molly weren't harmed?" said Mercy. "Not all harm is physical." She watched the little family as Molly picked at one of the bandages on her father's hands. It would be a long road to healing for all of them.

"I've been watching Victor and Bridget," Truman said quietly in her ear. "They can't keep their eyes off of each other."

Mercy had noticed it too.

"I got very anxious when I couldn't locate you today," he whispered, his words heavy with sorrow. "I didn't want to lose you again."

She kissed his cheek, holding her face against his for a long moment. "I worried about you. I knew you were experiencing that."

Mercy followed his gaze as he looked at Bridget pressing close to Victor. "She gave up everything to be with him," Mercy said. "She told me they had an I-will-follow-you-around-the-world type of love."

"I believe that."

His breath tickled her cheek, and she leaned into him, appreciating the weight of his arm around her shoulders.

"Do we have that?" he asked.

She met his gaze, loving the concern in his deep-brown eyes. "I have no doubt that's what we have. None at all. I'd follow you anywhere, and I know you'd do the same for me." She touched his face. "I knew when we first met that fate was at work. I tried to ignore it, but I knew."

A wide smile lit up his face. "I did too."

Kaylie and Ollie appeared in the doorway and hesitated, scanning the crowded area. Evan gestured for them to come in. "It's okay," he told them. "Their father needs to meet the two of you. Without you guys, this past week wouldn't have been doable."

They stepped inside, and Mercy frowned. Both of them looked ready to burst.

"What is it?" she asked Kaylie.

"It's this." Kaylie held up the sparkly backpack that she'd given Charlotte. "I opened it to see if my missing sunglasses were in it. Look what I found." She handed Mercy a postcard addressed to Victor.

Ollie could barely stand still. "Look what's on it!"

Mercy turned it over. It was a watercolor image of a brown bee with a forested mountain background. She flipped it back to the address side. There was no return address. "I don't understand."

"It's a wooden bee!" Evan said. "Holy shit. This was in Charlotte's backpack?"

"Is that important?" asked Mercy. Evan's eyes were wide, and Ollie and Kaylie were grinning like fools.

"'Where would it be?'" said Ollie, pointing at the card.

Mercy shook her head at him, not understanding.

"Charlotte," said Evan, "could you come here a second?"

The girl reluctantly pulled away from her father and joined their group, studying their faces in curiosity. Her gaze fell on the backpack. "Am I in trouble?"

"Not at all," said Evan. "Where did you get this postcard?" He showed it to her.

She smiled. "It was in the mail after Mom left. I thought it was cute, so I kept it." She glanced at him. "Is that okay? It didn't have anything written on it, so I assumed it wasn't important. The rest of the mail is in a kitchen drawer."

"Thanks, honey. You can go back to your dad," Evan told her. Once she'd left, he looked at Mercy. "Theodore told me they have a PO box in town. He picked up the mail once a week. This must have been sent separately from Chester Rollins's first letter."

Mercy finally understood. "It's part of the answer to the clues? Bridget said Alex claimed the first letter from Rollins about the treasure location was incomplete."

Truman touched a mountain in the background of the postcard. "See that little angel drawn on the hill? How much do you want to bet that's Angel's Rest? Ina told me it was a significant location to Chester."

"Ollie spotted that too," said Kaylie. "I'd thought wings in the poem referred to bird wings, but when we saw this, we thought an angel's wings. There are three places nearby with *Angel* in the name." She grinned at Truman. "You just narrowed it down to one."

Mercy caught her breath. "You mean the hunt is over?" She glanced at the Kerr family gathered around the hospital bed. No family deserved the treasure more.

"Almost," said Evan.

48

Three days later

"We are definitely in the pines," muttered Evan, quoting the treasure-hunt title as he and the kids reached the end of the three-mile hike. Charlotte had insisted Oreo come along. The little dog had trotted along happily for the first hundred yards and then sat, refusing to go any farther. Charlotte had insisted on carrying him. Another hundred yards landed the dog in Evan's arms for the rest of the hike to Angel's Rest.

Ollie, Kaylie, Theodore, and Charlotte were Evan's accomplices for what he hoped was the end of the treasure hunt.

Two deaths and multiple occurrences of trespassing and destruction of property were enough to persuade Chester Rollins's lawyer to issue a press release. In it he stated the treasure had been found and the finder wished to remain anonymous. There'd been an immediate outcry of people demanding to know where it'd been found and by whom. The lawyer had ignored their pleas. He agreed with law enforcement that it was time to put an end to the hunt.

Alex Kerr had been connected to Billy Serrano's murder by the recovered bullet and to Meghan's murder by a fingerprint lifted from her necklace's pendant. He still refused to talk, but Linda Kerr had spoken freely, implicating him and his mother, after making a deal with the district attorney.

Evan watched Charlotte out of the corner of his eye, her resemblance to Bridget no longer creating longing and sadness. Now he drank in her mischievous grins and the stubborn set to her brows. Having Bridget back in his life had eliminated a dark cloud that had hovered above him for fourteen years. Their reconnection had been instantaneous, almost as if she'd never been out of his life. And he was growing to appreciate his brother-in-law. Victor wasn't a controlling spouse. He was proving to be a good man who'd done what he thought was right to protect his family. The love between Victor and Bridget was unlike anything Evan had ever seen.

He was envious.

"Do you know what I want to do with the money, Uncle Evan?" Charlotte asked, a dreamy look on her face.

"I'll guess a massive shopping trip. Dresses. Shoes. Jewelry."

"Nope. Guess again."

"Ummm . . . a trip to Hawaii and Australia."

"Nope. Guess again."

"How about you just tell me?"

She took Oreo out of his arms and gave the dog a kiss on its nose. "I want to have a ranch for animals that don't have homes. Dogs and cats and bunnies. Maybe even horses. I'll hire vets and lots of kids to give them love."

Evan was touched. "That's a wonderful idea." Oreo had been officially cleared for adoption by the county. It'd simply involved paperwork; the dog had never left Charlotte's side. "I don't know what your parents would think of that. *If* we find the treasure, I think they want to save it so you can go to college."

"It won't cost me and Theodore two million dollars to go to college," Charlotte said pointedly.

"I hope not."

"There's enough money for dogs."

"That will be up to your parents. And remember, you're not to talk to anyone about this. It's a secret."

"I know. My mother told me that three days ago." She lifted her chin. "I'm not dense." Charlotte gave him a measured look. "How come you're not married?"

The change of subject made him stumble on perfectly flat ground. "I haven't met the right woman yet. It's a big decision to spend the rest of your life with someone."

She looked thoughtful. "Maybe I could use the money to create a dating service. I'd find you a nice woman. Someone who wants kids because you'll be a good dad. Although you're a little old already."

Ouch.

"That would be nice of you, Charlotte."

She skipped ahead to join Kaylie, who'd stopped at a bench overlooking a stunning view.

Evan took a drink of his water and wiped his forehead, then joined the others. The view was nearly 180 degrees to the east. Plains and farms and small hills. It went on forever.

"That's something," he said to Ollie.

The older teen ignored the stunning sight and paced around the bench, studying it carefully. Theodore watched his every move. The boy idolized Ollie. Evan had heard him use some of Ollie's unusual terms of speech and seen him mimic his gestures.

He could have a worse role model.

"This is the end of the hike," Ollie stated. "It's got to be here somewhere."

The five of them looked around. Evan had no idea what exactly they were looking for. He assumed they'd know when they found it.

"Truman said Ina talked about a big flat rock nearby," said Ollie. "Let's split up and look."

"No, stick together," said Evan. The last thing he needed was for any of the kids to get lost in the pine forest.

"'Where the brake would flatten her wings.'" Kaylie quoted the second-to-last line. "If we use the homonym theory, we might be looking for a break in the woods. And according to Ina, possibly a flat rock."

Ollie looked thoughtful and headed into the trees. The others followed, weaving among the tall trees. The ground was quite clear, mostly pine needles, sagebrush, and rock. They could easily see dozens of feet ahead. They had trekked back and forth for ten minutes when Theodore spotted a group of large rocks where the trees faded away. The rocks were definitely at a break in the woods, as the clue suggested. Most of them were jagged or rounded, but one was quite large and definitely flat. The trees had thinned around the rocks, letting the sun warm the surfaces.

Kaylie immediately sat on the flat one. "Now what?"

"Just look around," said Ollie.

"We don't even know if we're in the right spot," said Kaylie. "That postcard didn't indicate anything about rocks at Angel's Rest."

"I didn't see anything at the bench, which is the official viewpoint," Ollie told her. "It makes sense to look here. It's a break in the wood."

She shrugged and climbed to her feet on the wide rock, her hands on her hips as she surveyed the small clearing. Evan walked a slow circle around the grouping of rocks. Ollie and Theodore did the same.

"None of the clues could be interpreted as describing a rock formation like this?" asked Evan.

"I don't think so," said Ollie, uncertainty in his voice.

Are we wasting our time?

Maybe we're putting too much weight on Ina's memory.

Evan wanted to find the money for the Kerr family. Victor would have staggering medical bills, and there was speculation that he might have some minor brain damage. The money would be a safety net.

"Hey! Look at this!" Kaylie had crawled up onto another rock. The other four of them climbed onto the flat one and strained to see what she was looking at.

It reminded Evan of a hieroglyph. On the side of the tallest rock in the group, someone had painted a bee that was impossible to see from the ground.

"I'll be damned," said Evan. Surprise flashed through his veins. "'Where would it be?'" he quoted. "It's an actual bee."

They'd found the last clue.

"Where's it go?" asked Ollie. There was enough room for only Kaylie on the second rock.

"Hang on. I think I see something." She stretched out on her stomach and shoved her hand between the tall rock and the one she balanced on. "It's plastic."

She backed up, a heavy-duty plastic bag in her hand. It was smaller than Evan had expected. Only about twelve inches square.

"That won't hold two million dollars," said Ollie. "Is there something else?"

"No. This is it."

"Maybe it has a check inside," suggested Charlotte.

"Then whoever cashed it wouldn't be anonymous," countered Theodore. "Mom and Dad won't do it if it's a check."

Charlotte's face fell.

"Ollie, can you cut this? It's too thick to tear." Kaylie dropped down to the large, flat rock where the rest of them stood. Ollie pulled out a pocket knife and cut the thick covering.

"It's so pretty!" Charlotte said as a plastic box appeared. It was intricately decorated with plastic stones and gold swirls. Something a young girl would use to store her most precious items. It looked like a ten-dollar toy from Target.

That's it?

Kaylie opened the latches and looked inside as everyone pushed closer to see.

"Ohhh," exclaimed Charlotte. "Are those real?"

Kaylie lifted several rings, each set with a large diamond, and handed them to Ollie, who peered at them. "How do you tell if it's real?" he asked.

"I suspect they're real," said Evan.

Next was a small velvet bag that Kaylie upended, dumping the contents into the toy box. More diamonds. And sapphires and rubies and emeralds. But mostly diamonds.

Evan had no doubt he was looking at a $2 million pile of precious stones.

"I guess diamonds are more portable and easier to hide than cash," said Ollie.

"What if they were stolen?" asked Theodore.

"Chester Rollins was a jewel collector," said Ollie. "They're not stolen."

The five of them were silent, staring into the box.

"Now what?" asked Charlotte, looking up at Evan. Her eyes sparkled as much as the gems.

Evan smiled. "Now you get to persuade your parents to let you take care of homeless animals."

"*Yes!*" Charlotte shot a fist into the air and then squeezed her brother, making him gasp. "More dogs!"

Warmth spread through Evan. His sister was back, and he loved the family she'd brought with her.

A happy ending.

Acknowledgments

This book took nearly a year and a half to write. My previous books took about five months each. Simply put, 2020 was a rotten year; 2021 was better, but I still struggled to find the peace and focus to write.

I can't thank my publisher enough for adjusting my deadlines to accommodate my needs. Montlake has been my publisher for a decade, and the people there are simply the best. They have my back and always ask what they can do to help. My agent, Meg Ruley, is my biggest cheerleader and always has a shoulder ready for me to cry on.

I loved being back in Mercy's world. After writing *A Merciful Promise*, I received an unbelievable number of messages that begged me not to end the series. Readers wanted more from those characters. I admit I needed a bit of a break after writing six Mercy books in a row, and writing the first two books in the Columbia River series provided that rest. When Mercy popped up in *The Silence* as a secondary character, I knew I was ready to dive back into her life. I'd missed Truman, Kaylie, and Ollie, and even their pets.

Thank you to my fans for being patient and waiting for this book. There will be more.

ABOUT THE AUTHOR

Photo © 2016 Rebekah Jule Photography

Kendra Elliot has landed on the *Wall Street Journal* bestseller list multiple times and is the award-winning author of the Bone Secrets and Callahan & McLane series, the Mercy Kilpatrick novels, and the Columbia River novels. She's a three-time winner of the Daphne du Maurier Award, an International Thriller Writers Award finalist, and an RT Award finalist. She has always been a voracious reader, cutting her teeth on classic female heroines such as Nancy Drew, Trixie Belden, and Laura Ingalls. She was born and raised in the rainy Pacific Northwest but now lives in flip-flops. Visit her at www.kendraelliot.com.